# Dead Flies and Sherry Trifle

## By Geoff Le Pard

# About the author

Geoff (not Geoffrey, save for legal documents and to his mother) Le Pard is a former lawyer, an aspiring novelist, an enthusiastic blogger (at www.geofflepard.com), someone who enjoys walking and talking at length and lover of London. He will publish his second book 'God Bothering' in spring 2015 and his third, provisionally titled 'Salisbury Square' in summer 2015. After that the pace will slow.

# Acknowledgements

This book is the product of one summer's sweaty vacation in 1976, an Arvon course circa 2009, an MA (writing) at Sheffield Hallam 2011-2013 and many, many hours of love and labour.
Several people have been involved in reaching this point and to each of you I owe a debt of gratitude (and in some cases a debt). I hope just knowing that you are loved and cherished is sufficient. If not, then form an orderly queue.

## Copyright, etc.

Dead Flies and Sherry Trifle
Copyright © 2014: Geoffrey Le Pard
Publisher: Tangental Publishing
The right of Geoffrey Le Pard to be identified as author of this Work has been asserted by him in accordance with sections 77 and 78 of the Copyright, Designs and Patents Act 1988.
All rights reserved. No part of this publication may be reproduced, stored in any retrieval system, copied in any form or by any means, electronic, mechanical, photocopying, recording or otherwise transmitted without written permission from the publisher. You must not circulate this book in any format.
The characters and situations described in this book are the product of the author's imagination and any similarity to actual persons, living or dead and situations, past present or future is entirely coincidental.

For more information about the author and upcoming books online, please visit
www.geofflepard.com

Cover design by Peter Le Pard

For Linda

**SUNDAY 11TH JULY 1976**

## Chapter One

## Going South for Summer

I must be the last to leave. The hall of residence that has been home for my first year at university has a deserted feel, like a ghost town. My best mate Gary Dobbs (the Dobbin to one and all) left an hour ago, trying to cheer me up with a promise to write and a vague suggestion we go to France for a holiday before our second year starts. He left me Amanda as a sort of consolation prize because I was so miserable. She is a trophy from a rather boozy night after the end of the exams; a four-foot high cardboard blonde who he 'rescued' from outside Boots, where she was offering their twenty-four hour film processing services. The Dobbin named her Amanda after some former girlfriend.

Someone hammers on my door. Briefly I hope it's the Dobbin returned. I'm smiling as I imagine the 'Hey, Spittoon, fancy a last beer?' That's my nickname, which is ok when your real name is Harry Spittle.

It's not. Instead, blocking the doorway is Stephen McNoble.

We eye each other suspiciously. There's no way he's here to see me off with a cheery wave and wish me a happy holidays. For some unexplained reason, since Easter he has gone out of his way to get up my nose, trip me up, adulterate my food and generally be a pain in the arse.

If that wasn't bad enough, in the last two to three weeks, he's punched me twice, tried to twist off my right nipple and come within an inch of hitting me with a hubcap, which he said he was using as a Frisbee.

McNoble takes a step forward and closes the door behind him. I can feel the sweat beginning to pool behind my ears and drip down my temples; if he attacks now, no one will hear my screams. I'm only here this late because of Professor Bloody Bradshaw and his 'little chat' about my 'unique' exam results. If McNoble kills me I'll haunt Bradshaw.

"I just want a chat." McNoble's eyes bulge with the strain of not hitting me. As an afterthought he adds, "Harry."

That's another thing. I didn't think he even knew who I was until his reign of terror began and since then he's only called me 'bastard' or 'the bastard'. And the idea of a chat is a joke; since our first contact he's barely formed a complete sentence. He deals in grunts and thumps. There is something unhinged and inhuman about McNoble though it's difficult to say what exactly; he has the usual complement of limbs and facial features and he dresses like most university students. But if he's not a different species, then he has to be a different subset of hominid: *Homo Rightbastardus* or something.

Since I opened the door he has been moving towards me and I've backed away. I can feel my bed pressing against my legs and I'm just wondering what to do if he doesn't stop when an older man opens the door and steps into the room. "There you are." This stranger is a complete contrast to the muscle-bound McNoble: lean with greying, bubble-permed hair, a loud cheesecloth shirt and a droopy moustache. He and McNoble immediately ignore each other in such a deliberate way that they have to be father and son.

While I cross my arms to protect my nipples, McNoble begins to chew the inside of his mouth; in another life it could well have been my spleen.

Mr Skinny moves forward, hand outstretched. "Harry Spittle?" He has an oddly limp shake. He says, "I'm Charlie. Claude's Dad." He begins shaking his head, then nodding while grinning stupidly. "A Spittle, eh? Just think."

A lot of people laugh at my name. It is unusual, I grant you. It might have well-established Scottish origins but causes no end of mirth, though normally grownups manage to hide the sniggers. Not this one; mind you, if he's McNoble's Dad I'm not entirely surprised he's a jerk. It takes a moment to process that he has just called Stephen McNoble, Claude. I glance at the silverback; he looks even less chuffed than normal.

"Claude?" I do well not to laugh; probably a nervous reaction to the reprieve.

The man – Charlie – nods some more. "You'll know him as Stephen, won't you? Stephen's his middle name though."

"It's my only name." McNoble sounds so deeply pissed off that I think he might actually hit Père McNoble – which would be welcome if it meant he left me alone.

"Yes alright. His real name is Claude Stephen Jepson, only his Mother and I are divorced so it's Stephen McNoble, apparently. He's kept his Mother's maiden name. Silly really, not that I mind. Nothing special about Jepson, I suppose." His eyebrows shoot up, suggesting it's just a bit of fun, but the rest of his expression suggests he is deeply offended. He goes on, "I just wanted to say how-do because when I spotted your name last Easter – I was here to drop him off – I thought 'there can't be that many Harry Spittles'."

I glance at McNoble. He's taken an interest in Amanda and is pretending not to listen. There has to be a link between this man, Charlie Jepson, spotting my name and McNoble's campaign of hatred. Not that I have any clue what.

The nodding has increased. Something will soon come loose. Mr Jepson says, "You have your Mother's forehead. And eyes."

This is all rather disconcerting. He knows Mum? The idea I have some, albeit tenuous, link to McNoble's family is horrifying. Mr Jepson rubs his hands together. "So you off home? Still live in the New Forest?" He doesn't really pause to give me a chance to answer. "Great place for the holidays. All that lovely countryside, the peaceful lanes, the ponies, the pubs – I bet there are lots of free-spirited girls looking for a holiday romance, eh?" He winks. Just for a moment he looks like McNoble. "I bet you have fun with the girls, eh? Handsome boy like you."

I get this 'Isn't the New bloody Forest wonderful' blather from adults all the time, especially from those who have never visited.

What they don't understand is that it is full of gorse and scratching heather and brambles that ensure every walk is an experience in giving blood; and if you avoid them there are bogs that breed midges with bites like crocodiles and which, when you miss your step, as you do, suck off your shoe.

The revered ponies crap everywhere and block the lanes and occasionally drop their afterbirth where you're least expecting it. And, if by some mistake you get too close they will try and bite you in the belief you're a grockle offering food, or practise drop kicking you into the Solent.

And no one of my age willingly holidays in the Forest. There are two sorts who visit: ancient ramblers who dress in plastic clothes and have knees like fossilised sheep's turds and anglers with names like Leonard and Tony and Sid, who sit under umbrellas all day, eating cheese sandwiches. The pubs welcome these grockles, but refuse to serve anyone under twenty because someone who looks vaguely like you once threw up in their prize-winning window box and lost them Regional Pub of the Month for August 1974.

Anyway, how many girls are so desperate that they'll jump at a snog with a spotty, penniless nineteen year old with over-active sweat glands and bugger-all transport?

Mr Jepson pulls me back to the moment by taking hold of my arms and shaking me a little; he looks like he might burst with excitement. "Harry Spittle. I can see your Mother so clearly. And is that Arthur's nose?" He twists his neck, making it click and for a moment he stops nodding, like he's checking he's not accidentally made himself a paraplegic. "I suppose you're off home then?" He does like to repeat himself.

When I don't answer he looks around at McNoble, who holds up some keys and says. "These need to go back to the bursar's office. Could you take them, Dad? I want to say bye to Harry."

"Oh. Right." Mr Jepson glances at me. "Won't be a mo." And he's gone like a will-o'-the-wisp before I have a chance to beg him to stay.

As soon as the door has closed, McNoble lurches for me. I do the only sane thing and jump the bed so the mattress is between us. "Now, be calm... Claude."

"Don't call me that, bastard." He's primed and ready to spring.

"How does he know my family?"

"He grew up in the New Forest. That's when he met your parents. He asked me to mention him to you so if he asks, I did. Ok?"

"Ok. Why didn't you?"

He doesn't answer. Instead he begins to move left so I go right. It's like the wrestling with Mick McManus and Big Daddy only without the referee and no chance he'll accept a submission.

"And one other thing." He stops, breathing heavily.

"Yes?"

He goes right and I slid across my desk so it is between me and multiple dislocations.

He says, "The urn. Don't mention the urn. Or your shitty box."

"Why would I?"

"Just don't."

Once again he tries the old feint-left-and-dart-right manoeuvre but he tangles with my cardboard friend, Amanda, and falls backward onto the bed. I take my chance and grab the door handle only to find the exit blocked by Mr Jepson.

"Hey? You off?"

I step back, shaking my head. Mr Jepson surveys the scene suspiciously. "So what were you two doing?"

I manage a small smile; a mad urge overwhelms me as I say, "Oh just talking about the urn."

Immediately Mr Jepson's face crumples. The nodding takes on a more solemn aspect. "You know about Mother, do you? Claude mentioned her, I suppose. That's partly why I wanted a word. Since we'll be in the Forest for her memorial service, I wondered if your parents might want to come. Your Mother knew my Mother. They were quite close, once upon a time."

"Close?" I eye McNoble who is behind his Father and is making a sinister cutting movement with his flat hand across his throat. "Like friends?"

"Oh yes. We all were. A long time ago. I thought if I had your address I could drop them a line. Or maybe call round. There'll be a ceremony, a few drinks, that sort of thing."

"Ceremony?" The need to repeat oneself is catching.

"We will be spreading her ashes." He nods, more a wobble really. "So, your address?"

Reluctantly I give it to him. I want to lie but I don't have the imagination. While I'm wishing they would leave, Mr Jepson spies Amanda and bends to pick her up. He sniggers. It's such a ridiculous noise in a grown man. "And who is this?" He peers at the scratchy writing across her chest. "Amanda Spittle? Nice."

While he turns Amanda round in his hands, inspecting her a mite too closely, the room begins to fill with a sinister silence. Eventually Mr Jepson says, "Right, well we have to get off and meet with Claude's Mother for lunch. Can we drop you at the station?"

"No, I'm fine."

But he'll have none of my protests. He takes a case and I pick up my rucksack. I'm very keen to stick close to Mr Jepson but somehow McNoble is in my way. Mr Jepson is already some feet ahead. McNoble pushes me onto the bed and leans over me.

"I'll scream."

"Shut up, bastard. If my Dad does come and visit, just keep your Mum off him, right? And shut up about the urn or your crappy box or anything." He scans the room and his gaze alights on Amanda. He pulls out his red penknife, which I've seen a few times but this is the first occasion when I'm genuinely scared in its presence. McNoble looks seriously demented. "Otherwise..." He digs the knife into the cardboard, making a cross cut before pressing with his thumbs. There's a crack and a pop and when he holds her up, there's a new opening. "I'll do that to you, knife or no knife. I'll change your effing sex."

I've had enough. I begin to run after Mr Jepson who is whistling 'Goodbye to Love' by the Carpenters. He looks at me, misty eyed. "It'll be lovely to see Veronica again."

***

According to the clock on the dashboard, the journey to the station takes twenty-seven minutes. Mr Jepson keeps up a stream of chatter while McNoble stays silent. For my part I spend most of the time easing some flies that are trapped in the back out of the rear window. Mr Jepson catches me in the act as we wait at a traffic light. "Why are you doing that?"

I can't really explain why I have this thing about saving flies. Maybe it's because, as a young child, I saw Mum paint over a horsefly who'd bitten her while she was touching up the kitchen window frame. It squiggled and squirmed and I cried until she told me off. When Dad asked why I was upset, Mum told him I was a 'softie' and he said, in a stupid voice, 'Mum would never hurt a fly,' and they both laughed. It's such a vivid memory.

Mr Jepson nods, as per. "God knows where they've all come from. Maybe the box is attracting them." He catches my gaze in the rear-view mirror; I'm very aware from the way McNoble has tensed that he has to be talking about my box. Mr Jepson asks, "You hear about the accident?"

Even though he's looking away from me I can feel McNoble's stiletto stare just as much as if it was slicing into my forehead. I manage a shake. In extremis, I can lie it seems.

Mr Jepson goes on. "One of those things. It seems some oaf broke Mother's urn but Claude managed to get this lovely old box and she's in there. It's a nice touch and she would have liked it, but the fact the lid doesn't quite fit must be encouraging those little blighters."

McNoble turns slowly and meets my gaze. Something passes between us, like a righting of the scales, a restoring of equilibrium: he knows where I live, but he also knows that I know he has lied to his Father about the urn breaking (he ran into me when holding it – definitely his fault) and the box (I gave it to him to stop him beating me senseless).

When we've stopped and my bags are on the pavement I shake the wet fish that is Mr Jepson's hand again. "Have a good summer, Harry."

I watch them drive away and then pick up Amanda; she continues to smile enigmatically at me, promising to round off my holidays perfectly. As I head for the station the sweat cascades from my nose and chin. I think these summer holidays will be the hottest and shittiest since they invented the thermometer.

## Chapter Two

## Home Sweet Home

After four gruesome hours of train and hitching I reach Lymington. It's only another two miles, but there are sod-all lifts so I walk. By the time my house looms into view I'm saturated, exhausted and need food, even Mum's – cooking is not amongst her top fifty talents. My cheery 'hallooo' echoes back to me – no reception committee then. 'Home' is what's known as a 'New Forest Cottage', a pretty ridiculous title for a three-storied pile of ugly brick and old slate. The ancient roof fills Dad's waking hours with worry in the winter months and the whitewashed walls turn pink from the damp and algae every September and go back to white when they warm up in the spring. It is one of five houses in a small cluster by a T-junction, where a narrow lane meets the main road. Opposite there are a dozen large greenhouses for growing cucumbers but otherwise we are surrounded by fields, which act as a cordon sanitaire keeping the sodding Forest at bay.

Inside it is more decrepit than I remember – paint flaking off the skirting boards and cobwebs hanging from the lights. It is usually spotless; my parents run a B&B, you see. That means the first floor is out of bounds – we sleep in the roof space so I drag everything up the two flights. Even if I close my eye, I know I'm in my room with its smell of mouldering socks and mothballs. The bed hasn't been made and there are paint tins and rolls of wallpaper stacked against the far wall. A real 'welcome home, Harry.'

I tuck Amanda away – she won't last if Mum finds her – and head for the kitchen. Here I encounter the first sign of life: our malevolent cat, Rascal, lying on the boiler. The room is oddly hazy like there's a sea fret blowing in. My hunt for food takes me first to the fridge: there's a lump of extra hard cheddar that I suck to make chewable. Next I touch the oven. It's warm and optimistically I pull it open. A foul smelling miasma envelopes me, which probably explains the haze; as it clears I can see a roasting tin containing a block of coal carved into the shape of a leg of lamb – dinner. There's a pan on the stove that's also warm – it holds a strange lumpy orange soup that suggests carrots but smells of boiled handkerchiefs.

Before I go looking further, I heave up the sash window to get some fresh air and catch some aural crap floating in on the warm evening breeze. My kid sister is somewhere down the garden. Chewing my cheesy prize, I head off to find her. It's Emerson Lake and Palmer – like synthesized fingers down the blackboard. The volume alone confirms that neither Mum or Dad are about.

She's at the far end of the garden, beyond the gazebo. Dina may be sixteen, but in attitude she can veer from a snotty six to a smug twenty-six in the blink of an eye. She used to be pretty gross, a sort of human space hopper but this year the fatty bits seem to have migrated to her chest, which suggest she may be a female human after all. She never ever gets spots – unlike me – it's only her personality that's riddled with acne.

Dina is in a red bikini, lying on a towel. I'm still twenty feet away when I detect a familiar herby tang. I try out my 'Dad' voice. "Dina, what are you doing?"

I'm pleasantly surprised how high she jumps and the way her face is empty of any colour when her head spins round. "Jesus, cheese face, you might have killed me." With one hand she tries to bat away the stench of the joint while the other shoves the lid on an old tobacco tin.

I say, "Nice welcome home. Where's everyone?"

I'm ignored as she begins to collect up her things.

"I assume the burnt offering in the oven is dinner?"

She pulls a dress over her head and stands to face me. "The reason no one is here, and the reason dinner's become a sacrifice to the gods, is because Nanty is in hospital." Nanty is our Great Aunt Edna – Mum's Aunt.

With that she pushes past me and makes for the house. I follow a couple of paces behind. "What happened?"

"She fell." Dina speeds up but I keep pace with her easily.

"Is she ok?"

We reach the gazebo and she stops to pull away a loose board at the back. "She tripped over some of Mum's painting stuff – broke her arm," Dina stuffs the tin in a gap and pushes the board back in place, "concussion, loss of speech." She twists to glare at me. "Yeah, she's fine."

She's clearly intent on going indoors so I grab her arm to stop her. "Just hold on. What's up with you? When did it happen?"

She holds my gaze with a ferocious scowl until I let her go. It's like so many of our numerous standoffs from down the years. In the past it would probably end with her beating me with her fists, me retaliating and her crying to Mum. This time she just stares. One slow tear builds in the corner of her eye and slides down her cheek.

"Di?"

Her head drops forward and she shudders. "It's awful, H. Really awful." She only uses 'H' when things are bad – or she wants something.

\*\*\*

We sit in the gazebo; there's no air here and the sweat runs from my arms, down my fingers and makes dark spots by my feet. While I watch the dots grow and form a row of knuckles in the dust, she explains what's been happening: Nanty's accident followed the loss of all the bookings for the B&B, which followed some epic arguments between our parents, which followed the Mother of all battles between Mum and her sister, our Aunt Petunia, over my Grandfather's, their Father's, will. At least that's what I think she says because she snuffles a lot.

It is plain things have been going haywire for some time yet no one has mentioned it to me. I'm wondering why this is when I realise she's stopped talking and has leant right forward. Somehow she's pulled her foot to her and is chewing the skin by her big toe.

"Do you have to do that?"

She stops and looks at her toes and then up at me. "Is that all you can say? Haven't you been listening?"

"Yeah sure, but that's disgusting."

She picks out something from between her front teeth. "I knew you wouldn't care. You never write or call."

"Someone could have written and told me..." I can see her profile; she looks really miserable and suddenly I feel guilty at how I've ignored all her letters, everyone's letters. "I'm sorry. You're right. Ok. First, is Nanty going to be alright?"

She nods. "They say she'll recover but it may take some time."

"And why have the guests cancelled? July's always the best month."

She pushes herself up. "First come and see this."

We head, not to the house, but over to Mum's vegetable plot. I stop by a line of carrots and pull one up. It's twisted and full of holes. "Geez, these are pathetic. Is it this drought?" I look around. "Where are her pumpkins?" Mum grows prize-winning pumpkins; it's a family joke – that frankly is too close to the truth to be funny – that she pours more love into them than she does into her children.

Dina's sniffing reaches a gloopy conclusion; to stop the accumulated mucus enveloping South Hampshire, she gulps some air and wipes a snail-trail of snot down her arm. "She had to replant them down by the stream; I'll show you sometime. They're well hidden."

"What for?"

"To avoid the pumpkin vandal. Oh, we've had it all, H. Here, take a look at this lot." We're standing by a row of plastic bags and cloches. "Quatermass meets Percy Thrower." Inside the cloches are a range of different vegetables, some tied with odd bits of string and some in wire cages. She says, "So what do you think she's up to?"

"They've introduced an alien vegetable section in the Flower Show?"

Dina says, "Try again. And remember she's bonkers." She smiles enigmatically, reminding me briefly of Amanda; I shake my head hard – there's something wrong with my brain if it is linking my sister to the bikini clad vision in my room. While I continue to try and expunge the image, she stamps on one of the bags. "Stupid bloody cow."

I stare at Dina. She hardly ever – no, make that never – swears.

For her part she straightens the crushed bag, pulls her shoulders back and says, "Let's see if Dad's hidden any sweets in his shed – I found some sherbet bon-bons last week – and I'll explain."

"I don't know... he counts his sweets and..."

"Oh shut up, Mister Sensible." For the first time since I got home, she smiles – I'd forgotten how cheering her smile can be – and says, "You're a big girl's blouse, aren't you?" She brushes my arm with her fingers. "I'm glad you're home. Really."

***

Dad's shed is full of the detritus of his many passions: his collectables, his magazines, his correspondence, his 1957 edition of *Encyclopaedia Britannica*, his crappy record player and his collection of Elvis LPs and EPs. He seems to be making something from an old bean tin, like small cymbals. Soaking in a saucer is his spare glass eye; he lost his left eye while on National Service when he was involved in a nasty accident. For some reason the spare tends to go green if he doesn't disinfect it regularly. It's horrid, like part of him is still there, watching me as I go on a sweet hunt.

Dina settles into his old wing-backed chair, with her hands folded in her lap. She looks like she's presenting Jackanory. She picks at fluff on an old blanket draped over the arm. "He slept here last night. And two nights last week. It's not been good." She leans back and closes her eyes. "It started a few weeks back. June sometime. That group who come for a fortnight to fish at Hatchet Ponds…"

"Leonard, Tony and Sid."

"Yep. They cancelled. Sid was made redundant and Leonard had to have an operation or something. May was wet as well and the bank holidays were disastrous. I heard Dad moaning at her not giving the business her full attention but that was when the first pumpkins were attacked so she was dealing with that and this year she's secretary of the WI and heavily involved with its guest speakers and the summer concert."

"What's with this vandalism stuff?"

Dina deepens her voice, sounding like Mum, "It's all very sinister, dear – someone destroyed a lot of plants." She points at a shelf to my left. "Try that tin; he's hidden them there before. Mum set up some sort of informal policing – you know Mum, she got a bit carried away so Dad was left in charge of the B&B." She waits until I look at her; she's pulling a face. "He decided to advertise again..."

"Christ, he didn't? After all the fuss she made about his sign last year?" Dad painted this huge sign for the B&B which blew into a passing car, causing several hundred pounds of damage. Mum made this big thing about not needing to advertise; she believes we should rely on recommendations.

"Precisely. He didn't tell her. I only know about it because I overheard him talking to the paper about it. Of course she found out."

"Did she go mad?"

"You could say. Thing is H, she'd didn't spot it; the first thing she knew about it was when Aunt Petunia called her to crow about a mistake in our phone number. Aunt loved the idea it was Mum's incompetence."

"I bet she did. Poor Dad."

"It gets worse. While Mum had a real go at the paper and got the money back Dad applied to have us registered for Golden Oak Leaves – it's this new rating system for B&Bs."

"Surely Mum would love that. It would give her something to boast about."

"Dad didn't tell her so when this inspector came to stay and began complaining Mum gave as good as she got. You know what she's like. Then he got food poisoning and sort of said she did it deliberately."

"Oh God."

"And the paper got hold of the story – they made a big thing of it – Mum's sure it was sour grapes because she'd got a refund. Then the *Daily Express* picked it up..."

"Oh God. Was that Aunt Petunia?"

Dina nods, "Uncle Norman's nephew works there. After that – poof – no more bookings and a load of cancellations." Norman is Aunt's husband. "Of course she blames Dad and he says she made it worse."

"Bloody Aunt. She's a real cow."

Dina nods. "It all about Grandpa's will – don't ask me what exactly but even before the fiasco with the inspector there were a couple of really frosty family lunches – something about needing to change the bequests because they are so unfair. It all came to a head last Sunday. That's when Mum accused Dad of siding with Aunt and Uncle."

"Wow. That's a mandatory death sentence, isn't it? What's he meant to have done?"

She shrugs. "He's started helping Norman at the garage. Mum wants him here, redecorating, but he's told her Norman's needs are more pressing. Try that tin." Just to the right of my head there's a tin marked 'poison'. It's full of humbugs. We each take one and sit facing each other.

"So what's with the mutant veg?"

Dina takes out her sweet and inspects it; then she picks up the glass eye out of the jar and holds both the sweet and the eye in front of her face.

"God you're sick. Don't put the wrong one back."

She says, "Mum's trying to grow a carrot that looks like Bruce Forsyth or a tomato like Ted Heath, or a courgette shaped like a thingy. Her great idea is to send the best one off to That's Life. In her mind, she gets invited on the show, flirts with Cyril Fletcher, gets included in his Odd Ode and plugs the B&B; when she gets back her appearance is sure to be written up in the paper and then run in all the dailies. Free publicity, she says; Dad says she's a hypocrite because that is all advertising. He threatened to grow a ponytail if she succeeds."

She licks her sweet and says, "Dad's been working for Mr Anacide in his bike shop as well. He's hardly ever here." She takes out the sweet again and pulls a face like it has suddenly turned bitter.

I don't know what to say. Mum and Dad are always finding something to row about, so is this any different? Dina clearly wants me to agree with her, but all I can think about is Dad being at the garage.

You see, last Easter Nanty said I could help her with the garage admin during the summer holidays – Nanty does the book keeping for both Uncle's garage and our B&B; she's the only one in our family who really understands sums – Uncle says that the garage would collapse without Nanty doing 'the sodding admin'. That was to be my summer job – my money – but if Dad's involved it'll never happen. I can already hear him: 'Harry old son, it's pretty difficult this stuff – you'd better leave it to me.'

Dina wipes her nose again. She's said something, which I don't think I heard right. "What?"

She gazes back at me. "I said they're going to divorce."

## Chapter Three

## Biking for Boys

We find a rice pudding under some muslin in the pantry. A couple of dead flies are lying on the skin. The cause of their deaths becomes clear when we try and break through the surface: it's not so much set as vulcanised; they must have perished like kamikaze pilots of old. Dina offers to make us tea and toast while I go into the garage to check on my pushbike, my only hope of escape from home isolation.

Dina brings her cassette machine. It's playing Genesis.

I shudder. "Can't we have something else?"

Dina digs out the transistor Mum uses when gardening. After fiddling with the tuning an awful squawking echoes round the room. 'A Little Bit More' by Dr Hook. If you ask me, it's 'A Lot too Much' made worse by Dina singing along.

I attack the crusted mud on the bicycle, which comes away in satisfying chunks exposing acres of rust; I hope it wasn't holding the frame together. For a while I forget Dina's there as I tug at the chain and gears, liberally squirting oil where I can. We are treated to some America and Harry Nilsson. It must be twenty minutes or so before she says, "Janice says they're at a classic stage leading to divorce."

"Janice is what? Sixteen? Seventeen? Since when was she a divorce expert? A know-all, yes but not an expert. Can you grab the handlebars?"

The brakes do a neat impersonation of Demis Roussos. "They're not going to divorce. If they went on *Mastermind*, Dad would specialise in 'Winding Up Mum' and she'd have questions on 'How to Patronise Dad'."

Dina's knuckles have gone white as she hangs on while I try and heave the front wheel round. She says, rather breathlessly, "Janice's Mum and Dad divorced last year and she says they spent most evenings in their sitting room refusing to speak to each other. And then her Dad had an affair with the cleaner at his school…"

"Thanks. That's freed it." I look at her; she's definitely worried. "Who's Dad going to have an affair with? Colin Anacide? Those old boys he plays shove ha'penny with at the Wheel? Susan Glebe?" Ms Glebe lives in one of the other cottages across the lane; we're sure she's a lesbian because she wears corduroy trousers, smokes cheroots and likes opera.

"You don't understand, H. It's Mum I'm worried about. She's been going out loads with Mrs Martin. She even borrowed my eye shadow one time."

"That's your evidence? It might be proof of a lack of taste, but not divorce."

"I'm serious."

"I simply don't believe it." I lean the bike against the wall. "That'll have to do. Now, stop worrying. They're just on edge because of the lack of guests. And Nanty, of course."

She stares at her lap as she swings her legs to and fro but she's given up arguing.

I say, "Right, well, I'm going to wash my hands and then go and see Ruth."

It's rather disconcerting how that cheers her up. "Did she tell you about her and God?"

I'm bloody sure, from her expression, that she knows I don't know what she's talking about. I say, "I… we haven't had the time to write, what with exams."

She's off the bench and bouncing on the balls of her feet, all her energy restored. "Everyone knows. Ruth suddenly started going to the same Bible classes that Janice goes to and..." She misses my "bloody Janice" and ploughs on. "...and it's like she's gone all devout. Janice says she only goes to make sure her Mum gives her pocket money, but Ruth is really keen."

I don't want to believe her but it sounds just like the sort of stupid thing Ruth would do. "You can be a Christian and still have a boyfriend."

Dina twists her face into a grin. "Yeah but it won't be so much fun, will it?"

I spin the wheel to avoid looking at Dina. Is there something in the Bible that prohibits breast fondling? There's only one way to find out. I'm halfway to the door when Rascal sidles into the garage and studies me through yellowy calculating eyes. To reinforce who is the alpha male here he opens his right paw to inspect his talons.

Dina makes a purring noise. "He's come to welcome you home."

I have too many scars to believe that. As he slinks away I have this momentary picture of Rascal as a feline McNoble. They both inflict pain without a second thought. I wonder which of them would win if they fought each other? I suppose the truth is they'd just gang up on me.

# MONDAY 12TH JULY 1976

## Chapter Four

## Porridge

If ever I need a family motto it will be: 'Nothing good can come of a day that starts with having to get out of bed'. Sadly Mum's would be some crap about early birds or some such. It's barely ten to eight when she pushes open my bedroom door and tickles my feet.

"Morning, dear. If you want your breakfast before it gets cold, you'll need to pop down soon. Tea on your desk."

She leaves the tea just out of reach and disappears. I kick off my sweaty sheets and stare at the huge erection that has popped up overnight; I bet if I'd gone to Ruth's I wouldn't have one now, but Dina made me feel guilty about going out while Nanty was in hospital.

Instead we sat in front of the telly until Mum appeared, sometime after ten; she was in a foul mood because Dad had gone to his sister's, my Auntie Joan's, and wasn't coming home. About Nanty she said, 'not to worry' which meant I did just that; she muttered something about 'more tests' but refused to answer any questions, pleading tiredness and soon went to bed.

I sat up and watched some weird Dennis Potter thing on the box mostly because the *Radio Times* promised some nudity, but I must have dozed off because I didn't see any. And to cap it all, when I went to my room I found Amanda had been wrapped in an old sheet and stuck under my mattress. I assume that was Dina's idea of a joke.

I'm happily fondling myself when the peace is crushed by the cacophony that erupts through the wall. I've just about ignored the moron who keeps slamming the front door and Mum's fluffy slippers as they slush-slush across the hall carpet and I have years of experience blocking out the Today programme, which is wittering away somewhere downstairs. Even Rascal yowling as he eviscerates some hapless rodent causes me barely a twitch. But Dina's god-awful prog rock is too much – Wishbone Trash on an empty stomach is a cruel and unusual punishment – and if she's awake there's a real risk she'll stick her head round the door. There's no way I will risk being caught, red handed as it were, so I hobble to the bathroom to wash.

Mum's redecorating gubbins is everywhere – in particular the bowl of paste in the bath smells a little too much like her rice pudding. She's also hung this huge new mirror over the sink, which highlights a ginormous spot on my chin that's erupted overnight like a tumescent Krakatoa. Until the exams I'd convinced myself that I was growing out of spots but the stress of revision caused a resurgence. Clearly all I heard last night has set me back again. I'm halfway through probing it for its fissile qualities when Mum bellows for me to come and get breakfast. I just love Mondays.

***

Dina is reading the local paper; in her school uniform she's less the young woman and more the skanky sister I remember fondly. That cheers me a little. She says, mimicking Mum, "Have you washed your hands, dear?"

"Ha ha. Haven't you moved on from Wishbone Trash or are you stuck on the same old crap?"

"Harold…"

"Sorry Mum, but surely you don't like that mush?"

Mum stirs the pan in her hand. "I'm still rather sad that Glen Miller died. Now, porridge, dear. It'll set you up for the day. And it'll make a nice change from that awful institutional food."

My stomach reacts first and goes straight to the spin cycle. Mum makes porridge like a road mender makes tar - consistency and the ability to set under any conditions being more important than taste or nutritional value.

Dina is grinning nastily. "Fatten you up, eh? And that was Yes, you ignoramus."

"They all sound the same."

A car horn shatters the peace. "You're clueless. And that's Janice," Dina says. She ups and grabs her bag, offering me the paper. "Look at page ten. I've ringed some jobs."

"I've got one. At the garage."

Dina just shrugs and goes to give Mum a hug. Before she leaves she says, "And do you like his new hairdo, Mum? Very now."

Mum says, "Good luck, dear." When Dina's gone, Mum looks at me and raises her eyes to the ceiling. "I'm not sure Janice is a good influence. Her parents let her run wild; she even uses their car to go to school. And no I don't like your hair that long, Harold. It will give you headaches. And spots." She turns away and adds, "Did Dina tell you she has this beau?" Even with her back to me I know she's embarrassed.

"Beau? As in boyfriend?" I tip the bowl until it is vertical. The porridge doesn't move.

"She's far too young. Not that she'll listen to me."

"Who is it?"

"Jim James. Harold, it is food, not Plasticine. Put it down and eat it."

Jim is a totally harmless runt. Mum and his Mum have been friends for years. She's really scary - a Magistrate or something.

Mum is pulling on some rubber gloves while the water runs hot. "You couldn't have a word, could you? About precautions."

When I look across at her reflection in the window she has her eyes closed. I can't begin to imagine the effort it took to use the word 'precautions' in my presence. Before I can think of what to say, the phone rings. Mum sighs and says, "Would you answer that?"

***

The phone is in the dining room; Mum has always painted this room green (the rest of the house is a sort of puss-yellow) and it has the effect of sucking out all the light. Dina and I suspect this is to make it difficult to see what we are eating. Because the phone is here rather than in the hall or kitchen, it feels like you have some privacy. In fact anyone in the kitchen can hear every word. I've barely picked it up when a querulous voice barks at me. "Where the bloody hell are you, Arthur?" It's Uncle Norman.

"It's Harry. Dad's at Auntie Joan's—"

"Christ. When will he get here?"

"I don't—"

"No, you wouldn't. Bloody hell. I need him now."

"I'm sorry, Uncle but—"

"You lot are all bloody useless. You don't have the first bloody clue. You know what he's done? He's only gone and hidden the keys to the cars we have in to service. It's the last bloody straw…"

"Dad has this shoe box for his spare keys."

"He's taken them home? Jesus, that is typical. How cretinous can…?"

"I meant he may do the same thing at work."

"Hang on..." The phone is obviously dropped and a door opens and slams then opens and slams again. "That's it. Now, what about the invoices? Did he bring them home?"

"I haven't a clue, sorry."

"Oh bloody hell. How do you manage to run that B&B? Oh yes, I forgot. You don't. Without Edna you're sunk, aren't you?" His voice drops slightly. "We all are."

"I can help, Uncle. I talked to Nanty about helping —"

"You what? You think I'm having a second Spittle buggering things up? No way. I'm going to get Bert in, though it'll cost the earth. At least the bloody paperwork will get done."

"I can do it Uncle. Nanty showed me and I know —"

"If you see that useless Father of yours, Harold, tell him not to bother coming in. We'll cope better without him."

"But what about my job?"

"I'll tell you what you can do to be useful. Get Edna back on her feet pdq."

"But please Uncle..."

***

Back in the kitchen, the porridge has congealed.

Mum's voice is sharp. "Stop that, Harold."

Damn, I thought she'd gone outside.

"Porridge isn't good for cats. Take it out of his bowl please."

"But it's covered in his hair..."

"Think of it as fibre. You men need to ingest more fibre; it will improve your motions. What are you doing today?"

I pick up the local paper. "It looks like I'm job hunting."

She nods. "I'll drop you in Lymington. You can get your hair trimmed too."

"Can I see Nanty?"

She smiles slightly. "I'll ask. It may have to be later."

## Chapter Five

## Job Hunting

Mum drops me at the unemployment office to sign on, but the queue is horrendous. Instead of sweating in line, I take the paper Dina gave me and go looking for a phone box. The first one free is way down the High Street near the Angel Hotel.

There's not a lot, outside of farm or nursery work, but I'm determined to avoid castrating pigs or cutting cucumbers like I did last year. Dina has ringed three possibilities. The first is barman at Sharpner's Wine Lodge. While I dial, a fly cavorts and cartwheels around my head; at least one of us is having fun. The phone rings for ages and when it's answered the voice oozes suspicion.

"Who's there?"

"Oh, hello. I'm calling about the barman job. Can—"

"No." The phone is very clearly slammed down. When I replace the handset I see the fly again, sitting on Button B. As I watch he slips off, very clearly dead.

With my mood suitably lowered I try for bar staff at the Balmer Lawn Hotel in Brockenhurst. The person answering is polite, but equally negative. I'm about to try the third when there's a ferocious tapping on the glass.

"You've had long enough. I need to call the 'ospital." The gentleman is pretty ancient so I give up my place with good grace, not that he acknowledges it. In a way I'm grateful because I already feel exhausted.

"Harry? It is you. Small world."

Mr Jepson is striding towards me; in a panic I check for McNoble but there's no sign. Mr Jepson says, "I just knew we'd meet again. What are you up to then?"

"Where's, erm, Claude?"

"With his Mother. She's staying in Buckler's Hard." He shakes his head. "He prefers to stay in a pokey cottage than a four star hotel. He'll be over for the ceremony though. You can have a beer after, I expect."

"Ceremony? Is that your Mother's ashes?"

"That's right. We're scattering them on Hurst Spit. Bit of a trek, but it's what the old girl wanted."

There's an awkward pause while we watch the old boy in the phone box drop his change and fumble on the floor for it. Then Mr Jepson says, "So what does Arthur do these days?"

"My parents run a B&B."

"Really? I'd have assumed Arthur would have done something more practical. He was always good with his hands."

"He helps in a bike shop."

Mr Jepson laughs. It's not a nice laugh. "Yes that's more like it. Bicycle Repair Man." He glances at his watch and nods. "I'm in the accommodation business – hotels, a hostel or two, a couple of free houses. I might have a look at a few opportunities while I'm here. Maybe your parents could help? Seeing as they know the area."

I wish he'd go. After a moment Mr Jepson's gaze moves from me to the High Street, like he's daydreaming, so I turn my attention to sending hate vibes to the old geezer to get a move on. Eventually he leaves the phone box and marches off with not so much as a nod. "I need to make a call, Mr Jepson. I'm job hunting. I hope the ceremony goes well."

Mr Jepson blinks and smiles. "I'm sorry. Miles away. Job you say? So what are you after?"

"Ideally bar work, or waiting or something in an office at a push. Anything that doesn't involve animals or plants."

He laughs, "Quite right." His expression changes, like he's sharing a secret. "As it happens, I might know just the thing. Wait there." He squeezes past me and goes into the box. He isn't long. "That's lucky. Are you free now?"

"I'm meeting my Mum at twelve thirty. We're going to see my Great Aunt. She's in hospital."

"Is that Edna? Is she alright?"

I think I nod; he's not really looking at me, but at his watch. It looks very expensive. "Right. Good. We have an hour. I'll grab the car. Won't be a mo."

"What are we doing, Mr Jepson?"

"First you're getting a haircut; then you're getting a job."

## Chapter Six

## Hemingways

The inside of his BMW is better than the outside; it smells new. He makes me do up my seatbelt and says, "Hemingways. Best hotel around here. It's where we're staying. The owner is looking for staff so I've got you an interview." He glances at me. "Don't let me down, young Spittle."

I vaguely know Hemingways and it is very swish. I'm pretty sure Mum and Dad went to someone's ruby wedding party there. There's no way it'll want me as a waiter. "I thought Claude was with his Mother?"

His face clouds. "I told you he was."

"But you said 'we are staying'?"

"My wife. My current wife. We came down a few days ago; I just popped up to your hall to fetch Claude. If I hadn't he probably wouldn't have made it for the ceremony."

After a brief stop at the Universal Barbers where I sacrifice my much-loved tresses for the possibility of employment, we speed past Wellworthy, the big engineering company and up to the Forest. Mr Jepson keeps glancing around. He points at a side road. "I was born down there… Boldre. God, it was grim when I was fifteen. Bugger-all to do. Couldn't wait to get away."

"Is that when you met my parents?"

"Hmm? No, I met them in Salisbury, actually. It made us laugh when we worked out we had lived a mile apart and not met before."

"I didn't know they'd lived in Salisbury."

He's still distracted by his past because he barks out a laugh and points at a ramshackle pub sign. "Good God, is the Odd Fellows still going? It was the worst pub around though they did serve me my first pint when I was twelve." He pats my leg, making me jump. "Hmm. Jeans. I'll explain to Hemingway. This is a silver service waiting job; he'll want you smart. You know, black trousers, white shirt, that sort of thing."

What on earth is silver service waiting?

\*\*\*

Mr Jepson drops me at the gates. "It'll be quicker if you go in the front. I'll park and find you later." He twists a sort of smile. "I'll have you back before your Mum gets angsty." As he drives away, I realise how nervous I am and how heavily I'm sweating. I stare at the huge gates with tall brick plinths each topped by a vulture eying every entrant. Out loud I manage 'Get a grip, Harry'. From somewhere I find the energy to put one foot in front of the other and drag myself up the drive; on either side are unfeasibly (given the present drought) green lawns that scream 'Keep Off'. I try and walk steadily in case someone is watching from the huge impenetrable windows, but the deep gravel is designed for seriously expensive tyres to scrunch through, not nervy pedestrians. With each unstable step, my confidence begins to sag like my jeans, which seem to have grown, or I've shrunk since this morning.

When eventually I enter the front door, I'm slightly cheered by the rather pokey and tatty reception. There's a bit of peeling wallpaper behind the counter and a long black streak on the far wall. The furniture is covered in a ghastly orange felt. Though the door creaks loudly as I push it, the woman behind the counter doesn't look up.

"Hallo, miss. I've an appointment to see Mr Hemingway." The woman takes an age to register my presence; when she turns I'm startled because she has the most ferocious expression. She studies my face through narrowed eyes before standing and going into the back office and shutting the door. It's all a bit creepy and I want to pee rather badly.

"Harold?" My jump sends my jeans south and I grab at the buckle. The man who called my name has appeared from behind me; he is tall and disconcertingly asymmetric with crinkly grey hair and placid grey-blue eyes; he's clutching a clipboard to his chest. Close up I can see one nostril is almost closed while the other is the size and colour of a new penny. "You are Harold Spittle? Charlie... Mr Jepson mentioned you. Yes?"

"Er... Yessir. Mr Hemingway?"

"Right," he glances at his board, "Magda, do we have anyone else today?" When he looks up he realises Magda has gone to the room at the back. "Is that right, Magda? Magda?" She reappears. "Wasn't there an Enoch, and a Courtney?"

She shakes her head and disappears.

He studies me carefully; I'd guess from his expression I'm not exactly meeting his expectations. "So you're it?"

"Sir?"

"Why are you clutching your stomach?" He smiles slightly. "Not nervous, are you? Magda. MAGDA. Where is that bloody wo—?" Magda appears again. "Should we leave this until tomorrow? Until we have..." Her stare is unwavering and he peters out, his shoulders sinking. "I suppose you're right." He turns to me and smiles like an afterthought. "So..." He looks at the notes before glancing up. "Harold. Let's get this over with. You're Veronica's boy, are you?"

"Yes sir."

"Good woman. Salt of the thingy, you know. So, waiter."

"Sir?"

"The job. Think you can do it?"

"I..."

"Jolly good. There are forms of course. Bloody forms. Magda insists." He leans closer and whispers, still watching the room at the back. "Bloody tyrant that one. A stickler for forms. East German, you know?"

"I didn't."

"What? No of course not." He seems to have run out of things to say. After an awkward pause he coughs and moves towards the back office. "I'll... erm... right then..."

Is that it? Do I go? Abruptly, Mr Hemingway's head reappears round the door. "Black trousers, Harvey. And a belt. Especially a belt."

"It's Har..." But he's gone. Moments later the office door opens again but instead of the blank-eyed Magda it's a girl of my age. "Are you Harvey? Mr Hemingway asked me to give you these to sign."

"It's Harry."

She smiles. "Harry it is."

After I've filled in the forms she grins and then giggles as I heave my jeans up a notch. "I'm Penny. I'll show you around."

As we leave reception, Magda follows us with her creepy stare. I say, "Is she real? I mean she is a woman, isn't she?"

Penny nods. "Of course she is." She narrows her eyes. "Does she scare you?"

"No, it's not that."

"Well, she scares me. Guess how old she is?"

"Fifty?"

"Twenty-three."

"Never?"

"She's the youngest of the permanent staff; the rest are ancient." She leads me through the ground floor reception rooms to the restaurant and the kitchens. As we go, she says, "There are three of us students. It's really great fun. Mostly. You local?"

I manage a nod. "How long have you been here?"

"Two weeks. There's Natalie and me. We're at uni in Bath. Then there's Sven, the other student; he's local like you. He's a bit odd and…"

While she rabbits on I check her out as surreptitiously as I can. She has a chubby face framed by a mass of black curly hair that falls into her eyes. She's all curves and has very brown legs, which Nanty would call sturdy and blame on too much sport. She's different from Ruth for sure. Not stick-thin for starters; Penny goes out more than she goes in.

"…we all think Sven's loaded though he pretends he isn't. He says we can have a party at his place. Are you listening?"

"What? Sorry. Yes, go on."

Her smile is huge; she has more than her fair share of teeth. "I'll show you the gardens. We have this gardener, Cyril." She wrinkles her nose. "I think he's a creep but it's probably best for you to make up your own mind. So what music do you like?"

We chat about our tastes as we walk around the top lawns; the gardens spread away towards the Forest fence. As for music choices, she likes these female singer songwriters – Joni Mitchell, Joan Baez, Carly Simon – and I don't.

She snorts a laugh. "Your face is a picture. I wanted Carly Simon as my sister when I was sixteen." She spins round and grabs my hands, swinging me slightly. "Give me the summer and I'll make you want her babies by September."

She snorts again. "I shouldn't have said that, should I? I'll see you for breakfast tomorrow. Terry the Terrible will be after me if I don't scoot. He runs the restaurant... as you'll find out. Be here a bit before seven thirty tomorrow morning for his briefing. White shirt, black trousers and black bow tie. Don't be late or he'll eat you."

Alone in reception, I'm at a loss what to do when Magda appears. "Mr Jepson says 'e vill collect you by ze gates at quarter past. 'e is vith Mr 'emingway just now."

***

When Mum picks me up she's in a bit of a mood, partly because there's no real progress with Nanty, not that she tells me any details, and partly because Aunt Petunia has called her, demanding a meeting so they can sort out who is going to deal with the will while Nanty is incapacitated. She agrees to drop me at Ruth's; how much she is distracted by the upcoming sisterly discussion can be gauged from the fact she asks no questions about whether Ruth's Mum, Cynthia, will be there. I'm happy letting her drive in silence, when she seems to remember I've been job hunting.

"How did you get on, dear?"

"I got a job. Waiter."

"Oh well done. Where?"

"Hemingways."

"Really? That's... I..." After a pause she adds, "You must have impressed them, dear, with your boyish charm." She coughs. "And your nice short hair. Well done on getting it cut. The girls will come running now."

"It's not my hair, Mum. I bumped into this man when I was waiting by the phone box – he's the Father of someone I met at university – he's down here for some family business and he asked what I was up to. He knew Mr Hemingway and got me an interview. He even took me there and back."

"Really? How lovely. Is his son a new friend? You might have him round."

"No. Not really. More an acquaintance. That's all."

"Well that makes it even nicer of him to help you, doesn't it?

"He said he was from around here and knew you and Dad long ago. I think that's why he went to all that trouble."

"What's his name? Maybe I might remember him."

"Mr Jepson. Charlie Jepson... Mum, you need to turn here."

I have to grab the side of the seat as we squeal round the corner and come to a halt in the middle of the road. Mum is breathing hard, staring in the rear view mirror. Carefully she puts the car in neutral and starts the engine again. "I'm sorry Harold. I... I wasn't concentrating. Do you think you could walk from here? I really must get to Petunia's."

It's quite a relief to get out.

## Chapter Seven

## Sins of the Flesh

Seeing Ruth is both exciting (see-through cheesecloth top exposing white bra) and irritating (eyes half closed, whispering in a little girlie voice). "Hallo Harry. It's lovely to see you." She peers at me. "I thought you said you were going to let your hair grow long? I like long hair."

"I... I needed to get it cut for this job."

I make for a kiss, but she sways easily out of the way and says, "Come on. I've something to show you."

My brain advises caution but my penis is ever hopeful. Only once before, at Easter, have I made it as far as her bedroom, ostensibly to listen to her new Gilbert O'Sullivan album. It wasn't long before I was happily teasing her nipples into encouragingly firm peaks and struggling to control my erection when her bloody Father materialised outside her bedroom door, demanding to know 'what are you two up to?'

In the rush to put some distance between us, she used my throbbing nob as a lever; while she pacified her Dad I ended up in the bathroom, wanking into the sink. When I emerged I knew he knew.

"Are your parents about?" I ask.

She stops me at her bedroom door and grins. "No." Then she says, "Close your eyes." I'm led inside; in my fevered imagination she's undoing the buttons on her shirt with her free hand.

Of course I'm disappointed. On the far wall is this huge poster of Christ on his cross; on the wall to the left is a print of William Blake's 'God Judging Adam' that we had to 'interpret' in RE at school. One classmate, Nigel Sodding Parsons, suggested 'he looks like he's in the shite' which got a snort of laughter from Reverend Adams followed by yet another detention for Nige. I blot out the wagging finger and concentrate on Ruth's neck, which is inches away. As I move forward she says, "Do you feel His Love, Harry? Is it surging in you?"

I doubt He would approve of what is surging in me. My lips touch her moist skin and she jumps and whimpers. Soon enough my arms are round her waist and I'm nuzzling her neck. It worked well enough last time.

"No Harry, oh heavens don't." She moans and goes floppy, slipping out of my arms. I follow her across the room.

"STOP IT NOW."

I'm off balance as she turns and slams her palm into my chest sending me sprawling onto her bed.

"The vicar warned us that boys think… think these thoughts so we need boundaries." I'm not sure I want to hear what the boundaries are. She says, "I bet you haven't heard this." She turns away to her record player. "My cousin sent me it; he's working in New York. They're huge there. The Ramones." She looks at me like she's going to be cross. "They have long hair."

It is then this wall of sound hits me. It's fantastic and rather different to the Gilbert O'Grimbo she used to love.

"You've never heard of them, have you?"

"No. I bet they love the Velvet Underground."

I bend to pick up the sleeve as she sits on the bed and leans across me. "Kiss me, Harry."

Better. We kiss; it takes a while before she allows tongues and I'm sitting on my hands hoping that if I give it enough time she'll forget about boundaries. My willpower is only so strong and eventually I try an exploratory breast squeeze, which she doesn't stop. In fact she tentatively squeezes my nob, which bounces violently. I squeeze harder which makes her pull away. "We need to discuss boundaries, Harry." The record has ended and she flips it over. The B-side is even shorter and our next kiss lasts about as long. As silence falls she says, "The vicar says we must avoid the point of no return."

"No. Sure." Pause. "Which is where exactly?"

She puts on some Joan Baez. Hell, she can put on Jimmy bloody Osmond for all I care. We kiss and she squeezes me again, giggling. "He's very hard."

"Yes." I'm trying to breathe but with little success.

"We mustn't go too far." Another longer squeeze.

I swallow, gritting my teeth. I stand and pick up the Baez album cover. "This is great. How long have you had it?"

She looks surprised and folds her arms. "Don't you like it? I thought you'd like it."

I'm breathing and counting slowly. I sit down next to her and take her hands. "I love it. Only, if you carry on..." I place her hand back on my fly. "You'll have to get him out."

She jerks away and looks around as if someone has just entered the room. "NO..." Then, more quietly, "We must keep a boundary."

Everything is starting to spasm; this isn't good.

She says, "Do you want to squeeze my breast again?"

I don't know what to do or say. I try thinking about something neutral like shoe polish or umbrellas and squeeze my eyes tight shut. I suppose she misreads my straining for control as rejection, because when I look at her, she's sobbing.

"What's wrong?"

"You're so good. Is God telling you to stop? Is he setting the boundaries?" While she wipes her eyes and blows her nose, I turn the album over. As boring Baez protests her way through 'Come from the Shadows', we lie across the bed and stare at the posters, deep in our own thoughts. Even though she's not touching me my erection stubbornly refuses to shrink. When the last track comes to a scratchy conclusion she says, "I've been bad, Harry. That's why I've turned to God but I keep letting Him down. He's told me I must love myself and then He can love me, but before that I must seek forgiveness from those I've wronged."

"Who have you wronged?" I'm watching her right hand like a hawk; it keeps waving dangerously close to my flies.

"You. I've been tempting you, like Eve."

"No, really, I don't mind a bit of tempting…"

"Adam didn't mind either and look what happened to him. Reverend Sandal says the woman has to be the Drawer of the Lines." She surprises me by twisting off the bed and kneeling in front of me, like she's praying. "I've committed many bad acts: theft, sexual deviation, blasphemy, envy, cruel thoughts…"

"Sexual deviation?"

"I indulged in sins of the flesh." She scrunches up her eyes again. Was that me? Was that when we reached stage 2(b) at Easter? Her eyes ping open. "He told me it was my lascivious thoughts and that I mustn't lie…" She suddenly buries her head in my lap, which is really an unfortunate piece of timing, all things considered.

***

When I return from the bathroom, she's sitting in the corner of her room, tugging at her hair. "I stole, Harry. I was full of anger and hate and I took what didn't belong to me."

I have no idea what to say as I sit next to her. She allows me to put my arm round her shoulders. "Can't you give it back, whatever it is?"

She's shaking her head. When I bend to look at her face she's blinking hard. "I gave it to you. It was that box with the carvings; I took it from my Uncle."

***

She won't say why she took it only that I must get it back to her. I knew it was going to cause a problem. "I'll have a root around." I'm not telling her about McNoble.

That leads to a kiss and I'm allowed to reprise stage 2(b) for about ten seconds; in truth, having already shot one load, my heart isn't up to pushing for seconds. It's a bit of a relief when her Mum returns so I can leave; walking home I do wonder if having God as a rival is entirely fair.

## Chapter Eight

## Paying Your Way

Dad is on the old swing. We mostly avoid it, after Rascal's dirty protest for being shut out one evening. Dad doesn't mind; the accident that cost him his eye also did for his sense of smell and some of his hearing.

"Harry-mate. Your Mum said you were back. Good to see you, young shaver."

This Harry-mate and Harry-lad and what-have-you is quite new – since I left for university. It's because we're now officially 'friends' not just Father and son. He is always going on about how we should go to the pub 'for a good long talk'. Why we can't just have a swift pint and ignore each other like my friends do with their Dads, I don't know.

"Sorry about Norman. He told me about your call. He's getting rid of me too." At least he looks a bit sheepish.

"That's ok. I've got a job. Waiter at Hemingways."

"You? A waiter?" I think he must see my expression. "Not that you won't make a fine waiter. One day. It's just you need… well, co-ordination. And common sense. And…"

"I start tomorrow."

"How… erm, how much are you paid?"

"Thirty-five pounds a week. And I get three meals so I won't need any food here."

"Thirty-five? That's… well, generous." He plays with a frayed edge on the cushions, studying the wilting camellia to his right. "You heard we've no guests?"

I give a nod.

He checks to see if anyone is listening. "I have a plan; don't tell your Mother, but I may have a solution." He chuckles. "Yes, a grand scheme." His voice becomes serious. "Meanwhile I think – what with Edna incapacitated so we can't get your Grandfather's money just now…" I have a bad feeling about this. "Only short term – say twenty a week?"

"Twenty? Twenty what?"

"Pounds Harry-son. As rent, board and lodging, you know."

"But I'm eating at the hotel; I just sleep here."

Dad's lips pull into a tight line. "Lucky you. Twenty's fair. If I'm successful, you'll get it back. Some of it. Perhaps. You're nineteen now. You need to pay your way." He stands and adds, "If you see your Mother, tell her I won't need dinner."

***

The evening turns out to be rather difficult. Mum agrees to take me to see Nanty who's in a private room. When we get there she's fast asleep; while Mum goes to talk to the nurses, I chat away quietly about nothing and everything. She looks peaceful enough, smiling once, but then her eye tooth catches her lip, snagging it oddly; that smile has forgiven so many childish indiscretions and the idea it might never be the same is an awful thought. The more I try and bat it away the more the notion grows and the more I sniff back the tears. Outside her room I can see a TV with a programme about the Montreal Olympics that are due to begin this weekend; everyone looks happy and healthy and I hate them for it. I won't watch on principle.

After an hour, she's still asleep. I go to find the toilet. When I return, Mum and Aunt Petunia are sitting either side of Nanty's bed. The door is open and as I approach it is clear they are arguing, albeit in whispers.

Aunt Petunia: "I tried asking that stupid lawyer—"

Mum: "I won't discuss it now."

Aunt Petunia: "Arthur agrees. He said to Norman—"

Mum: "I won't have everyone bully me and I certainly won't have pressure put on Edna."

Aunt Petunia's voice softens: "That's why we need to talk to the lawyers…"

Mum: "Why are you so desperate for the money? Another hat? A new car?"

Aunt Petunia: "What about you? Arthur told Norman you had no guests."

"WE DO NOT…" Mum's loss of control pierces Nanty's snooze and she begins to stir. Mum and Aunt watch until she's settled back. "We do not need the money. It's just temporary."

"Daddy wouldn't want us to argue."

"So stop pressing. And how would you know what Daddy wanted? You never looked after him. You hardly—"

"I was working for my living."

"If you're implying that being at home is not a job…"

"All I'm saying is I pulled my weight and Daddy understood. He couldn't stand the oppressive way you tried to control him. That's why he gave us the garage business to run. He knew we would cherish his legacy."

"So why do you need the money? Your share's a pittance anyway."

"It is not. And it's mine. You can't stop me."

"If I can wait then…"

Aunt leans forward, putting her not inconsiderable weight on Nanty's bed. From where I'm standing it looks as if this is causing Nanty slowly but surely to tip towards her. "Everyone knows the will is unfair to me. Edna said so and Arthur has intimated as much to Norman."

"I WILL… I will not change it."

Aunt hasn't noticed that Nanty has now rolled over and is lying on her side, wide awake and staring at me. I'm about to intervene when I see Nanty wink and smile. Then she coughs and there's a bit of a commotion as the two sisters realise what has happened. A lot of clucking and patting and tucking-in ensues giving me the chance to enter the room without giving away that I've been listening.

Nanty smiles her old smile and taps the bed with her right hand. I go and give her a little hug and she mumbles something incoherent. When I look up Aunt has gone and Mum is looking thoughtful. She bends and kisses Nanty on the forehead and I follow suit. As I straighten up, Mum hugs me too. "I'm glad you're home Harold." She holds my arms as she steps back to study me. "A waiter, eh? I'm so pleased."

Mum leaves me with Nanty while she goes to see if Aunt has gone home or just for a cigarette. We sit in silence while a large, slow bluebottle swoops around the room, thumping the window occasionally. After a while it lands in Nanty's hair, on her left side where she can't flick it away. "I'll sort him out, Nanty." But she shakes her head and lets him settle. There are many reasons why she's my favourite relative and why I can't stop the tears this time.

**TUESDAY 13TH JULY 1976**

## Chapter Nine

## Terry

Mum hasn't grasped that I don't need breakfast. When I dash into the kitchen to grab a quick cup of tea, Dina is staring at a plate in the centre of the table, massaging her chin. She says, "Don't bite them, smelly. My jaw has dislocated."

"What are they?"

"Drop scones. Only don't drop them." Dina picks one up and feels the edge carefully with her finger. "Watch." She takes a used match from the edge of the stove and, with two swift swipes of the scone, cuts the match in half. "She said you'd need something solid for your first day at work."

"I'll get breakfast later; you can have mine."

"Oh no you don't." Dina stuffs two in the pocket of my jacket. "You can skim them on the Avon on your way to Hemingways. Give it a year and they may have softened enough for the trout to eat." She pushes two letters at me as she stands to go. "You're popular. And I don't like your hair. Makes you look about thirteen."

The fact Dina doesn't like the new short haircut convinces me it's probably a good thing. Maybe I'll see what Penny thinks about this whole long/short conundrum. One letter is from the university which I'll read later. The other is from Dobbin.

*Dear Spittoon,*

*Siobhan's dumped me. Mum has chicken pox so we're all eating frozen peas and spaghetti for every meal. I've a splinter in my finger which is septic and the puss just keeps on coming. Also I have a job. Fat Frank's Chippy. There's a girl with enormous bazookas too: Dotty. Just your sort.*

The kitchen door bangs open and Dad enters, a blanket over his shoulders. He looks miserable and just about manages a nod before he slumps in a chair and pulls the teapot to him, gripping it for warmth. He will be the only person this summer to suffer from chilblains.

I go back to the letter. *I was talking to my mate Jeremy about that rat who's stolen Siobhan and he recommended I curse him like in that ghost story – 'Casting the Runes' by M.R. James – that we did in the first term (not that you read it, I expect). Have you decided on a date for France? August 28$^{th}$ would suit me. Is your fat sister still mad? If you manage to remember, write back soon.*

*Dobbin*

*PS Have you heard the new Dire Straits album yet? It's fab.*

Silly sod. Mind you, if he perfects a curse I'll get him to send me one for McNoble.

"What's he mean? Probation?" Dad is holding a sheet of paper.

"That's my letter..."

Dad ignores my attempt to snatch it away. *While we set a pass mark of 40 per cent for the first year it is unusual for a student to manage exactly 40 per cent in each paper. As a result you will be on probation next year to ensure you are capable of completing the honours course. Yours sincerely H. Bradshaw (Professor and Dean of Faculty).* Dad blinks at me, his face expressionless. I know what he's thinking; the first Spittle to go to university and this is what happens. Carefully he reaches down to the floor and brings up a pair of highly polished black shoes, which he pushes across the table. He's stealing my wages and yet I feel like I'm the shit. Bastard.

\*\*\*

My bike is crap, despite my best efforts. The chain comes off at least six times in the first mile, most of which is up hill and I'm despairing of ever getting to work when I hear this pfutt-pfutt – a moped or something – getting closer.

The rider puts his machine on its stand and takes off his helmet: Nigel Sodding Parsons. Nigel is the bloke you meet on your first day at school and spend the remaining seven years trying to shake off. He's pug ugly, with a nose like Concorde and a set of teeth that druids would happily dance around to celebrate the midsummer solstice; he's also rich and a bird magnet. Not that the two things are linked, of course. "Bike trouble?"

"Yeah. My first day at work too. Hemingways. I'm going to be so late."

"Want a tow?"

"A tow?"

Nigel nods. "Coppold," he says, waving his elbow to make clear I need to grab it. I'm anticipating disaster, but it sort of works. We wobble a fair bit and he does seem to want to talk a lot, which doesn't make for a relaxing journey, but in no time we're at the entrance to Hemingways. Indeed by the time I let go and curve neatly in between the huge brick plinths, I'm feeling almost elated that I'm not going to be late after all; this lasts until I hit the deep shingle of the drive and the joy morphs into a bowel-loosening 'oh shiiiit' as I lose all control and crash into a small round bed of roses. While I lay still, triaging myself, a flashy car with blackened windows cruises slowly past; whoever's driving pauses to look at me before pulling away in a shrapnel of stones.

I take a moment to dust myself down and push the bike the final fifty yards; waiting on the steps is a tall, sallow-skinned man with stooped shoulders and hooded eyes. "Are you Harold?" This has to be Terry the Terrible.

"Yessir."

Terry's lips fissure his face. "You are late. You are staff. That," He nods to his right, towards a small opening, "is for staff and," he raises a long finger and points slowly at my hands, "you are filthy."

"I'll go and wash them now."

"Then you will be even later for my briefing."

"Er. Shall I do them afterwards?"

"You cannot enter the dining room like that."

"Er, what do you suggest I do? Sir?"

His expression suggests he would prefer having his prostate widened with a cucumber rather than tell me. He spins round and marches back into the gloom.

It's then I see Penny, standing by an arch, waving frantically at me. When I reach her she takes a step back. "How can you get so dirty and sweaty this early?" I start to answer but she waves me quiet. "Go and wash in there. I've got to find Natalie."

# Chapter Ten

## Breakfast

Terry's credenza, where we congregate, is this monstrous wooden thing. While the waiting staff form a horseshoe, Terry folds napkins and briefs us. "Right. We're full today, so no effing slacking about like yesterday. And no stupid giggling." He glares at Penny who is looking behind her a lot. "Any questions?"

No one says anything. No one looks at me. No one mentions my presence. As the others drift off to their stations I hop from foot to foot. Even Penny seems distracted and barely nods before she hurries away.

Finally Terry looks up, surprised I'm still there and snaps, "Jacket." He points at the back of a chair. It's white, heavy and stiff, more suitable for a trip to the South Pole than a steamy restaurant. Everyone else is wearing green jackets, save Terry who's in red.

"You're with Amos." He waves vaguely at this man with bushy eyebrows, a bug-eyed stare and frantic movements.

The restaurant is in two parts; the main area is down two steps from the credenza and holds some twenty tables; off to the right there's a smaller area up about six steps with maybe six or seven tables. Amos is running this section. Beyond Amos' empire there are double doors that seem to open onto a lounge with lots more of the orange furnishings I saw in reception.

Amos is affable enough. The first guests are an elderly Scottish couple. 'The MacThings' according to Amos. I know it's a trick and smile; it's good he's treating me like one of the boys. I'll find out their real name later.

Each step is explained out of the corner of his mouth while he does this head-tilt thing, bending it one way then the other almost touching his shoulders. Eventually his neck clicks; by rights he should shriek with pain, but he just grins showing very white if uneven teeth.

Amos plays his audience for all he's worth, his patter coming thick and fast. I'd reckon the guests get about half of what he says. His asides are waspish and probably insightful; his demeanour knowing one minute, unctuous the next. When we've collected the first set of dirty bowls and glasses he says, "Come on, time to brave the kitchen."

***

When Penny showed me round, the kitchen was eerily quiet; now it's a cacophony of shouts and clashing pans; Amos tries to explain the rules about which door to use, which sink is for which crockery, how to place and collect an order and so on; I take in about a tenth because I'm rather distracted by the most gorgeous looking blonde who's in one corner, partly shielded by some cupboards, as she struggles into her green jacket. It rucks up her shirt affording me a glimpse or two of a black lacy bra. "Harry?" Amos is waiting by the serving counter, which is manned by this huge sweating hulk in chef's clothes and a salt-stained bandana. "This is Beet." Amos flicks his head back to the blonde. "And the tart is Natalie." We all look across to where Natalie is standing; when she sees us she waves and sashays into the restaurant.

Amos has his hands on his hips. "You boys are pathetic. You're dribbling." He too sashays away. Beet waits for him to go. "What you think? Amazing knockers. Like bumble bees."

"Bumble bees?"

"You don't know how they stay up without help." He nods at the door. "Go on. Fuck off and work."

***

I'm set on making toast. All goes well until I realise there are only two slices left and they're soaking. I approach Beet for more bread. As if by magic another much shorter chef appears. Beet says, "What do you think Paul?"

He sniffs one of the wet slices, suspiciously "Yeah. You're right." He looks evenly at me. "Name?"

"Harry."

"Student?"

I nod and smile.

He leans towards me as if to get a closer look. "I'm Paul, the head chef. This is Beetroot. Beet to his friends." There is nothing friendly about the introductions. Something tells me that they are complete bastards. "So you were saying?"

"I... well, I need some toast, but somehow the last two slices have got wet and..."

Paul scratches his neck. "Yeah but how'd that happen?"

"I don't know."

"But you had them last. You saying we make shit wet bread?"

"No, but..."

"So?"

"I'm not saying there's anything wrong with the bread. It's just they've got wet."

Beet says, "You spilt something? Dropped them in the sink?"

I try and sound in control. "No. They must have been..."

Paul leans forward. "What do you think of Natalie? Cracking, eh?"

"Er..."

"Beet says you were gawping at her tits."

"No, it's—"

"Makes you horny, does she?" He jerks back. "Or you a poof like Amos?"

"No. No, I'm not."

Paul nods and Beet follows him. "We thought so. It's understandable you being a student and all."

I'm lost; I wait for him to finish. He waves me close to the counter and leans across. "You students haven't really been out in the wide world, see. You don't understand all the little rules, all them social conventions. But here, in this posh hotel, we don't wank into the toast. Not done."

"I didn't." I know I've gone red and I sort of know they don't mean it, but I don't know how to stop them.

Paul looks over my shoulder. "Here doll. Help us out." To my horror Natalie comes over with a tray and stands next to me. "Poor Harry ain't used to being close to girls, see. He had a little accident on his toast. My sense of smell ain't what it was. What do you think that wet patch is?" Paul offers her the slice. "Spunk?"

Out of the corner of my eye I can see Natalie recoil and then smile nervously. I can't take any more and grab the few slices I've toasted already and dash for the exit.

Amos knows something is up, because he takes the toast from me, tells me to go and clear the tables, before marching back to the kitchens. As he opens the door I can hear Paul and Beet's laughter. If I could run away without causing a scene, I would. I've been at work two hours and already I hate this place.

## Chapter Eleven

## Tips

I don't quit. Partly it's because Amos comes back and tells me they're bullies and wankers and I should ignore them; mostly it's because Natalie comes over to me while I'm laying the tables for lunch, and says she hated what happened and knows it was a stupid joke, but it was horrid. She kisses me lightly on the cheek. "There. Better?" She has such lovely chocolate buttons for eyes. She adds, "We'll have so much fun, Harry. We'll go to the beach later and have a swim. I bet you swim really well."

***

I'm to do elevenses with Sven so have to hurry my breakfast. Penny catches me as I'm leaving the staff restaurant. She whispers, "Harry, don't be cross, but someone said you smell a bit; all the sweating on your bike maybe? Have a wash before you serve the guests."

I nod, and don't say a thing, but I'm livid at whoever has suggested I stink and at Penny for believing them. I mean, thirty-three days without rain, a barometer that says 'fair' with a kind of smug confidence not usually associated with English weather instruments and I'm wearing a Nepalese winter coat: what does she expect?

I go to find the gents; my plan for a quick armpit sluice is thwarted by the presence of an elderly guest trying to pee. He jabbers away about ageing equipment and his urologist, making me turn on the taps, whistle 'Little Brown Jug' and flush the toilet twice before he succeeds.

When I finally emerge, Sven is leaning against the wall cleaning his nails. "Now that must have been an impressive dump, young Harold. You were in there at least fifteen minutes." He is tall, angular with thick white-blond hair spreading over his collar. As he leads me to the coffee station, he says, "Do you prefer Harry or Harold?"

"Harry's fine."

"I see. And Paul suggests you may be homosexual?"

"No. I'm, you know... not."

He looks at me like I've disappointed or maybe confused him. "Some people of our age are still unsure."

"I'm not a queer, ok?"

He holds up his hands defensively. "A matter of complete indifference to me, Harold. Now coffee..." He begins to move away before he says, almost as an afterthought, "You couldn't lend me a tenner, could you?"

***

He shows me the basic idea and disappears. My first customer is Mrs MacThing who is very understanding. She reminds me, with her permed orange hairdo, of Mrs Thatcher. My second customer isn't so pleasant. The man is sunburnt, hairy and impatient. As well as coffee, he demands two glasses of squash and some biscuits. If Mrs MacThing hadn't overheard us and pointed me in the right direction I would have been stumped. As it is, I'm soon balancing a tray on my right arm and going into the garden. The sun lounger I'm looking for is empty, but there's a slim woman lying face down on a towel next to it. "Are these for you madam?"

The woman doesn't look up but turns her head slightly towards me. I look towards the gardens; her swimwear barely covers the yards of bronzed flesh and I don't want to be accused of gawping. "Thank you. Just leave my cup on the floor."

"Shall I put your husband's on the table?"

"He's not my husband. You're new, aren't you? What's your name?"

"Harry, madam."

"Hmm. Age?"

"Nineteen, madam."

"God, so young." She turns her head the other way. "Always so young. And so handsome." When I've finished she says, "Could you rub some oil on my back? It's on the floor." As she's speaking she unclasps her bra strap. "Make sure you do the tops of my thighs. They burn easily." I'm still wondering where to start when a chocolate-smeared girl with blonde pigtails runs up to us.

"Me, me. Please, Monica, please... let me do the rubbing."

The woman sighs. "Yes Annabel, all right. Can you reach my purse, dear? We ought to give this young man a tip."

While the urchin sorts through the change, the woman peers up at me. "I'm sure you'll get another chance, Harry."

## Chapter Twelve

### Penny's Fears

When the coffees are done I go to the gardens for a breather; I already feel exhausted and there are two more meals to serve. Sven and Penny are on a bench under some forlorn looking cherry trees. Penny is reading and Sven is sketching. She smiles. "Well done for coping."

Sven doesn't look up. "Harold is the sort who copes, Penelope. He's been bred to make the best of things. And how was Mr Leaver? Still cuckolding Mr Jepson?"

"Sorry?"

"The angry man in the too tight shorts? Wasn't he with Mrs Jepson?"

"She didn't say her name."

"Well, her husband seems to disappear a lot and Mr Leaver kindly keeps Mrs Jepson amused. Rather like over-sexed rabbits."

Penny hits him with her book. "Stop it Sven. We don't know that."

Sven sneers at Penny. "I'd almost feel sorry for Mr Jepson if he wasn't such an arsehole. And he dresses like a pimp."

I say, "I met Mr Jepson the other day. He was from around here a long time ago."

"I believe my Father has something to do with his absence." Sven sneered. "A falling out. You don't fall out with Pater and stay around, not if you're wise."

I'm about to ask what he means when I catch Penny shaking her head vigorously. She says, "I saw Paul with Mrs Jepson yesterday."

Sven sniggers. "Oh please, Penelope, I think Mrs Jepson has better taste. And we know where Paul is directing his affections, don't we?"

Penny glares at him. "Shut up, Sven."

He holds his hands up. "Some people will do anything for a little cannabis…"

"I said shut up."

"Sorry, I'm sure. Now are you certain you can't sub me a note, Harold? I'm a little embarrassed just now and I do owe young Penelope here a few little green drinking tokens."

Penny shakes her head, "He's teasing, Harry. He's really loaded, but pretends otherwise."

Sven's syrupy voice hardens. "You know nothing about my personal circumstances, Penelope." He looks at me. "I popped my watch you see and if I don't have it back when Pater gets home this evening things might become unpleasant."

"Popped?"

"Oh Harold, please. 'Pop goes the weasel?' You know, I pawned it?"

Because Penny smiles, I laugh. That seems to irritate Sven who snaps his sketch pad shut. That's even better. "Here." I hold out the fifty pee. "My first tip; Mrs Jepson. You can borrow that."

Sven's face creases into a smile. "A tip? You'd better keep it, Harold. Oh dear."

I'm so confused by his reaction I don't notice Penny has stood up until she tugs at my sleeve.

"Come on. We... God. You are soaking, aren't you?" She sets off for the front door at speed leaving me to catch up. Sven calls out behind us, "And tell him about the biscuits, Penelope."

Penny only pauses to hold the door for me. I say as I pass through, "Is he always a prick?"

"Oh yes." She leads me back towards the restaurant, down a corridor with the bar on one side, visible through half height internal windows, and the toilets on the other. Just before we emerge by the credenza, Penny stops. I can just make out Terry's outline; he's folding napkins.

I say, "Why does he do that?"

"It soothes him. Stops him yelling at us. Come on." She walks up to him and says, "Harry has a tip."

Terry doesn't look up. "Has he?" He holds out a hand, his fingers clawing towards me.

When I don't move, she says in a flat voice, "Terry runs the tip box. We all contribute and Terry divides the tips at the end of each week. It's to ensure fairness. We each get a percentage." She pauses for breath. "If anyone failed to give in their tips, everyone would be upset and... and there would be consequences..."

"What's my share?" My fifty pee feels hot in my hand. Terry's fingers are opening and closing like a cuckoo's beak.

Penny can't keep still all of a sudden. "Harry, please."

I drop the coin into Terry's palm. It disappears with sinister speed, but there's no sign it's put in any box. As Penny pulls me away, Terry looks at me. I ask, "So what's my percentage?" He's still in shadow, but I'm pretty sure his bony fingers form a zero.

***

Penny takes me to a small windowless room behind reception where she digs in a cupboard full of jackets.

"Here, try this." It's a lighter weight though about two sizes too big.

"When you pass your test – to be a silver service waiter – you share in the tips. You get a green jacket then."

"When's the test?"

"Probably the end of the week; it depends when they think you're up to it."

"Never then. I'm useless at that sort of thing."

"You'll be fine. Just be a little careful to begin with. Don't go winding people up."

"I'm not."

She shakes her head, counting on her fingers. "Paul and Beet are chuntering about you, Terry won't trust you, Amos was moaning about the MacThings' toast and you've irritated Sven, which most people do."

"What was all that about his Father?"

"I heard from Chris – Christian, he's another waiter – that Sven's Dad's a bit dodgy. Though he's meant to be really rich. I suppose Mr Jepson had some run-in with him or something."

"Why's Sven trying to cadge some money if his Dad's so rich?"

"He's probably stingy too," Penny says, "Rich people are. It's well known." She sighs, "Look, Harry, just be a bit wary. There's a lot of tension around here just now. You'll soon notice it. Different cliques." She studies my face. "Sorry, I'm making it sound awful. It's not. It's great fun. You wait till you meet Chris."

"Is he local?"

"Yes." She does this lusting thing with her eyes, "He's so good looking. And a lovely person. He makes us all laugh, keeps us sane. You'll love him."

I hate him already.

Penny frowns. "Just remember the permanent staff resent us students. They worry that the more there are of us the worse the business is doing – bookings are right down – and the more likely this place might close."

She must see my skeptical look. "It nearly did last winter. They'd love it if one of us was sacked. Meantime they make our lives hell. Biscuits for instance – Paul controls biscuits so if you took them and he finds out, well, be careful what you eat."

"You're not selling this job to me, Penny..." My voice is a bit too whiny, but I can't help it.

She shakes her head and smiles. "My Father would say it's character building. Keep your head down for a bit and avoid people's toes. I'll try and help."

"Thanks." We both smile; there's something really warm that makes her easy company. Much more so than Ruth. I bet she likes long hair; I bet Christian has long hair.

## Chapter Thirteen

### Sand, Sex and Cereal

The trip to the beach, after lunch, perks everyone up. I'm not expecting to be invited, being the new boy, but Chris insists and we – Penny, Natalie, Sven and me – cram into his car and go to the beach near the cliffs at Milford on Sea. For an hour or so, we muck about with a ball – well, Natalie just stretches out on a towel – and then sit and chat. Mostly I listen. Christian, it turns out, was at my school two years ahead of me, not that I knew him. He has long hair.

After an hour, he and Penny stand and, without a word, move off towards the base of the cliffs. Sven must see my confusion. "They like their space, Harold. Though," he's watching them closely, "for someone so intelligent I find her choice odd."

That sparks Natalie into life. "Don't be a complete prick."

Rather than respond he sighs and picks up his sketch pad. It seems almost contrived that he heads in the opposite direction and settles to draw the sea.

I feel awkward, alone with Natalie and keep my eyes on my book. After a few minutes she sits up and asks what I'm reading. Soon we are talking about books, music, TV and films. When she says she loves Clapton I pretend to be sick and she throws seaweed at me. I throw it back and she makes for a pretend wrestle. I let her push me over, not sure if it's ok to touch her and, if so, where.

I'm sort of hoping this is a come-on when someone calls her name: it's Paul with Beet, coming towards us. My groan merely triggers a laugh as she says, "You just have to know how to handle them." With that she's up the beach and snogging Paul like a long lost lover. He, very obviously, gropes her bottom.

When they break apart she waves for me to join them as they settle on some rocks to smoke a joint but I can't face it and go back to my book, feeling useless. It must be about thirty minutes later that she returns, standing over me. "You're a prick too, you know. They're just mucking about. Come on."

I shake my head at which point she bends down and kisses me quickly. "You sure?" I feel stupid, hot and angry and I know they are laughing. When I don't move she says, "Your loss," and collects her towel before returning to join them.

*** 

Cycling back late, my legs weary from all the standing, I'm so engrossed in trying to decide what I think about Natalie that, when I wheel my bike in the back gate, I don't immediately register the noises coming from the gazebo. And when I do I'm not really thinking what they might be until I hear a gasp. Stupidly, even though I know it is Dina, I peer round the side.

There, right in front of me, is my sister propped on the back of the bench – she's facing me – while her bare fleshy legs dangle, like those of an untrussed chicken, either side of Jim James' angular, dimpled and pumping bare buttocks.

Dina spots me pretty much as I see her. "Oh Christ. Stop Jim, STOP. He's watching us."

Jim's bum clenches and looks like it might shatter under the strain of going so rigid so quickly. "Your Dad?"

"No, my slimy brother. Go away, raisin face."

The buttocks relax and resume their thrusting. I definitely prefer them stationary. I say, "I'm going. God, you're both mad."

I've abandoned the bike, but even as I hurry towards the house, trying to scrub my mind of the awful images, Jim calls after me, "Harry, you ok for Saturday?"

That stops me, though I keep my gaze fixed on the house. "What?"

I might not see anything, but I can hear the slow creaking and groaning from the bench as Jim maintains his rhythm. He says, "The cricket. Angus said…"

"Christ Jim. Not now. Ring or something." I up my speed, wishing to God I could block out the noises. As I yank open the backdoor there's this gloopy slurp like someone trying and failing to pull a Wellington boot from a sticky bog.

***

By the time Dina comes in a few minutes later I'm really angry, but she pretends nothing has happened. "Brrr. Where's the summer gone? So how's the job?"

"You're barmy. How can you do that, out there? What if Mum or Dad caught you? And Nanty is still in hospital…"

It's her turn to be angry. "You're never here. You don't know what it's like. Jim's the only one who understands. They're splitting up and you don't care."

She digs around in the cereal cupboard and pulls out the Sugar Puffs. She says, "Mum's left you dinner and said to make sure you finish it."

"She knows I get fed at the hotel. What is it?"

"Shepherd's entrails. It's in the oven." Dina sits at the kitchen table and spoons cereal into her mouth slowly.

"Where are they?"

"Mum went to see Nanty and then went out with Mrs Martin. She was all dolled up too. Like I told you."

I pull out the oven-proof dish. "Bloody hell. This could feed Southampton. Where's Dad then?"

"He went to the pub with Uncle and Mr Anacide. Darts I think. Mum wanted him to see Nanty, but he said he was busy."

"Oh great. The sod demands I give him twenty quid from my wages and then he goes and spends it in the pub." Dina doesn't seem interested. I say, "I saw Nanty yesterday. Did they let you in?"

"For five minutes as I'm only sixteen. They're a bunch of Nazis." She waves her spoon at the dinner. "You could try Rufus though he's been a bit choosy since we gave him her meatballs in May."

I try breaking off some of the crust. It's like plywood and the smell is pungently goaty. In the past we put out anything vaguely meaty for the fox (who has been called Rufus for years); if that option has closed off we are in trouble. Dina slurps a dessertspoonful of sweet milk. It's a bit too close to what I've just heard outside. She pauses, mid-mouthful. "She waited until Dad went out before she called Mrs Martin."

I don't want to talk about her suspicions so say, "You were right about Ruth and God. She's gone really weird and—"

"I don't care about her."

I carry on. "I'm not sure I can deal with this God stuff, you know? I may just dump her; there are others. A couple of the waitresses seem nice..." I take a glance across the table. "For Christ's sake, Di."

She's crying, hugging herself.

"Come on. They're not splitting up."

"THEY ARE." She rubs her eyes furiously. I don't think I've ever seen Dina so upset – well, not since I amputated Barbie's left arm.

I'm surprised how much I hate seeing her like this; it feels like I should put an arm round her shoulders, but fortunately I spy the dribble of snot leaking from her nose and remember who she is. She says, "You'll have to do something."

"Me?"

The snot grows into a silvery bubble, which she wipes on her sleeve. She says, "Yes, you. Dad hates her so it'll have to be you or we'll be orphans."

"He doesn't hate her. He's just a bit, you know, anxious about the lack of guests. Once that's sorted it'll be ok. And they'd need to be dead if we were to be orphans."

"I sometimes wish they were. They're always getting on my back."

Mum's face and the word 'precautions' pop into my mind. "Is this really about them?"

"Of course."

"You're not, you know, in trouble?"

"Trouble?" The sobs stop and she peers at me suspiciously.

"You know? You and Jim?"

Her look could strip paint. "NO I'M NOT." For a moment I think she wants to hit me; then she sinks back onto a seat, like she's been winded.

"Sorry, Di, I... she... they're just worried. You know."

One minute we're staring at each other, not sure exactly what we're meant to do, the next she lurches across the room, grabs me and hugs me tight, her face buried in my chest. I keep my hands high while she mumbles incoherently. I hope the damp sensation is her tears.

**WEDNESDAY 14<sup>TH</sup> JULY 1976**

## Chapter Fourteen

## Peeping with Cyril

Day two at work and it's better than day one. Christian, self-styled 'coolio doodio', lightens the mood considerably acting as a lubricant between the students and the permanent staff. I even remember my trunks for another promised trip to the beach. In my mind's eye I can see me stretched out on the sand while Natalie winds daisies in my hair and we talk about how great it would be to see the Doobie Brothers live – while agreeing Paul is an arsehole and she was wrong to kiss him. When lunch is over I wander off with my swimming stuff to wait for the others. Natalie is there, still in her uniform; she's staring into the distance out over the Forest heather.

"Hello."

"Hello Harry. This place has ancient rhythms, doesn't it? You can feel the planet beating here." She turns her dopey stare on me; is she stoned already? "I think the crust must be thin and we're feeling Gaia's pulse. Do you feel it?"

I can't tell if she's serious or having a laugh; if I get it wrong she'll think I'm a pillock. I play it safe with a considered, if slightly amused, nod. It seems to satisfy her. She says, "Imagine making love in that heather, all nature around you joining in the coupling." Her eyes are squeezed shut as she lifts her arms to the skies. Clearly she has no idea how unbelievably scratchy the heather can be.

Natalie seems happy to stay in that pose while I shuffle my feet. Finally Penny appears. "Christ, aren't you ready girl? Come on." She pulls at one of Natalie's arms, destroying her 'I am a waterfall' pose.

Natalie glares at her. "OK. Just stop being such an effing matron. Christ." She marches off towards the Rat Pit, leaving Penny looking from her retreating back to me.

She shrugs her shoulders and begins to follow. She says, "Make yourself useful and fetch Sven. I saw him with Cyril so I expect he's up to no good."

*\*\*\**

My Mum has talked about the gardens but this is the first time I've seen them. While the rest of Hampshire looks like the dust bowl on the front of the cover of the Steinbeck novel we studied for O-level English, this place is green and lush. Not that the riot of colour makes me any less hot and sweaty. And the distant squeals from the swimming pool don't help much either.

I'm on the verge of giving up when I come across the gardener. Cyril. I watch for a minute or two as he digs slowly, his lips moving silently. He surprises me by abruptly looking up and glaring at me.

"Hello. Cyril? I'm looking for Sven."

"Arrr?" He is as nearly spherical as a man can be. His sweat-stained shirt is straining at the buttons. He plants his fork and marches over to me, seemingly oblivious to the plants he's crushing. His eyes, sunken black dots, are joined by a deep crease over his nose like a pince-nez. "New boiy?" He has a melodious sing-song voice.

"Yes. Harry. I'm trying to find Sven."

His jaw circles like a cow grinding its cud, before he says, "Arr."

"Er. Do you know where he is?"

"Arr." He narrows his eyes for a moment before turning away. "Oi'll shows you what he loikes."

After a few yards he stops; he pulls out a radish and passes it to me. He watches as I try it; it tastes divine.

"My Mum would die to know the secret."

Cyril chortles and tugs at his fly. "I pizz on 'em."

What I've not already swallowed I gob out, managing not to gag on the rest. He hurries away and I have to run to catch up. "Is Sven…?"

Suddenly he stops, looks each way and pulls back some branches in a laurel hedge. He says, "This'll be a roight treat," as he eases me into the dark space behind. The hidey-hole leads to a small opening that reveals, some feet below, the pool and to the right a small compound with some deckchairs; it's separated from the pool by a thick hedge.

I begin to pull back when I'm poked in the bottom by his thumb. He says, "Wass you seeing?"

I look again. "Just a couple of families playing in the pool." There's a small warning voice telling me to stop, but I don't.

"Over to the roight. Wass up?"

"Er, two women playing cards. Wait, another is joining them." Penny told me about the women-only compound. As I watch, Mrs MacThing enters. She keeps her back to the card players and walks over so she's straight in front of me.

Behind me I can feel Cyril's damp breath and smell his musty odour. The thumb – I hope it's his thumb – is pressing me forward and he keeps mumbling what sounds like 'Phwoar'.

I'm transfixed as Mrs MacThing slowly lifts her colourful kaftan over her head to reveal her complete nudity. I don't know where to look, but my gaze is drawn to her pubes, which, like her hair, are a startling orange.

The spell is broken as Cyril pushes next to me and says, "Any titties?" I let him have the front and reverse rapidly out the back, onto the path feeling sick and rather disappointed. Waiting for me, smirking, is Sven.

"Oh Harold. And you such a 'nice' boy. I suggest you come and sit in the shade."

***

I try and pretend nothing has happened but I'm a crap actor. As soon as she sees me, Penny says, "What's up Harry? You look ill."

Sven says, his eyes half closed, "You had such high hopes of Harold, Penelope, but sadly, he too has succumbed to Cyril's wiles."

Penny's face is thunderous. "Jesus, I thought Hemingway said he would stop him."

Sven shrugs. "Cyril's uncontrollable. He's too essential to the business."

She glares at me. "I thought better of you, Harry. I hope you feel ashamed of yourself."

"I didn't realise what he was doing."

"You didn't realise? God, that's pathetic. Well, come on, you can back me up with Hemingway. This has to stop."

Sven says, "We men are so weak, Penelope."

"Don't talk rubbish, Sven. You should come too. This is disgusting. Come on, we need to tell Mr Hemingway." She makes to go, but Sven stays put and I follow his lead. She says, "Well? Are you scared?"

Sven sits forward. "I'm not sure I can explain this to you in a way you would understand." He seems earnest all of a sudden. "I've been controlled since birth and I hate it; so I've decided that's not the way I live my life and my philosophy is live and let live. He's not hurting anyone, is he? Leave him be."

Penny's expression suggests she might vomit any moment. "He's an evil peeping Tom, raping those women with his eyes. You can't let a pervert get away with it. If you do they just get cockier, peeping today... If I catch him peeping on me I will castrate him so help me. We need to stop him now."

The standoff between the two of them lasts only a few moments before Sven drops his gaze. "Each to their own. I like my job, Penelope, and the money is rather essential so I'm not upsetting any apple carts. You told Hemingway last week and what happened? Nada. He's made his Faustian Pact; he gets fabulous gardens and guests wanting to enjoy their beauty, and Cyril gets to polish Percy in a few quiet corners. That's hardly worth all this fuss."

I know I should help her but, in truth, all I can think about is whether it was really his thumb or his nob pressing in my bottom. When I look up, she's striding back towards reception; Sven is smiling at me. "Good to see you're a libertarian as well, Harold. She'll forgive you. Eventually. She's a realist and knows I'm right. As is she, of course." He pats me on the leg as he stands. "Come on, old man. There's Christian. He'll pacify the rebarbative Penelope."

## Chapter Fifteen

## A Night Out

Ruth and I go into Bournemouth to the cinema. The Last Detail is the main picture. She wants the middle row, but I lead her to the back. She wants to watch, but I manage a couple of snogs before her rigid posture and disconcerting way of stretching to look at the screen force me to give up. It's a grim film, which puts me off going to America any time soon. When we come out it's got quite cold as a sea fret is blowing in; Ruth doesn't have a coat, so snuggles up to me on the walk to the train station. I'm beginning to feel a bit more hopeful for the journey home when she says, "Did you dig out that box I gave you?"

    I don't know why, but that really irritates me. Stupidly I snap, "I gave it away. Does it really matter?" In a flash she's ten feet away. I have to run to catch up, pulling her to a stop. "Hang on. What's the big deal with this?"

    Her face is thunderous. "You promised. I told you I stole it and God won't forgive me if I don't give it back."

    She yanks her arm free, but I grab her again. "It's only a stupid box, Ruth. Come on…"

    She's wriggling like an epileptic snake. "It's STOLEN. That's a SIN. Let me go—"

"Will you stand still?" I let go and she stops immediately, breathing hard. "Ok." We stand apart, warily circling each other. "You said it was your Uncle's, didn't you? That's Mr James? Jim's Dad? Surely if you told him it was a mistake, then...?"

"NO." She steps back like I've pushed her hard. Her bottom lip is wobbling and her expression is changing towards tears. "He'll punish me." Her voice becomes even quieter. "You don't understand what he's like."

"I thought God was merciful. If you ask for forgiveness—"

The fury returns and she's on me, beating my chest with an incredible ferocity. "UNCLE, NOT GOD." She's sobbing and I think she says, "I don't want him to hurt me again."

"What? What do you mean 'hurt you'?"

She makes to go again so I grab her wrists. "Calm down, please. Tell me what you mean."

She yanks herself free; her face is an odd colour. It's like she doesn't know whether to beat me up or collapse in tears. Then, without warning she falls onto her knees. She looks up at me, like it's me who has hurt her and she's begging me to stop.

"Come on, get up."

She shakes her head. "No one believes me. My Mum didn't. The vicar said I was dirty."

"Why?"

She covers her face as the sobs start again. I'm vaguely aware that a few people are staring as they pass so I put a hand under her arm and say, "Come on. Let's... Ow... Bloody hell."

One minute I'm reaching forward with a helping hand, the next stars and shards of sparkly light fill my head as something hard sends me spinning away.

When I can see again I register an angry McNoble glaring back at me. He says, "What are you doing to her, you shit? I saw you throw her on the floor."

Out of the corner of my eye I can see Ruth has got up and is frozen in surprise, her hand covering her mouth. He turns to her. "Are you ok, miss? Is he hassling you?"

"Piss off McNoble. I'm talking to my girlfriend. Just back off."

With a trademark chop of his right hand he cracks my collarbone, sending me to the floor in a mirror image of Ruth's tumble. My knees take the full force of the fall.

"I wasn't talking to you. Miss?"

My brief burst of courage slips away. He's ignoring me anyway so I stand slowly and back off, testing my kneecaps for fissures.

He says to her, "It's Ruth, isn't it? Harry and me are at uni together. He's talked about you though from what he's said I didn't realise you were so beautiful."

I'm stunned he knows anything about her; I'm sure I've never mentioned her to him. And why would he take an interest anyway? I manage to growl, "You lying bastard, I never said anything to you."

I'm glad I've put distance between us because for a moment he looks ready to wring my neck; instead he turns back to her and takes off his leather jacket. "You look frozen. Here." He drapes it round her shoulders. "Are you going back to the station? When's your train?"

"Ten twenty-five."

We all look at our watches, each realising at the same moment we've missed it. Only McNoble smiles. "Oh dear," he says, "and I've only one spare seat in my car. You won't mind if I give Ruth a lift, will you Harry? She must be freezing."

They both stare at me. He can't do this. He can't take my girlfriend away like this. And she won't go with him. He's a stranger and a thug.

I nod and she takes his proffered arm, gazing at him like he's a fireman who's just rescued her. "Thank you," she says, in a really irritating baby voice.

I try a desperate, "We could get the bus…"

He spins towards me and instinctively I jump back. I hate his smile. He says, "Come on Harry. She's had a shock. She should get home."

I look at Ruth. She wants to go. Maybe she is in shock. I nod again and his smile is more than triumphant.

"Good."

At the bottom of the steps to the car parks, they pause. I'm sure she's going to look back and wave or something but she carries on up the stairs while he turns back, puts two fingers to his head and pretends to fire.

# THURSDAY 15TH JULY 1976

## Chapter Sixteen

## Guests of My Own

When I wake on Thursday it's to the sound of Mum shouting at Dad. By the time I've got up she's driven off somewhere and he's waiting on the drive with his box of Elvis records and a suitcase. By seven o'clock Colin Anacide has driven up in his old van and Dad's gone. There's a note from him for Mum on the kitchen table. I'm rather glad I don't have to confront them; I'm sure one of them will give me grief over the university letter about my probation. I tell myself not to think about it. I put Savlon on my knees, still weeping from last night's assault, and cycle slowly to work.

After an uneventful breakfast I find a quiet corner to practice for my silver service test. I'm hopeless, mostly because I keep thinking about Ruth and what last night meant.

I'm on the verge of throwing in the towel when I manage to pick up a napkin ring. I do it twice and then a third time. Both Terry and Mr Hemingway witness the last two successes; Mr Hemingway congratulates me, but Terry looks disappointed. I suppose someone else sharing the tips is his worst nightmare. He certainly says nothing about me having passed, and when I have a secret try at lunch I launch a croquette potato several feet in the air, so maybe he has a point.

After lunch everyone goes different ways. Penny and Christian are off somewhere, Sven takes himself to the tennis court to sketch whoever's playing and Amos stays in his room. I wander the gardens looking for Natalie and end up watching Sven. Mostly he likes sketching in silence, but after I fetch us some lemonade he says, "You like Natalie, don't you?"

"Yeah, she's ok. Bit odd I suppose."

"You know she and Paul have this thing? But of course, you saw them on the beach."

"Are they going out?"

He looks like he's considering this. "Not, I think, in any traditional sense, no. I don't think she wants to be tied down and Paul's very understanding."

"Understanding?"

"No need to sound so surprised. She kissed you, didn't she? And she's kissed me and she even had a go at Terry, but he's made of sterner stuff. Just her way. With Paul it's more a question of barter."

"Sorry?"

"Sex for weed. If you fancy her you just have to work out what it is she wants. He understands that."

***

Dinner is dull and only enlivened by Amos taking umbrage at a guest who sends the wine back as corked. I make the mistake of trying to joke about it; all that does is get me a towel in the face and ten tables to clear and set up for breakfast on my own. As a result I'm the last to finish; when I pick up my tray of dirty crockery there's no one about.

As soon as I push open the kitchen door, I hear voices. Paul and Natalie.

I creep forward to see Paul pressing hard against Natalie, who is bent back over the serving counter; he holds her head with one hand while the other is pushed up her skirt.

He says, "You fucking bitch. Since when did you know the word 'no'?"

I'm frozen and might have stayed that way but for her whimper. It's so pathetic I let go of the door and it bangs my tray. While Paul twists his head to look at me, Natalie takes advantage to push him off. There's a bit of a struggle, at the end of which she manages to reach the restaurant leaving him confronting me and me holding him at bay with my tray.

This frozen tableau might have gone on forever, but for the kitchen door swinging open to reveal a furious looking Magda.

"Vot is 'appening?"

Paul drops his arms and swivels to face her. "Just finishing up." He looks at me. "Turn the lights out when you go, Harry. I'll see you in the morning."

After he leaves, Magda says nothing until I've stacked everything away.

As I turn off the lights, she says, "'arry, I don't know vot 'appened, but I think you are a good boy. Be careful, ja?"

She smiles at me. "You a good-looking boy, yes? Girlies like you? Be careful, I say."

**FRIDAY 16TH JULY 1976**

**Chapter Seventeen**

**You're in for a Treat…**

I'm almost peeing myself when I arrive for breakfast, but Paul isn't there. My relief is such that I don't mind receiving a hairy eyeballing from Terry for knocking over his napkin mountain. Just in case Paul has left orders with Beet, I only eat leftovers. I'm on my way to the garden to read when Amos bounces over, holding a green jacket. "Surprise!"

"For me?"

"Oh, loosen up you miserable git. You're a commis waiter. Take a bow. Lots of privileges, but do try and stop pinching the guests' food. Makes you look like a Biafran refugee." He helps me take off the old white jacket and slip into the new one. It's much lighter and I feel pretty good. The word 'tips' pogoes around inside my head.

Amos brushes the sleeves of imaginary fluff. "Very handsome." He giggles. "I could eat you in that. Now, I want you in the bar fifteen minutes before the lunch gong."

"Why?" I can't help feeling rather awkward all of a sudden.

He smiles smugly and says nothing.

\*\*\*

There's a small group of staff by the bar. Amos, Christian, Sven and Rodney, the barman, who is feigning disinterest. On the bar there's something hidden under a bar towel.

We are made to wait to see if the girls will join us but Amos becomes rather impatient and says, after a couple of minutes, "The tradition is that when you're promoted you drink a drink of our choosing." At this he pulls away the towel, like a magician.

The chosen drink is green, amber and red. My stomach does a preparatory tumble. "What's that?"

"A traffic light." Rodney steps forward and turns the glass fractionally. "It's bloody awful. Crème de Menthe, Galliano and Cranberry juice. I suggest you throw it up or sit very still for a long time."

I'm sitting by the cherry trees, wondering if I should force a vomit, when the girls come over and bookend me. "Sorry, Harry. We missed it. What did you choose?"

"I didn't get a choice."

They giggle. While one holds a cup the other pours from a bottle. Neat gin or vodka I suppose.

"Bottoms up." They both look expectant. Oh well...

\*\*\*

When Amos calls me in my head is swimming. It's too late to chunder, not that I'm much good at vomiting on cue. Amos wants to regale me with tales of other promotions and the emetic aftermaths but since lunch is slow, I make an excuse and head for the windows, hoping some air will calm my tumultuous stomach.

The impact of so much weird booze on my vital functions is really intense; I can't swallow, my eyesight is impaired and if I raise my head I lose my ability to balance. The only way to survive is to lean against the top pane of the sash window while breathing through my teeth.

Eeeeeow... thump. I jump as an enormous black fly crashes into the glass next to me, mistaking the window for the freedom of the sky, before tumbling to the carpet.

Through the tiny slits that are all my eyes will allow, I can see it has settled next to the curtain; taking care to move slowly I ease the carcass under the hem with my shoe.

I don't know how long I'm like this before a hand pulls me back and eases me into a chair. It's Amos who offers me some water. "Sorry, Harry. I didn't realise how it would hit you. Do you want to go and lie down? I'll cover." He crouches in front of me. "You look awful."

I manage a nod. "I want to serve my table."

He smiles. "Ok. Stay here and I'll let you know when they arrive." Before standing he reaches down to where the fly crashed and picks something up. Still smiling he pops the something in his mouth and turns to go, chewing his prize.

I know I have an empathy with flies, but eating corpses isn't part of it. It's the trigger I've lacked. I stumble upright and head for the kitchen doors; the toilets are too far, but I might just make the bin compound.

*** 

The little walled area smells of rot and cigarettes. Christian is leaning against one of several galvanised zinc bins, smoking. While I pull myself over the lip of the nearest one he says, "Hey, man, you look grimbo." He pushes a crate towards me to stand on. "Technicolor yawns in there, man."

I let everything go; the vomit cascades onto the finger-fat maggots, covering them in a slime the colour of Charlie Jepson's car. Briefly I wonder why I haven't seen him; that leads me to McNoble and his stealing of Ruth. Another spasm triggers an image of Paul. I can't stop.

Christian steadies me with his right hand as he says, "What do you think of the girlies? I saw you clocking Nats. You dig the ladies, Harry-O? You could be in there. If you need some help, ask your Uncle Chris. That's everything, is it? You empty, man?"

I step down and sit on the crate, head in my hands. "Christ I'm dying."

"Man, you do look deadsville. Chill. You need a dee-straction." He hums then says, "You want to know a secret?" As with Cyril I just know I shouldn't hear this one, but nod anyway. He says, "They're orange."

"Orange?"

"Her nipples."

"Natalie's?"

He taps his nose, grinds out the cigarette and turns for the door. "Taken your mind off that lot, hasn't it?"

***

I do my best with my guests, a family of three. The man has a boxer's face, South London grammar and hides his old-school charm well. His wife is a fluttery nervous sort and the daughter, while possibly pretty, is wearing so much make-up it's difficult to tell.

"'Bout bloody time, boy. I could eat a stewed elephant."

I keep going until the main course, but the residue of the booze, my recurring fears and my lack of solids conspire to send me tumbling in a faint, slap in the middle of the steamy kitchen.

When I come to, Amos is splashing me with a wet sponge, Beet is holding a serving cloth to his forearm, which is oozing blood, and Natalie is looking on, pale and anxious.

"You are in a state." Amos smiles, no doubt trying to comfort me; sadly a small piece of fly-carapace is stuck between his front teeth and the last vestiges of my stomach's contents besplatter his green jacket.

I'm vaguely aware of some noise. It's Beet, swearing about his cut arm. He looks dementedly at me. I say, "Did I do that?" But I don't hear any response.

\*\*\*

I don't remember what happens next or how much time passes. I'm in the staff dining room, my forehead resting on the table. A chair scrapes back and there's Amos, with a plate of some sort of stew. I'm starving.

"You look awful," he says.

"I'm sorry about the sick."

"I've had worse," he says. I can't not stare as he tucks into his food. "When someone has rubbed dog dirt in your hair for being queer, a bit of vom on a jacket is nothing."

"I'm sorry."

"My fault; I never thought you'd react like that." He stops and points his fork at me. "Watch out for those chefs. They really have it in for you just now."

"Did I do something to Beet?"

"No idea."

"Was Natalie there?"

He pauses again. "Word to the wise, Harry. That tart isn't to be trusted. Oh don't look like that. She thinks she's being cute, but she's playing with fire with those two."

"Paul attacked her yesterday. He threatened me too."

Amos' stare hardens. "You were playing The Knight Gallant I suppose? Well don't believe in the little girl lost routine. It might explain why they're so mad at you though." He smiles and pushes his half full plate at me. "Go on. I can't eat any more. Too nervous."

"Nervous?"

"I've a date." While I gobble down the stew he drifts off somewhere. He says, dreamily, "He answered my advert. 'Hunky chunk wants to meet Slippery Dippery for sugar sucks and lollidrops. Sense of humour helps.' He's probably a skinhead, but I'll take my chances."

The food is so good.

"Don't worry too much. Paul's all mouth and trousers. He'll run away if you hit back; he's a coward really." He begins to stand.

"Amos?"

"Hmm?"

The bit of the fly carcase is still stuck in his teeth. I rub mine with my finger until he understands. He picks the fleck off, checks it and licks it away. "Thanks."

## Chapter Eighteen

## A Joint Enterprise

On the way home, I try and imagine an advert for a girlfriend – *'Boy 19, almost spotless needs... no, desires girl 18... hmm, 17 to... er 22 for fun and... Must love flies'* – but I can't concentrate. My mind turns to Ruth and whether I've been dumped. It's as I push at the gate I think about Dina and Jim and slow right down, straining to hear if they're there. The first thing that hits me is the scent of freshly smoked weed. It's a zephyr of pure bliss. Then their voices, giggling, float on the air. Dina is on the ground, leaning against the bench with Jim stretched out along the seat behind her head.

"That smells good."

She offers me a toke. "It's unbeliev-a-bubble."

"Where'd you get it?"

Jim says, "My Dad. He came ashore early – some problem with his cast – and brought a load with him."

"Cast?"

"He's entertainment officer on a cruise ship. The cast all quit so he has to sort out a new one before they go back to sea."

Dina reaches out for the joint and says, "Ship... ship ship shooray!! Reggie is a hero."

Jim grimaces. "He's a pain."

I have another drag. "He gave you this?"

Another grimace. "Not exactly. He was so stoned I stole some." He rolls on his back. "Does the sky shrink when you smoke a joint? The stars are really wobbly."

My brain is already doing some neat little somersaults like that Olympic gymnast the Beeb are wittering on about. I can't look at the sky, but the house swells and shrinks cheerfully. I can feel myself slowing down, calming down, slipping off. Pictures of people skip past my eyes, faster and faster. Dina shaking my shoulder brings me back.

"Who's McNoble?"

"What?"

"You just shouted out his name, called him a bastard."

"Did I?"

She pats my arm. "You need to go slow with this stuff. Reggie has this special recipe." She twists around. "I'll give you a massage."

Jim scrabbles behind me. "Me too."

I close my eyes, wondering why I called out. A hand slips inside my shirt and starts groping my chest. "Hey…"

It's Jim. They are both giggling. When they see my expression they become hysterical; we all do. We try and speak, but we can't. Then, as quickly as the laughter started it stops; I feel cold and then hot and panicky and start shaking. I push them away; they're laughing again and I race indoors.

*\*\*\**

I'm desperate for water so put my mouth under the tap and let it run. When I'm more than full I stand up and promptly vomit it into the sink. For a few moments I feel fine; then my face starts to burn again and I bend to the tap.

"What are you doing, Harry-lad?" It's Dad, wearing an apron.

"Bit hot."

He comes and looks at the sink. "Don't make a mess, will you? I've just cleaned this end."

"Why?"

"Just a bit of a spring-clean. Part of the plan." He taps his nose. "You do looked flushed. Come on, let's get the window up." He reaches past me to heave the sash up; there's a slight breeze, which we let fan our faces.

After a minute he leans towards the window. "Is that Dina? Is she in pain?"

I follow his lead. It's Jim not Dina. You can't mistake his nasal tones. As we listen his voice grows in volume, calling out 'yesyesyes' then 'nonono' before he makes this weird noise, like a choir of plugholes practicing the Hallelujah Chorus. Finally there is one very loud, very long 'OH GODDDDD'. After a few moments silence he says, "Where did it go, Di?"

Dad has gone rigid, except for the muscles in his cheeks. Time hangs heavily until the backdoor opens and slams and Dina appears. Dad's face is as red as a tomato. She looks from him to me and says, "It is hot, isn't it?"

She approaches the sink, I guess for a drink, but he blocks her way. "What on earth were you doing out there, young lady? As if I didn't know."

Dina pushes past him and runs the tap, bending, like me, to drink straight from it. "What do you mean?"

"I don't approve…"

She twists to face him, tears oozing from the corners of her eyes. "And I don't approve of you and Mum fighting and splitting up and…" Her fury makes her lose her thread. Eventually she turns and disappears, stomping upstairs.

Dad's face says it all; he wants to say something but years of avoiding any topic remotely to do with sex ties his tongue in knots. Finally he returns to his cleaning and I sit down and rest my head on the table.

***

I must doze off because when I come to, Dad has his coat on and the kitchen is back as it was. There's a small crust of vomit on my sleeve.

"Here. Wipe it up."

As I chip off the crusty bits, he says, "Do you know what she meant? About splitting up?"

"I think she's worried you spend so much time in the shed… and then with Mr Anacide."

"Really?" He sounds cross. "I'd better go. I've left a note for your Mother." He's almost out of the door when he adds, "And talk to her. She listens to you."

## SATURDAY 17TH JULY 1976

## Chapter Nineteen

### Utterly Potted

I have the oddest night. I must have fallen asleep almost immediately, but wake as Mum comes home. She's talking to herself as she comes upstairs. I think she calls 'night' through my keyhole, though I could be wrong because then I'm lying on the floor next to Amanda and the room is full of light. Amanda's lost her covering and I'm running my finger round the rough edges of her little hole.

I'm sure it's later when I next wake, but it's dark and an owl is hooting just outside my window. The curtains have been pulled and Dina's face is reflected in the glass.

Then it's light again and Amanda is on the bed, face down; someone has written her name on her back in green felt tip.

And finally someone's making a lot of noise downstairs, it's daylight and I've lost my pyjamas.

In the middle of the floor is a blue cardboard folder that was hidden under a loose floorboard: it contains the few pictures of topless women I've collected over the years. My favourite picture – a double page from the Times in which the saintly and totally naked Vivian Neves is brushing her hair, back arched, nipples pointing to the stars while she advertises Fisons fertilizer – is stuck to Amanda's back. It rips when I try and prise it loose. I must avoid that weed; whatever Mr James puts in it, it is lethal.

## Chapter Twenty

## History Repeats

Mum's in the kitchen, drinking coffee and staring into space. She wears this blue quilted nylon housecoat, which is usually buttoned to the neck. Today, it's flapping open, exposing her legs and the little blue veins that crisscross her left thigh. She's not looking very cheerful.

"Do we have any aspirin, Mum?"

"Top shelf by the sink. Have you been drinking?"

"No Mum."

"And do wash your hands, Harold."

"Mum, give me a break. I haven't stopped washing them…"

"Well, they're covered in flecks of paper or something and anyway, as long as you keep that awful cardboard thing in your room, you will do as you're told young man. I hope she's hidden."

When I come back from the downstairs toilet, Mum says, "I gather your Father was here last night."

"He was cleaning the kitchen when I got in. He had the whole of the dresser out on the floor."

"Arthur was cleaning?" She never calls him 'Arthur' at least not when she's talking to me.

"He was hard at it."

"Why would he do that?"

I shrug but she's not watching. I say, "I'll be off then. Early start."

I'm by the door when she says, "He left me a note saying he caught your sister with Jim. He won't say what was going on, but I assume it was something inappropriate."

"No idea Mum. I'll see you…"

"Wait. Come here."

I have no choice. I force myself to look at her. She says, "I asked you to talk to her. Did you?"

"Yes. Sort of."

"And?"

"God Mum. She's my sister for heaven sake. She doesn't listen to me."

Mum takes a moment then says, "She's young, Harold. It may surprise you, but she will listen to you. Not me, and certainly not your Father. I wouldn't want…" She closes her eyes and then looks at me again, "I don't want her making a mistake, doing something she'll regret. It's easier for boys."

I think she's finished so I nod.

She smiles and pats my arm. "While you were at university she did nothing but talk about you. If anyone can, well, make her think, it's you." She picks up her cup and goes to the sink. "I'd better call your Father and find out what's going on."

"When's he coming home, Mum?"

But she pretends not to hear me and goes to get dressed.

***

Mr Poseidon, the postie, hands me another Dobbin letter as I'm climbing on my bike. Because I'm early I head to the seat under the cherry trees to read it. I even begin to pen a reply. I like to read out loud what I've written.

*Dear Dobbin.* For some reason I'm mimicking Terry and force my voice higher.

*Work is ok. The people I work with are a mixed bunch. There are some real bastards who I'd like to curse if you ever get round to creating yours. I need four. There are two girls who are nice enough. Penny and Natalie – she has these fantabulous orbs...*

"Fantabulous orbs?" Penny is standing right behind me. She has a towel round her shoulders and looks like she's been swimming.

"I, er..."

She's giggling. "Sorry, Harry. I shouldn't eavesdrop. I won't tell her." She begins to rub her hair dry. "So who do you want to curse? Paul and Beet I suppose. Terry?"

I shake my head.

"Cyril?"

I nod; I know that's the right thing to do.

"So who's the fourth?"

"Never mind; just a bit of fun."

She gives me an odd look and says, "You want some tea? We have a kettle in the Rat Pit."

"Please. You been swimming?"

"I wish. Natalie and I are allowed to use the showers by the pool before breakfast. She'll be doing some yoga I expect so no staring at her 'orbs'."

## Chapter Twenty-One

## Keeping Abreast

Their home, the Rat Pit, is a flimsy box bordered on two sides by the ubiquitous laurel hedges. It looks damp and gloomy. Penny says loudly as she opens the door, "Hide your boobs, girlie, man about." I'm hanging back, yet again embarrassed in the presence of these women and not a little cheesed off at the way they both can so easily make me squirm.

Natalie is sitting on the floor in a painful looking pose. She's wearing baggy pyjamas and doesn't open her eyes.

"Hi Natalie." No response.

Penny meets my glance and shakes her head. "She's in a world of her own. So, tea? Like our pad? The Ritz, eh?"

"Cosy." The floor is strewn with clothes. There seem to be bras everywhere I look.

Penny begins kicking everything into a heap. "We're trying to hide the carpet, it's so disgusting. So..." The note in her voice has changed. "What happened yesterday? I heard you fainted."

I catch Natalie briefly opening her eyes; it's a flicker and she's quickly back to her trance. I say, "All that drink. And then Amos started eating dead flies and the kitchen was so hot..."

Penny looks over her shoulder. "Eating flies?"

"I'm not making it up. I was over by that big window – the one that looks over the tennis court – and there were these flies on the floor. He bent down, easy as you like and started eating one. A bit of its body stuck in his teeth..."

I grind to a halt as Penny's expression goes from astonishment to hysteria. Natalie's glances from Penny to me and back.

I say, "What's so funny?"

Penny takes a minute to compose herself. "Oh you nit. Some kid dropped a packet of Poppets or Treats or something at breakfast. We all had a few. Eating flies. Priceless."

My neck is getting hot; they are both laughing at me, at my stupidity and naïvety. Natalie is especially annoying, suddenly grinning. She's not said a word since I saved her from Paul. Sven's rubbish about him being understanding comes rushing back.

"So you've got yourself an 'understanding' with Paul then, Natalie?"

Her expression changes in seconds, the smile dropping into a scowl. "Sod off." She grabs the towel that's on her bed and makes for the door.

Penny turns to the kettle. "Nice one."

I can only slump on the bed. "Why is she so moody? You know I helped her with Paul, don't you?"

Penny says nothing until she's made the tea, then joins me on the bed. "She told me, yes." She picks up her brush and attacks her hair. "She's really grateful only…" She drops the brush and pulls her hair into a ponytail. "Just before we came here she was dumped by her long-term boyfriend." She reaches out to pick up her uniform. "They'd been going out for years and… she thought he was the one. Poor thing spent the whole of the first year turning down all these offers, saving herself, and now she thinks she's wasted her life. She's gone a little mad since and, with that shit Paul, she's learning a hard lesson."

She stands up, holding a black bra and skirt. "About turn, please." When I look up she has taken off her shorts and is holding the bottom of the hem of her T-shirt.

I cover my eyes, but can't resist a peek. Her back is to me and she's only wearing a pair of pink knickers. A faint white strap mark, halfway down her back is the only thing interrupting the smooth brown surface. As I watch she manoeuvres her way into her bra, her breasts flopping briefly in and out of my view. Before she turns I squeeze my eyes shut, feeling rather hot.

"Ok. I'm done." She smiles at me while she buttons the shirt. "You look so sad. Here." She holds out her hands. "Come on, stand up."

"Why?"

Penny has already gone to the cluttered work surface where she fiddles with a cassette player. A piece of classical music fills the room. "Strauss." She closes her eyes and skips to one side and then the other. "A proper waltz... though I love Latin too... the Cha-cha-cha and the Samba." She's spinning around, in a little world of her own, her face creased happily.

I say, "I've never tried. My Dad says it's the same steps, just different speeds."

"Now's your chance." She moves towards me, offering me her hands. I lose my mug on the floor and stand, feeling a bit foolish. "Just follow my lead, sonny." She takes my left hand and holds it out, while her left rests on my shoulder, before dropping quickly to my bum and squeezing. "Oops." Her grin is so easy. She's really infectious. I start to drop my hand to reciprocate, but she catches it. "Naughty. My Mum warned me about boys like you."

Before I can try again, she pulls me round and we spin clumsily in amongst the detritus of their wardrobes. After a twist left and a few paces back she eases her head close to my left ear. Her recently captured boobs palpate my chest as we circle once more. Her warm, easy breathing tickles my neck and her scent, sort of metallic, fills my nose.

She speaks quietly. "There, Harry. It's never that bad. We'll look after you, don't worry. You're one of the good guys."

**SUNDAY 18TH JULY 1976**

## Chapter Twenty-Two

## Under Pressure

I have a late start today so take my time heading downstairs. Dina looks surprised to see me. "Are you helping, then?"

"Helping?"

"Dad's grand plan."

"What's he up to?"

She smiles. "It's completely hush-hush. Mum's gone to the hospital – I bet Dad fixed that. This man from the council is coming."

"On a Sunday?" I fetch some cereal and sit down.

"So he says."

We stare at each other and then both burst into laughter. "This is mad." "Yeah, crazy."

She takes a bowl and we eat in silence. Mum's words about Dina listening to me drop into my head. "Di. About you and Jim…"

She's very careful not to look at me.

"I know it's none of my business, but you will be careful, won't you? They're… we're all just a bit worried…"

She glares at me and holds up a hand. "Stop. You're right."

"Good. I just…"

She stands and moves towards the door. "It's none of your business."

\*\*\*

At nine thirty Dad arrives, dropped off by Mr Anacide. Dina emerges from wherever she's been hiding. He says, "Hi Harry-fella. You going to watch then? I'll just put on something appropriate." He leaves us briefly before returning, dressed in his one suit and a garish red and green tie.

"Do I look ok?"

Dina nods. "You look great."

Dad checks himself in the small mirror by the kitchen door. "And your Mum is definitely out?"

"Yes."

"Excellent." He smiles at me. "Right, are we ready?" He leads us out front.

Dina stands next to him chatting amiably. I'm amazed at how they can be shouting at each other one day and be the best of friends the next; I'm more like Mum in bearing the sores for longer.

Eventually a car pulls up and a young man, not much older than me, climbs out. He's also in a suit and has a clipboard and a starter moustache. He and Dad shake hands and then Dad says, "Mr Harrison. These are my children. They help us here. Where shall we start?"

The man doesn't acknowledge us; he studies the board. He says, "Kitchen," in an adenoidal voice and follows Dad inside.

Dina is smiling as we walk after them. "He's sorted everything. He says he's found guests and that means everything will be fine again. Mum can stop being stupid."

We follow Mr Harrison as he walks round the kitchen. Dad says so only Dina and I can hear, "He's here to check we're suitable. They're keen, coming out at the weekend." Mr Harrison turns to us and we all smile for him. He looks threatened and holds the clipboard rather like a shield. "Bedrooms?"

Dad rubs his hands nervously. "Are the facilities acceptable? Will they be happy?"

Mr Harrison walks past him. "That will be in my report."

Dad scuttles after him, pointing the way with Dina and me in their wake. When we reach the landing, Dad is hopping anxiously outside the bathroom. I say, "Are these guests sharing the kitchen?"

Dad nods, his eyes rooted to the closed door.

Dina says, "What will Mum say? About sharing?"

Dad turns on us. "I will sort that out. Now, if you can't be constructive why don't you go away and play. I don't need you two upsetting him." He half turns and then says to me, "We need a word about that letter. I've being having some thoughts." Before I can respond Mr Harrison calls him away.

We go into the garden, naturally gravitating to the gazebo. Dina says, "Letter?"

I say, "University. A mistake over my exams. Have you any idea who these guests will be?"

Dina is picking at some flaking varnish. She says, "Dad says 'refugees'."

"Jesus."

***

Mum calls to say I can see Nanty after lunch. She is sitting up, eating with her right hand rather hopelessly. The nurse tells me the doctors are pleased with her progress though they are confused about her speech. While the nurse talks I watch Nanty; it is clear she is annoyed at what the nurse is saying.

When she has gone Nanty tries again to eat with her right hand but it's no better and she throws down the spoon. It's so unlike her and very upsetting. She even flaps away the bluebottle.

On my way out, the nurse says, "Can you make sure your Mother understands Miss Thoroughly must get complete rest." I wonder why she doesn't tell her herself.

I need cheering up so take a detour to the Wheel for a pint. It's just before they close and the only customer is Nigel Sodding Parsons. "Oi 'arry. What's you said to Ruthie? You split or sommat?"

He's the last person I need to debate my love life with but fortunately the barmaid appears and continues what appears to be a long-running flirt with the pug-ugly Lothario. I give him a wave, not that he notices, and retreat swiftly.

***

When I get home at about eleven after what has been, frankly, a rather dull day, Dina is waiting for me in the gazebo. She tells me we have passed the council's tests and the guests will arrive in a few days.

I say, "Who are they?"

"You remember all that fuss when Idi Amin threw out the British Asians? Well…"

"Oh shit, you're joking?"

Dina feigns shock. "They need somewhere to live."

"Mum will go bananas."

"That's only because she's narrow-minded."

"I know, but it doesn't change things. She'll hate the embarrassment. The neighbours."

"Ms Glebe won't care."

"You know I'm talking about the whole area. The WI, the Town Women's Guild, the Post Office, the RSPCA…"

"Why are you so negative?"

"I'm realistic but, you know what? I don't care. Let them make fools of themselves."

She bends and lifts the board that hides her tin of weed. "At least he's trying to sort out the mess they're in. All she does is have affairs and fight Aunt Petunia over that stupid will."

"I don't care. Really I don't. This place is mad. You're all mad. At least at work people are normal."

Dina opens the tin. "Really? Fancy a joint?"

"Yeah. No. That stuff you got from Jim's Dad is mental."

She says, "Seems Reggie grows this weird herb and mixes some of it with the weed to give it more oomph. It didn't affect me."

"Lucky you."

She smirks. "Jim says it's meant to make you feel randy." She waves the joint at me. "This one doesn't have any extras so you're safe, if you want a puff?"

After a couple of drags I say, "When do these guests come? I want to be miles away because Mum'll go off like an ICBM."

At that moment a car purrs to a halt in the lane, just the other side of the hedge from where we're sitting. Dina looks at me and frowns. I know she's thinking, like me, it's an odd place to stop. After a moment the car doors open and close and Mum's voice floats across to us. "I don't think you should come in."

"No, of course. It's been fun, Vee, hasn't it? You haven't lost it."

Mum laughs. "I'm too old for all that."

The man laughs as well. "Not at all. You're as good as any of those youngsters. You've still got your rhythm."

"Silly..." Mum's voice fades.

"I..."

"Vee..."

Mum says, "No, you first."

The man coughs. "I was serious, you know. I want to make up for lost time."

Mum is almost whispering. "It wouldn't work. You know that."

The man's voice is fading like he's moving away. "I really want to do something. It's been on my mind for ages. I'd never have had the courage if you hadn't called."

"No, don't..." Mum sounds like she might be crying.

Dina has gone rigid with horror.

The man says, "Hey, Vee, there's no need for that. Come here." There's a definite rustle of clothes before he says after a moment. "Kiss me." There's another rustle and then he says, "Sorry, I shouldn't have. I'd better go."

Mum says nothing more. The car door opens and closes, but it's only the movement of the headlights that tell us the car is moving away.

When the car turns into the main road from the lane, Mum says to herself, "Oh God. What now?" before very obviously lighting a cigarette. It takes us a moment to realise the noise is her heels clicking on the road, as she moves towards the front of the house.

Neither of us breathes until we hear the front door open and slam and see the light go on in the bathroom. Then we talk over each other.

"Where did they come from?"

"Who was Mum with?"

"She's smoking, isn't she? When did she start?"

"She's wearing heels?"

"Who was she with?"

"Who was he?"

"She never wears heels."

We stare at each other. Dina voices our biggest fear. "They kissed, didn't they?"

"I don't know." But I do. It was unmistakable, especially the slight whimper.

Dina is glaring at me. "I told you she was having an affair. Didn't I say? Who was that man?"

I can't tell her that I recognised the man's voice.

**MONDAY 19TH JULY 1976**

## Chapter Twenty-Three

## Sandwiches for Two

I can't face anyone this morning and fortunately Mum and Dad aren't about. Dina's starting her job at the florists today, which means I don't have her on my case about Mum and Mr Jepson.

At breakfast Penny is subdued and Natalie on autopilot. At one point, when Sven and I are waiting for our orders, Paul leaps over the serving counter like a greased Dick Fosbury to chase after Natalie, but she escapes easily enough.

I think it's only because Sven is there that Paul doesn't go for me.

As we sit for our own breakfast, Terry announces Natalie and I can have lunch off as we're going to be doing a special tea for fifteen pensioners from the Carefree Nursing Home at three o'clock.

When I look at her, hoping for some sign she's in a better mood, all I get is a look so utterly crestfallen that I hurry out to the garden to find somewhere to read and, frankly, to hide. I feel a bit childish, so, just before lunch I head to the Rat Pit, apology all prepared. Paul is already there, hammering on the door and hurling abuse through the woodwork; I creep away, wishing to God I wasn't such a coward.

I'm still alone when I wave off the rest to the beach. Natalie has already taken herself to the Forest boundary fence, staring into the dusty, heat-wobbly distance. I know I should go and say something, but true to character I sit on the car park wall and read.

I'm well into the bit in I, Robot where the Third Law of Robotics is being put under severe strain, when she makes me jump. "Harry. I'm sorry I'm such a moody cow, but would you help me?" She hands me a letter. "Penny said she explained about my ex." She sighs deeply. "He's a prick and I need to reply to this." She's holding a blank sheet and a biro. "Do you think you could help me think of what to say?"

I glance longingly at my book, snap it shut and pat the wall.

She shakes her head and points at the fence. "Over there."

There's a nice breeze and the insects are of the buzzy, non-biting type. Very soon we're laughing about her ex and his new girl, Shirley Price ('She's like cheap perfume, lingering too long'). It's like the first afternoon on the beach, with us giggling at everything. Twice her face brushes close to mine as she reads over my shoulder and her hair – her gorgeous hair – tickles my neck. I watch it swirl and flow as she describes her fight with Shirley at Easter. "I really wanted to thump her," she says. "She has huge arms though. Typical barmaid…"

I pull a face and put on my Mum's voice. "I don't think violence is ever the answer." I've closed my eyes as I speak, just as Mum does when she's being snotty so, at first, when I look up I don't register the frozen expression on her face. When I do and turn to look where she's looking, something thumps into me and knocks me sideways.

It's Paul. "Violence is just the ticket, arsehole."

I scramble to move as far away as I can but he follows.

"Stop it." Natalie tries to insert herself between us but he pushes her to one side and Paul and I face each other a few feet apart.

His gaze holds mine as he lets his fists swing loosely by his side. "Come on then. You've been asking for it."

Amos' words come to my mind: he's all mouth and trousers, push him and he'll run away. He is small and he doesn't look exactly healthy but I know from bitter experience that being bigger isn't any guarantee of success. "Please Paul. I didn't do anything." I sound pathetic to myself so heaven knows how it comes across to him.

Just then we are distracted by the arrival of the charabanc of pensioners, which coughs and grumbles its way through the gates. 'We' as in Natalie and me; Paul keeps his focus and like a seasoned fighter takes advantage of my lapse in concentration to hit me near my eye. It's bloody painful.

Stars fill my vision and I have to grab at the wall to stay upright.

"Oh shit. Shit SHIT." Paul sounds in real pain. When my world comes back into focus I see Paul is cradling his hand.

Natalie looks at me, then him. "Did he hurt you?"

We both answer in the affirmative, neither sure who she is addressing.

I surprise myself by asking him, "Are you all right?" and receive a growl. Natalie shakes her head at me and takes his elbow, leading him to reception, while I go and welcome our guests. Paul does appear to be in a bad way.

***

Paul goes to hospital in an ambulance. I'm left with the old boys and biddies; they treat me like some sort of dashing war hero to be fed scones and small sandwiches and asked the same question dozens of times. Natalie and I hardly speak to each other until they're gone. Once it is quiet she says, "I need a word," and leads me to the car park wall where we sit in silence for a while.

Eventually she picks up a piece of gravel and throws it as far as she can. "Shit. Harry, I know you want to help but you need to stop before you really get hurt."

"I—"

"Please. You really don't understand." She turns and peers at my shiner. "I wanted to be a nurse, but my Mother said I'd not stay the course."

"You'd be good."

Natalie pulls a face and pokes at my cheek. "Is it tender?"

It hurts to all buggery, not that I'm telling her. I say, "Why don't you tell him?"

"Stop." When she's sure I'm quiet she adds, "I don't want to talk about him."

"Penny said…"

"Penny said what?" She folds her arms tight. "Everyone knows what's best for me, don't they? Everyone except me."

We lapse back into an uneasy silence again. Then she sighs and says, "Do you like me?"

I know it's a trick question that I'll get wrong whatever I say. "Yes of course." And I add for good measure "I think you're gorgeous and…"

She's picked up more gravel and flings it away. "Exactly. You know nothing about me, about what goes on in here." She taps her head. "At least with him it's simple. Nothing unexpected. But with you," she turns and holds one of my hands, "with you, there will be expectations and complications and I can't be bothered, if you want the truth. Simple is good."

I can feel her staring at me, assessing me, and I can't think what I need to say to get across that I can do simple too. She squeezes my fingers. "Did Pen say I'm a mess?"

She lets out a coarse laugh. "Like her. Bloody hell, I mean – Christian. What's someone intelligent like Pen bothering with a dimwit like him?"

I try a smile back, showing I agree. I don't want her to let go. She's sexy and gorgeous and I can't imagine why she wants to spend another minute with a bastard like Paul.

Natalie drops my hand and pushes herself up. "They're back."

I stand and look where she's pointing. Sure enough, Christian's Ford Escort with its white boy racer stripes has turned into the car park and is coming towards us. Natalie twists her head and says, "I'm sorry, Harry. Here." She moves close, takes my face in her hands and pulls me into a kiss on the mouth, her tongue rubbing gently across my teeth before I can react. She smiles. "That'll make them think."

She leaves me standing by the wall, my heart pounding and my brain refusing to believe that this is some sort of consolation prize. While she trots over to the car, I scan their faces: Christian grinning, Penny confused and Sven winking. As I slowly go to join them, it occurs to me that everyone will soon be laughing at me but I don't really care. That kiss has to mean something.

**TUESDAY 20$^{TH}$ JULY 1976**

## Chapter Twenty-Four

## Snap!

Because of my swollen face, Terry wouldn't let me serve 'looking like a stewed lobster' and told me not to bother coming in until I looked 'as normal as I can'. The unexpected lie-in is welcome enough though I'm soon drenched as the unforgiving sun and my brushed nylon sheets start sucking the moisture from my flesh. Since I'm alone – everyone was gone by nine – I kick off my pyjamas, re-imagine the kiss taking place in my bed and massage myself an impressive erection. It's one of life's pleasures, nurturing the hollow feeling in the pit of my stomach that precedes a good wholesome wank, but I know it can't last; Mum said she'd be back after she'd done a few chores. So with a certain reluctance and firm friend in hand, I head for the shower to finish things off.

My face, seen in the mirror, is a mix of colours, mostly similar shades of purple to my penis. I hold that silly thought as I lean into the shower to turn it on.

No soap.

I head for the dressing table; the spares are kept in the bottom drawer. I crouch slowly, protecting my hard work and determined not to lose focus. As ever there's a pile of guff in here – Mum buys whatever gets her the most Greenshield stamps – and no sign of soap.

It's as I reach in the back of the drawer that I sense rather than feel something move behind me. I've just begun to turn when I explode in pain. The bloody cat has crept in, seen my rod and walloped it with a ferocity and malevolence it is hard to credit for a creature that is supposed to be domesticated. His super-sharp talons rip my nob from root to tip, snagging and tearing through the fleshy foreskin, leaving me rolling on the floor, blood oozing through my fingertips. Meanwhile Rascal bends to clean his anus, purring contentedly.

What has he done? All sorts of fears compete for priority: will it get infected and rot; will I ever be able to wank, have sex or even pee; will it stop bleeding?

I'm studying the damage when there's the sound of a key rattling in the front door. I just have time to stand and push the lock in place before Mum comes pounding upstairs.

"I'm in here, Mum."

"Well, come out. I need the toilet."

"Can't you use downstairs?"

"No paper."

"I'm in the shower."

"No you're not. You're leaning on the door. Please let me have the toilet first and you can shower after."

"Mum I..."

"NOW."

"Oh alright. Give me a moment."

I wrap my wound in toilet paper, drape a towel round my waist and hurry past her to my room. She gives me a glare but is too busy moving the other way to ask me awkward questions.

*\*\**

The bastard cat has left a V-shape rip that is oozing blood.

I'm certain I'll get gangrene so rather than follow my instincts and lie on my bed and whimper, I grab jeans and a T-shirt and head downstairs to the medicine box. I've not reached it when Mum calls, "I want a word, Harold."

Shit. "Later Mum. I… I need to check my brakes."

"It won't—"

Whatever 'won't' will have to wait. Pulling my trousers on – which is no joke – I hobble outside and collect my bike. I can hear her coming after me, so, bravely ignoring the discomfort, I make for the back gate.

Once on the lane, I'm confronted by the stern countenance of our neighbour, Ms Susan Glebe. Very definitely a Ms. She is in her forties, a writer of travel books and is short and bony – she would blow away in a strong wind. She waves me over. "Hello Harry. I thought I saw you were home. How's university?"

I manage what I hope is a polite nod and hope she'll let me go. No such luck.

"Tell me, has your Mother been attacked yet?"

"Attacked?"

"Surely you know? The pumpkin vandal?"

"Oh yes. No, I don't think so. She's hidden hers."

"Has she? Are they safe?"

"I…" Mum's voice is getting closer. "I'd better go. I hope yours are all right?"

"I lost a few. Everyone has, even Mrs Potts and she's very vigilant. All save your Mother." She waves me away. "Off you go. Tell your Mother I'll pop round soon." She turns for her front door leaving me with the feeling I've disappointed her in some way.

It amazes me how people can get so worked up over a vegetable though in truth the pumpkin patch is the chosen battleground between powerful village factions.

On one side there's Mum, Mrs Martin and a few long-term residents; on the other, Mrs Potts, Ms Glebe, Mr Poseidon and all the other newcomers. When Mrs Potts' late husband initiated an annual trophy for the largest pumpkin a few years back, he didn't know what forces he was unleashing.

Mum has stopped calling, but I'm taking no chances. There are some bushes further down the lane where I can go and check on the damage. I'm increasingly concerned that the increased throbbing – it's like a Led Zeppelin bass riff – is the precursor to gangrene. Once hidden behind some shrubs I ease out the wounded soldier; it's a mess but I've hardly touched it when a car slows to stop right next to where I'm standing.

For a few seconds I freeze, sure I'm about to be discovered. Then I take in the colour of the motor and the pain is forgotten. Bloody hell, it's Jepson. Curiosity beats infection hands down and I creep out to the lane and follow him as he heads for the back gate. He doesn't hesitate, easing it open and going inside.

When I reach the gate, now shut, I push it a fraction and stop. Mr Jepson and Mum are a few feet the other side, talking.

"I don't know where he's gone but his bike is not here. We mustn't be long."

It takes me a few seconds to realise they must be kissing. Again. I feel sick to my boots. Eventually he says, "God Vee that's—"

"Shh. What happened?"

"Yes. Ok. Well, I've agreed to speak to some people and I'm sure it will be fine."

"Charlie, this is madness..."

"No it's not. It's what you've always wanted. Come here. Look at me. I meant every word. You believe me, don't you?"

"Yeees. But—"

"Shh. Now, have you thought about coming? I'd really appreciate it."

"Are you sure? What about Monica?"

I don't hear what he replies because another car is approaching. As I stand back trying not to look too suspicious the car begins to slow. I assume it's so the driver can get round the BMW but to my surprise the car stops right next to it.

Opposite me, Ms Glebe times her appearance to perfection, shutting her front door and walking to her gate. As she pulls on some gloves – she must be melting – she pauses to watch me and the double-parked car.

It's takes a moment to place it, that car. I'm pretty sure it's the one that drove past me on my first day at Hemingways, when I crashed into the roses. The trees overhead make it difficult to see the driver. After what seems like an age, with both Ms Glebe and me held in suspended animation, the car crawls forward and stops right next to me. I can see the driver's head in silhouette. Whoever it is turns and stares at me before driving off at speed.

Ms Glebe brushes her coat, nods curtly at me and marches away. When I turn back to the gate the voices have stopped. They must have gone indoors. Taking great care I flop down behind some shrubs to wait until Mr Jepson leaves. It gives me plenty of time to build up a real hate for the man.

## Chapter Twenty-Five

## Driven to Distraction

Mum is singing opera when I return. She's ridiculously cheerful, offering to take me to Mr Anacide's bike shop to sort out my brakes. She even offers to pay. She adds, "I can talk to your Father. It's about time he explained his cryptic notes. You don't know what he means about new guests, do you?"

***

It feels like fate, what with me pretty much a eunuch, that Penny and Natalie should be the two people wandering past the bike shop while I'm waiting for my bike to be fixed. They both look serious, but Penny perks up when she sees me, full of concern over my injury – my face that is. Natalie barely nods.

    I suppose she's a bit embarrassed about kissing me like that in front of everyone. As luck would have it Mum has failed to track Dad down and appears just when they're about to leave. After the necessary introductions, Mum says, "We're going to pick up Dina – we're seeing Harry's Great Aunt – poor dear is in hospital. Why don't we drop you off on the way there? Unless you want to catch the bus?" Lift accepted and while we wait for Mr Anacide to finish up, Penny sits down and chats to Mum like an old friend. When I look for Natalie she's disappeared.

***

Dina's school is near the high street making parking difficult. Instead of risking my denting the car, Mum directs me towards the pull-in next to the village pond. While Dina settles between Natalie and Penny (she's loving the chance to be quizzed about me, by Penny), I'm confronted by my driving nemesis: the three-point turn. Mum increases my nerves with an unnecessary, "Slowly, Harold."

As I twist to reverse back, I can see Dina and Penny, heads close sniggering over something. It has to be me. I strain to hear.

"Let the clutch in now, Harold."

"Mum I know—"

Thump! Thump! Something hammers on the bonnet. Mum screams, Dina looks horrified and I go to jam on the brakes, though of course I jam on the accelerator and we shoot backwards; two bumps later and the back-wheels are sinking in the silty soil around the edge of the pond.

All heads turn to look out of the windscreen. Staring back at us is McNoble.

Mum's voice is shaky and full of barely suppressed venom. "What the hell is he playing at?" She glances at me; she must see my expression. "Do you know him?"

I nod and look directly at her. "Mr Jepson's son."

The colour drains from her face. I find myself saying. "I'll go and speak to him."

Mum just sits and looks at McNoble who hasn't moved. As I climb out, I can hear Dina asking who Jepson is and Penny explaining he's a guest at the hotel. I'm determined to stay in view of everyone, fairly certain I won't come to any harm that way.

He is playing with something in his pocket; his knife, I suppose. He says, "Is that your Mother?"

"What do you want?"

He keeps shaking his head. "My Father says he got you a job. I warned you to keep away."

"He found me. I..."

He puts his finger to his lips and I stop. He says, "He was really annoyed about the urn; really upset. When he saw that crack..." He smiles. "One hundred and fifty quid, he says. That's what it'll cost to fix it properly. You'll have to pay."

"Me? But—"

"You've got a job, Harry. He told me. In that posh hotel. You can afford it."

I feel horribly sick. "But one hundred and fifty pounds. Can't he buy a new one?"

"Ah well, you see it's been in the family years. Needs a specialist." He pauses before he adds, "A ceramicist."

"But that's ridiculous."

It's the way he smiles that tells me he's made up the number. Or at least I think he has. Not that I can see it helps me much.

He pats my arm in what might in others seem to be a sympathetic gesture. "I haven't told him you broke it. I did the decent thing, since our families are such friends, and told him it was me. So the least you can do is pay. Just get me the cash and we're quits."

He takes his arm away and says, like he's only just remembered, "He says he wants it by the sixth, ok?" His voice is all syrupy. "He loves that box by the way. He said, if he can't use the urn then that is a pretty good substitute."

My mind is spinning. "Box?"

He nods at Mum. "Is it hers? Because I don't see how I can get it back now. Not now her ashes have been in it. You understand, don't you?"

I'm so dazed by the idea that I have to find one hundred and fifty quid that it takes a moment to register that he is talking about Ruth's box. I'm vaguely aware that he has put his arm around my shoulders

"Don't look so worried, Harry. The ladies will think something is wrong." To reinforce his point he uses his free hand to grab my balls and squeeze.

Of course he doesn't know I've a lacerated nob and how effing painful his grip is. Penny reacts first to my grimace and is out of the car in seconds. McNoble lets go but not before she pushes him away.

"What are you playing at? He's in agony."

I thought I was being quite brave and the whimpering was barely audible.

He holds his hands high. "Nothing, sister. Just lads playing. Eh Harry?"

He turns and walks away. As he goes he says over his shoulder. "You've two weeks, arsehole."

***

Mum accepts the 'lads playing' explanation and goes to phone Uncle for a tow. The rest of us sit on the grass to wait. I'm sitting between Penny and Dina, while Natalie goes a way off and lies on her back, eyes closed. Dina wants to know what's going on. If we were alone I'd tell her to mind her own business but with Penny listening I tell them a version of the truth, leaving out Ruth and her box.

Dina is indignant. "You mustn't pay." But she knows what I'm like so then she says, "Are you going to earn enough at Hemingways?"

I shake my head. "Dad wants a contribution to board and lodging."

"He can't." But she's ever practical and she adds, "There's always Grandpa's money."

I shake my head. "I can't go pressing Nanty for a cheque, can I?"

I add, for Penny's benefit. "Our Grandpa died at Easter; he left us both some money but we haven't had it yet. Our Great Aunt – Nanty – is the executor but she's in hospital so we won't get it for a while yet." Penny is staring at the back of the car and doesn't seem interested.

Dina tries to offer alternatives but none make any sense to me. Eventually after we've been quiet for a few minutes, Dina offers to go and buy some chocolate. She asks Natalie, who ignores her. Dina shrugs, mouths 'moody cow' at me and disappears towards the shops.

When Dina has gone, I say to Penny, "What's up with Natalie?"

Penny blinks at me and pulls a face. "It's... she's a bit worried. It's nothing but... just try and give her some space."

I look across at Natalie, her face peaceful. She looks like a goddess; why do the beautiful ones choose prats for boyfriends?

"Harry?" Penny has turned right round and is facing me. Same with her; she's pretty too, and she's with Christian. QED. She says, "Are you related to the Jepsons or something?"

I stare at her. "No way. Why do you say that?"

"Close family friends?"

"No. I mean I think Mum and Mr Jepson were friends when they were our age but I only met him a week ago and that was the first time I heard they knew each other."

"Oh."

It's amazing how she can load one little word with so much hidden meaning.

"'Oh?' What do you mean, 'Oh?'"

It's like you can see her thinking the way her expression changes. She blows out a deep breath. "When I saw your Mum earlier I recognised her from the Crown the other night. I was there with Chris." She swallows. "She was with him."

I nod as casually as I can. "So? I knew they'd had a drink together."

She takes her time before she looks at me. "They seemed to be 'close' friends, you know?" She pauses. "Very close friends, that's all."

I suppose I should ask her to define 'close friends' but I don't need to. I'm still wondering what to do when Penny begins to stand; Mum is coming back.

\*\*\*

At the hospital Dina isn't allowed in and I only get five minutes alone because the ward sister is of the Oberleutnant sort. As I swap with Mum we're told that even though Nanty is not making the expected progress she should be able to come and stay with us shortly. When Mum has gone in Dina says, "Mum won't ask Nanty to write us a cheque. She got really snotty."

"I could have told you that."

"There must be a way to raise the money." She frowns to herself; like Penny I'm sure I can hear her little grey cogs whirring furiously.

The waiting room is stifling and I go to try and prise a window open.

Dina says, "By the way, what's wrong with Natalie?"

"Wrong? Nothing."

"Only she had this prescription that she was holding like it was really valuable."

"No idea." The sweat is cascading off me and I use the curtains to mop my face and arms. It smells dreadful. I say, "What I need is something I can sell; it's the only way I'm going to make the money."

"Your sex toy?"

"She's not a sex toy.

"Really? That's not what Mum thinks."

"Mum's spoken to you?"

Dina isn't listening; she's lapsed into a sort of trance. She says, "I think I may just be a genius."

"I doubt it."

"Ha! Your little sis may be the answer to your cash crisis and you get to keep Amanda and her perforation."

"I won't hold my breath." But actually, with Dina, I do hold onto a small sliver of hope.

\*\*\*

Mum makes Spanish omelettes that have the look and consistency of carpet. Paul may adulterate the food that I eat but it still tastes divine.

Dina and I watch TV until the news, and then I go looking for Mum. I have this idea I should ask about Mr Jepson. She's out with her mutant vegetables. I'm a few paces away from her when I see she's smoking. She's always hated smoking, mostly because Aunt Petunia smokes constantly. When she looks up, there's something in her expression that tells me Charlie Jepson is not a topic of conversation for tonight.

# WEDNESDAY 21ST JULY 1976

## Chapter Twenty-Six

## Drought

I call Magda to update her on my black eye and swollen face. She says, "Stay 'ome. I cover with Terry and Mr 'emingvay." I spend the morning finishing I, Robot and then the M.R. James ghost story Dobbin mentioned, the one with the curse in it. If only such things worked. Mum reappears after lunch and gets me watering the veg. They say Hampshire is the only part of the country without a hosepipe ban; not for long if Mum has her way. She's reasonably cheerful, at least until I ask if I should water her pumpkins. "What did you tell Susan?"

That floors me. "Ms Glebe? Nothing."

"She said you told her I had them hidden."

"I thought... is it a secret?"

"From her, yes. You know full well that anything you tell that woman gets straight back to Mrs Potts. I really don't need any more nonsense from her."

"Nonsense?"

I think Mum is about to explain but in the end she just walks away. About twenty minutes later I see her going down the lane with a watering can, a distinct vapour trail of cigarette smoke following her.

I don't see Dad all day.

**THURSDAY 22$^{\text{ND}}$ JULY 1976**

## Chapter Twenty-Seven

### Sherry Trifle

Hot. Baking hot. I am my own personalised swimming pool. Paul's having an operation to pin the break in his hand caused by hitting my eye. No one mentions it until Beet blocks my way to the staff dining room.

"I need a word." He pulls off his headscarf and wrings it out over my shoes as he says, "You know how much weight I lose in there every day?" Carefully he re-ties the kerchief. "I'm head chef. Always wanted to run me own kitchen."

He has this way of looking at me with one eye, like he's measuring me. "But it's a fucking nightmare. Paul will be back – arsehole – I get no extra dosh and when I said I needed help, all Hemingway offered me was some trainee bint from Bournemouth. A fucking girl."

He tries me with the other eye. "But you know what keeps me smiling?" He glares at me, both eyes wide open. "When he comes back, you're fucking dead. He's lying in that hospital bed, planning. He's got a lot of time to think, and plan. He's going to rip your guts out and hang you in the cold store by your skanky feet and every morning he's going to stick his cock in your mouth."

"'Scuse me, Beetroot old fella. I'm famished." Sven smiles coldly as Beet stands back to let him past. "Come Harold. I need a word." Sven pulls me away and leads me to the serving dishes, scooping out food for us both. "You need to find a way to disarm them, young Spittle. You could start by looking less smitten. She's really not worth it."

"I haven't done anything."

He sits down and forks up some eggs.

"And she likes me."

He sighs. "Oh don't be naïve. SO WHAT? She likes men. She likes sex. I told you, didn't I?" He pauses, I suppose waiting for me to speak. When I don't, he says, "My Father has done little for me, but one lesson I've learnt the hard way is giving into bullies doesn't work, but neither does fighting them. If you can't fight fire with fire, and you can't out run it… then find some water to damp it down."

"What are you on about?"

He lays down his cutlery slowly. "Sometimes you are deliberately obtuse, you know?" He picks up his fork. "Do try the eggs. They are sublime."

***

I'm a bit distracted come lunch. Sven's 'advice' remains impenetrable, Natalie ignores me completely, Amos is in a mood, I have four tables of my own and my nob aches horribly. One table is a large party of locals, corralled by this booming alpha male, bearded like an old sea dog. I manage not only to anger him, but also Beet over an order change, Amos over some vegetables of his that I took by mistake and Terry over a wrong wine request. It feels like I could be sacked at any moment.

We reach dessert; as I wheel over the sweet trolley, the woman to Mine Host's right side is simpering something about only having a coffee, but Captain Pugwash is having none of it and bullies her to have some sherry trifle.

Beet makes an incredible trifle, the cream piping a work of art and the sherry just sufficient to give it a truly distinctive flavour. It seems a criminal offence to touch it. Still there's a tip to be earned so I cut a neat portion and smile as I place it on the table.

While the pirate chief regales the multitude with a story of another trifle in another place, I turn to the trolley for the cream jug.

You know those moments, when a group realises, at pretty much the same moment that something extraordinary has happened? Time stands still. As I turn the woman spoons the creamy top towards her mouth. Everyone, apart from the storyteller is watching her. Just before the spoon enters her mouth she stops. She lowers her spoon and looks at it. Her eyes widen. There's a sharp intake of breath.

One of the party says, "Is that a currant?"

The currant waves its six legs and the woman makes a sick gurgling sound, places the spoon on the table, staggers to her feet and heads for the ladies, pursued by one of the other women. Blue Beard reaches across to pick up the spoon; he looks from it to me and back. He extracts the struggling fly and squeezes the life out of it. "You idiot." In one swift movement he stands, wipes the fly residue down my sleeve and heads for reception.

I'm transfixed by another unnecessary death. I'm not really aware what's happening until one of the waiters points me to reception. "The boss wants you."

Mr Hemingway is waiting for me by the front desk. He's dressed in black but carrying a pair of green Wellington boots. "Ah Harvey. Your Mother wants you. You can use my phone."

"It's Harold, sir. My Mother?"

"Your Mother wants you to ring home. Hurry, hurry."

Dumbly I duck under the counter, wondering why I haven't been sacked. As I wait for my call to be answered I see Mrs Jepson approach Mr Hemingway. She, too, is dressed in black.

## Chapter Twenty-Eight

### The Trouble with (Great) Aunts

"Mum? Mr Hemingway said you wanted me to call."

"Yes, dear. Now Edna is coming home today and will need some things but I have to go out. Mr Hemingway has kindly agreed for you to have the time to take them round so…"

"I'm working, Mum."

"He said you can have the afternoon off. He's the proprietor, isn't he? Now, I really don't have time to debate this."

"I can't just leave in the middle of my shift—"

"Harold, I have to go out, I can't get hold of Dina or your Father, of course. You want to help your Great Aunt, don't you?"

That's a killer. "Where are you going?" Not that I need to ask. She's off with that man.

"My lift has arrived. The bag is on the stairs. Thank you, dear."

I stare at the dead phone, unable to prevent my mind imagining Jepson and my Mother kissing again.

As soon as I exit the office, Mr Hemingway walks across to me. "You'd better get off, Harvey." For a moment he stares at me suspiciously, then shakes his head. "I've told Terry to arrange cover." Just then Mrs Hemingway, also in black, appears alongside Magda.

"'ere it is, zir. Safe and sound, ja?"

"Thanks."

Mr Hemingway reaches out and takes Ruth's box. I'd forgotten what it looked like but seeing it now, my stomach jolts. Mr Hemingway sees me looking. "Yes, sad day. We'll give her a good send off." He takes his wife's arm and walks to the front door.

I follow to the top step and watch as they walk to where Mrs Jepson is standing. She's next to the same car with blackened window that stopped by our back gate the other day.

As I watch she opens the boot and he puts the box inside carefully. They both look up towards the gates; a black car is driving slowly towards them.

A huge lump of a man, dressed in a dark suit and with enormous dark glasses gets out. He goes to the rear door and opens it, allowing a much smaller man with dark hair and a slight stoop to emerge. He vaguely reminds me of someone. This man shakes Hemingway's hand and kisses both Mrs Hemingway and Mrs Jepson on the cheek. Out of the corner of my eye, I see Sven approaching from the direction of the gents. He stands next to me and says, "Looks like something out of the Godfather, doesn't it?"

"Who's that?"

"My Father. Showing off. Probably trying to scare Jepson." He peers at the group. "Where is he?" Then Sven grins. "That'll piss Pater off. All that effort wasted." He sighs and looks at me as he shrugs on a black jacket. "What did I say about bullies? I should take my own advice." As he steps forward he says, "Once more unto the breach..."

Everyone watches Sven walk slowly down the steps. He shakes Mr Hemingway's hand and nods at Mrs Hemingway. His Father says something, but he just turns away and gets in the back of the black car.

***

Nanty is in her room, watching the TV with the sound off. The visitor restrictions seem to have disappeared as I'm shown through without a murmur. "Mum says you're coming home later? That'll be great. Are you feeling better?"

She smiles and tries to push herself up the bed with her good hand and fails. I slip my hands under her armpits and heave. Once upon a time she was a strong woman who could lift me easily; now she's just bones and sharp elbows. She looks exhausted just from me lifting her up, but she still beams at me before making a juddering grunting noise.

"How's the arm?"

She waves the cast at me. Her fingers are a mottled bluey red; I take each one and massage them slowly. I do the same for her good hand, all the while telling her about the mad people at the hotel. She watches me, smiling when I look at her. After a few minutes she motions for her pad and writes in wobbly child-like scrawl: 'what's wrong?'

"Nothing. Only… it's… I wondered about Grandpa's money, the money he left me." I can't look at her; I'm doing what I said I wouldn't and feel awfully guilty. "I just wondered when I might get it."

I've been talking at her hands; when I look at her face, tears are slipping down her cheeks. I've made her feel guilty. I lean in and, like I did as a child, rest my head on her chest while she strokes my hair with her good hand. "It's ok Nanty. Please don't worry. It's not a problem. I can wait." She can't see my tears.

When finally I sit up she points at her bedside cupboard. In it is an old photo album that she sifts through. Finally she finds the one she wants and points it out: it's Mum with Aunt Petunia when they were children; Mum must have been ten and Aunt a couple of years younger, both wearing white summer dresses and straw hats. They're holding hands.

I look quizzically at Nanty and she mimes a bit of boxing. I think I see; no money until they stop fighting. "I understand, Nanty. Let's get you home, eh?"

Nanty nods and sniffs hard; I hold a hanky to her nose and she blows. As she does so a fly, maybe the same one as before, is dislodged from her hair and circles the room before settling back into her curls. She glances up and then at me, and smiles broadly. We leave him be.

## Chapter Twenty-Nine

## Ice Cream Surprise

While I'm sitting with Nanty, I'm given two messages. One says Uncle Norman will be along to take Nanty to ours and the other is to say Dina is on her way. When she arrives, Nanty is having some final checks and we're told to make ourselves scarce. Since Lymington Hospital is old fashioned and smelly in a sort of boiled-fish-poultice-old-feet sort of way we head into the town, aiming for Carlio's ice cream parlour. It appears to be my treat, despite Dina knowing I'm the one under threat if I fail to find one hundred and fifty quid. While I'm buying two of Carlio's fruit fool ice creams Dina sits at the back studying the various flyers and adverts pinned to a cork board. One is for Eric Clapton's No Reason to Cry tour; he'll be playing the Gaumont in Southampton soon. As I sit I say, "Penny and Natalie love him. They're desperate for tickets."

Dina pauses; I can feel her staring at me. "You want to take Penny?"

"She's going out with Christian."

"Oh God, not Natalie? She's such a moody cow."

"She had some bad news."

"What? Some mirror told her she wasn't the fairest of them all?"

"Firstly it's too late to get tickets and second I can't afford it." I don't mention the third, namely that Paul will kill me if I ask her.

"I can get you tickets if you really wanted me to." She sticks out her tongue at my incredulous expression. "Janice's Mum's new man is in charge of the Gaumont or something. She said the other day he can get tickets for any show. Shall I try?"

"I can't afford it. I told you about McNoble."

"She'll get them for free. If she wants any money I'll tell her to wait until September."

I stare at Dina; I shouldn't even think about it. "Really?"

Ice cream dribbles down her chin and splashes on the red Formica table top. She scrapes most of it off with her spoon and nods. "Course."

Given what she's offering I feel I have to share a little too. "Di, I think I know who that man is. The one with Mum." I tell her about Charlie Jepson and the visit after Rascal's attack and the funeral. "They knew each other years ago. I met him on the last day of term; he said he'd been looking out for me."

"This is McNoble's Dad?"

"Yeah."

She takes her time to absorb everything. "They kissed, didn't they? Like properly?"

"Yeah."

She catches me looking and pulls a face; I can't help laughing. "It's not a nice thought, is it?"

Dina can't suppress a giggle. "Tongues?"

"Stop it. That's disgusting."

She goes all serious. "You have to find out if it's him, so you can tell Dad. He can't realise, can he?"

I lick my bowl. "It may be nothing."

But from her look it's clear neither of us believe that. She says, "There's a phone box on the corner, I'll go and check about those tickets. You can work out what we do next with Mum."

While she's gone I try and think about Mum and Mr Jepson, but my head clouds at the notion they are more than old friends.

Dina returns, still looking thoughtful.

"Any good?"

"Yep. She'll sort some out." She takes her spoon and scrapes at the dregs. "Janice said she saw Ruth at Bible class last night."

"Yeah?"

"She was in the shop, too. Something about a box."

"Oh for Christ's sake. What is it with her and that box?"

"Have you broken up?"

I risk a glance, sure she's gloating but her expression is unreadable. "I suppose."

I can feel Dina peering at me. It feels like she's trying to be understanding but that is so out of character I dismiss the idea as stupid. I simply don't understand girls. "Tell her I don't have it." My head has started pounding.

"Is it important?"

"God knows. Yes, I guess it must be."

Dina says nothing; the silence feels so awkward that I say, "She stole it, she says. Last Easter or something, and being Christian and everything that's a big sin so she has to give it back or she faces eternal damnation. If it was so important, why give it to me as a present? You don't usually ask for presents back, do you?"

"Maybe she thought she loved you when she gave it to you. And now you've split, she wants to give it back to whoever she took it from."

"Oh sure." Just then the conversation with Ruth after the cinema comes back to me. "You may be right. She said it was her Uncle's box."

"Reggie? Jim's Dad?"

"Yeah."

"Why'd she take it?"

"God knows. Because she's a loony. Actually I think he did something to really annoy her so she took it as a sort of punishment." I remember how she looked when she begged me to get it back. "He frightens her a bit, I think."

Dina frowns. "Jim says he's got a real temper on him. He's been a bit snotty since he got back home."

She spins her bowl thoughtfully. "Yesterday he went mental. Jim and I were listening to some records when he started shouting. Seems he needs to hire this new cast for the next part of the cruise and it's taking a long time. Jim says it's because he can't get stoned while he does the auditions." She pushes the bowl away. "So if you're not going to take Ruth, who'll you take? I got you four tickets."

"Four?"

"Janice offered. Jim and me'll come if you like."

"A double date? I think not."

"Yeah, well I think Clapton's useless so I wouldn't go if you paid me." She smiles, "And I'm sure I have an answer to your cash crisis."

"Yeah, what?"

She taps her nose, like Dad. "That's my secret."

***

When I get home, after serving dinner, Nanty is in her new bedroom downstairs – our old sitting room – with Dina on the floor, both watching the telly. As I take off my work shoes, Dad huffs and puffs up the stairs with a bundle of sheets. I ask, "What's he doing?"

"Getting ready for the new guests." Dina tries to smile, but her heart isn't in it.

"The local authority people?"

"Yes. They come tomorrow."

"Great. Mum?"

"Out." Dina's face is turned to the screen; she won't look at me. "He says she'll be fine."

"He's not told her then?"

"I don't think so." She looks at me then.

I say, "I think I'll go to bed early. I'm pretty tired."

She nods. "Me too. On my feet all day."

"I know." I look at Nanty who's smiling. "Will she mind? Mum?"

Nanty shrugs. I'd guess she thinks she's seen a lot worse but I'm not so sure. I'm about to leave when Dina calls me back. She's holding the old photo album Nanty had the other day. She says, "Nanty showed me this earlier."

She holds it out, open at a page with four photos on it; three are Mum and Dad's wedding day. The last is a different size and clearly from a different time. It's a group of people. Dad is second left, leaning on a stick. He still has his eye bandage on. Mum is stunning in a white dress; she's on the far right and she has her arm round the waist of a man who is in profile, staring at her.

Dina prises the photo out of the little paper corners and hands it to me. Someone, Mum probably from the writing, has written the names of the people on the back in pencil; it tells me the admirer is 'Chaz Jepson'.

"How'd you find this?"

"I asked Nanty if she knew who he was. What do you think?"

I don't say it but it looks like they were, at least back then, very 'close' friends.

**FRIDAY 23RD JULY 1976**

## Chapter Thirty

## New Arrivals

I'd much rather not be around for the new arrivals, but Dad is up and cooking when I come downstairs. "Right, Harry-boy. You need to get the garden chairs out please. You'll need to sponge off that old parasol too. Then—"

"I need to get to work. I..."

He looks at me beadily. "No, you don't."

"I don't?" I've been sacked after yesterday's incident. "Has someone called?"

"I spoke to Hemingway. You can miss breakfast and do a half day rather than have a full day off next time."

Not sacked! Part of me is pleased, part annoyed that my parents are constantly organising my life. I go outside with a small spring in my step, but Mum's expression soon dampens it.

She's digging with real venom, adding to her vegetable plot. It will soon dominate the garden. She sees me looking and obliterates a reluctant lump of clay with one swipe of her fork. With that she buries the tines in the ground and heads towards me; I know better than to turn away. She's wearing a pair of jeans I've not seen before and she beats the dust off her hands by slapping her legs hard.

"How far are you going with the digging, Mum?"

"Far enough. How long have you known about these guests?"

"Will it be just veg or are we going to have livestock?"

"Harold, stop prevaricating. You're old enough to know this will end in disaster. You should have said."

"Dad seems happy enough. So, what about livestock? Though there's Rascal to consider…"

"Stop blathering. You must see that the cultural differences alone will make it impossible." She rubs her arms like she's cold. "I would be grateful if you wouldn't conspire with him to keep secrets from me." Her arm-fold tightens so much that the veins on her forearms pop out like bicycle inner tubes. I try to be as small as I can as she swells next to me. "You need to tell me what he's up to." I keep my eyes on my shoes, waiting for the rest of the lecture but instead she sighs. "Excuse me. I need to freshen up for this charade."

She squeezes past me and disappears into the gloomy interior. When she's gone I give the bucket that holds vegetable peelings a good kick and say, "You're a fine one to talk." I kick the bucket again. "What about you and Charlie bloody Jepson then?"

"Pardon?"

As I spin round, Mum's head appears out of the downstairs toilet, comb in hand. I was sure she'd gone upstairs. Her fingers bend the comb as she says icily. "What did you say, Harold?"

"Veronica? Can I have a quick word, please?" Saved by Dad. He sounds cheery.

Mum doesn't. "You and I will speak later."

***

The guests are the Ojhas. A lady from social services has brought them in a van. There are a family of five: Mother, Father, two children, who mostly stay hidden behind their Mother and an old man who will be along later. Dad is in his element, grinning and bowing while Mum, her expression inscrutable, stays in the shadow of the front door.

After a few minutes during which all sorts of bags are pulled out of the van, she wipes her hands on her dress and whispers for my benefit. "This is going to be a disaster. Look at your Father… bobbing up and down like they're royalty. As for that council woman… look at her shoes. Red heels and no stockings."

She's stopped by Dad waving her forward. "Veronica, come and meet Mrs Ojha. I'm sure she'll be fascinated by your plans for the garden. And your pumpkins, of course. Do you like vegetables, Mrs Ojha? I believe they're very popular in India."

Mum wipes her hands again and lifts her head to ensure she's looking as far down her nose at Mrs Ojha as is possible. Mrs Ojha is a tiny woman, wrapped in her green and gold sari. Her arms seem almost brittle. She moves gracefully, although as Mum approaches she keeps her eyes focused on the ground. The sun catches a gold stud in her nose as she makes a praying gesture with her hands.

"Nice to meet you, Mrs O'jar." Mum's voice is icy. "I'm Mrs Spittle." The two women briefly touch hands before Mum's manners kick in. "I suspect a cup of tea might be welcome. Come through." She doesn't wait, but spins round and stalks past me.

Mrs Ojha blinks rapidly and sweeps her children in front of her, almost like a shield. The oldest is a skinny girl with the whitest teeth I've ever seen. After taking everyone in, her gaze settles on me. The other is a stocky little boy, sucking his thumb; he has a thick froth of black hair and a snotty nose. The way his sister pulls his arm has to hurt, but he's joined the 'let's stare at Harry' contest and ignores any pain.

Mrs Ojha smiles at me. "This is Sajid, my little boy. Pure mischief when he's not shy. And this little jewel is Noor." The girl, who I suppose is about nine, grins again and I can't help but smile back as Mrs Ojha hustles them to follow Mum.

***

As the porter I'm set to work heaving the bags upstairs. Dad and Mr Ojha follow me on the first trip leaving me to finish while they inspect the accommodation before turning their attention to the many gadgets Ravi, Mr Ojha, has brought with him. The last to appear is a fancy cassette player, with Dolby stereo, something Dad is always going on about.

As Ravi presses play, the mellifluous (at least to Dad) tones of Elvis fill the air. The two men sway to the beat and share a look. "Would you like to see my shed, Ravi?" Dad pats me on the shoulder. "Come on, Harry-my-solider, time to help your Mother."

I'd much rather avoid Mum but Dad insists. We find them in a stony silence, Mrs Ojha on the swing, I assume not through choice and Mum and Nanty in deck chairs on either side. The best tea service has been set out and the women are hiding behind their cups and saucers. Meanwhile Sajid is grubbing in the recently dug earth, sorting out pebbles while Noor jabbers away at him incomprehensibly. Seeing me, Mum says, "Sit Harold." She points at the swing. "Harold is on holiday from university."

Mrs Ojha smiles at me. "Oh, Oxford?"

"Er no. I failed the entrance exam..."

Mum says quickly, "He did so well in his A-levels. Such a credit."

"My brother went to Oxford. He read engineering," Mrs Ojha says, "he's now working in the Middle East. Oil."

"Harold's doing... reading English. He's doing ever so well." Dad can't have mentioned my probation to her. "We have a daughter, Dina. She's been doing her O-levels and will certainly go to university."

Mum tries to mimic Mrs Ojha's immaculate pronunciation, but is defeated by several decades of exposure to the wide vowels of Hampshire's indigenous population.

"You must be so proud, Mrs Spittle. Noor is a worry for us. She's so advanced no school seems able to cope with her."

"Lovely."

Mrs Ojha pauses. "I adored university. Bristol. Classics. Father wanted Oxford, of course, but they were so stuffy. My sex and colour, I suppose. Bristol was adequate academically, but the town itself... do you know it?"

Mum shakes her head, her chin sinking fast to her chest.

Mrs Ojha sniffs. "Bristol is rather a curate's egg. Lovely people, very straightforward, though the town is a trifle bourgeois. A seaport, of course, which lends it an earthy charm. So how is the long vac, Harold? Full of opportunities, I hope?"

"I've a job in a local hotel."

"Oh splendid. Ravi ran the Hilton in Kampala, before Idi Amin sent us on our way here. He was their youngest-ever general manager, you know. But here, in England, if he says he's experienced in the hotel business they think he must be a waiter or porter or cleaner."

Mum nods hard. "Oh I do so hate prejudice. You won't find any here I'm pleased to say. We're very cosmopolitan." I know she's deliberately avoiding looking at me. "Why don't you show the children the rest of the garden, Harold? I want to discuss cooking arrangements with Mrs O'jar."

Noor is of the same mind. "Please, please do." Sajid follows his sister's lead. "Please." When I look at him he immediately sticks his dusty thumb in his mouth. No one seems to mind and the little girl's smile is entrancing. I allow myself to be pulled away and we wander behind the temporary fences Mum has erected and up the garden toward the gazebo.

As soon as we are out of sight of their Mother, Sajid turns on Noor and begins kicking her in the leg. She lets go of my hand and with one swift movement twists his ear in a circle so he has no choice but to stop the kicking and grab the reddened flesh. Neither makes a sound. Once released, Sajid runs ahead. I'm only half watching him while Noor prattles on about her schoolwork and her love of jewellery.

"What are you doing, Sajid?" Noor lets go of my hand and races forward. Up ahead, Sajid has reached Mum's experimental vegetable plot and is rummaging in one of the plastic bags.

"Hey, no, stop that Sajid!"

Noor is already with him. She administers a fearsome blow to the side of his head and as he reels away silently, she prises something from his grasp.

"Noor, let me have that."

She smiles at me slowly and rather slyly, with a knowing sparkle in her eyes inappropriate for one so young. With a neat sidestep she avoids my grasp and is off, back up the garden, followed swiftly by her small snotty partner in crime. "Mummy, Mummy, they grow willies. They grow willies."

***

The appearance of the veggie-phallus is the ice breaker; when Mrs Ojha finds out they are for That's Life, the two women form an immediate connection. It's not that they have suddenly become friends or even friendly, but it allows them a neutral topic of conversation.

Before long they are discussing their favourite bits of recent shows and their mutual admiration for Cyril Fletcher as an underrated poet.

By the time the elder Mr Ojha arrives to complete our guests the atmosphere is almost cordial. Mr Ojha senior is called Asoka (though he prefers 'Papaji', which is a bit like Nanty I think); he wears loose white trousers and a tunic. His whiskers are a thing of fascination, especially to his grandchildren who each sit on a knee and twist and tease the strands into quiffs and cow licks. Dad and Ravi also join in and Ravi has us spellbound with the story of their dramatic and heart-wrenching deportation from Uganda. I want to stay, but work calls so I slip away to change. Mum is waiting for me at the bottom of the stairs.

I've been dreading this moment since my outburst, but she floors me by easing me into the dining room and closing the door.

"Charlie Jepson." She rubs her hands like they are cold. She says, almost to herself. "How to explain? Years ago we all knew each other. Charlie, your Father and me. Frankly I never expected to see Charlie again, for all sorts of reasons but... Anyway, he... he and your Father haven't always seen eye to eye."

For some reason she winces and shakes her head, "I mean, they aren't exactly friendly so when he popped by... given the way things are just now... it might be easier... just now... what with everything else that's going on, it would help if you didn't mention him just now. I expect he'll be gone soon, anyway." She pauses her rubbing and interlaces her fingers. "Has he said anything? About me? Us?"

Dad appears at the door. "What are you two planning?"

"We were talking about Harold's probation."

I goggle at Mum. Where did that come from? I suppose she's thought about it because Mrs Ojha mentioned her uni.

Dad frowns. "I thought you didn't want to discuss that?"

Mum shrugs. "You said we should make it clear that we expect better from him."

Dad looks at me. "You'll try, won't you, Harry-mate? Our Mum is right. We can't go on paying our part of your grant if you're just going to waste it. Can we?"

Mum says, "Your Father means you need to prove to us you are serious about university if you are going to go back in September. Now, Arthur, we have guests."

Dad hesitates but turns away; before I'm left alone Mum says, "If anyone is to tell your Father about Charlie it should be me. Please?" She pauses again but doesn't wait for an answer.

## Chapter Thirty-One

## Arresting Developments

My head is buzzing as I cycle slowly up Mothball Hill and past the goose farm. The only bit of Mum's speech that I liked was the bit about Mr Jepson leaving soon. I've just reached the last junction before the hotel (turn left and you reach the cattle grid that demarks the start of the New Forest; turn right and the road curves hard left to the hotel entrance) when I'm confronted by McNoble, cleaning his nails with his penknife. It's like he's waiting for me. Slowly he puts the knife away and saunters over as I dismount. I'm expecting him to stop and tell me what he wants but he just ploughs right up to me, yanks the bike away and punches me in the stomach, causing me to double up.

While I'm spitting flecks of something foul tasting that his punch has brought up he snarls, "What the effing hell is your Mother doing at my Granny's ceremony? It was like she was some sort of guest of effing honour, the bitch. I warned you before to keep her away from my Father."

I can't answer. He clouts me on the side of my head and I slip sideways. "It's bad enough having that cow Monica as a stepmum." Next it's a kick in the ribs. I roll into a ball awaiting the next blow but a car approaches and he steps away. When I glance up it is Christian's blue Ford. He pulls up alongside us and I struggle to my feet, holding my side. McNoble has backed several yards away and is watching us, a picture of innocence.

Christian says, "Hey, Harry man. You walking? Hop in or Terry will kill your karma." He smiles at McNoble. I can't climb in quickly enough. As we pull away, I glance back. My bike is upside down in a ditch and McNoble is already walking away.

Christian says, "Man, what was that all about? Who's the ghoul?"

I just shake my head and he asks no more questions.

***

Christian tells me to go to the Rat Pit while he finds Penny. Natalie is sunbathing, looking stunning as always. I flop on the grass nearby. She doesn't immediately acknowledge my presence but after a few minutes she rummages in her bag and offers me a half bottle of vodka. She watches me take a swig, cough and take another. It cauterises some of my worries and pain, and I lie back and stare at the clear blue sky.

She says, "Penny mentioned you've got some problems. Money, is it?" She's kneeling near me, partly blocking the sun, as she takes the bottle back. "Don't let the bastards get you, Harry." She raises it to her lips. As she lets the booze slip down her throat I think about Clapton. Do I want to ask this volatile woman? Of course I do. "Natalie—"

"Hey, you." Penny races up to us and snatches the bottle away. She looks furious, as does Natalie who takes a moment before she grabs her towel and shoulders her way inside. Penny caps the bottle before slipping in next to me. She keeps staring at the door as if she's expecting Natalie to come back any moment. "Sorry, Harry. I didn't mean to interrupt." She glances at me. "You ok?"

"What was that all about?"

Penny shrugs. "Oh, nothing. Chris said something about you in a fight?"

I'm not sure what to say and anyway the vodka is swirling through me, my empty stomach assisting its rapid distribution. "Just a little misunderstanding. That twit McNoble again."

"You need to speak to his Father. He's a loose cannon."

"Yeah, maybe." My head is beginning to spin and I close my eyes. I must doze off because when I next open them, she's lying on her side, her head resting on her hand; she's studying me closely. As she sees me looking, she smiles. "How come you're so composed? This thug tries to rip off your balls one day and is punching you the next and it's 'yeah maybe'?"

I close my eyes and smile. Me composed?

She flips onto her back and stares at the sky. "God I wish the rest of them would take a leaf out of your book."

"Me?" I feel really chuffed even though I know she's making a major character misjudgement.

She says, "If it's not Natalie with her 'he loves me, he loves me not' – even though he's a complete sod – it's bloody Chris pretending everything is cool, calm and collected even though he's just been arrested again for possessing cannabis and it's only because he has an Uncle who is an inspector in the local force that he's got away with it."

"Really? Arrested?"

"He... he had to see someone – over near Picket Post. He told me, like it was a joke, they were sharing a joint when the cops turned up. Christ Harry, it's the fourth time in as many weeks he's been caught. He thinks he's smart but his luck will run out. Men, eh?"

We lie in a comfortable silence until it hits me that I need to retrieve my bike. Penny decides to come with me 'to keep an eye on you'.

She doesn't say much until I'm in the ditch, trying to heave my machine onto the verge. "Harry, I know this isn't what you want to hear, given how much you need the money, but I think the hotel might be having some real problems."

"How so?"

"I overheard Mr Hemingway tell Magda the month's takings were 'a disaster'. We might get the sack after all."

I'm glad she can't see me; she'd soon change her mind about how composed I am.

**Chapter Thirty-Two**

**Pot Luck**

To back up Penny's fears about the business, I'm told I'm not needed at dinner due to low numbers. When I get home Dina and Nanty are in the gazebo; Dina is painting her toenails and Nanty is reading a Mills & Boon novel.

"What a crap day." I wave an apology at Nanty who nods my indiscretion away. "How's the flower business?"

No answer. I flop on the grass. "Where's everyone?"

Dina goes on painting. Nanty keeps nodding. After a minute, Dina says, "You need to talk to Ruth. She's moaning about that box again."

"Let her. She's the criminal, not me." I undo my shirt and struggle out of it. Even I can smell how rank I am.

Dina shoots me a look but says nothing. Nanty must be asleep as her nodding hasn't changed in five minutes and she certainly hasn't turned a page.

I rub my rib, which is very sore. My mind turns to McNoble and what I'm going to do. I flop back and close my eyes. Despite taking off my shirt I'm not cooling down either. "God I wish it would rain. I'm fed up getting sweaty and dusty." I glance at Dina. "Anything for dinner?"

She's stopped painting and is kicking at the dirt with her heels.

"Hello? Anyone home?" I push at her leg and she pulls away. The kicking increases in pace but still no answer.

"Who's the moody cow now?" I check Nanty; still asleep. "You ok?"

Nothing. I close my eyes again, wondering why she can be nice sometimes and a miserable git at others. Abruptly the kicking stops and the bench creaks. When I look up she's moved to kick some earth near where Mum has been digging.

The thing is, I think as I watch her, she's not moody like Natalie or Ruth. Not usually. She's more like Penny. Reluctantly I pull myself to my feet and go and join her.

She's swaying slightly, her hands held in tight little fists by her side as tears moisten her eyes. Her body is rigid, every muscle taut. I touch her shoulder. "Di...?"

She almost leaps at me and hugs me hard, sobbing into my chest. Whatever she's trying to say is lost in her gulping. I hold her to me, her wet face slipping and sliding against my sweaty chest. She has to be in a bad way to tolerate that.

***

My head is spinning. After a few minutes calming Dina down, she pulls me to the garage. As we enter I almost pass out; the place reeks of cannabis. On the old workbench there are three large bags stuffed to overflowing. While I struggle to stay upright Dina sits on the floor with her back against the old dresser. When I've regained some composure I join her. "Are you going to tell me what's going on?"

It takes her a while to speak and when she does her voice is tiny. "You know I said I had a great idea to raise money? I thought if I could nick a little of Jim's Dad's weed and sell it to my friends. It's got such a kick they'd really pay a lot for it. I could make say twenty, forty pounds that way, I thought. Maybe more."

I look up at the bags. "You stole that lot?"

She shakes her head. "I went round at lunch time; Jim had told me his Dad was out – up at Picket Post auditioning for his new cast and his Mum's in Southampton. I knew where he kept the stuff – it's in the roof of his shed – and I thought it would take me about thirty minutes all in to get it. But I was up in the attic space when he appeared." She hugs herself. "At first he thought I was the police and went mental when he found out it was me." She stops and swallows. It takes her an age to get going again. "When he calmed down he told me he'd just got away from the police and they were going to raid at any time. He told me, since I was there, I could help him hide his stuff. I thought… I thought he meant help him take it somewhere in is house but he meant I had to hide it here. He didn't give me a choice."

"Jesus, Di. You can't keep this lot. The place stinks for starters."

"Mum and Dad don't know what weed smells like."

"I wouldn't be so sure. Just because they're ancient and old fashioned doesn't mean they haven't had a joint."

For a moment she looks at me like I'm mad but the brief burst of energy goes and her head drops until it is resting on her knees.

I say, "What are we going to do with it?"

"Sell it. Well, some anyway. He said I can have a bagful as payment for hiding it."

My head is still foggy. I'm trying to imagine how we might actually sell it when I realise she's started sobbing again. It's not easy but I manage to prise her arms from her knees and get her to look up. "Hey, we'll find somewhere to put it. Come on, stop this." It's only then I see the red mark on her check, a bit like mine after Paul's punch. "Did he do that?"

She nods and twists sideways, pulling up her shirt. There's a nasty red scratch that runs from her waist up her side; it's still weeping.

"He forced... he forced me to kiss him. We... we brought the bags in here and he went for me. I thought... I thought he was going to hurt me... like you said about Ruth. He was pulling at my shirt when we heard someone – the postman I think – he told me that if I told anyone he'd tell Jim I... I had sex with him."

She can't look at me and I don't know what to do or say. Mr James? I hadn't believed Ruth, not really, but now... God, I'm so out of my depth.

"What am I going to do, H?"

"We are going to tell Mum."

"NO. NO WAY." She pushes me back making me lose my balance.

"Come on, Di. We must..."

She's scrabbled to her feet and turned away from me. "He'll deny it and, and... he'll tell Jim and Jim will hate me."

I pull myself up and go and look at the sacks of weed. Ever since I tried my first joint at thirteen I've struggled to get hold of the stuff. And now we have more than enough for a lifetime and I desperately want it to disappear. "We really should tell someone."

She shakes her head hard. "No." She says it in a way that is completely final and, in truth I don't want to argue with her.

"Ok. For now. But if he touches you again..."

Her silence is the nearest I'm going to get to her acquiescence.

We stay as we are for quite a while before I have an idea. "What about hiding this lot in the compost? Mum always has one bin that's closed for the summer. If we wrap it in paper and put it in one of her fertilizer sacks we could bury it. No one would look and no one would smell it."

"It might rot."

"True, but have you anywhere better?"

She doesn't. She's determined to keep her sack in the attic, which I can't say is a great idea but I don't want to push it and upset her. With that sorted I ask, "How are we going to sell yours? It makes me nervous just thinking about it."

She smiles for the first time. "I've an idea."

"What?"

She shakes her head. "It may not work and anyway, if I told you now you'd try and stop me."

I should be angry, but knowing my snotty arrogant toad of a sister is lurking somewhere inside the fragile woman leaning on the dresser makes me nod and smile.

***

It's late and I've just been in to kiss Nanty goodnight when, out of her window, I see a torch somewhere down the garden. I watch for several minutes. At first I assume it must be Dad creeping to his shed, but then a car's headlights illuminate the vegetable patch and there, staring at the fruit cage, is Mrs Potts, Mum's chief rival. I'm too tired to think what it means and anyway I've enough creeps in my world just now – Mr James, Cyril, McNoble, Paul – without adding Desiree Sodding Potts.

# SATURDAY 24<sup>TH</sup> JULY 1976

## Chapter Thirty-Three

## Oil on Troubled Quarters

Most mornings, between breakfast and lunch, we disperse for an hour's R&R – a towel by the Rat Pit, a discreet corner of the garden not visible to the guests, but nowhere is really satisfactory. However, today Amos proudly unveils his 'salon', which was formerly an outside store but is now a suntrap, bordered by the pool house and pump room wall on one side and laurel hedges on the others. It has cushions and a bench next to the wall. And space for three, at a squeeze, to sunbathe. After a few minutes of dithering, Amos, Natalie and Christian stretch out on the towels while Penny, Sven and I snuggle on the bench and try not to touch each other.

"Do my back, Pen." Christian is the brownest of us, but always covers himself in oil. Amos never changes colour and never oils.

"What about you, Nat?" Penny kneels by Christian's head and works his back from shoulders to shorts.

"Let Harry." Natalie's voice is muffled, but I don't mishear that.

Penny smiles and offers me the bottle.

I follow Penny's lead and kneel by Natalie's head, staring at her back and tiny bikini. "Here." Penny leans over and unclips the top. "Do everywhere, Harry. Like this."

I watch Penny's circling hands, aware she's grinning. Her hands reach down to Christian's shorts, pushing them slightly before curving under his sides. I stare at the tiny triangle of yellow material the only interruption in yards of flesh and wonder what I can and cannot touch.

"Shit." There's a sudden commotion as Natalie begins to sit up, tugging at the towel trapped beneath her knees. Sun oil is running down her cheeks and dripping from her chin. "You stupid berk." She fights the towel, finally freeing it. As she does so she sits back on her heels and scrubs her face. For what seems an age no one else moves; then Penny reaches across and drapes a towel around Natalie's shoulders. She whispers something to Natalie who grabs at the towel, covering her chest before the two of them stand and hurry away.

As soon as the gate slams shut, we all relax a little. Christian is the first to speak. "Wowza. Now that's what I call a pair of peachy pert titties."

Sven shakes his head. "Oh Harold. Oil in the hair? Rather passé, don't you think? But a magnificent display for sure."

Amos has barely moved. He says, "If you really have to see her topless, ask Cyril. He'll find a way for you."

The image of Natalie's breasts, bouncing free from her top as she rubbed the oil away, seems to have been burnt onto the back of my retina. My first thought is not guilt, but a curious disappointment that the nipples are not, as suggested by Christian, orange.

Christian slowly stretches out, his hands behind his head. He starts purring. "Chill-o. Harry is the MAN. Now I can, like, die happy."

"I'd better go and apologise."

Christian reaches out and catches my ankle. "I wouldn't, man. Not now. I'll explain to Penny-o. She'll cool it with Miss Titty."

Sven pats me sympathetically on the shoulder. "And just before my party. Looks like you've just pooped on your chances, young Lochinvar."

## Chapter Thirty-Four

## It's My Party, and I'll Get High if I Want to...

All afternoon I've changed my mind about the party but in the end I decide to go. Dobbin would say it's because I'm an irredeemable optimist but actually it's because Dina gives me a small tin of weed from the attic store and a jar of 'special marinade' she and Janice have made using some of the supply. "It'll be great on the barbeque," she says. I've also practiced a fulsome and grovelling apology that, with everything else, should do the trick. I do press her on whether this sauce is her plan but she's still keeping mum. All she says is, "Wait for Sunday."

"Sunday?" The cold is creeping back into my lower intestine. "What's happening on Sunday?"

She doesn't so much as blink though Janice has a fit of the giggles. I am beginning to get a bad feeling about this.

\*\*\*

Sven lives at the end of a private road. His parents' house, glimpsed through the fencing, looks huge. When I turn in through the gates, the drive curves away to the right. Each step makes me more and more nervous. I also get Penny's point about Sven being loaded; surely he doesn't need to work if he lives here?

I'm still musing on the enigma that is Sven when a growl makes me jump. "Izz vat you, 'arry?" It's Magda, in every sense dressed to kill. She is wearing a pink silky see-through blouse and a short grey skirt. That's the end of her femininity; her granite hard, chemically enhanced biceps and tungsten thighs glisten in the moonlight. She extinguishes her cigarette with her fingers and sticks the stub in her small bag.

"Zo. Ow izz your Aunt?" Magda pushes her helmet shaped hairdo off her face and offers me her hand.

"Thanks, yeah. She's fine. Back home."

Her grip has just a hint of a vice about it. She pulls me in front of her. "You save a dance for me, ja? Not just these stoopid girlies." She leans in and kisses me softly on the lips; her scent is sweet jasmine.

***

We walk together round some trees until the drive opens out. To our left is the bungalow, out of which loud music is pouring. A few people, some of whom I don't recognise, are mingling by the door. There's a barbeque out front. To the right is more drive leading to more trees. We're almost at the house when a rasping voice calls me.

"Oi, tosser. Here." Paul waves at me. Reluctantly I go towards him. "You allowed out this late?"

Beet, looming out of the smoke from the barbeque, says, "Oh shit. You're not going to wank in the salad, are you? People'll think it's the mayonnaise."

Paul's right hand is thickly bandaged. He says, "I want a word."

"So do I."

"Yeah?" He's immediately suspicious.

"I brought you this." I give him a small packet of the grass. "And this." The marinade. "My sister made it. Got a real kick."

He sniffs the packet and reluctantly takes the jar. "If you're pissing with me..."

"No. Not at all."

Paul tastes it carefully before offering it to Beet. They share a look and turn to me. Paul says, "You're still a wanker."

Beet adds, "Yeah and a know-all shite."

Paul narrows his stare as the smoke envelops us. "I heard you got the tart to show everyone her tits."

I keep watching him, wondering where this is going. Finally he breaks eye contact. "Your funeral."

"Yeah. Funeral." Beet looks confused as he echoes Paul.

"She's yours. I'm done with the dirty bitch."

He turns away leaving Beet looking from me to him and back. "Yeah, fuck off." Beet follows Paul back to the fire.

***

I wander to the bungalow, cursing my luck. I'm offered a free run just when she won't talk to me. Waiting by the front door is our host. He opens his arms. "Did you come with the Gorgon? You're a brave man, Harold Spittle, if you plan to make her your next sexual conquest; it might turn out you are part of some sinister reproductive experiment. Now let me explain the layout."

Sven's blond locks are swept back and held in place with a copper-coloured Alice band, of the sort that Björn Borg can get away with but Sven most certainly cannot. He's wearing baggy black trousers and what looks like a quilted silk smoking jacket in reds and greens, with a knotted cravat tucked in at the neck. If Noel Coward was moody, Swedish and an utter pillock this would be the look.

"And I see you've made friends with Paul and Beet. They aren't so bad, are they?"

"They're complete bastards."

"Oh my. Such strong feelings. I don't suppose, in your sheltered little world, you really know who is the complete bastard and who is just a little inadequate. May you never have to learn the difference. Now, drinks in the kitchen at the back; dancing first on the right with coats in the small room by some stairs. If you get lucky," he winces, "there's a bed in the roof space. Follow your nose if you need the loo; Mama said the cesspit chappie never showed up to pump it out. Oh, and don't go exploring the big house. There are some rather nasty four legged security measures prowling the park, just to ensure Pater's peace of mind."

He struts off, loving the sense of power that hosting the party gives him. Why can't I have his easy self-confidence? If he had four tickets for Clapton or a year's supply of grass, he wouldn't worry about a little spilt sun oil. Even Paul and Beet treat him like an equal. How does he do it?

\*\*\*

There's some frantic uncoordinated dancing going on in the first room which is jammed full. The music is Mungo Jerry or some such bollocks. The next room is dark and full of coats. I've just tossed my denim jacket onto what I assume is the heap when the heap convulses and emits this awful sound, rather like a tenor practising his scales while having a number of cigarettes extinguished on his buttocks. It sounds like Terry.

Back in the hall, an unusually sweaty Amos has his arm draped round a tall vacant-looking man with purple hair. "Penny was looking for you." He pulls a face. "In there."

The kitchen extends across the back of the house. At one end there's a large wooden table covered in a variety of bottles and paper cups; at the other there's an open door where most people have gathered to catch whatever breeze there is. The only person not by the door is Penny, sitting on the corner of the table, wine bottle in hand.

As soon as I enter Christian breaks off and hurries over. He isn't his usual ebullient self. "Man, I tried to chill-o Pen, but she's gone all doom-time mean mama, yeah? You dig?" He looks back at Penny. "She's like a carnivore tonight, Harry-o." He shrugs and goes back to his group.

Penny is studying a cup like she's panning it for gold.

"Hi Penny."

Slowly she peers up at me and waves her wine. "You are a total prick."

"I'm really sorry. It was an accident and—"

"Shurrup." She waves a hand and burps. "You're a stupid baby, aren't you?" When she tries to stare at me she loses focus and has to grip the table edge.

"I'm sorry."

"Don't whine you... you... pissy... thing."

"I really didn't mean to..."

Momentarily she perks up. "Oh come on. You boys are all the same. Christ, Harry, you know what she's been going through." She picks up the bottle and waves that at me, slopping its contents on her jeans. "She thought, we both thought, you know, here's a decent bloke who's... who's... decent. Not like most of the pricks who come at us like we're just meat... and then you pull that trick." Penny forces herself to look right at me. "She thought, you know, you liked her..."

"I do. I want to say sorry—"

The bottle passes under my nose, missing me by a fraction. "Too bloody late sunshine. She's off men for good. We both are. I'm getting drunk and she's blubbing her eyes out. Well done to all men, you pricks."

"What about Christian?"

"Stuff him. Stuff you all." She stands and wobbles off towards the hall.

"Where is she?"

I think her final wave indicates the garden.

Natalie is stretched out on a swing, like ours only newer and bigger and undoubtedly less smelly. It sits on one side of a terraced area. I can only see her profile; she's staring at the stars. There's a part of me that wants to march up to her and deliver my well-practiced apology, but there's another, more cautious part that tells me to roll a joint first, as a back-up plan. I slip quietly to a table a few feet from the swing and set to.

"Hallo. It is you." Mrs Jepson has appeared as if by magic and slides onto the chair next to me. She's wearing a long white dress and not a lot else. "How are you, Harry?"

I'm so surprised it's her that I automatically stand. The joint, freed from my grip, rolls towards her. Hurriedly I snatch it up and stick it in my lap as I sit back down.

"Do you smoke?" She opens her bag and offers me one.

"Er, no thanks." She must think I'm a complete idiot.

She lights up and looks at the bungalow. "I heard the noise and wondered what was going on? Someone's birthday?"

I manage to shake my head. "Just a party."

She nods, pushing out her bottom lip. "Well, I expect you'll have more fun than me. Charlie had to visit Robin and they'll be droning on for hours I expect." She smokes for a while before she says, "So this is Sven's, is it?"

I nod, glancing at Natalie. She looks asleep but I don't want her to go before I can say my piece.

"Have you known the Andersens long?"

"No." I'm rather taken aback by the suggestion. "I only met Sven a couple of weeks ago, when I started work."

"But you've known his parents for a while, surely?"

"No, I've never met them."

She's looking across the lawns towards the main house, blowing smoke out of the side of her mouth. "I assumed your family and the Andersens must have known each other for a while." She shakes her head. "I saw your Mother talking to Robin Andersen at the ceremony – Charlie's Mother?" She peers at me. "You knew she went, didn't you?"

I nod.

"Did she tell you what happened?"

"Mum? She's not mentioned it."

Mrs Jepson is already laughing. "When Charlie opened the box the ashes went everywhere. We'll all be wearing the old bag for weeks. Robin wasn't best pleased." She stubs out the cigarette on the cast iron table, seemingly oblivious to any damage it might cause. "Poor Charlie. There he is, trying to ingratiate himself and he ends up giving Robin a good dusting."

I'm conscious she's staring hard at me. "You do know Charlie and your Mother are old *friends*?"

I don't like the way she emphasises the last word.

Her stare and her questions are making me increasingly uncomfortable. That and the way her nipples seem to be growing and filling my vision.

She says, "You don't know their history yet you were spying on them, weren't you? By your side gate? What did you hear, I wonder? Something interesting?"

She lapses into silence while she starts and finishes another cigarette. When the second stub has been ground into the table she brushes ash off her dress and stands, offering me her hands. Even when I don't move she stays with her hands out and says, "Do you know I'm his third wife? He told me he'd left Hampshire, his family home, that awful Mother of his. Betsy the Bitch. Never to return, he said. And what happens? She dies and suddenly we have to go back to spread her ashes. Two days at most, he said."

With every sentence she leans a little closer, those rock hard nipples jabbing at me as if to emphasise each point. "He tells me it's too complicated to make it any longer. Dealing with Robin bloody Andersen for starters. And now we've been here, what, a week? Ten days? And he's negotiating with Robin to let him stay even longer." She moves forward and takes my unwilling hands, easing me to my feet. "And who does he spend his time with? His 'old friend', your Mother. Isn't that rather odd for 'old friends' who've not met in years? Apparently." She squeezes my fingers. "That makes me curious. What do you think, Harry?"

"I... I suppose it would."

"But then, it's maybe not so strange given he was her first lover. Given she is someone he wanted to marry. Someone who wanted to marry him."

My mind feels scrambled; it's like she's hypnotised me. Finally she breaks the eye contact and looks across at Natalie; as she does so the breeze pushes her hair across her face. She brushes it away with an irritated flick. "You'd imagine he'd want to spend time with his current wife, wouldn't you?" She lets me go and holds her arms wide apart. "He's got this. What's your Mother got?"

I stare at those proud nipples; not them for starters.

She rocks back and laughs. "It's not her physical attractions, Harry. Your Mother has one precious commodity that all Charlie's wives haven't had. With us, he's won, with her he lost. And Charlie hates losing."

There's movement from the swing and she looks towards Natalie again who has sat up and is staring at us. Dropping her arms, she says, "Have I interrupted your plans? Was the joint for her?"

"Joint?"

There's a pause before Mrs Jepson reaches to the ground and scoops it up. In doing so she brushes my fly causing my already bulging nob to leap forward.

She holds the soggy stick to her nose. "I don't know if it will light." With that she picks up her bag and swings away, over to Natalie. Natalie looks bemused as Mrs Jepson hands her the joint and moves on slowly towards the big house.

My nob is causing me a lot of grief because of Rascal's lacerations, which have refused to scab properly. While I half turn away, desperate to ease the pressure, Natalie stands up and wanders over; she's grinning broadly.

## Chapter Thirty-Five

## Snogs and Sick

We're both lying on the swing. It took her an age to light the joint, and that gave me a chance to re-dress myself. All that did was give my erection another boost. While she greedily enjoys the joint, I concentrate on trying to identify Cassiopeia.

Why is it that a damaged penis holds its shape so much longer than a sound one? Every movement seems to abrade it further. However the last ten minutes have taught me an important lesson: a joint says 'sorry' in ways words cannot.

As soon as it was alight she took her first drag and nuzzled up to me; after two puffs she snogged me so hard I damn near swallowed her tongue.

Working on the assumption that there are usually about fifteen drags in a joint of this size, I'd estimate that my excruciating tumescence will become intolerable well before we finish it. I'm already doing well not to whimper.

After the third puff, she gives it to me and rolls on her back. While I inhale carefully she says, "You know we'll have to fuck, don't you?" With that she prises it from my lips and takes another drag.

No constellations are going to help me now. I manage to whisper, "I can't, Natalie. I'm sorry but really I can't." I try closing my eyes and begin listing the Kings and Queens since 1066.

I've reached Henry V when she says, in a small voice, "Why?" She puts her hand on my groin, just letting it rest on the lump.

"I... I just can't."

She's crying. At least I think she is but it's taking every modicum of will power to ensure I don't give a new meaning to the expression 'growth spurt'. I ease her hand away and tug at my zip, hoping to ease the pressure.

I don't know what she thinks, but in moments she's on her knees and has taken over the tugging. I think she says, "So it's ok like this, is it?" She sounds angry. I try and push her off but she's too determined and has my fly down and is yanking my penis from my underpants in seconds.

"No, stop. Christ. DON'T. STOP! Oh shit!!"

Too late. The impact of her drug-dumb fingers on my penis is instantly percussive and my self-respect is ejaculated into my pants and my fingers. She pulls back letting me try and staunch the flow, unsuccessfully of course. While my full attention is focused on capturing the outpouring of every spasm, she clambers off the swing and looks down at me. She says, "He told you, didn't he? About having sex with me?"

I'm too mortified to respond. The goo has gone everywhere and I have no choice but to use the upholstery to wipe my hands. As I stand and ease my destroyed penis back inside my jeans, she moves toward the kitchen. I don't think I've ever felt more depressed – as well as a little guilty about the state of Sven's upholstery. I retrieve the joint and lie back to finish it off. What a complete disaster.

*\*\*\**

When, eventually, I go inside Natalie and Penny have left. Magda says Natalie 'shouldn't have tried to sex you' and drags me off for a bop.

We have a really rather good snog to Layla and for a moment I wonder if I should invite her to Clapton. She tells me twice how good looking I am (I don't believe her but it's nice all the same) and how she likes my 'manly' haircut, 'not girly long like Christian'. We share another joint and talk about East Germany (well, she does). She suggests we 'go upstairs' but given that I'm reprising the hot/cold/hot reaction to the Reggie-mix that hit me before, as well as the fact that my penis has no dermal layer to speak of, I decline. She says she'll get us a drink but before she returns I have to vomit. Once outside I know I just have to get home.

***

I'm horribly ill. As I hold on to the great white telephone for support and gradually empty my guts into it, my head feels too full of information and feelings that I don't know how to deal with. As another retch overtakes me I know only one thing clearly – tomorrow will be the most embarrassing day ever.

# SUNDAY 25<sup>TH</sup> JULY 1976

## Chapter Thirty-Six

## Hangover

A shaft of sunlight pierces my troubled sleep; the small deaths that are hangovers repeat inside my head like a series of planned explosions. As I empty my bladder, noting dispassionately my urine is oddly purple, I check on my penis. Pleasingly, last night's scouring has triggered some natural remedy and scabs have appeared. They itch all to buggery, but it seems a small price to pay.

Going downstairs, I'm sure that 'guilty' is scratched in my forehead, but happily the kitchen is empty.

Sellotaped to my bike is a note from Dina. *'Be at the fête at one thirty; Janice and I have solved your money problems'*. I read it several times; what does she mean? They're going to deal drugs at the fête?

I'm about to go and see if she's about when I catch a deep anguish-filled moan emanating from Dad's shed. Everything goes quiet and I'm wondering if I imagined it when it repeats, only louder this time and I rush to push open the door. At first all I see is Ravi Ojha behind Dad's desk, staring at his turntable and swaying to 'Heartbreak Hotel'. It takes a moment to spot Dad, who is with Papaji contorted on the floor. The air is putrid with sweat, joss sticks and methane. "You ok, Dad?"

"Harry-kiddo. Yes. I think. Asoka here is a sort of Yogi would you believe, and he's teaching me to find my inner calm." Dad is drenched, his pyjamas sticking to him like he's being papier-mâché-ed and every little twitch releases another odiforous fart. Each one receives a 'well done' and a clap from Asoka.

\*\*\*

I'm still thinking about Dina's note when I reach Hemingway's. I try and persuade Magda to let me use the phone, but whatever happened last night, and I'm not entirely sure this morning, hasn't loosened her up at all. I wander back to my station, trying to convince myself that Dina is pulling my leg.

There are four of us at breakfast. Terry is apparently in hospital with cigarette burns on his back and a groin problem, so Amos, looking like a cadaver, is in charge. Only Sven is chirpy.

"Thanks for that sauce. It went down a treat."

I concentrate on the place settings, but he won't take a hint. He says, "You had quite a time, didn't you? I saw you snogging Magda. Still got your whole tongue?" He follows me around the tables and says, "The weed was rather strong though I suppose you're immune." I head for the kitchen but I can't shake him off. "There's a real mess outside the Rat Pit. Hemingway isn't impressed. Poor Cyril isn't either."

He's still by the door when I re-enter the restaurant. "And what were you and Natalie up to?" He closes his eyes. "DON'T! STOP!"

"Fuck off."

"Ah, you can speak. So was that DON'T. STOP? Or DON'T STOP?"

As I push past him, he holds his sides and rocks with cartoon laughter.

\*\*\*

I'm called into the office. It's not a reprimand or the sack, but a move: I'm to be support barman to Rodney. No bloody chefs, no Terry, no having to work out what the girls mean, no effing Sven. I'm not listening to him as he witters on until he says, "Good to see your Mother at Charlie's little ceremony. I never knew they went so far back." His asymmetric nostrils seem worse today; or maybe it's me. "I suppose you'll be seeing more of him now." I can see one is blocked so the other, the larger is doing the work of two. It's awful and fascinating. "It'll mean quite a few changes."

"What will, sir?"

My speaking makes him jolt forward. He rubs his face and says, "God, I shouldn't have said, should I? Pretend I didn't say anything, Harold. All right? Mum's the word." He holds my confused gaze for a moment before looking down to read some papers. I creep away to find Rodney.

## Chapter Thirty-Seven

## Asking Her Out

I should have gone straight home; Rodney insists on an interminable induction. With every 'this is an optic' and 'here we have Guinness' my departure is put back. Then when I go to collect my bike, Natalie is leaning against the bike rack; Sod is working overtime. She is a horrid beetroot colour. "Harry, about last night..."

"Let's just forget it, ok? I really do have to go and... Are you ok?"

"Just a bit hot." She wipes her forehead. "Can I say something? Explain?"

I fiddle with the lock. "There's no need."

"No, there is. I spoke to Pen and Magda. I shouldn't have got so cross and blamed you. It's not your fault."

I pull my bike free and gingerly straddle it.

She says, "I just wanted to ask that, if you can, you try and forgive me." She doesn't wait on a response and makes for the hotel.

It's the way she walks, shoulders down, heels dragging, looking so dejected that makes me call after her. "Just a mo. I've been meaning to say..."

She's still walking away but slows down.

"Thing is I have a friend... well, she's Dina's really... anyway, her Dad works at the Gaumont..."

She's stopped and turned to stare at me. "Clapton tickets. I have four. You said you liked him..."

From desolation to joy in five seconds. Well, incredulity to joy. She begins to bounce on the balls of her feet and then starts clapping. I smile and another minute is wasted, but it feels worth it. "I really have to go, but have a think about who might want to come and let me know."

I love the way little creases that nick her forehead into a frown of uncertainty have melted so that I can now drown in her eyes. I want to stay and luxuriate in her gratitude, go to the Rat Pit and… I glance at my watch. "I really have to dash. We can talk about it tomorrow."

The next few moments are something of a blur. She runs up to me, nearly knocking me off my bike. She doesn't know whether to hug me or do a cartwheel she's so full of energy. "Penny of course – she loves him – and Sven is such a fan and Christian likes all live bands and has a car. That's four." She stops, a huge grin on her face which then dissolves into a little frown. "I do understand, Harry. I misread last night. I see that now. But thank you."

I watch her go, still walking slowly but with more of a spring in her step. As hard as I try I cannot process what has just happened beyond two simple facts: first, I have just managed to give away all four tickets and, second, she is convinced I do not want to have sex with her.

You plonker, Harry.

## Chapter Thirty-Eight

## Coining It In

If ever it was going to rain then the WI summer fête would trigger it, but despite the thickening clouds and muggy heat there's not a drop of moisture anywhere. The fête is already pretty crowded when I arrive. I scan the stalls and soon spot Janice. I trail her to a table that Dina is manning. Behind it is a small tent from which Dina is ferrying small paper packets; on the table are some jars like the one I took to the party. Nanty is seated in a fold-up chair with a box for the money. I approach with caution but Dina sees me and waves me over with a huge grin on her face.

"So what's going on? Are you using this as cover?" I try and sound light-hearted but actually I feel terrible.

Janice appears from the tent with more packets. She's smiling too. Dina says, "Sort of. These are teas, spiked with you know what – herbal teas, like camomile and mint – and the sauces are like the one you took last night."

"But, but..." Is she really selling illegal drugs? They throw away the key for that.

"Don't worry, I've organised everything. There are some neutrals of both teas and sauces. Anyone who wants extra asks for 'added spice'."

I look around wildly. "You can't... I mean, it's the fête. How did you get the table?"

"It was Ms Glebe's idea."

"Ms Glebe? Susan Glebe? She doesn't know, does she?"

"Of course she does. She's helped with everything. Oh hi..."

Just then a mass of Dina's school friends descend on us, as irritating as midges at sunset, giggling and asking 'for spice' and 'double spice'. Nanty joins in the fun with nods and grins.

When the last one has gone, I say to Dina, "Does Nanty know what you're doing?"

Dina smiles at nothing in particular. "I guess. I gave her some mint-plus last night and she loved it. Does it matter? She's not trying to stop us is she?"

"For Christ sake, how can you involve her? People of her generation have no idea about drugs."

Dina gives me her 'your IQ is in the 7 to 10 range' look. "You were the one who said Mum and Dad smoked joints."

"No I didn't. I just meant—"

"It doesn't matter." Dina is beginning to sound irritated. "We're here now and have a lot to do. Are you going to help?" She looks again at Nanty, who's now listening to three girls talking about some boy. "I bet Nanty has a few secrets of her own."

"Oh sure. Frankly if she could get me my money from Grandpa's will then we wouldn't need to risk prison like this."

We watch as Nanty carefully counts out some change with her right hand. It's very clumsy and slow. Dina shakes her head. "Well, that's not going to happen so this is the only way."

"There has to be..."

"Oh and Penny's coming to help."

"PENNY? You spoke to her?"

"Yes. You said she wanted to save your skin so I called the hotel. The receptionist was very nice and passed on a message."

I'm rather stunned and don't believe it. Dina takes advantage of my silence to go back into the tent, leaving me out front.

"HAROLD. DINA. I HEARD YOU HAD A STALL. FOR THE NEEDY."

Desiree Potts, the WI president, local power-broker and Mum's chief rival in all things horticultural, with a voice like the PA on the Isle of Wight Ferry, pulls alongside. Seeing her reminds me she was in our garden and I haven't told Mum yet. But that thought slips away as quickly as it comes because she's picked up a packet of tea with added spice and is sniffing it. While Dina materialises next to me, smiling, I petrify.

"SO WHAT ARE YOU CHILDREN SELLING?"

Dina says, "Herbal teas and a marinade."

"AH. MARINADE?"

Dina says, "I've given a jar to the Scouts to put on their chicken, if you want to try it?"

"CLEVER GIRL. A BIT OF FREE ADVERTISING NEVER HURT." Mrs Potts sniffs the packet. "NOW THERE ARE DEFINITE MINTY NOTES, BUT THERE'S SOMETHING ELSE, ISN'T THERE?"

I'm beginning to sway and will topple shortly; meanwhile Dina maintains an inhuman and rather chilling sangfroid.

Mrs Potts puts the packet down quickly, and leans close to Dina. "I DIDN'T BELIEVE SUSAN."

Dina smiles, Cheshire Cat-like.

Mrs Potts turns to look at me. "AND WHAT IS YOUR PART IN THIS, HAROLD?"

If I move I'll have a coronary.

Dina ignores me. "Please Mrs Potts, let's not pretend you don't know. We're all aware that what Ms Glebe knows, you know. You've had a disastrous growing year, haven't you? All Ms Glebe and I agreed was that, for this year only, I would fill the vacuum. We won't do this again."

The Dreadnought is the first to break eye contact. She picks up a jar and weighs it in her hands. "MARINADE YOU SAY?"

"If you want a taste, the Scouts..."

"YOU SAID." She and Dina exchange one of those impenetrable looks beloved of women. "YES, WELL LET ME THINK ABOUT IT." She adds, "OH AND HOW ARE YOUR MAMA'S PUMPKINS? ARE THEY ALL RIGHT? NO DAMAGE I HOPE? IT'S BEEN AWFUL."

Dina says, "She has them well hidden."

Mrs Potts heaves to, turning to catch the next tide. As she goes she says, "YES, I BELIEVE I HEARD THAT. AND I DO LIKE THE SHORT HAIR, HAROLD; I ALWAYS THINK LONG HAIR SUGGESTS A LACK OF SPUNK IN A MAN."

When she's turned the corner by the tombola I let out the breath I didn't realise I had been holding. Dina is smacking the side of her head. "Are your ears ringing like mine? She should be fitted with a muffler."

"Are you going to explain?" I watch the crowds praying that they keep away. "She might tell PC Peeltrap."

"Stop worrying. If there's one person who'll not tell the law it is Mrs Foghorn Potts. Ah, here come the pensioners."

I look behind me; a shuffling line of geriatrics is being jollied towards us by Susan Glebe. Dina is laughing. I don't know how she can be so relaxed. She squeezes my arm. "Go and try the marinade, will you? Judge the crowd's reaction."

***

The scout leader, Mr Paulbarer, whose most striking features are his vein-fissured nose and flat greasy black hair, parades anxiously in front of his troop of fawn-shirted minions. To one side the barbeque smokes with unsupervised abandon, more conflagration than cooking. One little scout is playing a sort of solo Grandma's footsteps.

"You're the Spittle boy, aren't you?"

"Yes sir."

"Your sister's marinade is quite something. The lads love it and it spices up the chicken a treat. Do you want to try a piece? On Us?"

I take the chicken barely believing she has given them the spiced version. I'm still staring at the wing when Mrs Ojha and the children appear out of the smoke.

Noor runs up to me and hugs my waist. "Can I have some, Mummy? Can I?"

"What do you recommend, Harold? The chicken?"

"I... I don't think it's really for children, Mrs Ojha."

Before I can stop her she leans in close and sniffs my piece. One dark furry eyebrow shoots up her forehead. "Oh, my sauce. Has Dina used the spiced version?" She wipes a finger across the surface and tastes it. "No, plain. Sensible girl."

I can't help goggling at her as my knees nearly give way. "I... er, how...?"

Her serious face suddenly melts and she smiles and nods. "Dina couldn't really hide the smell last night. While it was cooling I went and checked and found she'd made two versions. Takes me right back to Bristol days. We put pot in everything back then; I used to love it on Weetabix. Yes, Noor you can have chicken and Sajid can have a burger – though don't tell Papaji you had cow." She smiles at me and moves to buy the food.

## Chapter Thirty-Nine

## Marmite Madness

Dina and Janice are laughing when I return. It's all quiet. I say, "So, go on. Explain."

Dina shrugs. "Mrs Potts supplies the Evergreen nursing home with cannabis. She's been doing it for ages. She grows it in those massive greenhouses of hers while Ms Glebe dries and packages it for her as... guess what?"

"Herbal teas."

Dina claps. "This year, she made a huge mistake and didn't whitewash the glass properly and with all the sun we've had everything burnt. She's had a lot of upset geriatrics."

"How do you know?"

"You know me. I love spying. Ms Glebe was talking to Mr Poseidon about it. He delivers the supplies with the post. I'd thought about it before but it was only the other night, when we were in the garage that I plucked up the courage. She's very practical is Ms Glebe. We agreed that she could have half a bagful and in return she helped Janice and me make up the teas and organise the sales. She came up with the stall idea too. She gets thirty per cent of the takings for the WI hall restoration and we get the rest. She's brilliant; she even had the nursing home send a coach."

"Did you use all of it? Won't Jim's Dad want some back?"

Her face has clouded. "I don't care."

"No well maybe…"

She's getting really angry. "Just for once don't be a total wimp, ok?"

"And Mrs Potts? Can you trust her?"

She's getting fed up. "It's her pension. And PC Peeltrap is her nephew, isn't he? He's more frightened of her than you are of McNob."

"And Mrs Ojha?"

"Just SHUT UP." She swallows and says, "She's not going to upset anyone. While Ravi's unemployed she can't afford to." Dina looks over my shoulder. "You tell him, Penny." She marches back into the tent.

Penny is already shrugging off her jacket. "Did she say we spoke? What can I do?"

"You know what we're selling?"

"Teas and sauces laced with your super weed that did for everyone at Sven's. Is that true?"

"Pretty much. How'd you get here? Christian?"

She pulls a face. "Mr Jepson actually."

"Jepson? He's here?" Instinct makes me check around.

Penny says, "He's off visiting some old friend. Hi, are you Nanty? I'm Penny."

They're soon on first name/nodding terms. I busy myself restacking some packets until Penny joins me. She says, "Nats told me about the Clapton tickets. She thinks you're some kind of hero."

I find the restacking is very engrossing.

"Is it right you don't want to go?"

"Not my cup of tea."

"She's worried you don't like her."

I shrug and conveniently knock over a pile of tea packets so I have to scrabble on the floor to collect them.

"Sven was saying you and she…"

I peer round the table leg. "I don't give a f… stuff about what that ponce thinks, frankly."

"Jeepers, what's got into you?"

"Me? What about your rant about men? I make a genuine mistake with some sun oil and it's 'all men are pricks' and that includes Harry."

It's her turn to look embarrassed. "Sorry. I was mad at Christian for his stupidity with the police and then Natalie was in pieces and Magda moaned about Hemingway and… You caught the end of all that." She pauses and then says, "You will be nice to Nats, won't you?"

"Of course I will."

"Don't be upset. You can understand how difficult it's been for her. Now, what can I do?"

While Penny bustles about, I watch her closely. I don't understand her or Natalie in truth. In fact girls generally are pretty much a closed book.

***

It's soon clear that the girls are far better at this sales business than me so I sit on the grass next to Nanty and doze off. They nudge me awake when it's time to clear away. By half five, Dina, Nanty and Janice are off home and I'm waiting with Penny for her lift before I cycle to work for my first full shift in the bar.

"How much have you made?" Penny is sitting on the grass, clutching her packet of extra spiced.

I manage a shrug. "No idea. I can't believe we've got away with it."

"She's incredible." Penny pats the grass next to her and I sit. She shifts and leans against my shoulder. When I look she's closed her eyes. "Hmm, this is nice. I love this summer. I'm definitely a girl for a hot climate."

"I'd prefer it cold. I can't stop sweating."

Penny looks at my face and reaches out with a finger, wiping a line of drips off my forehead. She tastes it carefully. "Mint? Camomile? There's a special ingredient, isn't there? Now what is it?"

It's so very natural, our kiss. As our lips meet my first thought is there are no drugs involved, she really wants to do this. The kiss is careful at first, just our lips touching before her tongue pushes them apart, not that they aren't willing, and we dive in.

It takes a moment for me to register something isn't right but when it does I'm overwhelmed. The source of her oddly metallic smell becomes apparent: Marmite. If there's one thing I hate, it's Marmite. Actually, it's beyond hate and well into revulsion. And there it is, that faecal paste, everywhere my lips and tongue have gone. I'm covered in it. I really try and let my reproductive instinct rule – the base urge to snog – but the instinct to avoid being poisoned is stronger and I pull away.

"What on earth's the matter?"

I'm rubbing my tongue on my arm and spitting and hacking as hard as I can.

"Are you ok?"

I manage to gasp, "Marmite" before I stumble upright and into the little tent where there are some teacups. I finish the cold dregs from each one greedily.

When I look up, she's standing in the entrance, hands on hips. "Are you serious? All this over Marmite?"

I just about manage a nod when we hear her name being called. She glares at me, shakes her head and hurries away.

Old Mr Moreybund, the cattery owner, who wisely banned Rascal years ago, is waiting by the table, holding Penny's packet. "'ow much?"

I shake my head, still staring after Penny. "It's yours."

He follows my gaze. "Don't worry son. She'll get over it." I glance up to see his gap-toothed smile. "Nice titties that one."

***

I'm cycling through the village when I spot Jim sitting on a wall; he looks miserable.

"You ok?"

He nods.

I try again. "I meant to say. The cricket. I don't think I'll make it this year. Work, you know?"

He nods again.

"Are you sure you're ok?"

He looks up at me at that and shakes his head. "I don't know what I've done, Harry but she's been really cranky."

Poor sod. How on earth to tell him? "Look mate, go and see her." I swallow. "Tell her you love her, you know. She'll really appreciate that."

"You think?"

"Oh sure. If you tell 'em you really care they're putty in your hands."

He doesn't look sure but stands up and brushes his shirt. I say, "She's home just now. She's had a good time at the fête so should be in just the right mood."

He doesn't exactly spring into action but after a moment starts off towards our house. What a hypocrite, Harry. Follow your own advice, can't you?

# MONDAY 26TH JULY 1976

## Chapter Forty

## Barman

The day starts badly. Dina refuses to answer when I knock on her door and by the time I finish my morning's contemplation on the throne she's gone. I'm more than a little keen to know what we earned at the fête so curse her and my luck. On my way downstairs the first negative to moving into the bar hits me: no more breakfasts at the hotel. Happily Mrs Ojha has taken over the kitchen and there's freshly baked bread and honey plus some sort of paste, a curious bright green which is like a spicy marmalade. While Papaji massages Nanty's fingers, I let the children climb over me and listen to Ravi moan about the lack of work.

I'm not so lucky with the second significant negative of bar work. My shift finishes well after the others have left for the beach; as a result my lunch companions are Rodney and Cyril.

"Eh boiy. Yous got a minute arter?" Cyril smokes rollups with his meal, mixing ash with the stew. "Oi need a 'and with me caktuzzz."

"I'm busy, Cyril."

"No, you're not." Rodney doesn't look up from the Wincanton race card. "Have you seen his cactuses? They are wonders of nature."

What the hell? It's not as if I owe Penny any favours after her sneering contempt yesterday. But it turns out to be worth the effort; they are amazing.

I'm soon helping Cyril repot some tiny ones. He makes me wear these thick gloves even though he doesn't bother. "Dunna yous touch 'em spines. 'Ems a devil to get art yous fingurs. Em tweezees ain't no good neither. They's be all puffy if yous touch 'em." His own digits are gnarled and discoloured with angry red blotches.

When the last one is buried in soil and watered, Cyril heads for the door. "Roight, toime for a treat." He leers at me.

"What exactly — ?"

"You'll see." He just assumes I'll follow as he sets off without looking back.

It's not far. We've left the greenhouses behind us and walked alongside the hedge that borders the Forest. When he stops without warning I nearly pile into his back.

"'ere we go." He pulls at some of the thick foliage and squeezes through, holding it back for me to follow. Beyond, between hedge and Forest fence is a small grassy meadow. It's bathed in the afternoon sun and is completely hidden from the hotel grounds. In fact you would have to be standing on a step ladder somewhere near Setley Cross and using serious binoculars if you wanted to spy on us. He watches me take it all in. "See, boiy. Oi's been thinking about them girlies. Oi knows they loike to get 'em titties out so Oi thought, if yous tell 'em about thissum, all proivate loike, then they moight sunbathe and we could watch. Phwoar!" He shakes the front of his corduroys and releases a rumbling chuckle.

"How would you do that?"

He turns back and pushes through the hedge. As usual I have to trot along behind. We retrace our steps to the greenhouses; behind the last one, a truly decrepit affair that might fall down any moment, is the corner of the hedges. He holds back the top layer of branches and I can just make out the meadow.

As I scan the horizon wondering with a sick stomach at his ingenuity, he disappears inside the ramshackle greenhouse. Moments later he pulls out an old table and drags it up to the hedge. "See, Oi'll cut a proper 'ole. Then when they're there..." he plonks a mucky looking jar on the table and turns the label to me: Nivea. "Good for me 'ands." He winks.

I want to gag. Sven wasn't joking about him 'polishing Percy'.

"I have to get back: bottling up." I start to jog back up the path, feeling dirty and just a tiny bit aroused.

He calls after me. "Sees what yous can do, all roight?"

***

That evening Rodney takes his fawning to a new level with the latest guest: the Commodore. He wants a pink gin at precisely 6.25. Rodney obliges, unctuously takes the tip and then calls him a wanker behind his back while suggesting he's so fixated by being punctual that he must time his wife's orgasms.

Rodney pockets the tip; no tip box here. He says, "So how'd it go with Cyril? Did he show you any of his 'views'?"

I suppose it's best if I ignore him so I crouch down to push some fruit juices on to the lower shelves while he leans on the bar.

"God, you're not another poof are you?"

"No."

He puts on a stupid voice. "Is Harry a snooty little prude then? Harry doesn't approve?"

I'm in two minds what to say. In the end I bottle it; I have to work with him after all. "It's not my sort of thing, if you must know. He can get on with it as far as I'm concerned."

Rodney's tone changes. "So I've got this right, have I? You're happy to let Cyril have his little bit of fun? Live and let live?"

I ignore him. It's not worth arguing about.

"So, what'll it be sweetie?"

Penny's voice is icy. "Two dry white wines."

## Chapter Forty-One

## The Good Book

I just want to crawl into bed, but Dina is sitting in the gazebo, staring into the distance while she kicks her heels against the back board. Her radio is blaring out Luxembourg 208. Kid Jensen I suppose; what a tit. I almost walk past, leaving her to whatever mood she's in but there's the question of the cash so I turn back. Her heel kicking slows but she doesn't look up.

"How much did we make?"

There's something about the tense way she's sitting that screams at me to leave her be.

"What's up?" Then, "You ok?"

"No." She bends her neck every which way until it clicks. God I hate that, but at least it stops her kicking.

"So what is it?"

"Nothing."

"So how much did we make?"

That causes a hunch of the shoulders.

"Oh come on, Di. You must know by now..."

"*You* didn't make anything. *I* made it all." Her anger so surprises me that she's by the backdoor before I can think. She's right but it's too late to apologise now so I take her place, reprising her heel kicks. I suppose the foul mood is linked to her and Jim splitting up or something. Rascal appears out of the shadows and slips in through the flap, no doubt on his way to Nanty's bed. I close my eyes and think about Dobbin and France. It's another world.

\*\*\*

I must have dozed off because it's dark when I'm startled awake by our family Ford coughing its last as it is parked. The voices I hear are Mum and Dad's; for a moment I think it's good news they are together but then I catch Mum's tone and shrink back. Inevitably they don't head indoors but come round the back, to the swing: Mrs Ojha's recent cleaning spree must have worked to reduce the stench. Sadly it blocks my way indoors and I'll have to listen to yet another argument.

Mum: "And?"

Dad: "Why must everything be a rush?"

Mum: "That's just the way it is."

Dad: "'That's the way it is?' You're asking me to decide on the devil or the deep blue sea, for heaven's sake."

Mum: "Charlie says—"

Dad: "Can we not mention that bloody man's name for even one minute?"

There's a brief silence.

Dad: "Thank you. You must see how his turning up like that is a shock…"

Mum: "I thought you didn't want to talk about him?"

There's another silence during which the swing creaks into life. Someone must have stood up.

Mum: "Sorry. Carry on."

Dad: "Have you told me everything? About you and him?"

Mum: "Of course. What more could there be?" Pause. "I didn't go looking for this, Arthur, but now it's happened and I'm not pretending it doesn't excite me."

Dad: "Oh yes, you were both like children who'd just discovered ice cream."

Mum: "Don't be silly. He's just very passionate when he's talking about his ideas." Pause "Something you could learn... No wait... Sorry."

There's a sigh.

Dad: "I'm not going to be hurried by you or him." Pause. "If you want me to take what I heard tonight seriously then you need to think seriously about this family..."

"What do you mean?"

"The garage, for starters..."

The swing creaks like someone is rocking very hard.

Mum: "They are two entirely different things. We need to focus on what Charlie said, not my wretched sister."

Dad, sounding really angry: "You always tell me that you're the one who puts family first but here you are, wanting to jump into bed with Jepson."

Mum: "Your metaphors are cheap and squalid, Arthur Spittle. If Charlie was running that garage it wouldn't be bankrupt."

Dad: "No, it would probably be a front for something criminal."

Mum, almost shouting: "You want me to take the money Daddy left me and pour it into that bloody garage? Is that it? Well I won't. I won't pressurise Edna to pay their pittance from the residue and I'm damn sure I won't alter the will to give her a bigger share."

Dad: "We don't need it."

Mum: "We might..."

Dad: "What?"

I can just about see a movement; someone must have grabbed the swing to stop it moving.

Dad: "Jesus, Veronica, are you telling me you're planning on using your legacy on that man?"

This time the silence is prolonged.

Dad: "Oh, fuck this." It's the first time I've heard him say 'fuck' in my life.

Mum: "How dare you. I... Oh, that's it – walk away. Go to your bloody shed."

I watch as the lights go on and off in the shed and then the upstairs bathroom. I'm frozen by the time I creep indoors.

***

Dina's door is half open. Something makes me peek in and whisper, "You ok, Di?"

I can't see her face in the dark, just her vague outline. Her voice sounds so fragile. "I'm frightened, H."

"Di? What's up?" I begin to go to her, but she turns to the wall pulling the sheet over her head.

"Go away. Please leave me alone."

I put my hand on her shoulder; she yanks it away like I've burnt her.

"GO AWAY."

I back out quickly in case someone has heard.

In bed my brain whirrs with thoughts that won't still. Dobbin and France loom large again, but this time I push them away. Mum and Dad are so wrapped up they'll never see Dina, shaking in her bed; my dreams will have to wait.

## TUESDAY 27TH JULY 1976

## Chapter Forty-Two

## What Affair?

Now that I don't have to get up early to serve breakfast I'm completely awake at ten past seven. It takes a minute or two to appreciate how quiet everything is. No Today programme, no slammed doors, no God-awful prog rock seeping through the cracks in my consciousness.

Nanty is in the kitchen, sipping tea. It looks like she made it herself, which must be a good sign. As I pour myself a cup, I notice her photo album. She pushes it to me; there are a couple of pages flagged with strips of newspaper.

The first shows Mum and Dad around the time they married; him still leaning on a stick, her in a wide skirt, smiling broadly with her hand on his shoulder.

The second is a dance, with Mum holding onto Dad, who's still using the stick; they're both laughing. Nanty leans over and taps a man in the background. It's Mr Jepson. Underneath someone has written: *V and A's engagement.*

"Why these ones, Nanty?" She reaches out and rubs my hand, like she used to if I was anxious about something. Is she telling me they'll be fine? I let her keep rubbing; I wish I believed that.

***

At half past, the Ojhas appear en masse: the parents are chatty while the children spin around me like human tornados.

Mrs Ojha takes over breakfast; it's as if she's running the B&B. Ravi is clearly in a rush and is soon on his way.

Mrs Ojha watches him go and sighs deeply. She looks tired as she says, "Everyone keep their fingers crossed."

The children solemnly do as instructed.

She says to me, "An interview. Hall porter." She opens the oven to retrieve something. "I expect he will be 'overqualified' or 'too old' or 'too young'. Again." She offers me the dish she's holding. "Samosa?"

***

Just before eight the phone rings and Mrs Ojha shoos me to answer it.

"Lymington Six…"

"Is that you, Arthur?"

"No, Uncle; it's Harry."

"Thought you were waiting? You been sacked?"

"I'm working in the bar."

"Where's your Father?"

"I haven't seen him."

"He's in that bloody shed. Get him. Please."

"Can I tell him why you want him?"

"You his Nancy-boy secretary, too? Just tell him to come to the bloody phone."

***

In the shed, Dad is in his chair with Papaji cross-legged on the floor. Elvis is crooning as usual.

"Hello, Harry-my-man."

"Hi Dad. Uncle Norman's on the phone."

Dad seems to want a nap; he leans back and closes his eyes.

"The phone, Dad. Uncle…"

He sighs and rubs his face. "Your Mum says you've met Charlie Jepson. What do you think of him?"

I say, "I… I've only spoken to him a couple of times."

"Did you know we were in the Army together? National Service." He stands slowly and pulls his dressing gown cord tight. "Did she say we were 'friends'? Real pals, Charlie and me." He shakes his head and moves towards the door like an old man. Papaji watches him impassively.

I am concentrating on Dad as he walks across the terrace to the backdoor so don't notice that Papaji has moved next to me. He says, "A man needs hope, Harry. It feeds his soul." He follows Dad towards the house, leaving me none the wiser.

*** 

I'm ready to leave at nine forty. Mum and Dina are long gone so I hunt for Dad to say bye. He's still sitting next to the phone, staring into space.

***

Tuesday is the day for the guests to go on day trips organised by Magda with her usual efficiency, so the bar is pretty empty. Rodney is back on his stool, studying the form in the Racing Post.

I'm dispatched to the gardens to hunt out the remaining guests and try and tempt them to a cocktail. Mrs Jepson is the first I find, tucked away behind a lavender border, sunbathing on a lounger. I've not seen her since the party and feel rather awkward as I approach.

"Hello Mrs Jepson. We wondered if you wanted a drink. A cocktail perhaps?"

"I would love a Harvey Wallbanger." She smiles up at me. "How are you? Is the job change working?" Her evident interest relaxes me.

"Yes. Thanks; it's going well."

"And that girl? On the swing?" Her smile doesn't change, but I can feel heat radiate off me. "I won't pry." She closes her book. "I'll have the drink in the little courtyard beyond the tennis court."

***

The courtyard is surrounded on three sides by an old wall and, at the front, which faces down the lawns, there are some neatly clipped shrubs. She is alone, at a table in the far corner.

As I set out the drink I say, "Mrs Jepson—"

"Monica, please."

"Yes. Sorry. Can I ask you something?"

She gives the faintest nod and sips her drink.

"You said my Mum and Mr Jepson wanted to marry. Is that right?"

Another tiny nod.

I wish I hadn't asked.

"Sit down Harry." She pats the chair next to her. I shouldn't, not while I'm working but I'm grateful as I feel rather faint. She pulls her chair close and rests a hand on my knee sending ripples of excitement through me. "They were lovers. Nearly engaged." She takes her hand away. When I look at her, she's studying the climbing roses.

I swallow hard. "Do you know why he's spending time with her?"

I can't be sure, given her face is in profile but I think she smiles. "What do you think?"

I think about the kiss I heard with Dina and the second one when they were in the back garden. I never saw them but I'd swear they kissed twice.

"What do you want to do, Harry?" The hand has returned and is much higher up my leg. I try and suck my stomach in, tensing all over.

All I can hear is my breathing interspersed with the thwack-thwack-grunt from the tennis court the other side of the wall. Her scent fills my nostrils. The tiny blonde hairs on her arm vibrate inside the beads of sweat. A trickle of moisture slips from her collarbone inside her bikini top. "Does your Father know she's seeing him?"

I force myself to nod.

"What has he said?" She holds my gaze for an age but I can't explain, not in a way that makes any sense. For a while she seems about to speak; she chews the inside of her cheek. Abruptly she stops but rather than ask again she picks up her drink. "I shouldn't press you. I need to think, Harry." She smiles but even I can see it is forced. She holds my gaze. "It's easy to jump to conclusions, isn't it? None of us wants..." She shakes her head. "I'm sure we all want the same thing."

She turns in her seat to face me and offers me her hands like the other night. "Can you do something for me? Can you tell me if you hear anything? If you could talk to your Father... No, I suppose that's difficult. Here." She takes my hands and stands, pulling me to my feet; this time she eases me into her arms. "Don't worry. I expect it's nothing but just in case, let's keep our eyes open, yes?"

She squeezes me tight, her hip pushing hard on my groin before she releases me. "I know this must be difficult at your age but you're old enough to understand. Marriages need work. Even those that seem the most secure. Sometimes things happen for no reason – something innocent gets confused. We can help them, you and I. Stop things getting out of hand."

She puts her hands on my face. "You are a handsome young man. You should be chasing those girls, not worrying about your parents, but you can help them." Then she kisses me. On the lips. No tongues or anything but not like a visiting Aunt either.

I'm utterly and completely discombobulated.

She slips back into her seat and picks up her book.

I'm on autopilot as I turn away. The last thing I hear is her saying, "You still owe me for that tip. I'll need my back oiled this afternoon if you're free."

## Chapter Forty-Three

## Puncturing the Punctual

Mr Hemingway has a G&T at noon. Usually Magda is on reception and takes it to him, but today the counter is unmanned. Mr Hemingway is standing at his desk, his back to me. He's on the phone as I walk up to his office door. He says to the caller, "Yes, that's right. Arthur Spittle, Charlie Jepson and me... Yes it is sudden, but we need to convince Arthur... Look, you're the bloody lawyer, you can explain it better." He chooses that moment to turn round. "Hang on. Yes?"

I hold out the drink for him. As I back out of the office he kicks the door shut.

\*\*\*

The afternoon is a blur; the bar, when I open for the evening, is peaceful. But throughout my thoughts are troubled. What's Mr Hemingway got to do with Dad and Jepson? Whichever way I twist it, it makes no sense. I'm brought out of a latest daydream by a sharp tap on the bar door. It's the bloody Commodore after his pink gin. I forget the angostura bitters, leave the ice in the glass and, worst of all, I make him late. His family are waiting by the door; this appears to delight his wife and rile him no end. As he pushes the empty glass back at me he says, "I'm not surprised the bookings are down with this sort of service."

## Chapter Forty-Four

## Jepson

By seven I feel spent. And then Sven appears looking remarkably chipper given the unrelenting and stifling heat. "Two G&Ts please. One with no ice." He leans on the bar while I address the optic. "You're a strange fish, Harold Spittle."

"You're pretty odd yourself."

"I like to think 'eccentric' is the apposite epithet."

"Why do you bother working here?"

"I enjoy the company."

"No, seriously. Your parents are loaded and…"

His expression changes quickly. "Don't mistake my Father's ostentation with my affluence. I want nothing to do with his money."

"You live in his house."

"Technically and geographically that's not correct. It's Mama's bungalow though in truth that's to keep his assets clean. But what about you?"

"What do you mean?"

"It's the talk of the staff room. Do you fancy her or don't you?"

"Penny?"

"Penny? No – Natalie. Why did you think I meant Penny?"

"Nothing."

"You see, if you're confused how do you think she feels? One minute you're encouraging her to pleasure you, the next you're slapping her face with Clapton tickets."

The heaters must be on as I'm gushing sweat. "I didn't. I haven't…"

"So you're done with her, are you? Given her unfortunate history I suppose that's expected. Now it's Penny, is it? Then what? Magda? Finish the summer buggering Amos, perhaps?"

"Eff off, can't you?"

"With pleasure."

It's only when he's gone I wish I'd asked what he meant by 'her unfortunate history'. So many bloody riddles.

*\*\*\**

Come nine and I'm nearly dead on my feet. Then Mr Jepson swans in, all confident strut and cheesy grin. He takes an empty stool in front of me and bangs a coin on the wooden surface. "Remi Martin please, Harry. One ice cube." While I pour the drink he says, "A birdie told me you enjoyed yourself at the Andersen boy's party."

I force out a smile. It stops me screaming.

He laughs. "I wish I'd had your nerve when I was, what, nineteen?" He toasts me with his glass.

I wipe away the sweat that's built up on my temples; what is it with these hot flushes? To stop him going on about me and Natalie I say, "Did you enjoy the party?"

He sort of snorts a laugh. "Party? Hardly a party for me. I was doing a bit of business with Mr Andersen. We used to be in business together, way back." He shakes his head. "Some of us have moved on." For a moment he seems distracted before he smiles and says, "So when are you and Claude going into business together?"

It takes a moment to remember Stephen McNoble is Claude to Mr Jepson. "I... er, that is..."

He laughs. "It's all right, Harry. I understand you aren't exactly close, but just because you aren't bosom buddies doesn't mean you can't work together. You'd have complementary skills."

He hits people while I whimper in the corner. Perfect.

"I haven't had the chance to thank you for mentioning me to your Mother. I'm not sure I'd have had the courage to call her but when she rang it was... well, just like old times." He's bloody nodding again. I want to grab his head and make him keep still. "You know about us, I suppose?"

"Er... I... no, not really."

He pulls a face, like a wince of pain. "Arthur, I suppose? Of course. Delicate." More vigorous nodding. "You might put in a good word for me. Tell him I'm not such a beast. Got you this job, didn't I?" He laughs but it sounds hollow. "It's not like I'm trying to steal your Mum, is it?" He finishes his drink and pushes the empty at me. I refill it slowly wishing I could poison him. He carries on, "Did you know we were in the Army together, Arthur and me – way back – 1956? Your Mum was a nurse then. Stunning woman. Arthur and I were close. We tried a little business venture, you know."

He drifts off, sipping his drink, lost in memories of his time in the Army. If only he'd shut up completely; first he blathers on about Natalie and now it's him and Mum. I search for a neutral topic and say, "I hope the ceremony went ok?"

He stops nodding briefly. "It was very moving. Thank you for asking. Tricky venue, out on the Spit. Mother always said she had a soft spot for it, but it's pretty bleak even in the summer. Difficult controlling the ashes."

"I hope the box wasn't the problem."

"The box? No. Why?" He looks surprised and I suddenly regret opening my mouth. When I glance at him, his eyes have narrowed with suspicion. "Claude said a friend gave him the box – when he broke the urn she was in. Was that you?"

I can't read his expression. Does he know I was involved in the breakage and is angry with me? I'm struggling to think what I should say when he stands and holds out his right hand. He's beaming. "I knew it! It was you, wasn't it? Good God, of course it was. That's why Claude's been so evasive. It's yours!"

Just then the bar door swings open and Monica Jepson sweeps in; she's wearing a long silky dress bare to the shoulders. She looks amazing. She says, "What's yours?"

Charlie Jepson has a huge grin. "Mine's a G&T. No sorry, we were talking about Mother's ceremony. You'll never believe it but that box – the one Claude used when he broke the urn? It was Harry's. Isn't that good of him?" To me, he says, "Where did you get it?"

"It was a birthday present, from a friend."

"Really?" He looks at Mrs Jepson. "You said you thought it was from North Africa, didn't you darling?"

She definitely flinches at the 'darling' before she nods. "Definitely. I have one just like it."

She's watching me closely and I'm finding her gaze very disconcerting. She says, "It's a shame it went in, isn't it dear?"

"What?" Mr Jepson's grin dissolves. "Oh Christ. I see. Harry, we lost it. Did you expect it back? The sea took it, I'm afraid."

I nod dumbly. "It's alright. My friend has been asking about it but I'll explain."

Mrs Jepson finishes lighting up and says, "She must like you a lot. They're very unusual."

"I suppose. I mean, she was my girlfriend then."

"Not anymore?"

I nod.

She smiles a little. "That's probably why she wants it back."

## Chapter Forty-Five

## Monica Jepson's letter

At eleven thirty I'm just about to leave when Magda hands me a letter. "Mrs Jepson asked me to give zis to you." She looks really suspicious, but eventually leaves me alone so I can read it.

> *Dearest Harry. You should have told me about Claude and the box before. I'm cross with you. However, to show I'm very forgiving, I wanted you to know I still have it. I rescued it! Please don't tell Charlie; he might think it disrespectful given he was the one who threw it into the sea. If you're interested I'll even show you why your friend wants it back. I'm busy during the day but if you're working tomorrow evening I'll pop down and explain.*
>
> *Much love,*
>
> *Monica.*

I would much prefer to have nothing more to do with that bloody box but if I can get Ruth off my back then maybe it's worth meeting Mrs Jepson. At least it means one thing might be going right at last.

\*\*\*

When I get in, the house is eerily quiet; Nanty is in bed, watching TV. Rascal is sitting next to her, calculating the distance between us. Nanty pats the duvet but I pull up a chair. After a while she mimes turning off the box. In the quiet I tell her about the bar work, Rodney's betting, the Commodore and his pink gin. I massage her fingers while she smiles goofily and I lapse into silence. She's such a comforting presence I say, "You know, I've been wondering about those photos – Mum and Mr Jepson and Dad." I sneak a glance; Nanty is watching me closely and when she sees me looking she nods for me to go on. "I'm a bit worried, him being around."

She shakes her head.

"Maybe I should do something… say something?"

She shakes her head hard. I give her a big kiss, disturbing a slumbering fly. I wonder if she's brought it with her from the hospital. A few minutes later she's snoring gently and the fly has taken up residence on her cardy. With each breath she slips into a deeper sleep. Once upon a time she would watch me fall asleep; she was my protector, the family's protector. It's only just dawning on me that I can no longer rely on her to sort out my problems, to give comfort. Nanty's the one who needs the protection. And I'm bloody sure I'm not ready for this change in roles.

**WEDNESDAY 28TH JULY 1976**

## Chapter Forty-Six

## Flush

I come to with a start. I was in the middle of a dream that's left me feeling sick with guilt; I think Ruth was involved but I can't be sure. I try and ignore the growing sense that I've done something awful. In the end I slip into the dining room and phone her. Happily she answers, not her Mother.

"Hi. It's Harry."

"What do you want?"

"I have news about the box. I might—"

"Where is it?"

"I'm not sure yet but I just thought—"

Suddenly she's shouting, "I NEED IT NOW. GIVE IT TO ME."

"Jesus, don't shout."

She starts actually wailing, an awful incoherent noise.

"For Christ's sake, shut up... SHUT UP." I stare at the serving hatch to the kitchen, waiting for someone to throw the little doors open but nothing happens.

She speaks more quietly. "I have to put it back. I told you what he's like. Why doesn't anyone believe me?"

The sense of guilt roars back. "I do."

"So give me my box back."

"I... Come to the hotel at eight. We'll sort it then."

"But—"

"Eight. Ok? It'll be alright." I wish I believed that.

***

I have a shower and distract myself with thoughts of Monica Jepson and lots of suntan oil. In the kitchen Ravi drones on about the prejudice of local hotels while Mrs Ojha makes soothing noises. Mum appears briefly, chivvying Nanty into her coat and makes a cutting remark about my choice of reading material. Apparently science fiction isn't what she expects me to be reading if I'm going to show I'm serious about uni. She soon leaves. Nanty has yet another hospital appointment about her lack of speech. When they're gone, Mrs Ojha visibly relaxes. As she offers me toast, she tells me some of the greatest writers have dabbled in science fiction. I make some smart remark about her taking over the B&B, which I thought was a compliment but clearly upsets her. To try and make up for my stupidity I offer to take the breakfast tray to Dad and Papaji in the shed. On the way across the terrace I practice asking him a simple question: 'Dad, what's Mum doing with Charlie Jepson?' I'm still honing the stress on each syllable when I push open the door. The question dies on my lips and I do well not to drop the tray.

Papaji has Dad by the armpits and is lowering his naked bottom into the washing-up bowl, which is full of water. Before I can skedaddle Papaji says in a strained voice, "Harry, is that you? Come, take his arm. Quick, quick. Before he slips…"

Dad is facing away from me. "Harry? Christ. GO. NOW."

Papaji shakes his head. "No, Harry is young and strong. Take, take…"

"NO Asoka. He… Oh, for pity's sake."

The old man looks to be about to collapse, so I grab an arm and Dad tenses.

Between us, we lower Dad until his bum is about an inch in the water; happily I can't see his face but his neck has flushed red.

Papaji signals for me to stop. "Just a minute, Harry. Squeeze, Arthur. Squeeze. Now is good… soft and sucky."

"Enough, Asoka. Let me get up."

There's a bit of a struggle during which Papaji, Dad and the bowl become entangled. When the dodgy water starts creeping towards me, I back out. Mr Jepson can wait.

\*\*\*

I nearly kick myself as I open the back gate; I've forgotten the fête money. I decided last night that my best protection against another McNoble attack is cash; I prop my bike against the gatepost and hurry back inside, heading for Dina's room. I wouldn't dare do this if she was about – rule one of the sibling code: no entry to the other's room with permission.

Dina is a creature of habit: her precious things are kept in shoeboxes under her bed. The first has her diaries; the second a set of Valentines and letters; I'm just finishing the third (of six) which is full of tacky jewellery when I notice two small empty jars. I don't know what makes me pick one up, but as soon as I see the label I drop it like it is scalding. It's a pregnancy test; there's space for a name and the time and date of the sample as well as some instructions. I stare at the jar until the printing goes wobbly; when it comes back into focus it still screams 'PREGNANCY' at me. I can't leave quickly enough.

\*\*\*

As I cycle up Mothball Hill, my thoughts lurch from a conviction the jar is nothing more than some sort of precaution (or maybe she's minding it for Janice) to a firm belief she's pregnant and the child is Mr James'. That makes me alternately sick and angry. I'm surrounded by bastards: Jepson, Reggie James, McNoble, Paul, Cyril.

As if to reinforce the point, as I coast to halt in the service yard Cyril appears with his barrow full of vegetables. When he sees me he picks up a carrot and holds it in front of his fly, 'phwoaring' for all he's worth. Paul appears and pretends to suck on the end, saying, 'Oh Harry, you're so BIG' over and over. This disgusting mime, which is accompanied by them corpsing with laughter, hits me like a kidney shot. A red mist descends and I storm off without looking. Having taken a wrong turn, I have to back track. Cyril is in front of me with his empty barrow.

"Ere boiy. Sorry 'bout that. He's a bit of a sorront."
"Sorront?"
"Queer bastard. You got 'em girlies into them meadow yet?"
"Look, Cyril…"
"There's this other spot…"
"What 'other spot'?"
"Oi'll tell you if you gets 'em in them meadow."
"No, wait. Where?"

But he turns away, chortling to himself. This time I have to tell Penny.

***

Penny has already left the staff dining room but Natalie is drinking coffee and waves me over. "Harry, I just wanted to say—"
"Have you seen Penny? It's important."
"I wanted to find out when we should pay—"

"Later, ok. I must find Penny."

I'm already turning away when she bangs her cup down. "What is it with you?"

"Me?"

"Yes. Do you hate me? For *not* having sex with you?"

"I... I don't..."

She stands, just about holding back the tears. "It wasn't true, ok? So you didn't have to worry."

"I..."

She pushes past me. Amos is watching, a grin on his face. He doesn't have to say, 'I told you so' but that's what he's thinking.

***

I'm setting up in the bar when Penny appears, her face barely masking her fury. "What is it with you and Natalie?"

"Me? She's the one who went off like a sky rocket for no reason."

"She said you were really rude to her."

"I... I was trying to find you and I didn't have time to waste."

"Oh sure. You were just pushing her away because you think she's a slut."

"No I don't."

"Yes you do. All the men here do, poor thing."

"No I bloody don't. She's mental but that's different."

"What do you mean? Mental?"

"She said, 'it's not true so I didn't have to worry'. What's that all about?"

Penny peers at me like I'm a specimen under a microscope. After a few moments she says, "You must know. Everyone does."

I'm angry now and spread my arms. "Well, stupid Harry is the only one who doesn't."

"You know what her ex did to her?"

I hold the pose and say, enunciating each word carefully. "I have no effing clue."

She studies me for ages. My anger is fading and I want to put my arms down as they are beginning to ache. Finally she says, "He wrote and told her he'd given her VD."

Every little bit of righteous indignation drains from me. "Oh shit. You're kidding?"

She sighs and slumps into a seat, leaning her elbows on the table. "That day you picked us up – by the bike shop – she'd been to the doctors to get tested. The results came back today; she's clear. The trouble was he told her she needed to tell all her partners, anyone she'd been with so they could get tested. That meant Paul. He went and told everyone else. Except you, it seems."

"Why didn't you – ?"

"Because I thought Sven would. You and he talk all the time."

"You thought Sven would tell me?"

"He's your friend."

"You are joking?"

"No. He likes you."

"Jesus. He thinks I'm a prick. You're my friend. Why didn't you…"

"I'M SORRY OK."

We lapse into an uneasy silence where we can't look at each other. Finally she says, "Sorry. I should have said." Eventually she smiles. "Any chance of a vodka? It's been a crap morning."

I glance around. Rodney is leaning on reception, chatting to Magda; he could come in at any moment and if he caught me feeding booze to Penny I'd get a right bollocking. "Sure. I'll join you."

As I pour she says, "Nats said you were looking for me?"

"Oh yeah. Bloody Cyril. He's got a new peephole somewhere and he's found this private meadow where he's trying to lure you – or rather he wants me to lure you so he can watch you sunbathe. I wanted you to know so... so we can go to Hemingway and put a stop to it."

She takes the drink. She doesn't speak until she's finished half. I pull a chair up next to her and sip mine.

She says, "He's been spying on the showers – there was a loose board in the cladding. Someone complained – that's what Magda said – but all Hemingway did was tell Cyril to fix it. I mean that's like asking a burglar to fix the window he broke."

She's shaking her head. "There's no point, Harry. Even Magda doesn't care enough to make sure he's stopped and given the state this place is in, no one's going to sack him of all people."

"It's in a state, is it?"

"Apparently." She's on the verge of losing it so I put an arm around her shoulders and she leans in close. It's only for the briefest of moments before she pushes herself away and finishes her drink. "I'm sorry I didn't tell you about Natalie. She'll be mortified." She's leaning away as she says, "I'll tell her you still care, then? About her?"

Something about the Wadworth beer mat has her spellbound. If she'd look at me she would understand who I really care about. In the end I give up waiting and say, "Yes, I still care."

She peers at me through her hair, which has fallen forward. I wish I could read her expression. She says, "Great. I'll tell her then. She'll be so pleased. She really likes you."

Suddenly she seems in a rush to leave but before she reaches the door she stops to say, "Why don't you have my ticket? You can take her. I know she'd like that."

She doesn't give me a chance to respond and anyway what would I say? That it's her I want to go with? After the Marmite why would she believe me?

## Chapter Forty-Seven

## Ruth

Ruth has dressed up; her usual baggy shapeless clothes replaced by a tight white T-shirt, tighter jeans and cowboy boots; I almost don't recognise her. She agrees to wait for Mrs Jepson and has a white wine that she sips in silence. After forty minutes of increasing tension Mrs Jepson comes in with a large bag. Before she can speak I say, "This is Ruth James. It's her box."

Mrs Jepson looks at me, then Ruth and nods. Rather stiffly she says to Ruth, "Shall we sit there?" She indicates the far corner of the bar that is partly hidden by a column.

Ruth looks deeply uncomfortable but follows Mrs Jepson's lead.

Mrs Jepson says, "So this box..."

Ruth looks from her to me, a rather confused expression on her face. "Can I have it please? I'd like to go."

Mrs Jepson opens her bag and puts the box on the bar. "I gave it a wipe." She pushes it at Ruth.

It's as if Ruth can't believe she's seeing it again. It takes her a few moments before she reaches for it. As she does so, Mrs Jepson puts a hand on the top.

"Do you know much about it, Ruth?"

Ruth tries to pull it to her, but Mrs Jepson's hand is stopping her picking it up. Ruth says, "I just want to go. It's nothing to do with you."

Abruptly Mrs Jepson lets go. "Of course. Go. Though don't you want to check it first?"

Ruth frowns. "Check what?"

"The contents."

"But it's empty." Ruth lifts the lid and peers inside. I'm just as confused now.

Mrs Jepson takes it out of Ruth's hands; Ruth doesn't struggle. Mrs Jepson turns it upside down and pushes at something; there's a slight click and she rights it. A little drawer has opened which she pulls out. She looks at Ruth and then at me. "So whose box is it Ruth? It's clearly not yours."

Ruth has gone rather pale. She's staring inside the drawer. I want to have a look to see how it works, but I hold back. Ruth speaks very quietly. "My Uncle's."

"And you took it from him? Why?"

"Yes, yes I did. I was wrong. It's a sin and I want to put it back." Ruth's wheedling voice puts me on edge but Mrs Jepson's expression doesn't change.

"But why take it?"

"He... I was angry and wanted to do something..." She looks down as she dries up.

"Did you think it was valuable?"

She barely nods. "Uncle calls his boxes – he has loads – his pension. He owed me because... He..." She stops and covers her face. I really don't want to think about what has gone on between Ruth and her Uncle that might have led her to steal. She says, "It was empty – or I thought it was. That's why I gave it to Harry."

"But you want it back. Why?"

Ruth perks up at that. "I've seen the light. He's told me it's wrong and whatever has happened, this was a sin and it must go back." She picks it up and puts the drawer back in place.

"Who told you it was wrong?"

Ruth's look is defiant. "God."

Mrs Jepson couldn't look more surprised. I know she's doing well not to laugh but she maintains her composure. "It's not because your Uncle has found it's missing then?"

"No." Ruth looks horrified. "He mustn't know. He'll... I don't want him to find out." She glances at me and says no more.

Mrs Jepson is busy lighting up so I say, "Was there something in that drawer?"

"Why do you ask that, Harry?"

"Because it always rattled." I hold out my hands and Ruth gives the box to me. When I shake it there's no noise. "I thought it was badly made but there was something in here, wasn't there?"

Mrs Jepson takes her time to smile. "Bravo." She doesn't move.

I look at Ruth. She's looking increasingly anxious so I ask, "Can we have whatever was in there, please? It should all go back."

Mrs Jepson sits very still, studying me carefully. Her only movement is to take the cigarette from her lips to blow out smoke. After a good minute that seems like twenty she nods. "All right."

Ruth and I follow her every movement. When she extracts a little drawstring purse from her bag, I'm sure I can hear my heart thumping against my ribs. The contents are poured into her hand and held out for us to inspect.

Four glittery stones. "Diamonds?"

Mrs Jepson nods.

I'm so engrossed that I don't see Ruth's faint. I only look up as the stool screeches a protest and Ruth disappears from sight. Moments later there is a crack as her head hits the wooden floor.

\*\*\*

It's the blood that does for me. One minute I'm rushing round to Ruth's side to help. The next I'm on a stool feeling hot and then cold, watching her blood coagulate; it looks like Mum's toffee sauce.

"Harry, hide the box please." Mrs Jepson's voice is sharp and I'm grateful to do something.

After a lot of flapping, Ruth is helped to the office to wait for an ambulance. I'm back in the bar when Mr Jepson appears followed by McNoble. There's been a mix up and he's agreed to run Ruth to the hospital. It's no surprise McNoble is going too.

***

It must be getting on for ten when Mrs Jepson reappears. "I'm so sorry about all that, Harry." She lights up. "I had no idea she'd faint. I suppose knowing it held something valuable makes the sin worse." She blows out a neat ring. "And I suppose she doesn't want a scene with her Uncle either."

I wonder if I should explain about Ruth's Uncle but it seems too complicated.

"Will you give it to her? I'm sure she'll be pleased to know you're looking after it."

"I... can't you keep it? Until she's better?"

She grins. "Or we could sell the stones and split the proceeds?"

I want to look horrified but oh my, is that tempting? I manage to say, "No, that wouldn't be right."

"God worry you too, does he?" She digs out her compact and checks her makeup. "You're probably right."

I pick up the box from behind the bar and push it to her. She pushes it back and says, "No thanks, Harry. It's all yours."

"But I can't."

There's a bit of a standoff before she says, "I really don't want the box. I should have thought about it before but Charlie would not be pleased if he found me with it." She pauses. "I'll hang on to the diamonds if that's what's making you uncomfortable?"

I nod and take the twist of paper I put them in from the main compartment.

"Where's the bag?" she says.

"I don't know. Didn't you pick it up?"

We have a good look but can't find it. In the end I put the box under the bar again and she sticks the paper and stones deep inside her handbag. After that, she buys me a drink and we sit in silence for a while before she says, "I've been thinking about your Mother – well, your parents – and Charlie. If we're going to stop them making fools of themselves – and us – we need something to make them sit up and think."

It's fascinating watching her; as she smokes she doesn't knock the ash off but lets it build up until you're sure it must fall into her lap or her drink; then and only then does she flick the column into the ashtray. So far the least number of columns I've counted for a fully smoked cigarette is three.

She furrows her brow. "I have an idea. At that stupid ceremony, your Mother was introduced to Robin – Robin Andersen. It was pretty plain she didn't like him at all." She glances up catching me staring at her cigarette. The way she looks at me I instantly know that she thinks I'm gawping at her breasts. "You don't know who he is, do you?"

I'm annoyed she's made me feel so childish. "He's Sven's Dad." I know that's a daft answer but I don't care.

She's beginning to sound like my teachers.

"Apart from that. He's a local businessman with something of a dodgy reputation. I bet your Mother – both your parents – know it, too. So what I think is if they knew – if you told them – Charlie is negotiating with Robin to do some business here – if they know Charlie is involved with Robin again – it might make then think twice about him."

I'm beginning to hate her tone; it's the same sort of voice that Mum uses when I commit one of the repeat crimes that so bug her: 'Do you think you can manage to hang up that towel?' 'Do you think you can flush the toilet properly?' 'Do you think you can wash your hands?' Anyway, I bet neither of my parents have ever heard of Robin Andersen.

When I don't answer, Mrs Jepson finishes her cigarette and stands. "See what you can manage." Slowly she stretches her hands high in the air; in doing so her breasts push hard at the material of her dress, emphasising her lack of a bra and the shape of her nipples. She holds the pose before yawning and slowly lowering her arms. "Time to turn in." She picks up her bag and says, "If the weather's nice tomorrow, maybe we can find somewhere private to sunbathe together?"

\*\*\*

It's pretty late when I get home. Mum is drinking tea in the kitchen. I ask, "How's Nanty?"

"She's spending a night in hospital. More tests." Mum moves to pour the undrunk tea down the sink. "They want to get to the bottom of her speech problems." She rinses the cup and says, "While I have you, did Edna pay you and your sister your legacies?"

No softening up first. "No Mum. Not yet."

"Are you sure?"

"Yes."

"Have you any reason to think why Dina would get hers before you?"

"No. I'm sure she'd say."

"Yes. That's what I'd expect." She shakes her head and sighs. "I'd better ask the lawyer tomorrow. I can't think why Dina would make it up."

I'm not sure if she's finished so say, "I'll go to bed then."

I'm halfway out of the door when she asks, "Has she broken up with Jim?"

"I don't think so." I haven't spoken to her since I found her crying and saying she was frightened – nor have I seen Jim since that pep talk. Maybe my unexplained guilt dream was about those two as well as Ruth.

"She refused to speak to him when he called round. I thought he was doing her good."

I try not to show surprise after all she said about precautions and everything. While I'm musing on the subject of the inconsistency of parents she walks past me as if I'm not there.

**THURSDAY 29$^{TH}$ JULY 1976**

## Chapter Forty-Eight

## Bated Breath

Dina's gone by the time I get up. I check the boxes under her bed. No money and no jars. The missing jars worry me more than the money, which is a surprise in itself. I suppose she might have given them to Janice or something.

Dad is in the kitchen with an apron round his waist, just like old times. He seems to be cooking his speciality: scrambled eggs surprise with the surprise being some mystery ingredient like raisins or chopped walnuts or, once, stewed rhubarb. I try and sniff the pan, but he pushes me away.

Ravi is in a three piece suit, testing the children on their times tables. Papaji is at the sink; it is full of dark blue water and he is pummelling whatever's in there. As soon as Noor and Sajid spot me they start climbing up my legs like noisy ferrets.

Holding them at bay, I ask Ravi about his latest interview.

"No joy, Harry." He tries a smile and looks at Dad's back. "They wanted someone younger with more experience."

Dad sounds exasperated. "Bloody... sorry, but the racial prejudice around here is awful."

Ravi looks a bit embarrassed and says. "Come children. Time to have a wash and get dressed." Papaji picks up whatever it is he's been dyeing, leaving the bowl in the sink.

Dad returns to his cooking, whistling tunelessly. This is my chance, but how to start? I have a brainwave and return moments later with Nanty's photo album. While I find the page I want, he stirs his eggy mix.

I present him with the group photo I saw. "Who are all these people, Dad?"

Dad twists to look and then sighs deeply. "What is this fascination with Charlie Jepson?"

"Mr Jepson was talking about you the other night. When you were in the Army together. He said you had some business or something."

"Did he? His illegal still, I suppose."

"Still?"

"It's how you make alcohol and not pay any duty. We used plums." His shoulders abruptly sink like a deflating balloon; with one hand he turns the toast, while he shakes the pan with the other. He points at the soldier on the right. "That's him. Charlie. Then there's Greg Tonge and Barry... Barry... damn. What was his name?"

I stare at a confident looking Charlie Jepson, with no stupid moustache and a severe haircut; he stares defiantly at the camera. Dad, also with a short back and sides, is inspecting his shoes. Dad peers at the picture, lost in some memory. "It was years ago, Harry-lad. Ancient history."

I glance at the stove; the smell suggests something's burning. "Dad, the eggs."

"What? Oh heavens. Here..." He hands the pan to me and goes to the larder for some butter. There's a fork in the mix and I sneak a mouthful. It's delicious.

Dad takes the pan back and adds the butter, staring at the contents resignedly. "Typical." He puts the pan on the drainer and picks up the album, flicking over a few pages, shaking his head at each new picture. At one he whispers, "Jesus." Then he snaps it shut. "I don't want to talk about him."

But he's still distracted and stares at the cover, running his finger round the edge. The toast begins to burn and my mouth follows suit, a deep throbbing at the back of my tongue. "What's the surprise this time, Dad?"

He glances at me. "Chillies. Mrs Ojha recommended them. Not sure if I've used the right amount though." He takes a mouthful and chews it thoughtfully. It takes less than a minute for him to cough and then spit the residue into the sink. My eyes are watering and I'm beginning to overheat, like the toast. He pours the eggs into water left by Papaji; the blue dye colours them green. He adds the burnt toast and fills a glass with water. I follow and we both try and douse the flames in our mouths.

His voice is a croak. "I don't suppose he told you that he was the reason I ended up with one eye, did he? And my hearing and leg..." He coughs again and glares at the sink then me. "Are you crying?"

I manage to say, "Same as you."

He wipes his eyes and holds his forehead. "Barry Smithers." It takes him a minute to finish. "That's the other one. Smithers. Charlie nearly blew me to smithereens." Tears are flowing down Dad's face. "He died, years ago. Complications after he had his appendix out. I thought I'd be the first to go." He shakes his head and keeps swallowing. "I think... bathroom..." As he leaves he's trying to breathe very slowly.

***

My tongue has gone numb and no amount of water helps so I head for my room to lie down. When I get there, I'm conscious of a kerfuffle out front. Mum is there with Mrs Ojha and Mrs Potts; they are looking at something on the front drive. I can only hear Mrs Potts.

"I WARNED YOU VERONICA. THIS PROTECTION IDEA IS CAUSING PROBLEMS." Mum turns to gesture to my window; I don't duck down quickly enough and her wave is easy to interpret: 'Harold. Here. Now.' Resignedly I follow orders.

"Yes Mum?"

Mum says, "Did you see who did this, Harold? Or hear anything?"

"No, not a thing."

Mum kicks at the pulpy heap: it looks like two smashed pumpkins. "Has everyone gone deaf and blind?" She peers at me. "Are you alright? You've gone very red?"

Mrs Potts says, "EVERYONE WONDERED WHEN YOU MIGHT BE TARGETED. PEOPLE THINK YOU MAY HAVE PROVOKED THIS WITH YOUR GROUP, VERONICA."

"That's ridiculous."

Mrs Potts half turns towards the garden. "SHALL WE CHECK THEN? FOR YOUR PEACE OF MIND?"

To my surprise, Mrs Ojha pats Mum's arm. "Shall I Veronica?"

Mum hesitates and then nods. "Thanks."

Mrs Ojha walks briskly towards the garden leaving Mrs Potts staring after her. When's she's gone round the side of the house Mrs Potts says, "YOU TRUST HER, VERONICA?"

Mum has bent down to wipe the goo from her toe with a tissue. "She seems to have taken over most other things around here. God knows how she found out where I put them, but she did." Mum glares at me before she turns to Mrs Potts. "I'd like to chat, Desiree, but I have to get on. I'll let you know if either of these is mine, but from the sizes, I doubt it."

Mrs Potts drags herself away, clearly reluctant to leave before Mrs Ojha returns.

When she has driven off Mum says, "Did you speak to your sister?"

"What about?"

Her eyes go up in exasperation. "I asked you last night. About her and Jim." She sighs and says, "Fetch me a spade so we can clear this up, please. Then I would like a word."

***

Mrs Ojha tells us none of Mum's pumpkins has been taken. Mrs Ojha offers to make tea while Mum disappears to change. Mrs Ojha joins me on the swing and we watch Papaji beat his dyed trousers. To my surprise Rascal hunts out her lap and accepts her stroking with purrs rather than claws.

I say, "I'm sorry Ravi's not found a job yet."

"No, well… Your Father has said he will try and help."

I mutter, as quietly as I can, "I wouldn't get excited…"

She smiles to herself and says. "Your Mother too has helped him. They are kind caring people, your parents."

I mumble something about how little she knows but all she does is smile. We sit in silence until Mum appears. Mrs Ojha says, "We were having such an interesting chat about H.G. Wells. Science fiction is such a skill, don't you think?" Before Mum can answer, Mrs Ojha pushes Rascal off her lap and heads for the kitchen.

Mum watches her go as she sits down in the vacated space. "What do you think of the Ojhas?"

"They're nice."

"Nice? Yes that's bland enough. Your Father is besotted."

"You said they were helping."

"I said they were taking over. Mrs Ojha seems to think she's the only one who can care for Edna as well as cook."

"She said you are helping Ravi find a job?"

Mum glares at the backdoor. I think she says 'bloody woman' but I can't be sure. After a minute of painful silence she says, "Are you really reading H.G. Wells?"

"It's going to be my next book. Mrs Ojha says I should try one." I blow on the tea, hunting for any subject that doesn't involve Dina and Jim or university. "What's with the pumpkins?"

Mum is still distracted by something.

I carry on. "I saw Mrs Potts in our garden. Late at night. Last week."

It takes her a moment to look at me. "Desiree? Are you sure?"

"Yeah. A car went past and I saw her face. She was by your vegetables. The ones in the bags."

Mum nods slowly. "Mrs Martin has heard tell of a tall man in a balaclava. It's getting out of hand." She sighs and closes her eyes. "According to Desiree, I'm the only one who's not been attacked so naturally that makes me the prime suspect."

"But you've got your protection group."

Mum rocks back and bellows. "HAROLD, IT'S NOT ME, BUT THERE ARE THOSE WHO THINK THAT IS A CLEVER COVER." She smiles at me. "Quote, unquote. The old bag is determined to pin it on me."

I'm gob-smacked. Mum never uses expressions like 'old bag'.

She pats her legs. "Now, I need your help. You know about poor Ruth? Well, I agreed that she can stay with us for a day or two, just to help Cynthia out of a hole. She has to go and see Ruth's Grandmother."

"Ruth staying here?"

"Yes Ruth. Cynthia wasn't sure if you were still... friends?" I avoid her X-ray gaze. "I said I was sure you wouldn't mind. You'll be at work most of the time."

She's resting back against the cushions, staring down the garden. Side on, she looks like she did in some of those old photos apart from her hairstyle. She also looks very tired.

I suppose everything with the B&B and Aunt Petunia and Nanty must be weighing her down – and that horrid conversation with Dad about Jepson and then the garage business. Just then a car horn sounds out front. She smiles at me and stands up; she holds out a hand for me and eases me out of the swing, brushing my jacket lapels like they're covered in dust. "That'll be Cynthia with Ruth. Be nice to the poor thing. It sounds like she's had a bit of a shock." As she turns she adds, "And I know what she's trying to do with that nonsense about science fiction and it won't wash."

## Chapter Forty-Nine

## Nursing Care

I'm not sure who's more surprised; Mum seeing Mr Jepson or me seeing McNoble supporting a pale looking Ruth. While I hang back, Mum marches straight up to Mr Jepson and says in a tight voice, "Bloody hell, Chaz. What are you doing here?"

Mr Jepson's nodding like the toy dog in the back of Aunt Petunia's car. He takes Mum's arms; he kisses her on the cheek; and to my total disgust he pats her bottom. "Thought that'd surprise you, Vee. Ruth's Mum had to dash away so I said I'd be happy to act as chauffeur."

Mum glances nervously past me. "Arthur's still here."

There's a slight flicker of something from Mr Jepson before he says. "We won't be long and I'm just dropping Ruthie off, aren't I?" He turns to McNoble. "You remember Claude from the other day, Vee?"

McNoble nods coldly. "It's Stephen. Where's Ruth's room, Mrs Spittle?"

Mum seems to register me for the first time. "Can you show them the yellow room next to Papaji, Harold?"

As I lead, certain McNoble is going to clout me at any moment, Mrs Ojha appears, drying her hands on a tea towel. McNoble is right behind me so only I can hear. "You have servants, bastard?"

"Mrs Ojha is a guest."

"You let wogs stay? Christ."

I glance at Mrs Ojha; I know she heard him but her smile doesn't falter as she says, "Welcome, Ruth. Would you like some toast and honey? Soup?"

\*\*\*

It takes a good fifteen minutes to drag in Ruth's clutter, move the furniture twice and take her the toast. Each time I open her door, I brace myself for the inevitable assault but McNoble ignores me. He seems content to listen to her witter on. Mum and Mr Jepson have moved round the side of the house and I just catch him saying '…Monica is going to be trouble…' before Mrs Ojha calls me to take Ruth her soup.

Mrs Ojha ladles out a bowl of something delicious smelling. "Will that young man want some?"

"He doesn't deserve anything."

She looks at me, a serious expression on her face. "Now Harry, they are guests here."

"But he's a pig. He was so rude to you."

She smiles and touches my arm briefly. "He's a product of ignorance, Harry. Don't sink to those standards. You know better and must show an example. Here."

As she goes back to stirring the large pan, I stare at her hair, pulled into a tight bun and the bones in her neck pushing through the skin. She seems delicate but she's not. "Mrs Ojha…?"

"Go. Before it gets cold."

Ruth and McNoble are on the bed, Ruth giggling at something he's said. When she sees me she says, in her most irritating sickly sweet voice. "Can I have a little wordy, in private?" While she stands uncertainly, McNoble sniffs suspiciously at the soup.

Outside she leans on the door and asks, "Were those real diamonds?"

"Yes."

She squeezes her eyes closed. "Have you got them? And the box?"

"What's the rush? You can't return it while you're here and—"

She glares at me. "I just want to know it's safe. Where is it?"

"She kept everything."

"Please, Harry. Please get it. And the diamonds. Today." To my surprise she pushes me in the chest and I bang into the wall.

"Jesus. Get your new boyfriend to fetch them. She's his stepmum."

She shakes her head hard. "No, I can't. He mustn't know what I've done."

"Why not?"

"Are you mad? He's a Christian. If he knows how bad I've been he'll hate me." She does well not to stamp her foot.

"Him? A Christian? Pull the other one." I've barely moved when she grabs my sleeve again.

"Please Harry." There's something in her tone that reminds me of Dina saying she's frightened.

McNoble yanks open the door. "What are you two doing?"

We both stare at the dribble of soup on his chin. When his fingers find the dollop, he says, "I was checking it's safe; it's shit that foreign muck."

Ruth looks angry though whether it's with me or him I don't wait to find out.

*\*\**

Mrs Ojha is waiting for me by the kitchen door. "You wanted to ask me something?" Before I can frame a reply, the front door slams shut.

She taps my arm. "Your Mother needs to see the lawyers." She tries to look unconcerned. "It's nothing to worry about, Harry. So, how can I help?"

I shake my head; I can't trust her either.

***

I'm feeling so wound up that before I go to work I dig out some of the weed and hide at the end of the garden while I smoke a joint. All that does is make me lose track of time and I'm rushing when I collect my bike. Consequently I don't see McNoble until I nearly ram him. Inevitably, he's cleaning his nails with his penknife.

I force out an 'excuse me' but he blocks my way.

"Ruth likes you, God knows why."

I stand very still, conscious I can no longer see where his knife is.

His free hand shoots out and grips my right arm hard; the twist is agonising.

"If she didn't I'd effing stick you, you know? I told you to keep your effing Mother away."

I wish I could see his bloody knife.

"Why, eh? What's her plan?"

"I don't know." I yank my arm free and massage the bruising. "He's got Mrs Jepson. He's not going to want my Mum, is he?"

"They're both effing gold-diggers. You'd better do something or…" He waves his knife close to my nose.

"I'm sure it's nothing. Really."

For just a moment the tension goes out of him and he takes a small step back. As his hands are hanging loose by his side I take my chance; I yank my bike away and push it towards the lane.

It's a hopeless manoeuvre. One moment I'm trying to straddle the crossbar, the next there's a blur of movement, I duck and he's on top of me as we fall to the ground, with me the sandwich between him and my bike. He's a real weight and all the air is forced out of my lungs. Being winded is no joke and I roll away, sucking in oxygen.

"Shit." It's the tone of his voice rather than what he says that makes me look up. He's sitting on the road staring at me. He looks like he's in shock. It takes a moment to realise what's holding his attention: his penknife has pierced my black trousers and about an inch of its blade is embedded in my thigh.

"Agghhhh." I've been stabbed. Because I'm gawping at the knife I don't realise what he's doing until he yanks it out.

"FUCK!" The pain is worse than Rascal's talons. I continue to howl as he waves the bloodied blade under my nose.

"Shut up, dickhead. SHUT UP."

I really think he's going to have another go so, despite the agony, I somehow get on my bike and pedal away. I don't stop until the goose farm where I ease my trousers down. I'm a bit disappointed there's hardly any blood and only a small wound. I was sure it had gone in so deep. I try squeezing the sides. It's tender but there's no blood. I suppose it isn't as bad as I thought. Even so I'm taking no chances. He can have his sodding money – anything to keep him at arm's length.

## Chapter Fifty

## Bottled Up

I spend every spare moment thinking about the fête money; now McNoble has tasted blood he'll not stop. Like effing Shylock. As soon as my shift is over, I pass up lunch and race back home to hunt for it. I reckon with Dina at work until at least six I have enough time to search her room completely. Unluckily for me, and just when I've pulled all her boxes out into the middle of the floor, she pushes her door open. Seeing me is like I've punched her: she looks like she might throw up.

I try to brazen it out. "I need the money for McNoble. Kind of now so I thought…"

My speaking frees her to drop to her knees and shove me away. "These are my things. GET OUT." She scrabbles to put the lids on.

I make a grab for her arm. "I need it, all right? Where have you put it?"

Her face is full of fury and something else. "FUCK OFF."

It's like she's slapped me. She's never used that word before. I recoil but manage to say, "Hey, he attacked me, today. With his knife. He stabbed me so…"

"Stabbed you? Where?"

"My leg. It's nothing really."

"But have you told Mum?"

"Look I need the money."

"It could get infected."

"Just give me..."

From being worried one moment she goes floppy and says, "Please. Just leave me alone."

I'm about to press again for the money when I see that the box she's now cradling is the one that held the jars.

"Di, are you ok?"

She won't look at me; she just rocks with it tight to her chest.

I swallow hard. "I... I looked the other day. In that box. I saw those jars."

She lifts her head and stares at me, squeezing the box to her chest.

*\*\*\**

Neither of us move for an age. Finally, and mostly because I cannot stand the noise coming up through the floor from Ruth's room – Caravan's Cunning Stunts – I dig out Genesis' The Lamb Lies Down on Broadway and put on side one. At the first chord she starts talking – she can't believe what's happened; it's her stupid fault not Jim's; she didn't think it was possible; she was so careful. On and on. Then she says, "I haven't dared to do the test."

"Why?"

"Doctor Martin will tell Mum."

"He can't." But we both know he will.

"Does Jim know?"

She shakes her head hard, so hard I'm sure her neck clicks. "I can't face him. His Father had another go at me, and Jim saw. I can't see him again."

The side ends and I flip it over. I say, "Can't you go to a different doctors? There's a practice in Lymington."

She looks like she's got no strength left. Side two fades away and we still haven't moved. On goes side three.

"Di, where's the fête money?"

"It's gone." She looks up then. "Mum took it."

"Mum?" My brain has stalled; for a moment something vital seems to have drained out of my ears.

She says, "I left it in the drawer; Janice changed it into tenners and Mum found it. I said it was Grandpa's money and she said it couldn't be so she took it. I couldn't stop her."

When side three ends it is Dina who puts on side four. "Do you really need it?"

I can't begin to tell her about McNoble's knife. All I manage is, "He's been here, with Ruth. I know he'll want it."

"We'll tell him to get stuffed." I know she knows I won't. God, why am I so feeble? When I look at her, she looks so forlorn I find myself saying, "Maybe I can ask Penny to pretend the sample is hers?"

"Really? Would you?"

I have to nod even though I know I won't be able to.

She manages a smile. "Penny really likes you, you know. She told me at the fête."

I should be cheered by that but Dina doesn't know about the abortive kiss.

***

Cycling back to work, my mind wanders here, there and everywhere. I've just reached the crest of the hill by the entrance to the goose farm, my wound is throbbing again and I've just thought how it's impossible for things to get any worse. It's then that my subconscious proves how wrong I can be. An awful thought hits me so hard I nearly fall off. What if Jepson is my Father?

A fog descends and logic gets lost. Jepson and Mum were nearly engaged; Dad and Mum were married really quickly, when she was pregnant with me. Jepson said he was in the Army with Dad in 1956; Mum and Dad married October 1956 (Dad once called it a 'whirlwind romance'); I was born in March 1957.

However hard I look for a flaw, the idea won't shift. My hair, my eyes, even the shape of my nose: they could all be Jepson's. I'm standing in some green slimy runoff from the farm and force myself to breathe in the ammonia. My head clears briefly until it hits me: if I'm right, McNoble and I are brothers.

**FRIDAY 30TH JULY 1976**

## Chapter Fifty-One

## Where There's Harry, There's Hope

I've decided to stop thinking; I'll just exist. Thinking hurts and makes me ill. I'm dreading seeing either Mum or Dad this morning – should I still call him 'Dad'? Dina slips me the jar; I barely register it's still warm. My brain races along, unlike my wheels. Will they want me to live with Mr Jepson? Adopt me? Make me change my name? I'm on autopilot as I cycle straight to the Rat Pit. When Penny answers the door, bleary eyed and tousle-haired, dressed in a baggy T-shirt, I take in the rather tired smile, the jeans, the male shoes but make no real connection. "Oh hi," she says, "You're early. Nats is having a shower…"

I'm not capable of speech; I dig out the pot and hold it in front of me.

She looks surprised as she takes it and reads the label. "What's up, Harry?"

I want to speak but I can't.

She hands the jar back and says, "Wait. I'll grab my shorts."

It doesn't take her long, but in that time I hate her, love her so much it tears my guts; I reconcile myself to a lifetime of ruing my antipathy to effing Marmite.

"Let's try the Salon."

It's empty and she makes me sit. "Tell me."

Finally I manage. "Dina."

She's a genius. She nods. "She thinks she's pregnant and you want me to pretend this is mine?"

"How...?"

She snorts with laughter, but then looks serious. "If it was some sort of bladder infection – well, maybe not VD – she'd tell your Mum. It's hardly unusual; where I'm from they always say: 'Married and not pregnant – now there's posh.'"

The funnies are not working today. She must realise because she puts her hand on my arm. "I'll take it." She frowns. "Sure this is Dina's? Not that girl who came to the bar?"

"Of course." I know my protests sound fake and my neck starts itching with embarrassment but Penny doesn't press. In fact she shuffles to me and hugs me.

"Not many brothers would do that for their sister. I'll pop it in today. Come and have some tea. Maybe Chris will be up by now." She stands but I stay seated. "He can't go to Clapton after all. And Sven's dropped out. Looks like we can both go. So, tea?"

Her smile is the nicest thing I've seen in ages. I nod.

"Good. Can you find a home for the other one?"

I nod again but right now I don't give a stuff about it.

\*\*\*

It's odd how one short sentence can do so much good. 'Looks like we can both go'. I'm full of energy all of a sudden; I force the question of my parentage from my mind and turn to the issue of money for McNoble. A crazy plan came to me as I served Sven; he was moaning about the need to raise money to redeem something. So once the bar is shut I go hunting for him. Happily he's drawing today, not at the beach. I know better than to disturb him and sit and watch for twenty minutes until he puts his pencil down and says, "Have you nothing better to do than gawp?"

"Can I ask you a question?"

He rubs out a figure in the background. "If you must."

"I think I need to use the pawnbrokers."

"That's a statement, not a question. And you make it sound like you want the toilet."

"You said you pawned your watch. I wondered…"

He remains silent.

"Sven?"

"I'm still waiting for the question." He picks up his pencil but stares at me. "Even you can master this skill. You go to the front door, open it and say, 'I want to pawn this please.' You hand over your item and he gives you money."

He is easily the most irritating person I've ever met.

"There's Frank's in New Milton. By the station. I use him. Tell him I sent you; he might be generous, though don't bank on it."

I mumble my thanks.

He turns to his pad. "Perhaps you'd leave me alone now."

"You think I'm stupid, don't you?"

"Naïve and ridiculously self-conscious. Most of the others are stupid."

"Do you like anybody?"

"Here? No. It's a job. It gets me away from my family while I'm on vac. The money is useful, too, so I don't rely on Pater. And don't pretend you'll be in correspondence with anyone come September. Maybe, in your case, one, but me? I don't think so."

I leave him be. One? Does he mean Penny?

\*\*\*

All I have to do is see Mrs Jepson, get the diamonds and pawn them. I've convinced myself that, since Mr James hasn't missed the box yet, he won't before he goes off on his cruise.

So if I give Ruth the box, with a suitable rattle, she'll sneak it back without checking. She's happy and I can pay McNoble. I can sort out redeeming them later, when I'm flush. Foolproof. Or proof I'm a fool.

Naturally Mrs Jepson is out all day. I'm pretty near exploding when I see her return, happily alone, collect her room key and disappear upstairs. I've had plenty of time to devise a strategy that swings into action.

First a brandy and water; second I tell Rodney Mrs Jepson wants a nightcap. Third I make for the stairs. That's the point when my courage evaporates. If the Commodore and his wife hadn't chosen then to go to their room I might have crawled away. As it is their querulous voices propel me to her door.

"Harry?" She's pulls her silky gown closed. "What do you want?"

"I brought you a nightcap. And maybe I could just grab those diamonds."

She's already walking to the window, leaving me to follow her inside. "Shut the door." While I set the drink down she lights up, blowing smoke outside. "Charlie doesn't like me smoking in the bedroom."

"Is he coming back?"

"Not tonight. I think he's in Southampton. He told me he was going to take your Mother." She looks at me. "As brazen as you like. Maybe they are having an affair. What do you think?" Her voice is so bitter I'm really taken aback.

She's staring out of the window, into the dark. "I don't suppose you spoke to either of your parents, did you?"

She blows smoke out of the side of her mouth, before tossing the part smoked cigarette onto the roof below and turning to face me. In doing so her gown flaps open, exposing her naked belly and small triangle of pubic hair. She tugs the gown closed quickly and says, "Do you know what he did when I asked about your Mother?"

I'm feeling rather ill and wish I hadn't bothered to come.

She twists away from me and hitches her gown high. First she exposes her legs and then her bottom, the white mark from her bikini standing out vividly. "Look." She points at a mark the size of an orange centred on the white flesh. She lets the gown drop and lights a second cigarette. "He used his nine iron. His 'rescue club', he calls it."

"Jesus. He hit you?"

"Are you surprised? Shocked? You have no idea, do you?" She blows smoke out of the side of her mouth. "If you're going to be sick, use the bathroom and if you're going to faint sit on the bed."

I take the bed. "Why...?" My brain is scrambled

She stares hard for a moment then laughs. "Why? Why does he do it? Because he can. Why don't I leave him? Because he does the leaving." She picks at the corner of one eye with a highly polished nail. "Whatever he's planning, I'm not going to stop him. If your Mother is planning on being with him she'd be well advised to think twice."

"Can't we do something?"

"Such as? If you think I'm risking another beating you need your head examining."

She walks over to a chair opposite me and sits. She's still smoking, Charlie's 'no smoking' rule seemingly forgotten. I feel distinctly unwell and find it difficult to maintain my balance. I can't stop worrying about Mum.

We sit in silence until she finishes the cigarette and stubs it out. She stands and moves to sit next to me, taking my nearest hand. "It's not your fault."

"I could speak to Mum, or Dad, about Mr Andersen. Like you said..."

She squeezes hard to stop me. "Don't. He's too clever. He'll have an answer. There's no point you getting caught up in this."

"But… but… what are you going to do?"

"Stay put. Keep smiling. Be the perfect wife. And when I can, leave the bastard. I…" She lets go of my hand. "I'll have a word with Claude's Mother, Pat. She still has some influence with Charlie. Mostly because she can get Claude to behave and he can't. At least we can find out his plans. Maybe." She strokes my cheek. "Poor Harry. Now what did you want?"

I want to go but manage to say, "The diamonds."

"The…? Oh yes… the ones in the box. I'm afraid…" She stops like she's lost her thread. When I glance across her face has creased into a frown. "You put them in that piece of paper, didn't you? And gave it to me?" She doesn't wait for an answer, but moves quickly to the wardrobe; in moments she's pulled out her bag and is rummaging inside. "Yes!" She holds up the twist like she has found buried treasure. "Take them. Quick, before I change my mind. Are you giving them to Ruth?"

My hands are shaking as I peer inside the paper; four little stones twinkle back at me. When I look up she's already by the bathroom door. "You'd better go." She goes inside and shuts the door. Moments later the bath starts running; I can't leave quickly enough.

***

With every turn of the pedals, the visit to Mrs Jepson's room takes on a more and more fantastical air; it is only the little paper twist in my pocket that convinces me it happened and sends me to the shed. "Dad, I…"

Dad is sitting in his chair. In one hand is a bottle of Bells; the other is stuck inside his pyjama bottoms. He blinks myopically at me.

"Oo's zat? Harry?" He tries to stand but slips back. At least the hand comes out to steady himself. "'Ave a drink."

He waves the bottle at a glass. While I hesitate he wobbles upright again and makes for the desk where he slops me a measure. "S'mudinyereye."

I toast him back and swallow, trying to blot out the image of the parental fumble.

"Sooo. Waya been up to then? With some girly, eh?"

"Dad, I need to talk about Mum and Mr Jepson."

"Charley-boy?" He waves his glass again. "Christ what a piece of work."

"Do you know what's he doing with her?"

He tries to focus on me. "Yer Mother? She's planning." He goes to tap his nose and misses by quite a distance. "Yep. Scheming and planning."

I take the biggest breath ever. "I think I heard them kissing."

"Kissing?" He frowns with a lack of comprehension. "Kissing?" He says the word like it's new to him.

As Dad slumps back into his chair, I press forward. "I spoke to his wife. Monica. She says it might be an affair. Dad, did you hear me?"

He starts shaking his head. "Affair? Your Mum?" He blinks for focus and patently fails. "Affair?"

"Dad, please, we have to stop them." His eyes close briefly and I shake him. "Dad, listen. He's violent…"

Dad squints at me. "Affair?"

I so want to slap him, but I say very carefully, "Mr Jepson is doing something with Robin Andersen. Something dodgy. Dad, do you understand?" This is exhausting.

"Kissing?"

"Oh Christ." I scan the shed for water. Nothing. I grab a glass and go outside to the water butt that Mum keeps topped up whatever the weather.

When I return Dad is lolling in his chair. I steady myself and throw the water over him. He shakes himself like a dog, growls and half stands.

"Bloody crook. Nothing kosher. Booze, brothels, protection." This little speech seems to exhaust him because he topples back into his chair and closes his eyes.

I try twice more but he hardly registers the water.

I'm nearly in tears with frustration when I go to bed, knowing I'll never sleep. There's so much to ask and the sod passes out on me. Who's my real Dad for starters? I tuck the diamonds under my pillow, ignoring the guilt that grips me briefly. Ruth can bleat to effing Stephen if she needs protection, I'm doing things my way.

**SATURDAY 31ST JULY 1976**

## Chapter Fifty-Two

## I'm Not Paranoid

When I awake around five, I'm sticky with sweat. Only it's not sweat; I've wanked in my sleep. The self-disgust rolls over me as I scrabble to clear up; where's my self-control? I try and console myself that this is my first pain-free wank since Rascal's attack but fail. It's only as I puff up my pillow I remember the diamonds and the guilt hits me: I'm dumping Ruth in it to save myself; I've tried to force Nanty to write me a cheque to save my own arse; I've let my sister deal in drugs for the same reason; I've done nothing to stop Mum making the biggest mistake of her life; I've done nothing to protect Dina from Mr James; I've let Cyril get away with peeping even though it really upsets the one girl I care for... I'm officially pathetic.

In the hall there's a letter from Dobbin. He wants money for the ferry that I don't have: another reason to feel guilty. In the envelope are four slips of paper. *Here are the curses you ordered. I re-read the M.R. James story and spoke to my Dad – he knows all sorts of stuff – and we copied out some runes to make them look official. When you decide who you're cursing, you need to write on the back what's to happen to them – buried alive for instance – add a date when it will happen and give it to them. Unless they give it back to you they're done for. Guaranteed.*

He's bonkers but I'll give them a try.

\*\*\*

The kitchen is full: all the Ojhas, plus Dad and Ruth. Ravi is a man-tree with Sajid and Noor hanging from his arms. Dad looks ill; he's nursing a cup of coffee in one hand and his head in the other. Ruth is tucked in the other corner, looking unsure whether she should be there. She smiles weakly at me, making the diamonds burn in my back pocket.

As Ravi catches sight of me he says, "There's your next challenge, Saj – Harry! I must dash. Wish me luck."

While Sajid attaches himself to me like a limpet, Mrs Ojha begins serving me some orangey porridge. I catch a glimpse of Ruth looking disgusted; I pointedly savour a mouthful.

After a few minutes, Mrs Ojha takes the children to their room to dress. Once she's gone Ruth says, "Janice said she got you four tickets for Clapton. Are any spare?"

"Yes. You want to go?" The guilt is making me weak.

"Not me, Stephen. Mum and I already have tickets but he's desperate to go."

Of course, it would have to be McNoble. I try and imagine him swaying to 'Layla' or 'Badge'. Nope, he's more your typical head-in-a-speaker-stack sort of music lover.

I look at Dad. He can barely lift the cup. "Where's Mum, Dad?"

"Hmm? Southampton Hospital. She wanted to see the consultant."

"She left early."

"No. She went yesterday... stayed with my sister."

Now I'm really confused. Maybe Mrs Jepson misunderstood, but if so why did Mr Jepson hit her? I finish my porridge in silence and check my watch. There's no reason to go to work this early but I don't want to spend any more time with Ruth than I have to. Sadly, when I go outside to fetch my bike she's waiting for me.

Ruth says, "I really want you and Stephen to be friends." She keeps up with me as I head for the back gate. "You mustn't be jealous of us."

"Jealous?"

Her face glows likes it's backlit. "He understands, Harry. He's a Christian now but he's been tempted too."

I do well not to vomit. She tugs at my sleeve to stop me. I know what's coming. "Have you…?"

"No. Not yet but I will, ok?"

She says in her worst whiny voice, "You promised."

"No I didn't, but I will get you the box and you will be able to put it back – ok?"

"When?"

"There's no rush is there? He's not missed them, has he?"

"Oh Harry. I can't stand the guilt."

*\*\*\**

I'm in my own little world as I pull the back gate closed. So much so that I don't immediately notice Ravi standing on the far verge. He nods and says, "My lift is late."

He checks both ways before walking over to me. It's pretty unnerving the way he stares at me, like he can read my mind; it also makes it really difficult to try and go. So we stand facing each other awkwardly. He's really tall with a mass of black hair, so unlike Dad with his wispy trails. And he's not the sort to confide in, unlike his wife who I know could help me if only I had the courage…

"Be patient with your parents, Harry. You must trust their experience and wisdom."

His eyes are much darker than Mrs Ojha's. He's leaning slightly forward and the combination makes it feel like he's trying to force me to agree.

"It is important to respect your elders and betters and wait for them to decide what is best for your family."

Because of the conviction with which he delivers his speech it takes a moment to realise what a load of rubbish it is when applied to my parents. Not that I'm telling him that.

Having shared his own wisdom he makes this praying gesture with his hands. I'm wondering whether this means I can go when a car turns into the lane and moves slowly towards us.

"My lift." He turns quickly and moves away.

There's something about the car that's familiar, but the overhanging trees mean I can't see inside the windscreen. Once Ravi has climbed in, the driver effects a neat three-point turn and drives away, back towards Lymington. As the car turns I catch a glimpse of both driver and front passenger. The former is, without doubt, Magda; the latter I'm less sure about but I'd hazard a guess at Mum.

I'm still staring at the space left by the car when Nigel Sodding Parsons rides up on his motorbike. "Hi 'arry. 'Eard you're going to Clapton. We should make a party."

Nigel and McNoble. What a perfect combination.

My face must communicate my lack of enthusiasm because he says hurriedly, "Must dash. See you."

***

The rest of my day is a bit of a blur. I go to New Milton in my break but the bloody pawnbrokers are shut until Monday. Hardly anyone comes to the bar, which means I've plenty of time to dwell on anything and everything and work myself up into a froth of anxiety.

By the time I head for my bike at ten thirty-five I just want to get home and go to bed.

Penny is sitting under the cherry trees, watching the hotel. I'm hoping she's just trying to get cool before bed; the night is another sticky one. No such luck; as soon as she sees me she walks over.

She says, "I couldn't go to the doctor's today."

I can tell there's more.

"How is Dina coping?"

"She's been off work. Sick."

She sticks out her bottom lip and says, "Did you find a home for the spare ticket?"

"Spare? Oh yeah."

"Oh? Good." She looks at me, but I don't tell her who; it'll only prolong things.

She seems to have finished so I roll my bike out of the rack and turn for the exit. "Night." I've gone a few feet when I glance back. She's not moved and I can't just walk away. I prop the machine against a tree. "You ok?"

She's hugging herself, sniffling as she does so. "Cyril's starting peeping in our windows. I was dancing on my own and he frightened me so much…" She wipes her face. "I can't stand it, Harry. He just stood there leering as I screamed at him."

"Were you, you know, naked?"

"NO. What's that got to do with anything?"

"Sorry. I just thought…"

"What? That it only counts if he can see my tits?" She leans her head back, staring at the stars. "I told Magda. She said Hemingway is too busy right now and my 'leetle problem' will have to wait." She wipes her nose on her sleeve.

"What about Chris?"

"He's useless." She shakes her head. "I told him the first time it happened. He said he'd sort him out, but then I catch the two of them sharing a cigarette, laughing. He told me he thought the softly-softly approach worked best." She looks completely defeated.

"I'll do something, Penny. Really." She lets me hold her; I know she doesn't believe me – I don't believe myself – but she knows I would if I could and that makes me feel better. A bit. Still guilty though.

*** 

Dina's in her room, listening to Leonard Cohen's New Skin for the Old Ceremony. Things must be bad. When I knock (no reply) and then stick my head round the door, she's swigging cider. I've never seen her drink alcohol before. She offers it to me and we share a few mouthfuls while Mr Misery winds to an end.

She stands and selects Peter Frampton's Frampton Comes Alive! It's something we both like. "Seen this?" She tosses me the local paper. "Page four."

The headline is 'Pumpkin Wars' and there's a picture of a distraught Susan Glebe with a smashed pumpkin on her drive. I struggle through the article; it talks about intimidation and the annual competition getting out of hand. A source is quoted as saying there are people who take it too seriously. That is followed by a picture of Mum holding the cup from last year with a line saying she will keep the cup if she wins it this year.

"They're blaming Mum," says Dina.

I try and re-read the article. "It doesn't say that, does it?"

"S'obvious. And why not? She's a total cow."

"Mum? No, it couldn't be her."

Dina's eyes are losing focus, putting me in mind of Dad last night. At least she's his daughter, I think sourly. I say, "I'm pretty sure you're right about her having an affair. With Mr Jepson. McNoble's Dad. They were engaged, way back."

She takes a while to compute this before shaking her head. "Nah. She's a raddled old bag. No one would have her."

"She stayed with him in Southampton last night."

Dina flops back onto the bed with a thump. "I feel terrible." She belches and looks rather green for a moment, but then begins beating her bedcover with her fists. "I hate her. I HATE HER. I HATE THEM ALL..." She stands and stares at me, wide eyed. "I'm moving out."

"What? Where?"

"Janice's."

"You know that won't work. It's the first place they'll look. You need a better—"

Before I know it she flies at me, pummelling me with her fists; it takes all my strength to push her off. Just as quickly as she started, she stops. She stares up at me from the prone position where I've pushed her. "Did you find out?"

I'm about to shake my head when she turns sideways and vomits neatly onto my jacket where I dropped it. We both watch as the yellowy liquid soaks into the green material.

**SUNDAY 1ST AUGUST 1976**

## Chapter Fifty-Three

## Legal Niceties

Mum wakes me at eight. "I need you to come with me to Petunia's"

I manage a croaky 'why?', but all I receive in reply is a curt 'cover her up, please' aimed at Amanda.

***

She tells me nothing more beyond 'it's to do with Grandpa's will' and someone called Michael – the lawyer apparently – has put himself out to be available on a Sunday. It's only after she's lit up – she's no longer bothering to hide the new habit – that the questions start. "Tell me about work. What are the staff like?"

"They're ok."

"Everyone friendly? Good at their jobs?"

"I suppose."

"Come on, Harold. Give me a flavour…"

"Mum, it's barely dawn. What's with the inquisition?"

"I'm interested."

I can't believe it; weeks of indifference and now this. "Our best waiter is a poof; the head waiter is fixated on his tip box and folding napkins; the two chefs are bullying psychos; the receptionist is recently escaped from a gulag but is very good; and the gardener is a peeping pervert who can't be sacked."

I hesitate, trying to decide if I should tell her Sven is Robin Andersen's son – just to gauge her reaction – but she starts probing about Paul and then Magda and she doesn't pause until some walking dog food trots in front of us causing a sharp stop. As the pony craps massively, Mum takes a few calming breaths before treating the steaming pile as a roundabout. At least the questions stop.

\*\*\*

The silence in Aunt Petunia's dining room hangs heavily. There are four of us: Mum, Aunt, this lawyer – a grey haired old boy, who I'm to call Mr Lewis – and me.

Outside, pottering in and out of his budgie cages at the end of the garden, is Uncle Norman. As always, Aunt's house is operating-theatre clean; she's invested in plastic covers for the seats that squeak every time anyone moves.

Eventually Mr Lewis stops reading some papers and says, "Shall I start?" He doesn't wait for permission. "First there has been some confusion about George Thoroughly's will, mainly whether Edna paid out either of Harold or Dina's legacy?" I could answer easily, but Mr Lewis continues with barely a pause. "Neither legacy has been paid; well, not to the children…"

This time the pause elongates; Aunt fills the silence. "Is this relevant?"

He peers at her over his glasses for a long moment before reverting to his papers. "Yes, Petunia, as you'll hear."

Aunt isn't so easily quieted. "This is a waste of time, if all we're here to discuss is the children's legacies. We should be sorting out the will… oh I know, you don't need to look like that Veronica. You've made it plain you won't change anything. Even so you know we need to free up the residue. Half of it is mine and we need it now…"

Mr Lewis holds up a hand, like a traffic policeman. "Petunia, if you'll let me finish. It's important that Harold understands the background."

Aunt begins to swell; that's not a good sign. "He's a child, for heaven's sake. Why on earth did you bring him, Veronica?"

Mr Lewis won't be put off. "If we are to appoint new executors, Harold, as an 'of age' legatee has to be involved."

"New executors?"

"Exactly Petunia. That's what you want, isn't it? It will speed things along. So if I may…"

"We should be changing the will. That's what we should—"

"Enough Petunia." I like the old boy, even though I'm with Aunt wondering why I have to be here. When he's sure she's stopped he looks straight at me and says, "Your Grandfather's will left a sizeable legacy to your Mother, individual bequests to you and your sister and the residue after various expenses to be shared between your Mother and Aunt. Understand?"

"Yes sir. Though…?"

"Yes?"

"Didn't Aunt have a legacy too?"

"A very good point…" Aunt is furiously smoothing the tablecloth flat.

Another hand signal and a growled 'Petunia' before he turns to me. "Your Aunt received her share four years ago. When your Grandfather retired he gifted her the garage. There were some tax advantages… well, so he hoped." He gives Aunt another warning glance. "Edna was put in charge of sorting things out; they were quite complex, but even so I would have expected a full payout by now. Her accident has exposed some, erm, issues."

While Mum studies her nails, Aunt grips the table edge as if to hold herself in check.

Mr Lewis smiles briefly; I bet he's relishing his captive audience. "All Veronica's money is safe, in the Estate account. Unfortunately the rest has, umm, gone."

"Gone?" Aunt glares at Mum. "You knew about this?"

Mum nods. "I heard yesterday when…"

Aunt puffs herself right up. "This is outrageous. That's my money." She turns the glare on Mr Lewis. "Where is it?"

Mr Lewis takes yet another sheet and smoothes it on the table. I think he's deliberately winding Aunt up. I do like this man. He says, "None of the money for the children's legacies, the expenses, my fees and, of course the residue is in the account." His face droops a bit at the mention of fees. "About two thousand pounds in total."

Both Mum and Aunt stare at Mr Lewis like the amount is a surprise to them. I suppose we are all stunned by the idea our money has just disappeared. Mr Lewis picks up a peach from the fruit bowl and looks at it longingly before putting it back. "I'll call Norman. He should be here for the next bit."

When Uncle comes in, he looks rather upset. He opens his hands and lays a small greeny-coloured budgie on the table. Aunt swiftly puts a coaster under it. "Bernard died last night. He was the best grey-green I've ever seen."

Aunt clearly doesn't give a stuff about the budgie. "But where's the money?" We're all back looking at the lawyer, but it's Uncle who speaks.

"Is this about the Estate money, Michael?"

Mr Lewis nods while Uncle sits heavily. He says, "Back in May the Bank sent a threatening letter. We'd lose the business if I didn't pay off half our loan. They gave me two weeks. You two were at each other's throats about the Estate and how unfair it was so I talked to Arthur, to see if he had any ideas."

He pauses, glancing at Mum. She says nothing.

"He let me have a little money, but I needed more. He asked Edna – she has savings – and she was prepared to help only everything was tied up for a while in some bonds or something. So we – the three of us – agreed she would use the Estate money – just as a loan. When Edna's investments were cashed she'd replace it and no one would be any the wiser. And I'd repay her when the garage turned the corner…" He rubs his face. "Then she had her accident." He blinks at Mum. "You're an effective bodyguard, Veronica."

We are all looking at Aunt who's mimicking a goldfish. Uncle says, "Sorry, pet."

Aunt is deflating. "But… but you told me they'd given you more time. You said we had two months."

Uncle is shaking his head. "I couldn't pay what I needed to pay, not even with the two thousand from the Estate. They gave me an extension. To the end of this week."

Aunt turns on Mum. "Now do you see why we need that residue?"

Uncle slams his hand on the table. "It's gone. Weren't you listening?"

"Well, we need Edna to sell her bonds and pay it back. It's her fault and—"

Mum reaches across and puts a hand on Aunt's arm, shushing her. "This isn't about Edna."

Aunt's jaw works hard but she's run out of things to say.

Mum keeps hold of Aunt's arm. "Arthur made me speak to Michael. When he explained the situation I realised what a fool I've been. Everyone is trying to save Daddy's business while you and I fight, Petunia. Poor Edna. She must feel awful…"

Aunt's expression slips easily from stunned to thunderous; she snatches her arm away. "Poor Edna my foot. She's the one who's made this mess."

"No, Petunia." Mum looks up, her voice firmer. "Her health is the most important thing."

"Aren't you listening? What about the business?"

Mr Lewis coughs. "I spoke to Edna's brokers, Petunia. They told me that her investments are not sufficient to cover the loan. It's possible Edna knew and that's why she's been avoiding the issue."

Aunt must be getting dizzy, swivelling to look at each of us in turn. "What do you mean? That she's putting on her illness?"

Mum says, in a quiet voice, "The hospital told me they felt sure Edna's speech problems were psychosomatic rather than physical."

Aunt's gaze moves rapidly from Mr Lewis to Mum and back. The painful silence is broken by a sob from Aunt, followed by, "Oh God. Norman?"

Mr Lewis coughs. He says, "To cut through this, Veronica agrees we need to resolve the executor issue, pending Edna's recovery and…"

But Aunt isn't really listening; she's staring at Uncle. "There's no money? What will we do? We can't lose the garage. We just can't."

Even though Aunt is on the verge of hysterics, Mum keeps her voice calm, turning to Mr Lewis. "You said my share was still there? How much will be left after you take what you need for the expenses?"

Mr Lewis says, brightening visibly, "About three thousand."

Mum rubs her hands. "So, let's sort out the executors, shall we? And—"

Aunt's sob turns into a growl; spittle flecks her chin. "Oh lovely. That's why we're here, is it? You get your money while we go to debtor's prison."

Uncle splutters, "Petunia, that's not fair…"

Mr Lewis says, "You don't go to prison for a debt."

Aunt is almost on her feet, her righteous indignation magnificent. "I don't care. It's typical of her…"

Mum grips her arm, making Aunt sink back down. "If I allow you five hundred pounds from *my* share to be paid to you on account of your share of the residue, will that help? Norman?"

Aunt turns to stare incredulously at Mum. Mum says, "I want to help."

"You do? Since when?"

Uncle interrupts. "Don't be churlish, Petunia. That's very generous, Vee. It's not enough but…"

Mum only has eyes for Uncle. "How much then?"

"Er, nine hundred and twenty seven pounds as of Friday."

"Ok. A thousand then."

We all stare at Mum. Finally Mr Lewis breaks the silence. "Why don't you talk it through? Harold and I will make some coffee."

***

Mr Lewis takes his time over the drinks. I say, while he fiddles with the kettle, "Will I get my money, do you think?"

"I can't say." He turns to smile at me. "Your Mother indicated yesterday that neither you nor Dina need it. Perhaps you and your sister should assume for now it's gone and be pleasantly surprised if it turns up."

How can he be happy, when all he does is bring bad news? Maybe I should become a lawyer.

He goes back to watching the kettle and says, "So how is the B&B? Blooming?"

***

As soon as we are back in the car Mum lights up. After a couple of puffs she says, "Why did you give Dina all your wages?"

"What do you mean?"

"She had one hundred pounds in her drawer. If she's not had her money from your Grandfather, then it must be from you. It can't be her savings; she needs me to sign if she wants to withdraw from the Post Office."

"It's the fête money. We made it at the fête."

"Don't lie, Harold. You sold some of Susan Glebe's teas. No one is going to buy that much."

I fold my arms. I'm not saying any more.

"Harold, this won't do. What are you and your sister planning? Is it to do with Jim?"

I stare outside, knowing I must be going red.

"You can't keep secrets about important things, Harold. We have a right to know."

My anxiety turns in a second to anger, her words repeating in my head: 'keep secrets… right to know…' "What about you? You and Dad?"

"Don't be silly, Harold."

But when I sneak a glance, she's staring out of the windscreen and gripping the wheel tightly. After an awkward few moments she says quietly, "I… we are only doing what we think is best. For the family." She ends by glancing at me.

This hard lump has stuck in my throat. I just about manage to say, "Me too."

She stops at a junction and turns to look fully at me. "If there's something wrong, you would tell me, wouldn't you? With you or Dina?" She sounds really worried.

I just about nod. It may be the way the sun catches her gaze that makes it look like tears. We both retreat into our own little worlds, unable to find words to break the heavy silence.

## Chapter Fifty-Four

### No Reason to Cry

Lunchtime is slow. I put 461 Ocean Boulevard on the tape machine to get myself ready for Clapton tonight. No one minds apart from me because it's dreadful. I'm just thinking how much 'Let It Grow' is such a poor man's 'Stairway to Heaven' when Paul marches in, bristling as only he can.

"What's all this crap about Hemingways closing then?"

"Closing?"

He leans so far across the bar I have to press against the back fittings to avoid him touching me. "You're the only Spittle here, ain't you?" Up close I can see he's lost several teeth in the back of his mouth. "I like this job; easy money, easy women, easy source of weed, and I'm not losing it because of you, shithead. If your lot have ideas to fuck me over then they can think again."

Paul looks like he's going to come round to my side, but a noisy group enters the bar and he leaves, still fuming.

***

When I push open the door to the bar at the Gaumont, I know immediately my evening is doomed. Nigel Sodding Parsons has somehow found Penny and Natalie and is chatting to them. How does he know?

As I walk across it's clear they are already smitten with his combination of rustic gormlessness and free dosh. Natalie, in particular, is laughing at everything he says. I've barely said hello when he offers her 'a little look at me boike' and they've gone.

At least Penny stays behind but she's more interested in talking to Ruth's Mum, Cynthia, about Clapton. Meanwhile Ruth and McNoble snuggle in a corner and begin eating each other – whatever happened to boundaries? While Penny and Cynthia compete to shower the most praise on Eric the God, I slope off into the auditorium to listen to the support. Even when they join me, Cynthia is still continuing her eulogy. I stand it for another five minutes and then head to the bar to get more drinks.

***

With the bar empty it looks like a war zone. The carpet, when I step on it, has the look and feel of a Jackson Pollock before it's dried.

"Three pints of lager please."

The guy serving me is Australian. "How's it going, mate?"

I shake my head.

"Seventy-two pence."

"Jeepers. How much?" I dig out the cash while he pours. I'm still watching the bubbles fizz to the surface and die when an arm reaches past me and picks up a pint. "Hey!"

Penny finishes it in three swallows, belches and slams the glass down. "Come on. Time to dance. Drink up."

"One's for Cyn…"

She glares at me. "Just come on."

I give in. The barman smirks as I'm dragged away.

***

We end up at the front. Natalie and Nigel join us but in the crowd we split apart and for several numbers I lose sight of everyone. At some point, when I'm next to Penny again, Clapton changes the mood and everything slows; the couple next to us start snogging and I slide an arm round Penny's shoulders. She doesn't stop me but doesn't come in close either. After that the pace picks up and we all end in the usual frenzy of stomping and sweat. As the crowd breaks we make for the exit to wait for the others.

We stop by a fire door. While Penny scans the faces I say, "I really enjoyed that."

She stops bobbing about and looks at me. "Really? So why'd you let that prick hog Nats?" When I don't answer she says, "She begged Chris to give up his ticket for you. She shouldn't have bothered."

"I..."

She turns away; I think she says 'stupid'.

I can't take my eyes off her neck. I want to kiss it, lick it, but it's protected by a force field. I can see the beads of sweat just waiting to be sucked away. Why doesn't she understand it's her I fancy? I say, "I can't do anything right, can I?"

Abruptly she turns and walks right up to me. "No, you can't. When were you going to tell us?"

"Tell you what?"

She couldn't hate me more just at that moment. "Your parents? The hotel?"

"My parents? The hotel?" I seem to have become an echo.

"There aren't many Mr and Mrs Spittles around, are there? Will they close it? Paul says everyone is getting the sack."

She folds her arms across her chest while I put both hands on my temples and press my thumbs in my eye sockets until I see stars.

When I stop Penny is watching me blankly. "Please tell me exactly what you mean."

At last she looks unsure. "Magda told us she overheard Mr Hemingway talking with your Mother and an Indian man. She said they're buying the hotel."

"That's impossible. It's a wind up. It has to be." But it's actually not a surprise – it makes sense – this is what Mum's been doing with Jepson. "It's rubbish, Pen. She can't afford it." But Jepson could – and that would let Mum run a hotel. Even though she's never said as much, I know it is what she's always wanted.

Penny doesn't believe me. "Paul says you've been spying for them all along."

I can't think of anything to say that won't sound false.

"There you are." Natalie bounces up, holding a reluctant looking Nigel Sodding Parsons by the hand. She is as alive as I've ever seen her. "That was brill. Thank you Harry. I know you didn't want to come, but thank you." For a fraction I think she wants to kiss me but she controls herself.

Penny has folded her arms. She looks miserable. "I think I'll go back. I've a bit of a headache." No one tries to stop her.

Natalie looks a little disappointed but rallies to say, "Are you coming to Nige's? He says he has loads of grass."

I shake my head. "I think I'll go home, thanks."

She hesitates a fraction, but Nigel positively beams. As he eases her away, I can't help wondering if she realises he's talking about his Dad's silage.

# MONDAY 2ND AUGUST 1976

## Chapter Fifty-Five

## Punch and Judy

I'm awake at six thirty, my ringing ears stopping me going back to sleep. When I peer out of the kitchen window I nearly have heart failure; McNoble is curled up on the swing. I suppose he's waiting for Ruth. Some sixth sense makes him look at the house at that moment. Like a waking anaconda he unwinds himself and comes to the backdoor.

***

He's quite at home in our kitchen. While I make tea he sits at the table.

"Ruth's a sweet thing, but fucking dumb. It took me until last night for her to tell me why she's always worried."

I put his cup down and sit opposite. At least there's a table between us.

"That stupid box." He shakes his head. "God you're something. If it was me I'd sort you out but she won't have it. So this is what you'll do. You'll go fetch the box, and give it to me and Ruth will be happy again." He sips his tea.

I watch his hands, still wrapped round his cup. There's no sign of that knife. A voice in the back of my head wonders if he knows about the diamonds. I'm sure he can't or he'd mention them. Cautiously I say, "Did she say anything about it?"

"Like what?"

Dina appears, rubbing her eyes. "What are you doing here?" She pours herself a cup.

"Bog off, bitch." McNoble turns to me. "She said you had it."

I can feel the sweat trickling down my spine. Dina sits down next to the thug. "What does Harry have?"

"Her box."

"Not that stupid thing? God, Ruth's obsessed with crap."

He slams his fist on the table, making everyone's cup jump. "Shut your gob, can't you?" To me: "She wants it now."

Dina laughs as she stirs her tea. "Well, she'll be disappointed then."

Something snaps. In one typically swift movement he grabs her throat and hisses "Shut up, can't you?"

Dina's amazing; she doesn't so much as blink until he lets her go; then she massages her throat and says, "How brave. Picking on a girl. What would Daddy diddums say?"

He loses it completely and raises his fist. To my surprise, and probably everyone's, I shout 'no' and lunge across the table at him, but my legs are trapped and I fall well short. McNoble isn't so restricted and clouts me on the side of my head.

I'm trying to shake off the stars and sparkles when he cries out. "Fuck. Bitch."

I'm guessing Dina has thrown his tea into his face because he's wiping it hard as he grabs her and throws her to the floor. I stumble round to their side and there's a lot of lashing out and thrashing about at the end of which both Dina and I are on the floor with him standing over us. We're all panting hard.

I just know he's planning on what particular pain to inflict, but Mrs Ojha appears, tugging her dressing gown closed. "What's going on?"

McNoble uncurls his fists and sneers. For a moment he looks like he's about to have a go at Mrs Ojha but he pushes past her. Seconds later the backdoor slams and he's gone.

It's like nothing has happened. Mrs Ojha picks up a broken saucer, wipes the spilt tea and takes the bread from the breadbin. "Toast?"

I can feel the blood trickling from my nose and a bruise has already appeared on Dina's cheek. We both stare at Mrs Ojha's back as she switches on the stove and then we're both in fits. Oh I love you, Mrs Ojha.

***

We take our food to the swing. Dina checks my face and says, "What is it with this box?"

I close my eyes, faking a wince. "Do you think it's broken?"

"No. The box – it's ok if you don't want to say."

I can feel the hurt in her voice. If I tell her the truth she'll make me give the diamonds back. Instead I say, "I heard something really weird last night. There's this rumour that Mum is buying Hemingways."

Dina looks as stunned as I felt yesterday. "Mum? On her own?"

"Penny said Mum and Ravi were talking to Mr Hemingway about it."

"That's mental."

"I know. She said everyone thinks I'm their spy."

Dina can't stop shaking her head. "She can't run the B&B so how could she run a hotel?" Another thought strikes her. "And she's always saying we're broke so where's the money coming from?"

Something Penny said is nagging at me. She said 'Mr and Mrs Spittle', but she can't mean Dad. That wouldn't make sense.

Dina jolts me back to the now. "Has she heard?"

"Sorry? Has who heard what?"

Dina looks down at her feet.

I begin to repeat my question but she jumps off the swing and heads indoors. "Bye."

I watch her go, wondering why she has to be so weird when it hits me: the bloody test results. I should go after her but, just now work seems more pressing.

## Chapter Fifty-Six

## That Bastard Child

There are three drinkers this morning. If I wasn't so overwrought I'd be bored. Penny is waiting for me when I close up. She doesn't smile. "I'm off to the doctors. Do you want to come?"

"Sure."

There's clearly no thaw and there's no conversation. We part by the surgery, me mumbling about needing to go to the shops.

The pawnbrokers is more a shed than a shop and not at all welcoming. I have several moments of doubt up to and including standing on the threshold; it's then I see Mrs Potts crossing the road and dart inside.

The man behind the counter is stooped, his skin an odd bluey colour. Despite the sweltering heat he's wearing corduroy trousers, a thick wool shirt and a cardigan, which looks filthy enough to be a breeding ground for maggots.

"Yes?"

"Are you Frank? Sven Andersen suggested I come."

"Ah Master Sven. A good customer. Are you redeeming for him?"

"No, I want to see how much I might get for these."

I pull out two diamonds. Frank puts one on a glass sheet and screws an eyeglass in place, prodding the stone with a pencil. He then picks it up firmly in tweezers and scratches the glass. He repeats with the second.

"Look real enough. Where'd you get them?"

"A gift."

"Really?" He looks again. "I'm no expert, but these look like Sierra Leone blues; the legal route is via Belgium where they're all cut. So these uncut beauties must have been brought in illegally." He peers at me through the eyeglass. "Sure you didn't smuggle them in a sock to avoid the duty? We get lots of that around here, being near the sea as we are."

"No, no, of course not."

Frank leers at me; the eyeglass emphasises his squint. "I know the local bobby. Could give him a quick call. Just to check your paperwork's ok?"

I stare at the stones. "I… they came from my Gran. Old family heirloom. Years in the family. No papers." After a swallow I add. "She's dead. Can't confirm."

It takes Frank a moment of further prodding before he nods. "Twenty quid each. If you don't repay me after a month I'll keep them."

"Twenty? Surely they're worth a lot more?"

"Yeah? So what were you expecting?"

"Maybe… Maybe a hundred. Each."

Frank holds my gaze for what seems an age. "Yes, you may be right." He turns away and begins reading a book.

"So one hundred each then?"

"Fuck off. I said twenty."

"But—"

"Don't push your luck, sonny. You know you aren't in any position to barter. Twenty or find somewhere else. If you want it, fill this out." While he disappears in the back to fetch a jewel box I pull out the rest.

"How much for the lot?"

He looks at me carefully. "Hmm. Ninety."

Reluctantly I push them forward. He says, "Nice though."

While I make up a name and address he counts out the money. He says, as he hands it over. "If you've any more I'll take as many as you can get me."

\*\*\*

I sit on the surgery wall to wait for Penny. I feel light-headed. I've not enough to pay McNoble; everyone at work hates me; my family is coming unstitched; my face throbs; the hole in my leg is getting sore; the tear in my nob is taking ages to heal. What else can go wrong? I look up; Penny is marching towards me. Her expression tells me exactly what else has gone wrong.

\*\*\*

Penny takes charge. It's like last night is forgotten. "You can tell her after work; right now you're coming back to the Rat Pit for medicine."

All I recall of the bus ride is her saying 'she could have an abortion'. She feeds me sips of neat vodka. I vaguely recall her telling me Natalie is still with Nige. She leads me to the bar and makes me open up.

\*\*\*

I only register the tall redheaded woman with a million freckles and loads of wrinkles when she asks, "Are you Harry Spittle?" She offers me her hand. "Pat McNoble. Charlie's first. Stephen's Mum. Though I dare say you know him as Claude?" She's laughing at something, not that I see anything funny. "Do you always stare like that?"

I look away.

I know she's studying me; all I want is for her to go. She says, "You're very like your Grandfather." The only other sound is the clock ticking in reception. "Stephen has mentioned you."

"Really?"

"He's angry at his Father and you feature somewhere, not that he made much sense." She has these deep lines down her cheeks that grow with each smile. For a while she's happy with the tick-tock before saying, "He says Charlie's spending a lot of time with your Mother." She speaks quietly but to me it's almost a shout, an accusation.

It's really unsettling the way she just watches me so I turn my back and fiddle with the bottles.

"Is he?"

I'm torn between answering and telling her to leave me alone.

"I take it this annoys you as much as Stephen?"

I feel ready to explode. If I could leave my post I'd walk away.

In the mirror behind the bar I can see her fiddle with a compact. She says, "And Monica says she's spoken to you. Did she tell you she called me?" She's watching me in the mirror. "Turn round, Harry."

I do as I'm told.

"How much do you know about your Mother and Charlie? Not a lot, I'd guess."

I force myself to hold her gaze. She drops hers to put her compact away. "Pour me a G&T and I'll give you a history lesson." When she has her glass she says, "I married Charlie Jepson in April 1954 and we had Stephen in March 1956. Charlie met your Father in the Army. National Service. Maybe 1955 or thereabouts. You know Charlie is from around here, like your Dad?"

I nod.

"Good. They were friends... opposites attract I suppose. Then came Arthur's awful accident. In fact both of them were hurt, not that Charlie knew how badly until later, but Arthur nearly died." She pauses. "He lost an eye, didn't he?"

I manage another nod.

"Your Mother was a nurse. That's how they both met her. Charlie fell for your Mum... he couldn't resist a pretty woman... especially pretty and intelligent. Don't look like that, she was pretty. He proposed... even though he was married to me." She waits for a moment. "He never told your Mum about me, back home, pregnant with Stephen. It was all rather horrid." The ring on her right hand becomes her sole focus for a moment. "Anyway, Charlie's Mother and your Grandfather became involved... your Mum was very upset, or so I heard. We both were, of course, though looking back I think I knew, before then, our marriage wasn't going anywhere." She looks up at me. "In a way, your Mother was the catalyst, though it wasn't her fault. At the time, Charlie's Mother tried to stop us divorcing – she was Catholic you see – she never forgave him for being damned like that. I suppose that if it wasn't for Betsy, he might have left me then and gone off with your Mother."

While she's explaining I try and imagine asking her if she thinks Jepson is my Father. I can't.

"Betsy was a dreadful old woman – completely controlling. She tried to tell him what to do most of her life. She tried to tell all of us. She drove a wedge between Stephen and Charlie with her constant accusations. Not easy for a young boy to hear such bad things about his Father."

Something clicks. "Did he know about my Mother and Mr Jepson?"

She holds my gaze and smiles. "Oh yes, Harry. Only too well."

She goes on, "At the start Betsy tried to indoctrinate him, about how sinful they both were. I... I would have loved to have told her what I really thought but in the early days it was only her money that kept Stephen and me afloat." She looks away, I suppose thinking back to battles in the past. She says, "It took maybe ten years – after she met your Grandfather and heard a different side to the story – before she understood your Mother was as much a victim as me. But by then Stephen was at boarding school and I had moved into a flat in Southampton. I suppose Stephen has never really forgiven either of them."

She finishes her drink. "So? Does that help? Any questions?"

She just stares; it's like she knows I have a question and she is prepared to wait as long as it takes. I'm determined not to ask, but then she reaches over and takes my hand. "Come on, Harry. What is it?"

"Do you think — ?"

The bar to the door slams back against the banquette and a flushed Monica Jepson enters. "Hello Pat. I thought you were coming later?"

Mrs McNoble lets me go. The two women greet each other awkwardly. "I had an early shift. It's given me the chance to meet Harry; I even told him some ancient history."

Mrs Jepson smiles awkwardly. "Did you? Perhaps we should let him work and go and sit over there." She points at a table.

I'm about to lose my only chance to ask my big question. I take a deep breath. "Mrs McNoble, do you think Mr Jepson could be my Father?"

Both women stare at me. Mrs McNoble is the first to react. She says, "Why do you ask that?"

I feel dreadful and want to sink into the floor. "I know it's true, isn't it? They wanted to marry. She was pregnant when she got married to Dad and he was just out of hospital. That's why he's come back, isn't it? He's found out and… and that's why she's buying the hotel. He's paying for it, for her."

I'm vaguely aware that Mrs McNoble looks astonished. But it's Mrs Jepson's reaction that startles me. It's absolutely clear she knows all about the purchase. She manages to cover it quickly and while Mrs McNoble is still somewhat dazed she eases her to the table. Neither of them come back to speak to me, and they leave after an hour. So much remains unclear but one thing is plain – at least I know now why McNoble hates me and why paying him off will not end my troubles with him.

\*\*\*

Two hours later, after I've locked up, I take the keys to reception. Mrs Jepson is perched on the edge of one of the ghastly orange sofas, reading a magazine. I join her, as I know she expects. We don't talk until Magda goes into Mr Hemingway's office.

"I'm sorry Harry. I should have said."

"How long have you known?"

"A while. It's why I was worried about him seeing your Mother. That's why I confronted him and why…" She drops her gaze.

"Can Mrs McNoble help?"

"No. He relies on her to make sure Stephen keeps in contact – he's very loyal to his Mother – but she also gets money from him so it's not easy for her." Everything about her says she's run out of ideas.

"Why didn't you say when you knew? In your room."

"I hoped it wasn't true. But Mr Hemingway confirmed he was seeing your parents and…"

"Is my Dad involved?"

"Of course."

"But if they're having an affair, how come Dad—"

She stops me with a gesture. "It's not about an affair. Not for Charlie."

"What do you mean?"

"I… It's better you don't know."

I grab her arm and tug her to face me. "It's my family. I want to know."

She takes an age. "I can't be sure but I think it's a front. You know I told you Robin Andersen and Charlie used to work together? Well, when they fell out, years ago Charlie promised never to do business down here. But recently Charlie has been having some problems and I think he and Robin having been talking again. I really don't believe Charlie is involved because of some old love for your Mother."

This is all getting too horrible. I can't think what to say or do. After what seems like a lifetime Mrs Jepson says, "If it's any consolation I don't think – and neither does Pat – that Charlie is your Father."

"Jesus." I cover my face and begin rocking. I'm only vaguely aware that she's pulled me to my feet and is holding me tight. I can feel the tears and wipe them away furiously. Then she holds my face and kisses me. On the lips. She leans in close and whispers. "Come on. Come with me. We'll go to my room. He's not coming back tonight." Her lips brush my ear and electricity pulses through me. "I think you need a hot bath and a massage."

I'm totally discombobulated but there's something in the way she glances over my shoulder that makes me turn round. Magda and Penny are watching us. Mrs Jepson pulls me slightly but I stand my ground. Instead of pulling harder she says, in a soft voice that still carries, "I'll run that bath. See you in a few minutes."

Neither Penny nor Magda say anything; while Magda continues to stare at me, Penny storms into Mr Hemingway's office, closing the door with a slam.

# TUESDAY 3RD AUGUST 1976

## Chapter Fifty-Seven

## Setting the Trap

I've become quite adept at the 'creep and sneak' exit, but today I'm foiled by poor timing; as I reach the bottom step, Noor and Sajid emerge from Nanty's room. Their noise and general kerfuffle brings Mrs Ojha and Dina from the kitchen.

"Are you off already, Harry?" I'm happy to hold Mrs Ojha's gaze.

"Yes. I… we'll be busy I expect." I try and wipe Sajid off my trousers like a stubborn stain, his adhesion being the perfect excuse not to make eye contact with Dina. When he finally drops away, some force beyond my powers to resist makes me look at her; her stare is as blank as any canvas and it triggers a quick head shake. All I mean is 'not here, in front of the Ojhas', but she turns away with what I'm certain is a slight relaxing of the shoulders.

I'm about to follow her, to correct the mistake, when Sajid kicks me hard in the shin. By the time Mrs Ojha has apologised and administered suitable chastisement, Dina has gone.

*\*\*\**

At work, different groups have formed though I'm not allowed into any of them. Even at meal times I'm excluded, except by Sven who asks me loudly if I've 'had' Magda yet.

I really want him to have the first curse but I never see an opportunity to give him one.

***

After lunch I take my latest book, The Second Foundation by Asimov, and go to find somewhere quiet in the gardens. There's a hot nipping wind blowing up some dust and keeping the gardens pretty empty. It's a surprise when Mrs Jepson appears in her silk robe with towel under her arm, clearly intent on sunbathing.

"I'm sorry about last night. Do you forgive me?"

"I… yes. Of course."

"I was rather down, you know." She sits next to me and blinks the dust from her eyes. "It's never as bad as we think, is it?" She turns her face away. "We can't sit here. Let's find some shelter." She stands, clearly waiting for me.

"I'm fine here. Thanks."

She blinks hard again. "Don't be silly. The gardener told me about this private meadow. We can go there. It's very sheltered."

A nasty little ball of sick starts melting in my stomach. "Where?"

"Over there. There's this little gap. I've used it a couple of times and it's very good. Don't you think it's kind of him to tell just me? He knows I like to sunbathe and it does give me some real privacy." She adjusts her towel and bag so she can take my hand, giving me a tug. "Come on, Harry. I won't eat you. It's time you oiled my back, as you promised."

I just goggle at her. I just know she's topless under that robe; I also know Cyril will be somewhere watching her, waiting to see where she goes.

"Are you coming? Maybe we will think of some way to warn your parents. Two minds are better than one they say."

I'm in a total fug of confusion. I make an excuse, telling her I need to get a towel and watch as she slides through the hidden entrance into the meadow. As soon as she's out of sight, I hurtle back, past the greenhouses, certain of what I'll find.

***

Cyril is standing in the viewing space he's made, staring into the meadow. On the bench next to the gap is the tub of Nivea. Even without the regular, low-level 'phwoars', his rhythmic arm movements give away what's happening.

"Cyril…" I hiss, hoping Mrs Jepson is far enough away not to hear me. "Cyril, you must stop."

"Jesus, boiy, 'ooo made me jump." He's furious as he turns round, one hand shielding his nob.

"You can't watch Mrs Jepson. She's a guest."

"Fuck orf. I ain't hurting no one." He narrows his eyes and says, "Oi bets you want a look. She'll be fiddlin' hersel' soon." He shudders, so excited he can't even 'phwoar'.

"No. This isn't right…"

He's angry now. "Look, boiy, yous can wait and have some winky-wanky arter Oi'm done or you fuck orf." With that he snatches up the tub from the bench and turns back to the hedge.

"NO. No, you mustn't." I make a grab for his nearest arm but he's far too strong. He shrugs off my hand and bodily lifts me off my feet. In seconds he's carried me to the nearest greenhouse and tossed me inside, shutting and blocking the door with the bench.

I'm desperate to get out and warn Mrs Jepson but the bench is really hard to shift.

As I struggle he keeps up a running commentary. "She's got nice titties boiy. Chroist, she's taken her cozzy orf. Ow Gawd..." There's a scratching sound before his face appears by the window. "Where's the new pot? Thissun's empty."

In the struggle I seem to have knocked his new tub of Nivea onto the floor; the lid has come loose and white gloop is oozing on to the dirt.

"Gie's me tha' new tub. NOW." He sounds demented and the last thing I need is him throwing me around again. I scrabble on the floor, scoop up as much as I can and hand it to him.

As soon as he turns away, I return to fighting the door. I'm pretty frantic because, while I can't see what's happening I can bloody hear. First it's his breathing, like a kettle beginning to boil; then there's this slopping sound, like a trawler landing its catch. That lasts until I manage to shift the bench sufficiently and struggle outside. Just as I squeeze free, everything goes very still and quiet before Cyril emits a roar that would make the *Saturn V* launch seem tame. After that there's an ominous silence.

***

Cyril's engorged and now perforated penis is a dreadful sight. It seems still to be swelling, but not in a good way. It's laying across his palm, glistening from the cream with the little black cactus spines, which I must have swept up with the spilt contents, very obviously embedded from the tip to root. His face is the same plum colour as the be-spined bell-end.

We're both transfixed and it's only Mrs Jepson asking if everything is alright from the other side of the hedge that sends Cyril scuttling back towards the hotel. From behind he looks like a determined competitor in an egg and spoon race.

As he goes he hyphenates yowls of pain with almost indecipherable curses.

"Harry, are you there? What's going on?"

I take a deep breath and step into the space Cyril has vacated.

"Are you there? Harry, was that the gardener?"

I can see right into the meadow. Mrs Jepson is only a few feet away, hands on hips, completely naked.

"Harry? Are you there?"

It's odd that I can be so close but she can't see me. I step back slowly so as not to make any noise.

"Harry? Don't play games. Come round here. We need to talk."

***

I don't go to her; rather I head for my bike, to cycle home. I want to go; of course I do. She's beautiful and naked and has pubic hair that doesn't remind me of a politician. God knows what might happen. But I can't; she's a liar. She didn't tell me about the hotel purchase when she could have done. She didn't tell me the truth about Mum and Mr Jepson; I had to meet Mrs McNoble to find that out.

And that night in her room, when she told me Mr Jepson had hit her with a golf club and showed me the bruise? She lied about that, too, because as she turned in front of me, exposing both hips and buttocks, there was no bruise, no mark at all, just pearly white skin. She must have drawn it on – with her make-up or something – just to confuse me. One minute I'm feeling like I may have done something right, in stopping Cyril; the next I feel like a fool again. I know what I should do. I should be home, facing Dina, helping her. God knows what I'll say but I won't lie. Not anymore.

## Chapter Fifty-Eight

## All Hell

I'm marginally calmer when I push open the back gate. Mrs Ojha is on the swing, knitting, while Nanty holds the wool between her knees. There's no sign of anyone else.

"Is Dina about?"

"She's still at work."

I look at my watch. Why didn't I work that out? "What about Mum? Or Dad?"

Mrs Ojha shakes her head. "You won't have heard. She had to go to the police. Your Father went too." She must see my surprise. "It's nonsense, of course. Someone has made an outrageous accusation that your Mother is the pumpkin vandal. I really find—"

Just now, pumpkins are the least of my worries. "Mrs Ojha, I'm sorry to interrupt, but I need to ask you both a question." She looks rather affronted, but, after a minor hesitation, bows and goes back to her knitting. Nanty smiles at me. I take a very deep breath. "Have either of you heard about Mum buying Hemingways? Maybe with Dad? Or Ravi?"

Mrs Ojha doesn't move but Nanty doesn't hesitate. She nods. As she does so, Mrs Ojha lays down her knitting. "Who told you?"

"Is it true?"

"Ravi and I wanted to say something to you but your Mother swore us to secrecy."

I'm fuming. "So it is true?"

She nods.

"And is Mr Jepson involved? Is he?"

For the first time, Nanty drops her gaze. Nanty has always answered my questions openly and honestly. I give her a chance to say something, or nod but she won't look at me. Mrs Ojha pats my arm and stands. "I'll make us some tea."

When she's gone, I reach forward and hug Nanty while she strokes my hair. I say, "I know he is, Nanty, and I don't trust him."

To my surprise she says, clearly, "I know, darling." They are the first proper words I've heard since I came home and I suppose they take an enormous effort on Nanty's part. She pats my head again, buried in her lap; it must be the cloud of lavender dust that brings the tears back to my eyes.

***

An hour later, I'm listening to the Allman Brothers in my room when the front door bangs open. Dina's voice calls out and her feet pound up the stairs, followed by her bedroom door slamming.

I force myself to go and knock, to open the door on hearing her permission, to stand and stare at her. I've run through what I'll say many times already but I can't act for toffee and as soon as Dina looks at me she wails and buries her head in her pillow.

Her howling like a wounded animal brings Mrs Ojha, then Noor. I feel utterly and completely useless. Mrs Ojha takes in me, then Dina, and says, "Was it positive?"

I stare at her and nod. How did she know?

Mrs Ojha pulls Dina to her; after initial resistance, Dina allows herself to be cuddled. "Oh, you poor thing." Mrs Ojha looks at me over the top of Dina's head.

"Harry, take the children and set them up in the kitchen, please. There are reading books there. Then call the Angel Hotel and tell your Mother to come home as soon as she can. Tell her it's what she feared." She goes back to soothing Dina.

Noor's tiny dry hand takes mine and pulls me away. She sits a compliant Sajid at the kitchen table with a glass of milk, two Jaffa Cakes and his Billy Goat Gruff book and then takes me to the dining room. There she sits me down and pulls out the Lymington telephone book. She finds the hotel, dials the number and hands me the phone. Mum's not there. They take my frankly incomprehensible message with good grace.

Noor stares at me with her two solemn brown eyes. "Mummy says she's pregnant."

"Does everyone know?"

"Mummy said she thought she was when Dina was sick every morning this last week. Is Jim the father?"

Jim. I need to tell him. Poor sod. Noor follows me to the backdoor. The sun is a flaming red and purple with a tail of green and gold streaking across the sky; it's like the start of the Apocalypse even though I know it's just the effect of sunlight on a release of something toxic from the Fawley Oil refinery.

## Chapter Fifty-Nine

## Stand Up and Be Counted

Jim's house is about a mile from ours, in the village, not far from Uncle and Aunt's garage. As I turn by the post office, I see Jim and his Dad, Reggie James, looking at the cars for sale on the garage forecourt and have a panic attack. I'm certain if he sees me he'll know I've pawned his diamonds, but before I can turn and run Jim waves me over.

"Hi Harry; you know my Dad?" Jim looks at his Father, a brown-faced tubby man with long hair in a greying ponytail. "This is Dina's brother."

Mr James doesn't look away from this American car with huge fins. All he says is, 'nice girl', but it's enough to make me want to scream.

"Can I have a word, Jim? Now."

Jim looks at me curiously while his Dad walks over to another car. He says, "What is it?"

"It's rather private. Jim, can we...?"

His Dad stops and looks at me; he is highly amused. "No secrets in our family, mate. Tell us."

He moves again, to the other side of the car he's looking at, so he can't see me; I mouth at Jim 'Dina'. Jim nods and points at the gravel drive that leads to the WI hall. As we walk away his Dad says, "Oi, you two, I could do with a laugh." But at least he doesn't follow.

When we're out of his hearing Jim says, "Sorry about that. I can't wait for him to go; he's a real arsehole." He leads me round the back of the Scout Hut, to a small shed sandwiched between it and the WI hall. When Jim pulls the door open, the scent of recently smoked weed makes my eyes water. There are a couple of old chairs on which we sit, hidden from the world. Before I say anything Jim says, "What's up? What's she said?"

I take a deep breath. "It's a bit complicated Jim. I need you to just listen and—"

Jim jerks a finger towards where we left his Dad. "It's him, isn't it?" He shakes his head. "They thought I couldn't see, but I did. She... they were kissing." He looks dreadful, on the verge of tears. "He made her, didn't he?"

I nod, feeling just as sick as him.

He covers his face. "It's like Ruth." It takes him a time to explain. "Last time he was home. Easter. She came round when Mum was out. I was revising in the garden and – I don't think he realised I was there – I could see right into his study." He shakes his head. "What did he do to Dina?" I have no idea what to say. He must take my silence as an accusation or something because he says, "Does she hate me?"

"No mate. She loves you. That's... oh Christ."

"What?"

I find myself wishing Mrs Ojha was here; she'd know what to do. There are wasps flying in and out of a crack under the eaves, getting more and more frenzied to the point where they'll lash out at anything. I know how they feel. "It's like this..."

**WEDNESDAY 4<sup>TH</sup> AUGUST 1976**

## Chapter Sixty

## Salad Days

When I get up, Mum's on the phone giving someone a hard time. In the kitchen, Papaji and Nanty are playing cards. Nanty is using both hands. I was so over-wrought yesterday, what with Cyril and the hotel purchase and everything, that I never noticed her original lumpy plaster cast has gone; in its place there's a much lighter bandage allowing her to move her fingers. When I pick up her hand and inspect it solemnly, she smiles before glancing over my shoulder.

"That is a sight for sore eyes, Edna." Mum kisses her on the cheek before taking Mrs Ojha's hand and squeezing it. There's a nod from Mrs Ojha who offers Mum a tray with tea and toast. Mum shakes her shoulders and sighs. "Thank you."

I study Mrs Ojha for some sign of pleasure at this new attitude from Mum but she remains as placid as ever. She says, her back to me, "Dina is lucky to have such a Mother at a time like this."

"Have they decided what to do?" I ask.

She turns slowly and stares. "Do?"

"I... you know, what happens to it. The baby."

I can feel three pairs of eyes boring into me. Suddenly I'm not wanted. Mrs Ojha says, "If I were you, Harry, I'd concentrate on persuading your parents you are worthy of their support. Have you been trying to improve your reading?"

Bloody hell. Why is everyone out to get me?

***

Just in case I pocket a battered copy of The Time Machine and stick it in my pocket. By comparison with home, everyone at work is on edge. The sense that something is about to happen is pervasive. Rodney scowls at me and chunters to himself. He spends ages in the kitchens, no doubt fermenting revolution. Even the guests seem affected and no one bothers to come into the bar before the lunch gong sounds, other than Sven. "So your latest conquest has deserted you, I see."

"Who are you talking about now?"

"Are there so many? The insatiable Mrs Jepson."

"She's gone?"

"Yes. All of a sudden. According to Magda she had a terrible fight with Mister and then checked out in a hurry. Big sunglasses, even indoors. Maybe hiding something?" I know the pause is just to see if I'll react; I don't give him the satisfaction. "One vodka and orange and one slimline tonic. No ice in either."

Gratefully, I turn away to fix the drinks.

He says, "Frank tells me you've used his services. You impressed him, which is not easy."

"Did I?"

Sven picks up the tray with the drinks. He says, "Harold, you need to be careful. My Father has been asking after you. You may not know my Father?"

"No."

"You don't want to, believe me. I'd start to worry when 'asking after' turns into 'taking an interest'. If Mr Jepson put you up to the diamond thing then you need to watch who you help." Sven gives me a curious look and wanders away with his drinks, leaving a nasty cold chill in his wake.

***

I'm still trying to grapple with what Sven meant when I'm distracted by raised voices from the dining room. Well, one raised voice: Mrs Potts, who sounds very peeved. Intrigued I pick up my tray, ostensibly to collect empty glasses and go and have a look.

Mrs Potts is lunching with Ms Glebe in Amos' section. Amos and Mrs Potts are in the middle of a standoff.

"I SAID A CAESAR SALAD, YOU STUPID MAN."

Amos' bug eyes are even more distended than usual. "Yes madam. That is—"

"NO, IT IS NOT." The chandeliers rattle. All conversation has ceased. "A CAESAR SALAD HAS…"

"Madam, this is a classic—" His voice is a squeak, which stands no chance.

"…EGGS AND TUNA AND…"

His cheeks are almost translucent with fiery red speckles. "Madam, a Niçoise—"

"ARE YOU CONTRADICTING ME?"

Amos bangs his head with his hand, an understandable if unsubtle reaction to her explosive consonants. "If you'd let me ex—"

"I DO NOT WANT YOUR FEEBLE EXCUSES. I WANT MY SALAD."

Amos pauses and watches.

She says, "WELL?"

"You have it, Madam. What do you expect me to do with it, Madam?"

"DO WITH IT? DO WHAT YOU LIKE."

Amos is beyond recall. "Right. If you won't eat it, you can fucking wear it." He tips the bowl over her head. Crispy lettuce and croutons drip from her light blue perm onto her shoulders and thence to the floor. Ms Glebe appears to be practicing making the perfect 'o' with her mouth.

Sven pulls Amos away. To my horror the old foghorn recognises me. "HAROLD, HELP ME!" With a mayo dressing, her normal formidable appearance has gone; she's just rather pathetic. "HELP ME! I MUST SEE CUTHBERT."

"Cuth...? Oh, Mr Hemingway. Of course." No one else comes to my rescue; all the waiters, Penny included, are watching me with undisguised contempt. Christian is nearest the door as I help Mrs Potts from the room. He hisses as I pass. "Man, you really are the Centre of Evil. Bad Vibes, dude."

***

Out of the public gaze, Mrs Potts marches to the reception desk. Magda bars the way, but the first 'CUTHBERT' brings Mr Hemingway to the door and he waves her in. Magda closes the door and says, "So vot 'appened?"

I explain, ending with 'everyone thinks it's my fault'.

Magda takes my arms in her iron grip. "Grow up, 'arry. Vot do you expect? Zey 'ear your parents are buying 'emingvays and zey fear zey are losing zere jobs? Zat's vhy Amos is zo angry. Mr 'emingvay vill not tell zem vot is 'appening."

"Are they losing their jobs?"

Magda shakes her head; does she mean they're not or she can't tell me? I'm still pondering on that when Mrs Potts sweeps past us and out of the front doors.

Mr Hemingway follows rubbing his temples. "God that woman. One crisis after another." He notices me and glares. "Yes, and while I'm on the subject of crises, Harold, what did you do to Cyril?"

Why, I wonder, does he only remember my name when he's angry? "Me sir?"

"Yes, of course. He was incoherent with rage yesterday... well, he's incoherent most of the time. But he was pretty clear that you had some role in the injury to his thingy."

"Sir?"

The phone rings and Magda answers it. She offers it to Mr Hemingway. "Mr Jepson?"

Mr Hemingway shakes his head as he leans close to me, whispering. "I'm beginning to wonder what you're up to. Charlie said he thought you and Monica were trying something. Well you listen to me, my lad. If I find out you're also behind Amos' mad interlude well woe betide. Christ..."

Magda repeats, "Mr Jepson."

"Yes I'm coming." He comes in even closer. "Cyril's threatening to resign because of you. And after her complaint, Amos will have to be dismissed. Apart from Paul, they're what keep this place afloat and Charlie knows it. If he starts chiselling me on price because of you then..."

"Sir, Mr Jepson."

"Coming." He sweeps back into his office.

Magda looks at me. Another crack-brained idea hits me. "Magda, just stop him sacking Amos, ok? Give me a chance to persuade her to withdraw her complaint. Please."

"You can do zis, 'arry?"

"I have no idea, but I'm bloody well going to try. I just need to stop the old bag."

Magda holds the flap up. "Go. GO." She pats me on the bottom as I race past. "Go on, 'arry."

For once God is on my side; said old bag is waiting by her car. As I race up she presses a small lace hanky to her eyes.

"YES DEAR? DID I FORGET SOMETHING?"

"I... Mrs Potts... I need an enormous favour. A really huge favour."

Her hanky disappears to be replaced by a beady stare. "A FAVOUR?"

This is not going to work. "Amos? That waiter? I need you to drop your complaint."

Her eyes narrow. "WHY WOULD I DO THAT?"

"I can get you some more of that super cannabis."

She grabs my arm, checking to see if anyone is listening. "REALLY I DON'T KNOW WHAT YOU MEAN."

"But Dina said…" My hopes are fading rapidly

She looks around and whispers urgently, "I want to see your Mother's pumpkins destroyed."

"What?"

"If you can destroy your Mother's pumpkins then I'll think about it."

"But Mrs Potts—"

"Either you say yes now or the poof is history."

She leans back, happy to give me time. I nod. "All right. I'll do it tonight and let you know—"

"I WANT TO SEE IT DONE FOR MYSELF."

"What? Oh all right. When do you—?"

"TEN O'CLOCK. I'LL BRING A FRIEND TO HELP. BE BY YOUR BACK GATE."

"You must tell the police it's not Mum who's the vandal."

She ignores me and waves Ms Glebe over. As she gets in her car she says, "DON'T LET ME DOWN."

***

When I turn back to the hotel, I'm confronted by the same view I had on my first day. When was that? A decade ago? Walking down the steps is Penny. She takes her time reaching me. Her expression gives nothing away. "Sven said—"

"It's not true."

"You don't know what I was going to say."

"I don't have to. He lies instinctively."

I wait but she says no more. Eventually I brush past heading for the staff entrance.

She says to my back, "What about Mrs Jepson?"

I spin back; she has her hands on her hips. "What about her? She's a guest. She's left. End of story." Again I give her a chance to reply but she doesn't so much as twitch. "What about you and Chris?"

Red dots appear on her cheeks. She says, "He's just a friend."

"Of course he is. That's why he was staying in the Rat Pit."

She laughs briefly. "That? He was stoned. He couldn't get home." She kicks her foot into the gravel. "He's not interested in girls. Not really."

"He's a homo?"

"God knows. He... never mind. All he cares about is acting and that goes for his relationships as well." She walks over to me and we head for the hotel. "What did you do to Cyril?"

"Nothing. Well, not deliberately."

"Cactus spines in his willy? I don't want to imagine how that happened. And Magda just told me you're trying to save Amos' job?"

"I... maybe..."

"How?"

When I explain, she looks unsure. "Won't your Mum go mad?"

"Probably. It's a price worth paying. She's got it in for me anyway."

"I bet she hasn't."

"She wants to stop me going back to uni." When I explain she shakes her head.

"That's plain silly. Now, have you got a camera? You'll need a record if your plan with that woman is to work."

She smiles. "You can borrow mine if you like? There are ten shots left. Maybe Dina can..." She stops. "Oh God, how is she? Have you told her?"

"She's ok... I suppose. Mum's taken charge."

Penny looks horrified. "She must be distraught. I can't imagine anything worse. Do you think she'd like me to have a word?"

"Would you? That would be fab. I mean, thanks, that's..."

"I'll talk to your Mum about uni as well, if you like?"

"I'm not sure. She may not like it."

"Well there's only one way to find out. Come on."

"But my shift? I can't just leave the bar."

Penny grabs my arms, and glares at me. "Who's going to sack the boss's son? Don't look surprised. Magda told me you didn't know a thing about the hotel sale; it's only because I believe her that I'm talking to you at all." She puts on a spurt of speed. "Wait by the car park; I'll get Nige's keys. We'll 'borrow' his bike."

I watch her go; Nigel Sodding Parsons must have stayed over, which means only one thing. I'm surprised that I really don't give a damn.

***

When we arrive home Dina, Mum and Mrs Ojha are on the swing with Nanty in a garden chair. Dina looks tired but delighted to see us – well, Penny. After a few pleasantries the two girls disappear to Dina's bedroom ostensibly to listen to a Yes album.

Mum hugs me. She's lost weight; definitely no longer spongy. "I'm sorry darling. I...we, your Father and me never meant to worry you both. I had a good long talk with Dina last night. You've both been amazing."

While I take Dina's seat, Mrs Ojha puts her knitting down. "I'll just take Nanty to powder her nose. Tea?" Mum and I nod.

Mum seems completely content to sit in silence; the Mum of a day or two ago – on edge, smoking, lecturing me about secrets – has been replaced by this calm, reflective woman. I don't really recognise either as my Mum. So I ask, "Are you really buying Hemingways?"

I watch her profile carefully. I think she colours a bit but it might just be the strong sunlight. She gives nothing away as she says, "What have you heard?"

"Just that. It's common knowledge at the hotel."

She twists to look at me, a crease of worry across her face. "Really?" She rubs her face like she wants to get rid of sleep; she's no longer relaxed. "If I tell you, promise me you'll be discreet?" She pauses for me to speak or nod but I just keep watching. "I suppose it's difficult for Cuthbert to keep it quiet. Yes, your Father and I are planning on buying Hemingways."

"Is…?" Suddenly this is very difficult. "Is Mr Jepson involved?"

It takes her an age to answer. "Has someone mentioned him?"

"He is, isn't he?"

She won't look at me.

"Why do you want to do this with him?"

"Why?" She looks at me with a scrunched up face like I'm mad. "It's our chance, our opportunity. Don't you see? Not a pokey little B&B but a hotel with such potential. I've always wanted this. Always and… Don't you see?"

"But why with him? With Jepson?"

"Charlie has a lot of interests, particularly in accommodation. This is a chance to spread his portfolio. He doesn't want to be involved day to day. That's us. He's very much a silent partner. We... with Ravi... You know, I wasn't going to go ahead if Ravi hadn't dropped into our laps with all that expertise. I don't think... no, we couldn't have contemplated it. Serendipity. Your Father's coup, that. Charlie provides most of the funds – we will pay him for our share over time and Ravi will buy in eventually – and we..."

"Mum. Stop. He lied to you. And Dad. He wanted to marry you and he was already married. He ruined his first marriage, didn't he? How can you trust him?"

The frown is back. "Who's been talking about Charlie?"

I feel sick. "Mrs McNoble. And Mrs Jepson."

Mum is nodding. "Pat and Monica. You mustn't just believe what people tell you, Harold. Sometimes they... well, they have their own reasons. I agree there's some history but that's in the past. Charlie is prepared to put in some money, that's all. It's a business deal for him."

Can that be right? Just a business deal? No affair? It doesn't fit with the kisses. "And Dad? He's happy?"

"Of course." She pats my leg; another patronising parental gesture. "It's been hard for him; he's not a risk taker by nature but, yes, I would say he's keen."

We sit in silence for a while. Then I say, "I wish I'd known. It's been very awkward at the hotel."

"That's why we didn't tell you. It had to be hush-hush. Charlie's very astute. He knew there was a risk of the price being pushed up if news got out that Mr Hemingway was selling. This is an off-market deal, Harold. It means no one else is involved. Charlie is very shrewd like that. If others knew, well they might make a higher bid that we couldn't afford. But we're nearly there. That's why we never said."

"You don't trust me, do you?"

"That's not it. Of course we do. But you work with these people; if you knew... if you let something slip. It would have been intolerable to ask you to carry that burden."

"Well, that's pretty much where I am now. They all think I'm your spy and they're going to be sacked."

Mum does look genuinely surprised. "But that's plain silly. We will close for refurbishment at the end of September, but they'll all be needed when we reopen, assuming they haven't found new jobs. I think the only one we plan to get rid of is the chef, Paul – especially after what you said on Sunday though Hemingway isn't to know; he treats him like a son."

She looks at me in a way that says, 'there, I trust you'. She's facing me now, a gleam in her eye. "I've always dreamt we'd run a hotel. I know we can do it." A noise makes her turn. Mrs Ojha is coming with the tea. Mum stands. "I must just pop to the toilet."

While Mrs Ojha ferries the tea things I try and work out what is true and what's not. I can't. It even looks as if Dad's been suckered into it. Maybe it isn't anything other than a business venture? Maybe it's another Monica Jepson lie.

When I look up both Mrs Ojha and Nanty are smiling at me. I'm in some sort of Panglossian nightmare – all's for the best in the best of all possible worlds – and look what happened to Candide. But sod this gushy love-in; I refuse to smile. Until I know who my real Father is I'm not smiling again.

Mrs Ojha taps me on the leg. "Harry, your Great Aunt has something."

Nanty pats her lap. It's a cheque to me for one hundred and fifty pounds, on Nanty's bank account, signed in a rather wobbly but entirely readable way by Edna Thoroughly. Mrs Ojha says, "Dina did a lot of talking last night, before your Mother got home. She explained about that boy Stephen and why you were fighting the other day."

I look from one woman to the other. Mrs Ojha says, "Dina told us about that boy. Pay him and be done."

"I didn't do anything."

While Nanty grips my hand Mrs Ojha says, "Think about your Mother, Harry. It's not going to help her, you fighting with his son, is it?"

They think it will smooth things out. If only they knew why he was so mad they'd realise it won't make the slightest difference.

## Chapter Sixty-One

## You Have Got To Be Joking

When I knock on Dina's door, Penny answers.

Whispering seems best. "How is she?"

"Ok. Sort of."

Dina is on her bed, reading an album cover. She says, "I can hear you. Did you like Eric?"

I say, "Yeah he was fantastic. I was really surprised how good—"

She turns the cover over, saying, "Penny told me I can get an abortion if I want."

Penny looks at me, pulling a face. She says, "I just went through the options; adoption is also possible..." She slips next to Dina who leans against her shoulder.

Dina says, "Mum expects me to have the baby. She doesn't care what I want." She's looking at me, waiting on my reaction, and I've no idea what to say. After a minute of awkward silence she says, "I just want to get away from here, but that's not going to happen now, is it?"

Penny hugs her. "Course it is. You can do your A-levels and go to uni if you want."

Dina is still staring at me. I'm really rather hoping one of them will tell me I can go. Dina says, "Do you want to be an Uncle, H?"

I assume nodding is the right answer but all that gets is a blank look from Dina and a glare from Penny. Dina says, "You'll be around, won't you? You didn't mean it when you said you'd leave for ever? I can't do this without you."

I nod again and try and look enthusiastic. Penny says, "There are still a lot of choices, Di, really. You—"

Dina pulls away. "God, let's stop talking about this, ok? Let's talk about something else."

Penny pulls herself upright and waves me to a chair. "I think Harry has something he wants to ask you, Di."

"What?" "What?"

We both look at each other, then Penny who is holding a small camera. "He wants your help."

## Chapter Sixty-Two

## Night Exercise

Dina is really keen, despite my misgivings. As a result the two girls are much more relaxed when Mum calls us downstairs. She's standing next to Mr Jepson, trying to look happy. Mum is busy, organising everyone to various seats, with Mrs Ojha's help. While this continues, Mr Jepson sidles over and says quietly, "Can we have a quick word, Harry? In private?" He doesn't wait but heads off for the side of the house. As soon as I turn the corner, he stops me, checks to make sure no one is following and grabs my shirt, banging me against the wall of the house. If all the air hadn't left my lungs I'd have cried out; as it is I just gasp, vaguely aware of a dopey wasp, disturbed by this violence, buzzing by my ear.

"What the fuck are you playing at?"

By way of reply I gurgle. The likeness between him and McNoble is suddenly very plain. He says, "I can take you winding up Hemingway about his fucking gardener and that poof of a waiter – keeps him on his toes. Monica too, stupid cow. She's learnt her lesson." He jerks his face in close so his spit sprays my cheek. "I'm having an affair with Veronica, am I?" He rams me back against the bricks. "Am I?" He lets me go a little. "Are you a cunning little shit or just fucking dumb?"

I try not to move, but I can't stop the shaking. I don't think I've crapped myself but I can't be sure about piss as my legs are both very warm. Out of the corner of my eye, I catch a glimpse of Rascal's ginger fur and green eyes. He must be loving this.

Mr Jepson lets me go completely and I slip to the floor. He crouches down in front of me. "You're just dumb, aren't you Harry? You don't have the brains." He pats my cheek. "If I didn't need Veronica I'd…" He twists his mouth into a smile. "I never thought I'd say this but tomorrow you are going to get us out of a little spot of bother."

Someone calls our names. He pushes himself upright and offers me his hand to pull me to my feet. "Come on." He dusts me down.

My throat won't work properly. Somehow I manage to squeak out, "What's this about, Mr Jepson?"

He may have been about to tell me but there's a blur behind him and he collapses onto the ground, howling and swearing. "FUCK. OW! CHRIST ALIVE." While he flaps at his legs, Rascal administers a series of vicious swipes, instantly drawing blood. The cat only stops when Mum appears, leading the others. While they cluck sympathetically, helping Mr Jepson up and promising ointments and cosseting, Rascal slinks away and I follow. Rascal may be a mean-spirited furball but at least he's ours.

\*\*\*

If it wasn't for the Amos Redemption Plan, I would be in my room speculating about what has got into Mr Jepson. As it is, Dina is ready at nine thirty and I'm waiting by the gate at ten when Mrs Potts' car pulls up. The promised friend is Mr Poseidon, the postman. He pulls a spade and torch from the boot while Mrs Potts joins us. I lead them in silence down the lane to the secret pumpkin patch Mum has made by the stream.

Mrs Potts starts sneering almost immediately. "PATHETIC." She turns to Mr Poseidon. "SPADE."

Even though I know the flash is coming, it still surprises me. Mr Poseidon starts swearing while Mrs Potts stumbles and falls over. The flash goes several more times until there's an agonising scream from Mrs Potts. "WHO'S THERE? STOP IT AT ONCE."

While Mrs Potts berates Mr Poseidon and flaps around I slip away, back to her car. It is twenty minutes before they appear. Mrs Potts walks right up to me and stands inches away. "I WANT THE NEGATIVES TOMORROW."

I manage to say, "You must tell Mr Hemingway first. So Amos isn't sacked." For the second time today I urgently need a piss.

"GET HIM TO RING ME."

"And you need to tell the police…"

"DON'T THINK YOU CAN BLACKMAIL ME, BOY." She yanks open her door and begins to manoeuvre herself inside. Once seated she bangs on the dashboard and Mr Poseidon pulls away hurriedly. Left alone I walk to the ditch and pull down my fly.

"That went well."

"Jesus." I turn away from Dina, splashing my shoes in the process.

"Sorry." She starts laughing. "You alright?"

"I'll be better if you let me finish alone."

She goes back into the garden, giggling. Even though I'm drained of energy and annoyed at her interruption, I'm also relieved to hear her laugh again.

As soon as I push open the gate, Dina flies at me, holding me tight. When I manage to unwrap myself she holds out the camera. "Did you hear her as well?"

She says, "Bournemouth heard it." We're both shivering now. "You were brilliant, H. I'll never forget her face when the flash went off, Penny's camera is fab."

"I hope this works."

She leads me to the seat. She says, "You should be in a Marvel comic. In the last couple of days you've maimed a pervert and out-blackmailed a blackmailer and... and..." She stops and looks serious, "You've been amazing. I like the new you." She squeezes my hand and just for the briefest moment I feel safe. But then thoughts about McNoble and his money, Mr James and his diamonds and Mr Jepson's worrying threats intrude. Dina actually believes in me, believes I've done the right thing for once. Is it only me who knows it was just another fluke?

**THURSDAY 5ᵀᴴ AUGUST 1976**

## Chapter Sixty-Three

## Take the Money... No, Open the Box

Mum is by the stove. "Breakfast, Harold."

I peer at the pan; it looks like hot viscera. "Is there any bread?"

"In the bin." She keeps stirring. "Here."

Thankfully it's just a small portion of boiled intestine.

She says, "Did I hear you talking to Desiree last night?"

I take a mouthful; it's really good.

Mum's laughing. "What did you do?"

"Nothing. This is great."

"Mrs O'jar left it. So it has nothing to do with that stupid man Peeltrap calling to say his enquiries are closed?" She puts a lid on the pan and wipes her hands. "Can you call Ruth? She left a message for you."

"Ok."

"Jim's parents are coming this morning. Can you stay and say hello?"

"I..."

"And your father wants to talk to you about university. He thinks you should leave."

"Leave?"

But she's already halfway to the stairs, neatly ignoring my reply. What does she mean?

\*\*\*

"I'm sorry, Harry." Ruth doesn't do small talk. "I didn't want to."

I just hold the handset waiting for whatever the bad news is. It's very bad.

"Stephen made me tell Mum about the box. He said I mustn't carry the guilt anymore. She's told me I must put it back or she'll tell Aunt."

My brain is spinning; I really thought I'd get away with my plan. "How long before she tells?"

"She doesn't like waiting."

Great. I do some rapid calculations. Now I have Nanty's cheque to pay McNoble I can probably get the diamonds back, but maybe not in time. "I'll get the box back, I promise." I'll just have to fake the rattle and sort out the stones later. I tell myself it'll work out fine, but I'm not convinced.

When she rings off I'm left staring at the sideboard, looking for inspiration. Mum pokes her head round the door. "There you are. Mr and Mrs James will be here shortly. I don't think Mr James believes the baby is Jim's, so it might be a little fraught."

"Do you really need me?"

"I can't expose Dina, Harold. Not in her condition. It would be very helpful if you could take Jim away. He doesn't need to hear our discussions."

***

Forty minutes later I'm in my bedroom when Jim is ushered upstairs. As he walks in looking like a puppy who's peed on the carpet one time too many, I have a brainwave. Of a sort. "Jim, can you do me... well, me and Ruth an enormous favour?"

He nods, with no enthusiasm. While I rummage under my bed for the box I explain how Ruth stole it – using her awful experiences as the reason – and how her newly found Christian beliefs mean it has to be returned. It's probably pretty close to the truth.

"You see, your Dad will be a bit uppity if he finds this box is missing…"

"Christ, don't I know it. He goes mental if he thinks we've been messing with them. What's in this one?"

"It's empty."

Jim reaches out to take it but I hold on. He says, "Nah, it's not. They all have something. Sometimes they have these secret compartments…"

"Oh, yeah, well it rattles. That'll be it." I'm extemporising rapidly, wishing I'd already sorted it out. "I'll go and find a bag for it. Won't be a mo."

Once on the landing I try and think what to use. I'm by Dina's door: her crappy jewellery. When I try it's too noisy without the little drawstring bag; it needs wrapping. Another brainwave: the sod can be the first to have a Dobbin curse. I tug it out of my wallet, scribble 'buried alive' on the back and tomorrow's date and stuff it in the little drawer. If he finds it before he goes on his cruise maybe Dobbin's promise will save me.

Jim agrees to put it back; he sounds confident his Dad will never notice but I don't have that much good luck.

***

When the James family leave, Mum goes to wave them off, leaving me with Dad, who has been dragged from his shed for the showdown. He seems subdued. He says, "She told you about the hotel, then? You're keen on the idea, I imagine?" He looks like he's a hundred years old.

"Honestly? I hate the idea."

He looks genuinely surprised. "You do?" He strokes his chin. "Your mother thought, as you like it so much just now, you'd want to work there. Get a trade. Work your way up. Given that you want to leave university."

"I want to do what? That's crazy, Dad. I'm desperate to go back." I realise how bad that sounds. "Of course I'd love to stay and all that but I... I don't want to waste my chances."

He starts nodding. "Well that's alright then."

I'm so angry about him and Mum trying to decide my future that I say, "Why are you letting that man Jepson into our lives? Didn't he nearly kill you? And marry Mum even though he was already married? He's a crook too."

He's still nodding, albeit more slowly.

"Are you keen, Dad? On the hotel? With Jepson? Mum said you are."

"Did she?" He rubs at the lines on his forehead as if trying to remove them. It's suddenly clear to me that he hates the idea.

"Dad, you mustn't let him win."

"Who?"

"Jepson, of course."

"This isn't about winning and losing, Harry-son, it's about a long term future for the family and an opportunity..." His voice peters out. Then he tries again. "She's set her heart on this. It's really a done deal."

Monica Jepson's face comes to me, urging me to speak to Dad, to stop this scheme. I say, "Dad, did you know Robin Andersen is involved?"

"Andersen?"

"I told you the other day, Dad. You were a bit worse for wear..."

He looks rather sheepish and says, "Andersen. Are you sure? The one with the large house over towards the old Roman fort?"

"Yes. That's him. I work with his son, Sven. And Mr Jepson's wife Monica told me Mr Andersen is involved. With the hotel."

Dad is frowning harder than ever. "Are you sure about this?"

I manage a nod, not really sure what I've done but it has changed him somehow. Mum re-appears at the backdoor. "There you are. We need to get a move on, Arthur. The meeting is in thirty minutes."

Dad stands but stops by my chair as he leaves. "I'd better go. But…" He grins down at me so only I can see; it seems he hasn't grinned in weeks. "Thanks Harry. And say nothing about this to your Mum. Ok? We will sort this out."

No 'Harry-mate' or 'Harry-friend'. Maybe he's trying to be a parent again. I just hope 'sorting this out' includes me getting back to uni

## Chapter Sixty-Four

## Time to be a Man

Charlie Jepson is reading the Financial Times in the lounge when I open up. I'd pushed yesterday's assault to the back of my mind, hoping it was a misunderstanding or something, but he soon puts me right. He follows me into the bar and orders a G&T. While I mix it he says, "Right, now listen to me you little shit. After you close we're going to see this man. You know his son, Sven. He's going to ask you lots of questions about those diamonds you pawned. So before we go we're going to make sure you have your story straight, all right?"

I somehow manage to put the glass down and stay standing. It really is no mean feat.

"So whose are they?"

My hesitation is fractional, but it's enough for him to push his face across the bar at me. "I said whose diamonds?"

"Mr James." I can't stop thinking about Mrs Jepson – how she said he attacked her, about what Sven said when she left, hiding behind large dark glasses. "He's Ruth's Uncle."

"Little Ruthie? But she's a Christian." He shakes his head and says, "Never did understand them. So how'd you get them?"

"He has loads of boxes – he collects them – and she took one. I… she never really said why. It… it had the diamonds in it. I don't think she knew they were there."

"Hang on. Do you mean that box you gave Claude? The one we used for Mother?"

I nod.

"Christ. They were in that?" He looks confused, on the verge of being angry again. "But... why did you share them with Monica?"

"Share?"

He finishes his drink. "You pawned, what, four? And she pawned fourteen so..."

"I didn't know."

He narrows his eyes. "Tell it your way, why don't you? How did you get those four and pawn them."

So I do. What do I have to lose?

He's smiling when I finish. "You mean I nearly threw the little fuckers in the sea? Priceless. Mind you, it would have made things easier if I had." He retreats into a little world of his own from which he emerges very abruptly. "She tried to screw all of us, you know? Stupid cow. I was furious when I heard she'd gone to this man in Bournemouth to sell them. I didn't get it – why sell them now, down here? There are plenty of places up in London. She told me she brought them back from Morocco last winter and decided she had to sell them. It's obvious now, isn't it? She wanted to cash them in before this man James realised they were gone. Only she chose one of Andersen's people, didn't she? I had a real mountain of grief because of that, I'll tell you. I thought I'd made it clear how unhappy I was and then you go to Andersen's man in New Milton with stones from the same fucking mine. Of course Andersen thinks it's me and I thought it was her – Christ, she'll not make that mistake again." He stares hard at me. "Nor will you. Robin Andersen is suddenly all our problem, ok? You'll tell him you and she were acting together and it had nothing to do with me. You'd better hope he believes you." He looks at his watch. "I'll be in my car when you close. Don't keep me waiting."

I pour myself a Scotch when he's gone. It's what they do in the films but it just makes me feel ill. It's clear he did hit her – she must have covered the bruise with sun cream or something. Maybe she wasn't lying after all. All I want to do is cry, hide or run home, but none of these options are available so at three I pull down the shutter and head for the car park.

## Chapter Sixty-Five

## Pinned to the Board

The drive to the Andersens' house passes in a blur. Somewhere to the north of the Forest there's a pall of smoke from a heath fire. I hope it's not prophetic. We skirt Sven's bungalow, pass through a grove of trees and reach this enormous house with Tudor-style wood beams and white plaster. There's a game of croquet being played out front by half a dozen or so people. Before we get out, Mr Jepson takes a deep breath and says, "I knew nothing. Got that?"

A man is approaching; this is the second time I've seen him and this time I know who he reminds me of: my old French teacher, Ratty Reynolds, even down to the crooked right eyebrow; I'd guess though that his preferred punishment regime doesn't involve conjugating 'avoir' numerous times. His speech is slow, almost a drawl.

"Charlie. Good of you to come. And you're the Spittle boy?" He holds out a hand. "Robin Andersen. You work with my son, I believe?" His fingers are fat with three gold rings and hairy knuckles; in his open shirt and shorts he does seem rather genial. "Let's leave these good people to their game and go for a walk."

He takes me by the elbow and eases me across the lawn. No one comes with us as we head for some trees. I'm shivering despite the heat. He leads me through a gate and up a track, much like a Forest ride, which is buzzing with insects and full of flashes of fleeting colour as butterflies ply their trade. "Do you like butterflies, Harry?"

"Yes sir."

He pulls what looks like a black muslin ball from his pocket that he twits and a butterfly net springs into shape. "Neat, eh?" He makes a swift darting movement and flips the net over. "What's this one?"

"Erm. A White Admiral, I think?"

"Good. Do you collect?"

"No sir."

"It's very satisfying; the chase, the capture of your target and the careful arrangement of your prize for future display." He smiles as if to himself. "A summary of a successful business strategy, don't you think?" Another smile; this is aimed at me. "Though mostly in business you don't kill the target."

We start walking again. "1976 will be remembered as a good year for Clouded Yellows. I'm taking my boat around the Island on Sunday, to see if any are blowing in." We're out of sight of the others when he stops and turns to me. "Do you understand the idea of a monopoly, Harry? The idea of having complete control over certain things?"

I manage a rather brave nod considering my stomach is melting and shortly its contents will join my trousers in sticking to my legs.

"It's what any businessman wants, ideally. And in certain areas I have achieved that. You can imagine how upsetting it can be if someone else tries to muscle in." He flicks the net again and reaches inside. "This is a Duke of Burgundy Fritillary. My favourite. It's so delicate both in its structure and its camouflage. It's endangered and has no way of fighting back; here there's no monopoly, just lots of predators prepared to do what it takes." He rubs the life out of the little thing like he's brushing dust off his fingers. "So I don't like it when someone tries to break into one of my little markets, in this case uncut diamonds. You did me a favour, pawning those gems with Frank. Charlie tells me he knew nothing about them, but, well, Charlie tells his own version of the truth, doesn't he? Is he telling the truth, Harry?"

His gaze never leaves my face; I'm squirming. Whatever I say someone is going to suffer.

"Or is this another of his stories to try and get himself out of a hole? How old are you?"

"Nine... nine... nineteen, sir. Mr Jepson didn't know about them. Just me and his wife."

He turns back to the house. "I believe you – and Charlie. He's not stupid enough to use my people. So," he glances at me, "whose are they and why were you pawning them?"

I walk a pace behind, saying nothing.

"Harry, you're young. Life's uncomplicated. Don't make me change that."

"They belong to Mr James. Mr Reginald James. I needed the money."

"A relative?"

"No sir."

"What do you think Mr James planned to do with them? I think, maybe, I should ask him myself. Is he around?"

"He's going abroad, sir. This weekend. He works on a cruise ship."

Mr Andersen turns back, looking at me quizzically. "Does he? And how will he react when he finds you tried to pawn them?"

"I don't know, sir."

"You don't think he'll be a little angry?"

"Yes sir. I expect so."

He walks on, with me falling further behind. "Come on. Let's see if there are scones for tea."

***

Things become surreal: I'm introduced to Mrs Andersen with her angular tanned beauty and kindly eyes; then Sven's sister, Marita, who is short and dark, like her Father, and nervous, unlike him. The others watch me without approaching. Mr Jepson has disappeared.

After half an hour Mr Andersen returns with some tea. "I think we will both meet this Mr James. I need him to understand you did me a favour. I'll let you know when I need you again." I nod while he sips his tea. The silence feels awful and I wish he'd say I can go even though I've no idea how I'm getting home. Mr Andersen peers across at the game as if his eyesight is letting him down. "Oh good shot. Ah, your lift."

I'm shocked and surprisingly relieved to see Sven walking across the lawns towards us. Mr Andersen says, "Charlie had to go so I asked Sven to help. He'll amuse himself for a while so let's go and see if we can have a hit."

As before I walk just behind him. He says, "So your Mother is George Thoroughly's daughter, is she? Does she own the garage?"

"My Aunt."

"George was a difficult man. Still sad to hear the business isn't doing well." He stops to stare at me. "When Charlie appeared, to lay his Mother to rest, I did wonder, you know. He's a slippery fish is Charlie and… well, we have a bit of history."

We join in a game; our opponents are either useless or desperate to lose so we make rapid progress and have to wait for them to catch up.

"He talks to me about maybe doing something together but then it all goes quiet. And I hear about him with your Mother, old friends I'm told. And then I hear they might be buying Hemingways." He glances at Sven, then me. "No, Sven didn't tell me. And I ask myself where on earth might they get the money?"

Suddenly he is right in front of me, staring hard at me. "Charlie?"

I stare back. I try not to breathe.

Just as quickly as he forced the eye contact he breaks it. "Let's go and put this lot out of their misery."

***

Eventually Sven eases me away and we walk to his bungalow in silence. There's a motorbike there. As he offers me a helmet he says, "You don't listen, do you? I tried to warn you."

"I didn't understand."

"Well, don't blame me if you end up as part of the foundations for this new M27 motorway… Joke, Harold. That's old hat." He pauses, halfway to pulling on his own helmet, and says, "You do realise my Father is a crook – a gangster if you like – don't you? Of course he looks legit… Christ, are you going to be sick?"

I shake my head, but I am anyway.

He peers at the puddle with distaste. "He told me you and he will be meeting someone called James?"

"I don't know why I have to be there."

"Pour encourager les autres, dear stupid naïve Harold. Once you see how he works, you will be forever determined to ensure you do nothing that might cause him to 'take an interest' in you ever again. Now, if you've stopped spewing, put the helmet on."

My hands are shaking so he has to do it up. I say, "What will happen to Mr James?"

"He may need some minor surgery." He holds my stare. "You think I'm joking, don't you? He tells me everything, Harold, because he wants me sucked into his empire. I'm the chosen successor, but I'm not playing his game. Not for long anyway. I hate who he is and what he does. And yes, I'm scared of him. And I work at Hemingways, I go to that stupid university just to be as normal as possible. As soon as I can I will leave forever..." He glances back through the trees towards the house.

"Your sister?"

He turns towards me, his helmet hiding his eyes. "Well done. Yes. There's no way I'm letting her put up with what I've had to put up with. She's eighteen next June. He's not an easy man to leave, but we'll find a way." Sven climbs onto his bike and kicks it into life. "Just make sure you do what he wants."

\*\*\*

Sven takes me to the bank. The manager plays shove ha'penny with Dad and is prepared to cash Nanty's cheque. While we wait for the money I ask, "Has your Father talked about Hemingways? And my parents?"

Sven's been drawing on a blotter. He pauses, frowning. "No. No he hasn't. Are they?"

"I... I think so. Yes, that's what I've heard."

"They don't tell you? Is that it?"

"I suppose."

"Why would my Father talk about it? You think he might want a piece?" Sven is staring at me and I'm wishing I hadn't said anything. He says, quite slowly, "Is that why you spent time with Mrs Jepson? Because he's involved? Jepson?" I try desperately to look anywhere but at him. To my surprise he holds my arm. "I didn't know. Please believe me but it begins to make some sense. I'll try and find out more."

"Why? Why would you help me?"

He shrugs and goes back to doodling. "I'm not doing it for you." He glances up. "Do you want this hotel purchase to go ahead?"

I shake my head hard.

"Good." He picks up a pencil.

"What should I do, Sven?"

He twists his head to check the picture from a different angle. "Do? You've done enough."

***

When I get home, after a dreadful evening full of praise for my saving Amos, I feel awful. Mrs Ojha tells me the police have dropped the charges of pumpkin vandalism. Mum is nervy, fussing about everything. She lets slip there is a party on Saturday to announce the hotel purchase but then contradicts herself and says it's 'all down to your Father'. Dad is with Ravi at the lawyers. Dina is with Jim, shut away in her room, so I watch TV with Nanty. I want to talk to someone, explain what's happened and see if they can work out what's going on but there's no one. I'm all alone.

**FRIDAY 6$^{TH}$ AUGUST 1976**

## Chapter Sixty-Six

### It's an Ill Wind…

Dad shakes me awake at six. When I come to, he's looking at Amanda. He peers through her little hole. "Dad, please."

"What? Oh sorry." He props her against the desk and shakes his head. "I hope your Mother doesn't see her. Listen, Harold. I'm having some difficulties with what you told me. Are you absolutely sure Mr Andersen is involved?"

His one good eye is always a little out of synch with his glass one but today they appear to be looking in opposite directions. "I thought so, but…"

As I say 'but' his head drops and he pushes himself up. "I see." He brings his gaze back to me. "Never mind. It's… I'll probably be at the hotel today."

"Mum said it will be announced tomorrow."

He nods. "Unless there's a miracle." He stands to go.

"Dad, about uni…"

"Later."

\*\*\*

I'd prefer to stay at home; today's the day McNoble wants his money. I know I shouldn't pay him, but, after what Mrs McNoble told me about his childhood, I doubt he's going to be very forgiving.

A vivid memory of him stabbing me comes to mind and I rub my thigh where the knife went in. It might have been accidental but given how often he hits me I'm taking no chances. I sort of understand why he's so angry. I'd be angry, too, if his Mother or Father had destroyed my family. I might not be a psychopath but I'd definitely not invite him to any house parties. The journey to work is awful: every car that passes is McNoble about to run me down; every shadow in the bushes is him, ready to pounce. At the hotel every creaking floorboard or slamming door is McNoble. By the end of lunch I'm a wreck. I decide to hide at home; no one's about. The phone rings about four. Reluctantly I answer it. It's Ruth.

"Have you sorted the box?

"Yes. Jim put it back yesterday."

"Oh thank you. Thank you. I'm ever so grateful."

If only she knew. "Yes, well, I'd better go..."

"There's just one little thing."

"What?"

"Stephen said... he said he wanted a word with you, now it was back. I thought... I thought you'd like to know."

\*\*\*

The rest of the day is one twitch after another, but I still haven't seen McNoble when I reach home at ten thirty (Rodney sends me off early – 'big day tomorrow, youngster' – he's not usually so thoughtful). As I get in the phone rings and no one else is keen to answer it.

"Harold Spittle?" Whoever it is talks very slowly.

"Yes. Who—?"

"Reg James. Jim's Dad."

My stomach lurches.

"I've just had an odd call. Someone wants to meet me at your house tomorrow at twelve thirty to talk about diamonds? They asked me to call you but not tell anyone else."

Oh shit.

"You still there? Have you any idea what this is about?"

"No Mr James."

"I don't see why I should waste my time."

"No. Though if it's diamonds it may be worthwhile."

"What? I suppose..." Mr James sounds very tired and it occurs to me he's probably stoned.

"I'll see you at twelve thirty." Somehow I make myself sound chirpy. It takes me a few moments to realise he must have rung off or fallen asleep. I put the phone down carefully and then leave it off the hook.

Tonight is the hottest night of the year; that plus thinking about Saturday stops sleep. In the end I head outside and lie on the swing. Rascal sniffs at my feet a couple of times, but even he goes indoors, leaving me alone, wide-awake and snivelling.

**SATURDAY 7TH AUGUST 1976**

**Chapter Sixty-Seven**

**Curses**

I did not expect to sleep but I do because I'm woken, not by the tiny flies that populate the pre-dawn but by Dad creeping out of his shed. He is so intent on whatever it is he has in mind that he never sees me. First he goes to the kitchen and then the back gate. As he pulls it closed, I hear low voices, then a car door slams and it accelerates away. It is five forty-five. If I wasn't so nervous about today I'd wonder what he was up to, but I blink that away and go hunting for some tea.

One of my worries has been how to meet Mr James and Mr Andersen when I know Mum and Dad will expect me to be at the party at Hemingways, but I needn't have bothered.

Whatever it is Dad is up to, Mum is not party to it and as soon as she reads the note he's left propped against the milk jug she goes into a funk, one minute angry the next anxious. So when I offer to stay behind, just in case he comes home, Mum accepts with speed if not grace.

Dina isn't so easily fooled. "What are you up to?"

"Nothing?"

"Are you meeting him?" It's clear she means McNoble. I hate lying. "Yes."

"What if he attacks you? You mustn't be alone."

"Don't worry, Di." I pat a pocket. "I have the cash."

I can see she doesn't believe me but she doesn't press.

At nine thirty Mum drives Dina, Nanty and Mr and Mrs Ojha to Hemingways. Papaji and the children have already been taken for a day's riding at the local stables. I'm alone and I feel grim.

\*\*\*

After a futile hour wandering around the house trying to find somewhere to relax I end up back on the swing with Rascal who lets me stroke him. It's like he knows I'm condemned.

I keep thinking about the tortures and punishments that Mr Andersen may be planning on inflicting; when Rascal twists to clean his anus a memory of a history lesson involving some ancient King and a red hot poker sends me scurrying indoors for a dump.

When I return I'm stopped in my tracks by the sight of Penny, on the swing, with Rascal on her lap.

"Hi. What are you doing here?"

"I thought you could do with some company."

She turns and smiles and at that precise moment I faint clean away.

\*\*\*

She makes me stretch out while she washes the graze on my head. "Dina wasn't happy leaving you alone. I was in the office when they arrived and I managed to cadge a lift on Nige's bike. He's doing a job for his Dad somewhere nearby."

"Was my Dad there?"

"I didn't see him. Your Mum seemed a bit anxious."

I'm not aware of it but I must shake involuntarily because Penny suddenly holds my shoulders. "Shh. It's ok. Are you going to tell me what's going on?"

"Nothing." I can't meet her gaze.

"That's not what Dina said and... and it's not what Sven said."

"Sven?"

"He was late for breakfast and spent time with Mr Hemingway. When he came out of his office he told me he was worried about you though he wouldn't say why."

I know she's waiting for me to explain, but I feel too tired to speak.

"Here. Medicine." I wasn't aware she'd moved; now she has two glasses of Scotch. "In one." She downs hers and after a moment I do the same, coughing violently. She waits until I've wiped my eyes before saying, "So," she leans in and kisses me on the lips, "spill it."

She squeezes my hand. I think that's what frees my voice. Out it all pours; McNoble, Jepson, James, Andersen and my crazy family. When I finish, she's frowning. "Do you really think you're Jepson's son?"

"I've no idea. I'm beginning to wonder if anyone really knows or cares."

"And those people are due here in a couple of hours?"

"Yeah, and McNoble..."

She waves a hand. "He's not the worry, Harry."

"But he stabbed me..."

She ignores that and stands. "Can I use your phone?" She doesn't wait to be given permission. She's gone fifteen minutes. "Sorted. Come on."

She holds out her hands.

"What do you mean? Sorted?"

She grabs my reluctant hands. "Come ON."

"Where?"

"Your bedroom. If I'm getting naked it's not out here."

I let myself be pulled to my feet, mostly because I don't really believe what I've heard. "Naked? But these awful people are going—"

She grabs my face and kisses me hard. When she lets go, allowing me some air, she says, "You need to be distracted, not sit there and worry. I can't think of anything better than sex." She kisses me again, massaging my nob with her right hand as she does so. "Well?" She's grinning, her cheeks are flushed and she's all glittery eyed. "I've been wanting this for weeks. Even on that first day when your trousers kept falling down. But there was Ruth and then Natalie and that bloody Mrs Jepson and Magda…"

"Except there wasn't. And what about Christian?"

"There was never Christian." She pulls at my hands. "Who cares? Let's not waste time."

As she pulls me indoors I look at Rascal; it occurs to me that, as with Rascal and the stroking, Penny is favouring me with sex as a sort of last request for the condemned man. It doesn't dissipate my growing ardour that is pushing hard at my flies.

***

I'm not sure what's worse – the day's old clothes on my floor, the smell of stale farts or the fact my bedroom is the hottest room in the house. While I kick the mess to one side and pull the crusty bedclothes off the bed she picks up Amanda.

"Dina mentioned your cardboard friend." She peers at me through Amanda's artificial fanny. "Impressive radius…"

"Come here and check the original."

That's the trigger; suddenly she's pulling off my clothes and me hers and all that's left are her pink knickers and my less than white underpants. I suppose I'm not surprised her nipples are orange, but soddit, who cares?

She says, "What about precautions?"

I glance at the door, which is ajar. "Yeah, you're right. I don't need Rascal lacerating my balls again."

"Sorry? Who's Rascal?"

"Long story."

She shrugs. "I was talking about contraception."

"Contraception? Damn. I haven't got any thingies. Don't you have a pill or something?"

She snorts out a laugh, which does wonderful things to her breasts. "Christ, what do they teach you out here in the backwoods? You have to take the pill daily, moron, and, yes, I am on it, but my Mum insists on double cover so I use a cap if a bloke doesn't have a rubber."

There's so much in that sentence that confuses, excites and sickens me that I just nod.

She rummages in her jacket pocket and pulls out a small blue box, which she waves at me like it explains everything. "I'll use the bathroom. Won't be a mo." Before she goes she pulls at the front of my pants, looks inside and gives me a squeeze. "Hmm. Keep him cooking."

My penis nearly somersaults and keeps trampolining. Rubbing against my pants isn't helpful so I pull them off while reciting: 'Amo, Amas, Amat…'

While I fight for control and the sweat floods out of me I stare at Amanda grinning back. The words 'impressive radius' beat in my head. Contrary to a number of people's assumptions I have yet to stick my penis through Amanda's little aperture, but at that moment it seems like a good idea.

I turn to face the door, ready for Penny's return and ease Amanda over my erection. While the fit is flatteringly tight, the way the frayed cardboard rubs on my recently flailed scrotum triggers more, largely uncontrolled penile gymnastics; the result is the throbbing and thrumming grows exponentially.

I try a soliloquy from Macbeth, then the periodic table but by the time the door opens I'm at about T minus three and launch is imminent.

"Geez. Would you look at that?"

My eyes have been squeezed tight shut for several minutes so it takes a moment to focus. Any illusion I might have had that she was talking about my erection is soon dispelled; what has caught Penny's attention is this ginormous salivating horsefly, perched on the very tip of my purple bell-end.

I've hardly had time to spot him before he impales the soft tissue with his steel-tipped mandibles. It's bloody excruciating. I flap rather feebly, not because of any hardwired antipathy to hurting the little bleeders, but because I know if I so much as disturb the air near my nob I'll ejaculate all over Penny.

Penny is unaware of the risk; she nips the fly in half, which, while avoiding my worst fear does mean my penis is covered in my blood and his guts. It's an unfortunate reminder of Mr Andersen and the butterfly and leads to an instant loss of penile pressure.

She wrinkles her nose at the mess. "You get yourself unplugged and I'll find some loo paper." While she darts out again, I tug at Amanda. Penny's voice floats back. "I'll kiss him better if you like."

That's not what I need. I'm rueing my stupidity and wondering if I'm the first man in history to be disappointed by how large his penis has grown when the doorbell goes and it deflates like a punctured Zeppelin. I grab my T-shirt and jeans and head downstairs, fearing the worst.

***

It's Nigel Sodding Parsons. "Hi 'arry. You gotta mo?" He waves towards the lane. "I'm buggered. You couldn't giz us a 'and?"

He's the last person I need so I push him outside. "I'm really busy."

"Won't take a mo. It's me silage delivery to yer farm across. I'se not driven this 'ere beast afore."

The problem is clear when we reach the lane. He's jack-knifed his tractor and trailer across the width of the road. "If yous giz us directions, maybe I'se can sort 'im out."

He fires up the 'beast' and begins to move back and forward while I call out directions. But with my mind elsewhere, I don't spot the danger until there's this fearsome crack as the top bales catch a branch of an oak tree. Everything tilts alarmingly.

"You pillock, 'arry. Now what?"

"HARRY." Penny's voice cuts across his panic with some of her own.

Instinctively I sprint for the house. Nige calls after me. "I need to phone me Dad."

"In a mo. You watch this lot."

Penny, hands on hips and legs akimbo is blocking the front door; at least she's pulled on my T-shirt, but her pink knickers peep from below the hem rather undermining her Amazonian pose. On one side is Mr James, hopping from foot to foot and clearly angry. On the other are Mr Jepson and McNoble, neither of whom is giving anything away.

I hurry across to Penny. "You go inside. I'll deal with this."

She shakes her head at me. "Not a chance, buster." She looks at the three men. "So how can we help?"

Mr James looks at each of us in turn. "Well, I want a private word with Harry." When no one moves he leans in close. "I checked this morning. My 'property' wasn't where it should be. You any idea about it?" I'm sure he wants to throttle me.

Before I can think what to say, Penny says, "Are you talking about your cannabis or the diamonds?"

He gawps at her, like she's slapped him. "The diamonds," he says dumbly.

She carries on like she's organising a meeting. "Well, that's fixed for twelve thirty. Harry can fetch the weed now, if you like? Why don't you wait by your car? Then we can deal with these other gentlemen."

I think both Mr James and I nod.

"Good. Harry, can you fetch it?"

I'm so gob-smacked I turn for the back garden. It takes me five minutes to dig the bag out of the compost bin; it feels warm and smells rotten but when I hand it to Mr James he seems happy to have it. As directed he goes to his car, an open topped Triumph, and puts it in the boot.

When he's moved away, Jepson laughs. "So Robin's coming here? To teach him a lesson?"

I nod.

"Twelve thirty?"

Another nod.

He checks his watch. "Well, I don't think I want to see him twice in one day so I'll say this quickly. I know you told him I was involved in the hotel purchase; it can't have been anyone else. So the sale is off which no doubt pleases you. Your Mother is devastated, of course, but I'm sure you don't care about her, do you? I'm annoyed because it was a good deal – a stepping stone, if you like – but I'll survive. What I want you to understand, you little shit, is this isn't over. Robin may have the whip hand for now but one way or the other I'll be back and both you and he will suffer. Understand?"

All this is said in a quiet voice while he smiles at me then Penny.

I've forgotten about McNoble until Jepson turns to him. "So, Claude, you said you wanted a word with Harry, too. What's wrong?"

McNoble is staring at his Father, his mouth hanging open. "It's off? This hotel deal?"

Jepson looks annoyed. "Yes, because of him and his plotting. But don't worry, he'll not get away —"

"Good." McNoble is glaring at me, gimlet eyed.

"Good? What's good?" Jepson looks confused.

McNoble turns to face Jepson. "It was a stupid idea. If Harry has stopped you making a fool of yourself again, then I say well done."

"What do you mean? It would have been a perfect way to get back at Andersen. Didn't I explain that? Didn't you get that? We use her and that Paki as a front and begin to build a business stream here, right under his bloody nose. I—"

"Shut up, Dad."

Whatever was about to pass between them is interrupted by a large black car that cruises up and parks next to Mr James' Herald. We watch as a huge man in dark glasses steps out of the driver's side while Mr Andersen climbs out of the back.

"You said twelve thirty." Mr Jepson stares at his watch.

Mr Andersen looks at us and waves us over. Mr Jepson, McNoble and I dutifully walk across, but Penny stays put.

I'm petrified, sure that in a matter of minutes I will not comprise the same number of limbs as I do now. As I glance around, I catch McNoble looking at me; it takes a moment to realise the expression on his face is a smile.

*\*\*\**

What happens next is a bit of a blur. After Mr Jepson does the introductions and explains he's only at my house because McNoble wanted a lift to see me, Mr Andersen asks Mr James about the diamonds: where he got them and what he's planning to do with them. Before Mr James says anything, Mr Andersen pulls out a little bag and tips the contents onto the folded roof of the Triumph. Mr James goggles at the stones and then at the rest of us. Having looked around rather wildly, his gaze stops on me.

"You shit. You stole them, didn't you? You and your tart of a sister."

I think, at this point, he makes a lurch for me, but the heavy grabs him by the jacket and jerks him back. However he's caught my sleeve and pulls me with him. We all lose our balance and fall, with me bouncing off the car and crashing to the tarmac. Someone puts a hand on my throat and there's some swearing and shouting. Briefly the hand tightens before there's a scream in my ear; the next thing I know is Mr James standing next to me, holding his hand which is dripping blood and McNoble pointing his penknife at him. Everyone falls silent.

This diorama lasts a few seconds before a police siren rips the quietude to pieces; then everyone starts shouting and moving at once. I'm so dazed I'm still on the floor but a meaty hand – McNoble's – drags me to my feet. "Go and look after the bird." He pushes me towards the house.

Penny is in the dining room, watching the action unfold. She looks excited rather than scared. "I called Chris earlier and he said he'd speak to his Uncle."

Out on the road two police cars have stopped, one blocking the road to New Milton, the other blocking Mr Andersen's car. As the police pour out, the Triumph reverses away; its tyres screech as it shoots round the corner and down the lane.

"Oh God. Nige." I brace myself for the inevitable scream of ripping metal. A deep silence follows before Nigel Sodding Parsons appears, squealing like a piglet.

***

It takes us all a while to free Mr Andersen and Mr James who are both buried in silage and the branch of the tree. Mr Andersen is out cold while Mr James appears to have a broken leg. He's moaning fit to bust.

There's some confusion when the diamonds are missing; eventually Mr Jepson produces them after McNoble has a quiet word with him. He was 'keeping them safe'.

If the rest of us are subdued, the police are pretty excited; not only do they have some dodgy diamonds and a local crook with them, but also a large quantity of cannabis that they can tie to another recent suspect. Mr Jepson doesn't seem to arouse any suspicion beyond his attempt to sneak off with the stones. Ambulance men appear to help the injured while the police commandeer our kitchen as their office. Everyone who is fit is interviewed, me first, then McNoble, Penny, Nige and finally Mr Jepson. I'm encouraged to give a full statement though I omit the bit about storing the weed; I'm not getting Dina in trouble.

While his Father is being interviewed McNoble comes and sits with Penny and me in the garden. There's a horrid silence while I wait for him to demand his money. Finally he says, "You're a slimy shit, Spittle. I have no doubt about that. But stopping that hotel crap," he nods towards the kitchen, "and pissing him off – I never thought you'd have the balls. So…" To my surprise he offers me his hand. "Forget the money. Just keep out of my way."

I can just about stutter. "Thanks for helping out there."

He frowns. "What do you mean?"

"Sticking Mr James when he was strangling me."

He shakes his head. "I just wanted to stop him getting those stones."

"Did your Father… did he mean what he said?"

"About getting back at you? Oh sure. It's not me you need to worry about." He nods at Penny and walks away.

Penny gives me a hug though there's not much she can say.

When Mr Jepson appears he looks sombre, like he's been told some really bad news. I think it's only because the police inspector is watching that he doesn't hit me. He says, "Looks like Andersen will be out of action for a while. I suppose I should thank you." He hesitates then holds out a hand. "No hard feelings, Harry."

When I take it he eases me in close and whispers. "It's only half time, shit." Then he smiles and leaves.

The police inspector has been watching and comes and sits with us. "I don't know much about him though one of the older coppers in our nick say he's a slimy piece of work. I don't think you should worry about him though. Ok?"

I sort of nod but I'm convincing no one.

***

Penny makes me phone the hotel while the police finish up. Dad speaks to me first. He sounds so relaxed it's like Dina has made him smoke a joint.

"How's Mum?"

"Oh, alright."

"No, really. She must be upset."

"She was but when I told her Andersen was behind Charlie's money she knew it couldn't happen."

"But he wasn't."

Dad laughs. "Harry-man, you're too young to understand but he called me last night. I went and saw him today and he said he realised it wasn't a good idea, said he'd spoken to his son who had been speaking to you, and he pulled out. Charlie had to stop then, if his backers let him down."

"But..." I can't begin to explain. Instead I ask, "Why did that help Mum? I thought she was set on the hotel?"

"She was – is – but her Father had problems with Andersen over the garage. Protection money, Harry. Your Mum would never have anything to do with him. Charlie had told her he wasn't involved – she did suspect when she saw Andersen at that funeral thing but Charlie had convinced her. So when I told her about my meeting she knew Charlie had let her down and we couldn't proceed." He's never sounded chirpier.

"Mr Hemingway must be disappointed."

"Cuthbert? Not really. All he wanted to do was get away from the day-to-day grind. Now he's met Ravi he's going to appoint him general manager. He spent years in India as a young man and has a great fondness for the place and people. He seems quite excited at what it might mean."

I try and visualise Paul working for Ravi. It'll never happen.

Dad's still talking. "Nanty isn't over her problems and Dina will need a lot of support so your Mum will keep busy."

"Will everything be ok?"

He sighs heavily. "Everything? That's a tall order. I'll certainly give it my best shot, Harry. As I'm sure will your Mother. Especially with you and Dina's support."

"Of course."

There's a long pause before he coughs. "Umm, Dina said… she said you might have been a bit worried about your Mum and Charlie. About their… umm relationship and…" He coughs again. "You."

I'm glad I'm sitting down.

"Thing is Harry, you don't have to worry on that score. The explosion… the one that did for my eye? It also injured Charlie. He didn't know it at the time, but some shrapnel hit him and severed something in his groin; he has penile dissy-wotsit. He could never have children, not after Stephen anyway. Thought you should know."

I make a noise to stop him saying any more. It works because he says, "Dina's worried about you. Are you ok on your own?"

I look at Penny. "Sure, tell her I'm fine."

"She's been telling us about how much you've looked after her. We're really grateful, you know. She couldn't have a better brother, she said." He coughs. "And Dina said I need to make it clear that we're behind you going back to uni. She said you were worried about it."

How did she know? "Thanks Dad. I will work hard."

"Of course. Just get off probation. That's all we ask,"

When I put the phone down, I can't move. I just stare at a patch of Mum's woodchip paper that's peeling away from the wall.

"What's up?" Penny is studying me intensely. "I've been here for a couple of minutes and you look like you've seen a ghost."

"I'm a fraud, Pen. Dina's been singing my praises to Mum and Dad but..."

She waits, giving me the space to hang myself. I tell her about Mr James and his assault and Ruth's story and my complete failure to do anything about it. I suppose I'm expecting her to be sympathetic, to give me a hug and tell me I've really done all I could be expected to do but instead she reaches out and takes my hand. "Come on."

"Where?"

"You're telling the police before they go. That way..."

I pull away. "I can't..."

"Shit, Harry. Hasn't Cyril taught you anything? If he thinks he can get away with it, he'll go on and on."

"But..." There are times when I am completely incapable of reading expressions, especially girls', but hers is plain: fail this test and my chances of getting laid is zero. "OK. OK. I will."

"Right." She holds out her hand and reluctantly I let myself be led away.

***

It takes another hour; the inspector is very patient with me because it's really embarrassing to explain with Penny there, but eventually I tell him all I know about Mr James and what he's done with Dina and Ruth. He listens carefully, making a few notes. When I've finished, he sighs. "Does your sister want us to pursue this? And the other young lady. Ruth, is it? It could be pretty upsetting."

"But he assaulted them. And he's smuggling diamonds and drugs…"

"They're very separate issues, Harry. The diamonds, drugs – that's easy, but this," he taps the notes, "this is more difficult. Their word against his, you see. No independent witnesses and if he says they wanted to, they were willing…" He shrugs.

"I saw the scratch and… and… his son – Jim – saw him, with Ruth."

"Did he? And he'll speak out against his Dad, will he?" He must see my disappointment. "Look, son, you're young and don't understand how this works…"

I think it's the way he puts a hand on my shoulder, like Dad does when he's patronising me. Anyway I'm pretty angry. "He hurt my sister, don't you see? I won't let him get away with it. So you'd better do something, ok? Or I will."

I've stood up and the policemen follows suit, towering over me. For a moment I'm sure he's going to force me to sit and lecture me again but he smiles and offers me his hand. "Good for you. And I'll see what I can do." He glances at Penny. "One way or another we'll make it uncomfortable for him. I promise you that."

When he's gone and we're back on the swing, I rest my head on her shoulder. "What do you think he meant? Uncomfortable?"

She doesn't answer. All she does is whisper 'you stink' before she leans in and we kiss. "You were great," she says, when we break for air.

"Not really."

We kiss a bit more; I'm pretty sure she's hinting that I should go further but then again I don't want to bugger up my chances by pressing fast forward if, in fact she means I've reached a boundary. She says, "What are you thinking?"

"Oh nothing." We shift around to try and get more comfortable. I'm trying to interpret her expression but I'm still not sure.

I say, "I was thinking about Di and the baby and how she must be feeling. And what's she going to do with it. And I hope the police beat the hell out of Mr James, even though he's Jim's Dad. And what fantastic lips you have. Yes, definitely the lips are brilliant. And it's a bummer that Jepson gets away with everything and I hope he forgets about me and even if McNoble changes his mind next term I'm not paying him a penny. And come what may I'm going to make sure I survive Prof Bradshaw's probation because if I end up back here I'll probably kill myself and, since I don't want to stop kissing you, ever, I can't do that, because everything about your mouth and tongue and lips and teeth are just perfect. And then I thought maybe I've completely ruined my parents' chances in life though I don't really care so long as they stay together. And come tomorrow I'll probably be sacked but I don't care about that either because, tomorrow, I'll still be kissing you and that's all I want. That and I'd really really like to, you know, say hello to your breasts again. But only if you want me to…"

She laughs, takes my hand and places it where 'X' should be on her T-shirt. "Kiss me, you lucky sod. Before I go cold."

"Me, lucky?"

She leans back and I take my hand away, in case she's giving me some mysterious sign. "You could fall in a barrel of shit and come up smelling of roses."

I burst out laughing. "I've just thought of something. Did I tell you about my mate Dobbin and his curses?"

"I don't think so."

"I gave one to Mr James. I put it in his box where he hid the diamonds. It said he'd be buried alive today and blow me, that's exactly what's happened. Who'd have thought Dobbin has special powers."

She leans towards me to put a finger to my lips. "Shut up, Harry." And then we are ripping off each other's clothes and we're both naked and our sweaty limbs are slipping and sliding over each other as the swing tries to dump us on the ground. Finally, Penny takes control. While with one hand she holds the frame, she makes me slide on top of her and rest my hands by her head. She has this serious expression as she holds my gaze and with her other hand she gives my penis a squeeze. We both moan and she closes her eyes.

A dozy little housefly circles her face and lands on her lips. Her tongue flicks out and knocks the little fella away. This time he settles on her left nipple, his jaws working overtime to lap up the small beads of sweat. He stops and looks at me. I'm sure he's telling me to forget boundaries and just get on with it. When I lift my gaze, so is Penny. So I do.

If you have enjoyed Dead Flies and Sherry Trifle, here is the first chapter of God Bothering.

## God Bothering – an extract

### Chapter One

*San Francisco - December*

Looking back I should have stayed in bed. I had no reason to get up. While the rest of California was basking in uninterrupted mild December sunshine, San Francisco was coated in a ball-numbing fog. I had spent two days up near the Russian River with my bastard father; it felt like every waking minute had been filled with his monotone voice, droning on about his journalistic successes – effortlessly making unflattering comparisons to my career. I left him when I couldn't stand it any longer and there I was, huddled in a lumpy bed, wondering if I could change my flight home. If I'd closed my eyes, or read a book, or taken a dump…

Capricious fate was about to pay its hand. Mistake number one: I picked up the TV remote and scrolled through the channels.

There they were, two of the old man's current bête-noires, neatly linked up on the local TV – in one corner, Isaac Beaumont and his Church of Science and Development and, in the other, Ernest Opache, shyster lawyer to the rich and unworthy. Did Dad know they were going to make the news? Did he set me up? Nothing would surprise me, looking back.

If I am totally honest, if you'd asked me why I climbed out of bed just then, I couldn't have told you. I knew Dad hated both of them, but not really why. I blanked out most of the detail of his monologues. Something to do with Beaumont's preaching style and Opache's liberal bending of the truth. But I knew this was an opportunity. It was like I'd just discovered a faith in a journalistic god who was pointing me at a story. I had to make the effort to find out more. Even if there was only the smallest chance it might lead to something tangible; even if, as an English investigative journalist who specialised in the misdeeds of the British Government and local celebrities, there was unlikely to be an outlet for whatever I found. I had to try.

First I needed coffee and some directions. The TV in my room gave a sketchy outline: a ProLife demo outside Opache's offices, against something called Prop Ten. The Church of Science and Development was one of the sponsors of the demo along with some other wacko Churches and ProLife nutters.

The coffee shop was packed but they were efficient with the double espresso and the girl who served me ('Hi, I'm Marlene, your barista') pointed out the bus I needed.

As I stood at the stop, my rational mind screamed 'Get indoors, moron' but I was too far gone; my long dormant faith gene had taken over and I believed; I'd lucked my way into a story which would show the old shit what I was really made of. And that, frankly, was incentive enough.

***

On the bus I googled Prop Ten: as I understood it, it aimed to liberalise the laws on the sale of human embryos for genetic experimentation – California wanted to lead the way in the field of research, focusing on how this might aid the eradication of some awful diseases and genetic flaws. The State's enthusiasm might have had something to do with the recently announced Federal grants' program.

Opache worked for some very influential supporters and funders and was the front man for the campaign. Opposite them was a coalition of faith groups, who focused on the ProLife aspects: this was a test case as a number of other States were watching what was happening here; if Prop Ten passed then others would introduce their own legislation. Thus a lot of out-of-state groups had joined in the opposition. The reason why the Church of Science and Development had been highlighted was easy to understand. First Beaumont's Church had just broken the record for the amount of funds raised in a calendar year through his Tele-Evangelism. Second, the science faculty at the Christian University of Beaumont – sponsored by the Church – had recently recruited some professor to run their own Genetics department. And the self-same professor was known to support the liberalisation. Conflict of Interest? Hypocrisy? Good business? Who knew? The article I read hinted at a deeper antipathy between Opache and Beaumont but I didn't have time to dig into that before the bus pulled up and the driver told me it was my stop.

Opache's law offices were downtown and glitzy and new. Security was ever present so my recently concocted plan A – go grab a few words with Opache – soon morphed into plan B – find the Church's reps and get a few rent-a-quotes to use to parlay my way into Opache's, to see if that threw up the bones of a story.

Even I could see it wasn't a great plan. I needed to know a damn sight more of the background to ask the right questions. Fishing trips are all well and good but they rarely pay the bills; but while there was a chance I might knock some of the egregious complacency out of my father, I ploughed on.

It didn't take long to wish I'd stayed in bed: the risk of hypothermia was far too real and the protestors were dispersing a damn sight quicker than the fog. My newly acquired faith was being tested to destruction. I asked ten people to point me at the Church of Science and Development's contingent but they stared at me like I was barking.

I was about to walk away when mistake number two occurred. I had spied a warm and friendly looking bar and was turning towards it when...

"Sorry." The young woman who I'd walked straight into bent to pick up the clipboard I had inadvertently sent flying. "I should have looked." She was wearing a long wool coat and a white beanie; one of her black pigtails caught her mouth and she flicked it away. I remembered thinking they were an odd conceit – pigtails were the sort of thing the under tens wore yet this woman was in her twenties I guessed.

"Here," her pen was rolling away and I scurried to stop its bid for freedom, "you'll want this."

She smiled at me as she clutched the clipboard to her chest, like she could draw heat from it. I held out the pen; she reached for it and between us our frozen fingers conspired to drop it so it could resume its rolling. This time we both made a grab for it and knocked into each other again. The momentum made me stagger to one side which I tried to cover with a swift foot shuffle.

She laughed "You dance well, sir."

I made a small bow. "One final turn around the floor, Miss, then I really must go."

She smiled, little less than the humour deserved and began to turn away.

"Do you know where the people from the Church of Science and Development are?"

She stopped and turned back. Her eyes, already quite narrow from the cold made suspicious slits. "Why'd you ask, sir?"

"I was talking about them to someone the other day and they intrigued me. You know, Prolife but close to a University that sponsors genetic research. I heard they were here."

She squared up to me. "We are a Church, sir. We are ProLife. There is nothing inconsistent with the two positions."

"You're from the Church? Great. Any chance of a few words." I waved vaguely at the dozen or so remaining protestors. "Looks like you're winding up here anyway."

She didn't speak for a good few moments. I let the silence hang, even though I just wanted an answer and quick – I really didn't care what it was, in truth. Then she smiled, this time exposing a mouthful of the most perfect All-American teeth. "You're a journalist?"

I waved at the office building in front of us. "What's Ernie Opache done to annoy you?"

The smile stayed in place but it looked like it was an effort to keep it there. "His firm represent the major funders of the campaign supporting Proposition Ten. If that is passed it will be the single most significant factor in the inevitable increase in underage abortions without parental consent." There was something mechanical in the way she spoke.

"How'd you work that out, Miss...?"

"Maybe you should read our literature and then call for an interview. Dan would be happy to oblige."

"Dan?"

She nodded at a grey haired man marshalling the troops. Several of them were looking our way. "He can explain everything, better than me."

"Right. But what about a, erm, younger perspective? What about we grab a beer – or a coffee - and you can fill me in?" I motioned to the bar; it was looking friendlier by the minute. "Thirty minutes and you can tell me all about Opache's latest crimes while I get warm. Also about your Church; I'd love to find out more."

"I'll have to pass, sir. We need to move on to City Hall. The protest is reforming there." She smiled again; I liked her smile even though it struggled to reach her eyes; frozen cheeks I suppose. "You could come with us."

I looked at Dan, their leader; he was staring at me, as was this blond gym monster. "So Isaac Beaumont isn't leading the charge then?"

"My father..." She stopped herself abruptly, like she'd been caught in a lie.

"Miss Beaumont?" What had I read about her? It escaped me. "Come on. A few minutes. Please. You can give your side of the story."

The albino ape appeared out of my peripheral vision and took her elbow. "We need to be getting on, Lori-Ann. Dan is anxious we don't miss the arrival of the mayor."

She nodded but I noticed how she pulled away from his grip. "Sure. Another time, Mr....?"

"Oldham. Maurice Oldham."

"You're not American are you? Australian?"

I winced. "British. Just visiting but always looking for a story, you know."

"I can't imagine this would interest your British readers." She flicked a glance at the gorilla. "I'm sorry you wasted your time."

I couldn't really disagree, but pride kept me going. "If you change your mind." I dug out a card. It wasn't even mine. "Can I borrow that pen?"

She gave it to me and I wrote my name and mobile number above Mervin's details – he worked for the Independent; god knows why I had his card. "Call me. If you want to get your side of the story across."

The lump of muscle said, "Who'd you write for, sir?"

"London papers mostly. But these stories, they're universal." Yep it sounded weak to me, too.

She tugged out a flyer from the clipboard. "Read this, Mr Oldham. If you still want an interview then the Church's PR team will be sure to fix it up."

I dutifully folded up her flyer, slipped it into my notebook and watched until she disappeared. I bet myself she would drop the card the first opportunity she got. She was cute – nice arse and I'm a connoisseur – but hard to like. Too cool and collected.

I headed for the bar. Over a Bud I read the flyer. It hardly added to the store of human understanding.

### The Church of Science and Development

### The Modern Way to God

*In 1935 GOD spoke to Joseph Beaumont in a dream. Up to that moment Joseph struggled with traditional Church teaching. Joseph believed GOD was benign and loving, HE was OUR FATHER. He understood that, after the FALL in the GARDEN, MAN was condemned to rot and decay and GOD sent HIS SON to save Man and allow him to pass to GOD's HOUSE.*

*Yet GOD had given Man many TALENTS and INSTINCTS: to survive and prosper, to have progeny, to be inquisitive, to use his reason. So he asked GOD: why give Man these TALENTS and INSTINCTS if all Man needs to do is be good and then die to reach HIS HOUSE? Why give Man these conflicting signals: use your TALENTS and survive but delay your arrival in MY HOUSE?*

*GOD explained to Joseph that Man had failed to understand GOD'S PLAN but he shared THE REAL PLAN with Joseph. MAN was to take all his TALENTS and strive to perfect his situation. He was to use everything around him to live longer, be stronger, to develop.*

*Eventually, when all those TALENTS were used to the maximum Man would ascend to GOD's HOUSE as he would have done before the FALL: without rot and decay. When Man had eradicated disease and want, had removed injustice and wanton destruction, when Man no longer feared or expected death, then he would ascend directly from his earthly state to GOD'S HOUSE.*

*Every discovery made by Man and every invention created by Man was directly ordained by GOD to achieve this goal. Science was at the center of GOD's REAL PLAN.*

*Joseph realised the BIBLE needed a fresh modern interpretation to reconcile it with GOD'S REAL PLAN and that became his Life's Work which he achieved through the First Iteration of the Testaments of Truths in 1947. Further iterations followed (they are now in their Fourteenth Iteration).*

*These BRILLIANT GOD DIRECTED INSIGHTS have given succour to countless souls clamouring for an interpretation that reconciles the BIBLE and JESUS' MINISTRY with the major scientific, cultural and social developments of the last two Millennia. Since Joseph's epiphany the CHURCH'S PHILOSOPHY has challenged both scientific thought and more traditional Christian teachings which have positioned themselves at odds with each other.*

*Under Pastor Isaac Beaumont's LEADERSHIP the BEAUMONT CHRISTIAN UNIVERSITY has become a world renowned center for Science and Philosophy. Isaac has been recognised as the GREATEST EVANGELLIST of the age. He draws MILLIONS to his regular bi-weekly broadcasts.*

*His CONVERSION RATE is phenomenal and the generous and farsighted donors are now enabling the CHURCH OF SCIENCE AND DEVELOPMENT through THE BEAUMONT FOUNDATION to invest in a wide range of projects and programs for the benefit of Man. Using ethically sound principles Pastor Beaumont has led the University in developing one of the most imaginative and forward looking scientific research programs in the Country.*

*If you want to find out more about our Church please visit www.churchofscienceanddevelopment.com. Please feel free to mail us for further insights into how you too can make your way to GOD's HOUSE in your own lifetime with GOD'S GOOD HELP and GUIDANCE.*

You had to smile; these people didn't do modesty. I glanced on the back. Some stuff about their opposition to Prop Ten. I had a second beer. While I sipped, I did what all self-respecting journos do: looked the Church up in Wikipedia. Of course, in the case of a real story I'd check my sources properly. Yeah, right. I should have known a Church like this one would have its own PR team working on its entry. Probably the same sycophant who wrote the flyer. Take this nugget...

*…. its theology treats the Bible as a work in progress. They view it as part of a continuum of Christian thought that believes each new generation should improve and enhance the old so that, in time the human race moves forward on its God directed journey to its ultimate fulfilment.*
*While Jesus is central to their belief he is but a stepping stone and not an end point. Christianity is not static but organic; God's aim in sending His Son was like a gardener watering his crops. Man needs to grow and to flower; that is God's Plan.*

*Man must use all his resources, all the powers he has been given to better himself so that, generation by generation, he creates a better world. That way he will pass straight to Heaven, fully aware and fully conscious.*
*To do that Man must understand all he has been given, he must come to understand what God wants and why. The difficulties and uncertainties that plague us will fall away at that point and there will be a Utopian elevation of all believers to Heaven.*
*So science is central to its belief system; it is by the enhancement of scientific thought and the continued development of scientific understanding (which embrace, controversially the principles of Darwinian evolutionary biology) that Man will achieve this goal.*

Happily someone, who I imagined planned taking a different route to God's Good House, had also taken the trouble to add his (or her) four-penneth...

*Despite its apparent modern interpretation of the Bible and the insistence that it is a work in progress, the Church still holds rigidly to Old Testament ideas on the place of women in society, that homosexuality is unnatural and a sin and other religions have no place in the modern world. Further its core tenet that God intended Man to develop from the Diaspora of the Ten Lost Tribes of Israel to reach ultimate fulfilment as God directed indicates a limited world view of those who will be chosen and, to some commentators, smack of eugenics.*

Ten Lost Tribes? Just reading that brought back long forgotten and much dreaded Sunday school lessons when I had struggled to stay awake. While I waited for the Testaments of Truths to download, just in case I bothered to study them later, I tried to imagine an interview with Miss Lori Ann Beaumont. She would give nothing away.

Outside the fog had lifted at last. The sun was shining and I had more pressing issues to focus on: like my marriage, telling my mother what I'd found and sorting out my life. Nothing important, then. Go home, Mo, I told myself as I paid. Go home and stop running away. And that was the last time I thought about the Church, Opache and cute Lori Ann Beaumont for quite a while.

Made in the USA
Charleston, SC
14 November 2014